THE RANCH HAND AND THE SINGLE DAD

ALSO BY JACKIE NORTH

The Farthingdale Ranch Series

The Foreman and the Drifter

The Blacksmith and the Ex-Con

The Ranch Hand and the Single Dad

The Wrangler and the Orphan

The Cook and the Gangster

The Trail Boss and the Brat

The Farthingdale Valley Series

The Cowboy and the Rascal

The Cowboy and the Hoodlum

The Cowboy and the Outcast

The Cowboy and the Dealer (Preorder)

The Cowboy and the Hacker (Preorder)

The Cowboy and the Wheelman (Preorder)

The Love Across Time Series

Heroes for Ghosts

Honey From the Lion

Wild as the West Texas Wind

Ride the Whirlwind

Hemingway's Notebook

For the Love of a Ghost

Love Across Time Sequels

Heroes Across Time - Sequel to Heroes for Ghosts

The Oliver & Jack Series

Fagin's Boy

At Lodgings in Lyme

In Axminster Workhouse

Out in the World

On the Isle of Dogs

In London Towne

Holiday Standalones

The Christmas Knife

Hot Chocolate Kisses

The Little Matchboy

Standalone

The Duke of Hand to Heart

THE RANCH HAND AND THE SINGLE DAD

A GAY M/M COWBOY ROMANCE

JACKIE NORTH

MM Romance Author

For all those who know that love is love...

And to Jamey D and Julia T, who, when I asked "Can I do it?" replied "Yes, you can!"

"Solutions to problems often come from knowing when to ask for help."

~~ Buck Brannaman

CONTENTS

CLAY

On Saturday nights, the Rusty Nail was hopping just the way Clay liked it. There wasn't a band, but the jukebox was blaring a Journey song while couples danced in a way that signaled they'd rather be getting into each other's tight blue jeans than dancing.

In the alcove, cue balls clicked, a staccato beat, and all around, from booth to table to bar stool, beer glasses and whiskey glasses and rock salt-rimmed margarita glasses glittered while chatter rose and fell all around. The smell of hops and glass cleanser make the perfect perfume.

Clay absorbed it all as he eased himself between two barstools and smiled at Mr. Grey Suit, who was drinking a whiskey and probably feeling like he was overdressed.

The Rusty Nail catered to truck drivers, ranch hands, cooks, farmers, grocery store clerks, and laundromat attendants, and not, generally, city boys from Cheyenne, who thought they might have a better time at a country bar than a city one. In such an environment, Clay had very good gaydar, and could spot the kind of city boy he wanted.

"You finishing that?" asked Clay, smiling, knowing his dimples were like a lure to some men.

"Why?" asked Mr. Grey Suit. "You want a sip?"

Mr. Grey Suit held out his half-finished glass of whiskey, which Clay knew Eddie, the owner of the Rusty Nail, watered down as much as he could.

Clay took the glass, winked, and polished it off, then licked his tongue along the rim. That was his message to Mr. Grey Suit, who could either agree or disagree to a dalliance with Clay, who'd picked out Mr. Grey Suit an hour ago, the second he and Levi had arrived at the bar.

Currently, Levi was moping over his beer at a table furthest away from the jukebox, which was rather loud. While Levi, the head cook at the ranch where Clay worked, was always up for a visit to the Rusty Nail, he usually sat and drank his beer and looked glum, as though he was waiting for someone who would never arrive. He almost never said no, though, and seemed willing to be the designated driver if Clay had too much to drink.

"Fancy a stroll?" asked Clay. He could use another whiskey to make everything feel relaxed, to allow his hopes to fly to the sky, but he'd wait for the next guy. One whiskey was enough for now. Later, after he and Mr. Grey Suit had hit it off, he'd have another, maybe with a beer chaser.

"With you?"

Mr. Grey Suit had friends with him who were also wearing suits of various shades of lush brown, sophisticated black, and serious grey. Nary a speck of color, nothing out of place. City boys, for sure. Those friends were raising their glasses at the other end of the long bar, as though congratulating Mr. Grey Suit on his taste in men.

"Yeah, with me," said Clay. He knew he was something to write home about. He knew the draw his body presented, knew that his dimples were a siren song, and his blue eyes were as bright as water beneath a sunlit sky. He was on the thick side, thicc, as the cool kids said, and that, along with his round, firm ass, and dense thighs, was also a draw.

He was a catch, pure and simple, just like the big stuffed purple octopus in the ring toss booth at the county fair. Except while the octopus cost many, many tokens, Clay could be had for a sip of whiskey. He just wanted to get laid. He just wanted to be loved.

"Yeah, okay," said Mr. Grey Suit.

"Well, don't get too excited," said Clay, which made Mr. Grey Suit look worried that the offer might be withdrawn. Which was when Clay knew he'd be getting what he needed from Mr. Grey Suit inside of ten minutes. Or, with the way Mr. Grey Suit's pupils became dark when Clay tugged on the cuff of Mr. Grey Suit's grey suit, inside of five. "This way."

There were several doors in and out of the Rusty Nail. For the kind of activity Clay was proposing, the door from the pool table alcove was the best one, for it led into the darker part of the alley, out of sight of the windows overlooking each of the booths along the wall. Clay had to shoulder his way through the pool sticks and hard-core pool players, still holding onto Mr. Grey Suit's cuff as he got them both outside.

The alley was like most, dank with oil-scummed puddles from the last recent rain shimmering in the streetlights along Second Street. That light made it most of the way into the alley, but there was one spot behind the back door of the Rusty Nail, just beyond the dumpster that now reeked of onions and yesterday's hamburgers that even Eddie wouldn't dare sell. The smell of all of this, oil and water and onions, plus something unknown that layered just beneath, something more rank that Clay couldn't identify, got him hard inside of a minute.

This was his spot, where he came on Saturday nights to get what he needed. At the ranch, where he worked long 12-hour days, Leland, the ranch's manager, had a non-fraternization rule. You weren't supposed to sleep with folks you worked with, and oh, how Clay had tried.

The rule, of course, applied to him along with everybody else at the ranch, but he didn't want it to, and so had ignored it while checking out each employee, one-by-one, in turn. Who could he have sex with? Who would laugh with Clay while they cuddled afterwards?

Who would bring him coffee in the mornings? And who could he adore, in return, all the days of his life?

Leland had been Clay's first crush upon arriving at the ranch at the beginning of last season. And who wouldn't have a crush on Leland? He was tall and broad shouldered, long-legged, and powerful. Confident. He looked like those old advertisements with the Marlboro Man and his rugged jawline and far-seeing gaze. Those long legs of his were eye-catching, too.

But though Clay had flirted at the start of his first season, all excited and almost panting over Leland, Leland had quietly and without words disabused Clay of the notion that there would be any fooling around going on. After which, Clay had quickly found that Leland's quiet, steady nature made him a good man to be around, to look up to, despite there being no sex between them.

When Clay needed advice, Leland had it. And when Leland needed a sounding board, more often than not, he turned to Clay. What grew between them became a solid friendship, which Clay found he rather adored and treasured more than he thought he would have.

Not to mention that at the start of the current season, a drifter had arrived at the ranch. And while Leland disliked drifters, due to their itinerant nature and tendency to bolt at the first sign of hard work, he'd not only hired this drifter, Jamie, he'd fallen in love with him. Thus went Clay's luck in that direction.

He liked Jamie plenty fine, and found that being with Jamie was like having a kid brother instead of five older sisters, like he had back home. Clay was the baby, yes, indeed. And while the rest of the family were corn farmers back in Iowa, Clay had always wanted to be a cowboy, which had rankled his dad something fierce.

In the end, Clay had been allowed to go west and work on a ranch once he'd graduated from college. Clay's dearest dream was to ride horses for a living and, since he'd come to Farthingdale Ranch, to one day own a ranch of his own. Guest ranch, cattle ranch, horse ranch, whatever. The wide open spaces were the place for him.

After his non-existent dalliance with Leland, Clay had attempted to woo Brody, the ranch's wrangler. Brody was his type, moody and quiet, broad shouldered and confident, going about his job being the most amazing horse whisperer, as if it were the most ordinary thing in the world.

Brody was cool, too cool to even acknowledge he was cool. Those dark eyes of his, filled with faraway thoughts, always shifting colors so quickly Clay couldn't get a bead on them, drew Clay like a mystery. His lanky body, thick dark hair, the odd scars on his upper arms that he never talked about—gah. He was perfect.

Clay wanted to figure Brody out. And to do that, he needed to sleep with Brody. But Brody, after one awkward flirt from Clay, wanted none of it. He never spoke of it, either, never joked about how Clay had practically thrown himself at Brody after only one beer at the Rusty Nail. It was like it never happened.

In return for Clay leaving it where it lay, Brody would sometimes come to the bar to sit and be moody with Levi, though Brody never seemed to be waiting for someone who would never arrive. Rather, he seemed to be waiting, out of friendship for Clay, for when they could just go home, back to the ranch. He was a good wingman and, sometimes, he too went into the alley with a boy from the city. Levi never did.

"Here," said Clay. "This is a good spot."

"Scoped it out, did you?" asked Mr. Grey Suit, looking at their surroundings with dubious eyes.

"Second I laid eyes on you tonight," said Clay, smiling because they both knew that was a lie. The confidence with which Clay had led them both there spoke volumes: this good spot was Clay's spot.

Mr. Grey Suit was looking at Clay with eyes that told Clay he suspected that perhaps three of Clay's friends were lying in wait to jump out and hornswoggle Mr. Grey Suit out of all his world possessions, along with whatever he had in his wallet. Maybe they'd take his city-fancy shoes with the tassels, too. It was up to Clay to reassure his new short-term friend what the alley was good for.

"I like to get my cock sucked good and hard," said Clay in a low, conversational tone. "I like to suck cock, too, and if you want me to stick my fingers or dick up your ass, I'm good to go. What d'you say?"

He was hard inside his blue jeans, and getting harder as he watched Mr. Grey Suit swirl these ideas in his city-boy brain. Maybe where Mr. Grey Suit was from, people had hangups, or maybe he'd been caught in the act before in an alley just like this one, somewhere in Cheyenne. Regardless, Mr. Grey Suit licked his lower lip, his eyes gleaming as he reached for Clay, hand shaking a little bit as he curled his fingers around the back of Clay's neck.

It might have been a testament to Clay's allure, or it might have been his own healthy ego, but Mr. Grey Suit clasped Clay's shoulders and sank down to his knees in the grimy alley like he'd just come to a shrine he regarded as holy. As Mr. Grey Suit unzipped Clay's jeans and tugged on the gap in his tighty-whities, Clay planted his hands on the brick wall behind him and grinned and sighed and waited for that first whisper-soft rush of breath across the head of his cock.

That's what Clay liked. That was the moment of reverence, of delight, when someone pulled his cock out to suck on it.

Clay might not have a foot long or one as big around as a baby's arm, but he had a pretty one. The doctor who had circumcised him had worked with steady hands and an artist's eye. The result had been a picture perfect penis, rosy and sweet, lined with strong veins, ending in a sturdy root.

And no, he'd not examined himself in the mirror, not at all, or at least not hardly. He'd just made sure, more than once, that what he had on offer was something another guy would want. Maybe even salivate over. He could never bring himself to fully groom the bushes, so to speak, as other guys did, though sometimes he used a small pair of scissors to keep his pubic hair under a dull roar.

Mr. Grey Suit's sigh was audible, and the lave of his tongue along the underside of Clay's cock was slow and warm and shivery good. The mouth that enveloped him was soft-slow but sure, sending ripples up the backs of Clay's legs, a low, steady evolving of warmth and heat in his belly.

As Mr. Grey Suit sucked hard and then soft, using one hand to coax Clay along, Clay drifted into the moment, the growing focus on his body's pleasure, the growing distance of the world around him.

There was no way Mr. Grey Suit wanted more than this, of course, but in that moment, it was enough. The suck-suck-suck of Mr. Grey Suit's mouth was practiced and equally spaced, sprinkled in with darts of his tongue along the slit of Clay's cock.

Mr. Grey Suit had learned this method from somewhere, Cheyenne, perhaps, or even as far away as Denver. It was a good method, effective, as Clay was hard and his balls were drawing tight beneath him as though preparing for a leap from a rather tall cliff.

When he came it was with a bang, an uncoiling of his muscles, a gut-deep curling and uncurling, and all the while Mr. Grey Suit sucked and licked until Clay's cock was soft in his mouth. Then he released Clay's cock with a pop and a smile as he stood up.

"Shall I fuck you or let you suck me?" asked Mr. Grey Suit.

This was not Mr. Grey Suit's first time at the rodeo, even if it was his first time in Clay's Good Spot. Shame. Clay liked to introduce guys from the city as to how cowboys in the country liked it. And while he'd done that, done it good and proper, in fact, there had been more than one city boy in Mr. Grey Suit's past.

"Whatever," said Clay. He was still shivering, still coming down, and while he would have liked to have been held and petted, it was Mr. Grey Suit's turn.

Mr. Grey Suit reached into the pocket of his sharp grey trousers and brought out a crinkly packet to show Clay.

Clay squinted to look at it, then nodded. Pre-lubed was fine with him.

"Want any help with that?" he asked, like he was offering to open the door for Mr. Grey Suit.

"Just turn around," said Mr. Grey Suit. "And pull 'em down."

It sounded very much like Mr. Grey Suit had his own Very Good Spot in another town where he was used to going to fuck whoever was willing. Well, Clay was willing, so he turned to face the alley wall, smiling as he tugged on his already-undone jeans and slithered them, along with his briefs, down to his knees. Planting his hands on the grimy, sharp-edge bricks, he leaned forward and stuck out his ass, then smiled some more at Mr. Grey Suit's appreciative sigh of pleasure.

He listened to the crinkle-crinkle of the packet being opened, then the slick, plastic sounds of Mr. Grey Suit unrolling the condom up over his cock, which Clay could now imagine as he liked, since he'd not yet laid eyes upon it. It'd be thick and strong and long and as Mr. Grey Suit snubbed the head of his cock against Clay's ass in a bit of a hello and warning all at once, Clay realized Mr. Grey Suit's one-eyed-wonder was wide. And that was just fine with him. Nothing he liked better on a Saturday night than a pounding up the ass. His ass. Him getting reamed in his Very Good Spot.

Pressing against the brick wall, Clay braced himself as Mr. Grey Suit pushed in, withdrew, then pushed in again. The first breech was always a little tight, accompanied by a snap of pain, the fraught tense feeling that maybe he'd picked the wrong guy and he'd end up in the hospital with a ripped up ass. Bleeding out while he called Leland to explain exactly why he wouldn't be at the Sunday morning meeting.

But that didn't happen. Mr. Grey Suit was steady and careful as he went in, his cock filling Clay, solid and slow. Then as Mr. Grey Suit sped up and began pumping, Clay bit his lip and closed his eyes and sank into the moment. Being pushed into. Being full.

He shivered at the feel of Mr. Grey Suit's pubic hair scratching the back of his ass cheeks, the slippery feel of Mr. Grey Suit's silk-lined jacket whisking across his bare hips. At the sound of Mr. Grey Suit's fancy belt clinking. The sigh of another man behind him, pleasuring himself, a damp hand on his hip, one on his shoulder pulling him close for each pumping thrust.

The pleasure-garden in Clay's head was disrupted by the front door of the Rusty Nail banging open and the chatter of happy patrons spilling out onto the sidewalk. They wouldn't be able to see the two men fucking in the alley unless they came all the way into the alley and stepped across the last barrier between light and shadow.

Where Clay and Mr. Grey Suit were was dim and secret and, while not quite private, was a long way from being public. But Mr. Grey Suit must have gotten a case of the nerves for he sped up and pounded into Clay and gripped Clay's shoulders almost painfully when he came. Then, like a gentleman, he withdrew his cock slowly. Unlike a gentleman, as Clay turned to face Mr. Grey Suit, he took the condom he'd pulled off his cock and tossed it in the alley.

Clay didn't say anything, but he wanted to.

"Good?" asked Mr. Grey Suit.

At the end of the alley, bathed in the streetlights, were Mr. Grey Suit's friends from the bar. They must have all known each other well enough to clock Mr. Grey Suit to the minute as to how long it would take him to suck and then fuck a stranger.

"Yeah," said Clay as he tucked himself away and straightened his clothes back into their proper places. "Thanks."

With a chin-jerk of farewell, Mr. Grey Suit turned and walked down the alley toward his friends. Leaving Clay, his body still singing with the effects of their encounter. Ripples of pleasure still moving in his belly, sparks of reaction racing down the backs of his legs.

And from somewhere, from that place he could never find and maybe didn't want to, came that slender spider web-thin bit of sadness. It might have been nice had he and Mr. Grey Suit gone back into the Rusty Nail to share that beer and have a laugh or two. Maybe compare notes about the sizes of their respective cocks, and whether Mr. Grey Suit fully groomed himself, like all suit-wearing men seemed to do.

But it was not to be, so Clay went alone back into the swell of noise and movement and light that was the Rusty Nail on a Saturday night. He'd have another beer to drink and after that maybe a whiskey all his own, which he would ask Eddie not to water down.

2

AUSTIN

The moving truck had just picked up the single metal pod that Austin had packed with all the things he was keeping from his marriage, including his grandmother's hand-built wedding chest that Mona, his now ex-wife, had hated from the first moment she'd laid eyes on it. The remainder of the pod contained the rest of whatever he'd collected in his life from before he'd met Mona and married her.

Everything else, all that they'd acquired together during their ten years of married life, Mona got in the divorce. This included the house, which had more rooms than two adults and a child needed, along with the Mercedes Benz Mona had talked him into buying brand new, and all of their friends—none of which he'd had the desire to fight for after discovering Mona's betrayal.

Their marriage and everything that had come with it had been a lie, after all, and everything to do with Mona was now toxic. It was best to make a clean break, so he had, even to the point of quitting the accounting job he discovered he'd always loathed. At least since Mona received the majority of their combined assets, his alimony payments to her were reduced.

The only thing he'd wanted was shared custody of their daughter

Beatrice, Bea for short, and this he received, with Mona receiving full child support from him. Visitation rights seemed to be in the control of Mona and her lawyer, Mr. Bledsoe, but Austin didn't have the energy to get that arrangement to a more balanced state, so he'd just have to leave it, at least for now.

He would not miss the house. It was three thousand square feet of middle class with aspirations, done in what Mona considered classy golds and beiges, wood trim, marble kitchen counters, stainless steel everything. To him it had been cold, but because Mona had so enjoyed the decorating of it, he left it to her. Now, as he stood in the driveway with his two suitcases and his backpack, he felt as though he was leaving behind an ice cold cave full of plumbless depths of unfeeling interactions.

Well, that was one way to describe it. When he and Mona had over-borrowed to purchase the home shortly after they got married, it had been a structure full of promises, of hopes and dreams. But now, even if the house wasn't exactly hell, it was a place he was glad to be leaving, to be moving on from, to be moving out of.

His gut churned with uncertainty as he looked at Mona and Bea standing on the top step. Mona had her arms around Bea's shoulders, and whether it was to comfort Bea or hold her in place so she didn't run to her dad, he couldn't be certain. Probably it was both.

Mona loved being a mom. At least that's what she said. She probably loved Bea, in her own way, but Austin privately thought Mona mostly loved the status that came with having a daughter.

To Mona, having battle scars that needed to be exercised away, moisturized away, bragged about, made her one of a very special band of mama bears. It had been her dream since high school to be a mom, to have a family, and she'd chosen Austin to help her with that.

In his senior year in high school, Austin had been planning on a quiet career in accounting with the aim of becoming a CPA. He'd had no thought in his head for girls at all. Had never attended the dances, had never asked anyone out on a date. Pleasure came with close male friends and Friday night pizza, b-ball on a Sunday morning, and the occasional camping trip to the Sand Hills in Nebraska when the weather was warm.

That all ended when Mona had, evidently, sized him up and determined he was the answer to her prayers. She wanted out from the confines of her little life in podunk Sterling, Colorado, and as none of her football boyfriends were currently in the running for college careers, but instead were looking at local stockyards, feedyards, and the sugar beet factory for jobs, Austin had become her next best option.

Of course, this awareness in retrospect had been gleaned from ten years, fourteen years if he included the years they'd dated during college, of listening to her chatter with her girlfriends, and listening politely to her parents at Thanksgiving. Listening to ex-boyfriends who were so drunk they probably didn't realize they were giving away all of Mona's secrets.

Austin had prospects, a future. Mona wanted out. That Bea was born nine months to the day after their wedding, or even that the wedding had been all about Mona, hadn't bothered Austin as much as the fact that she bragged to everyone there about how they were moving closer to Denver, to Thornton, so Austin could advance his accounting career more quickly. Like it was a done deal, though Mona had not consulted with Austin. But to keep her happy, he went along with it.

He'd not wanted to leave Sterling, not really. He enjoyed the slower pace of small town life, and didn't mind that the grocery store only had three brands of peanut butter. Didn't care that there was only one movie theater. Didn't mind that there wasn't a Starbucks and that the old-timers hogged the one good coffee bar on Sunday mornings, filling up the space with their low chatter and worn, time-seamed faces. Didn't even mind that the bars all served Coors and Budweiser beer.

At one time, he would have wanted to sketch those faces, to capture the weary exhaustion, the camaraderie among them. He wasn't good enough with pencil to capture that and watercolor seemed too obnoxious, as he couldn't imagine being that obvious about it, bringing even a small watercolor kit to the coffee shop. In the end, he never drew them, and anyway, Mona disliked him fooling around with anything that wasn't her. Didn't like him to focus on anything other than work, family, and home. Which is what he'd done, losing all of his friends in the bargain.

Now he was alone. Truly alone as he stood in the driveway, two suitcases at his feet, backpack over one shoulder. Briefly, he checked his phone. A taxi was coming to take him to the Motel Six along the highway, and after that, he wasn't sure. A few interviews via Zoom, and then dinner at the nearby Denny's.

"Mr. Bledsoe will be calling you about visiting Bea," said Mona. Her grip on Bea got tighter. Bea was only nine and, as far as Austin could tell, was overwhelmed and scared by what was going on. Only Mona had never seemed to talk with Bea about the divorce, at least she hadn't during Austin's last week in the house. "Maybe once a month?"

"C'mon, Mona," said Austin, keeping his voice level, even as rage beat in his heart. "It's got to be more than that. Be fair."

Mona's mouth was a firm line and, even from this distance, Austin could see she wasn't giving in. Oh, the stories she was probably telling to her mama bear clan about how awful Austin was. The details she would share about them, about their marital relations, were absolutely going to be less than flattering. What she would leave out was the fact that one—Roger Colchet—had been coming to all the backyard parties for the neighborhood Mona liked to throw. And the fact that when Austin had been out of town for a CPA conference, Roger had spent the night with *Bea* in the house.

That's when Austin put his foot down. That's when Mona had asked for a divorce.

All the rest of it, the expectations of a suburban life that Austin never seemed to appreciate, the sighs of disappointment that Austin never joined in with the neighborhood husbands in betting on football games, the slightly lackadaisical way Austin tended to the grass of their expansive front lawn—in short, the never-ending stream of criticism, Austin could have shrugged off. Just like he'd shrugged off the shudder of disgust she'd make when, after he'd pointed out that going down on each other should be mutual, she'd give him a blow job, then spit everything out, then make the face she'd make because, as she told him many times, when he came, he was icky.

He'd go down on her, he loved pleasuring her, loved making her feel good. He thought her body was beautiful, if on the skinny side, and he applauded her attention to self care, and paid the credit card bills for her endless waxing, mud treatments, and massages.

She was constantly fraught with anxiety over pubic hair, and got a Brazilian wax every other month, if not more often. Legs waxed. Underarms. Upper lip. Every little hair that wasn't on her well-coiffed head went under the strip to be ripped off.

The effect was smooth-skinned Mona. The side effect was her disgust that he simply would not shave down there, would not get his balls waxed. He told her no a hundred times and never gave in. He groomed himself, sure, but it was his body, and he would do with it what he liked.

It didn't matter to her he kept fit by working out at the gym, went to the fancy Cherry Creek hairdresser for his haircuts, like she liked for him to do, wore the bespoke suits she picked out for him. She might have designed him to be the perfect accountant husband, but his body was his own. He'd even resisted her suggestions that he get the freckles on his shoulders bleached. No, no, and no.

It was only in retrospect, perhaps even while standing there as the taxi pulled up, that he realized it wasn't just his pubic hair that disgusted her, but all of him. From the top of his dark, ginger hair to the tops of his ginger-hair flecked toes, all of him elicited a sneer from Mona. Unless she had to, she never touched him.

Sure, when there were people around, he got hugs and tender pats, but even those had been in neutral places, his waist, his shoulders. In bed, when it was just the two of them, Mona would welcome sex, but then she wanted another child so she could have a matched set.

Sex was the way Mona wanted it, missionary style, with a few variations. She did not want anything weird, and she most certainly did not want his *thing* in her face every other minute. She did not want anything to do with nasty butt sex, either, and though she would, from time to time, use her well-manicured hand to jerk him off during her period, to avoid blood on the sheets, those fingers never strayed, never lingered, never caressed.

She'd never once touched his ass except by accident. When he found out via a credit card bill that she'd bleached her anus, it was a mystery to him who that bleaching was for, since she never wanted him straying from her lady parts, which was what she called them.

Except for regular, straight up missionary style marital relations, he might as well have been a virgin. And, as he watched the driver load his suitcases into the trunk of the taxi, he felt very much like he'd been kicked out of his own life.

He did not know what that new life would look like. Other than the Motel Six, he did not know where he would lay his head. Who he would talk to as he ate. With his degree, CPA certificate, and all of his experience, he was sure to get a job almost right away. But a job wasn't life. A family was life, only his family was now in tatters.

"I'd like to hug her goodbye," said Austin. "I'd like to say goodbye properly. Please?"

Austin would have bet a million dollars that the only reason Mona nodded permission and released Bea was because the taxi driver was there. He was a witness to the kind of mom Mona was, the kind of divorcee she was. In Mona's mind, the grapevine was a lusty conduit of gossip and talk and reports, and what you were seen to do was very, very important. Mona's reputation was important to her, thus she allowed Bea to leave her side.

Bea raced down the steps and into Austin's arms like she had a hundred times, no, a billion times before. She loved to dash, loved to hurry, her long strawberry blond braids flying, cheeks flushed, arms wide open.

"Dad, dad, dad." Bea's voice was muffled against Austin's shirt, her arms going around him as far as they could reach. He bent down and hugged her to him, kissed the top of her head, calmed her fair hair with his palm.

He had about two minutes before Mona called a halt to this outrageous show of affection between father and daughter. He had that long to make sure Bea knew he loved her with all of his heart.

Before Bea had been born, he'd been terrified at the prospect of being a dad, of being responsible for a tiny human being. The moment Bea had been placed in his arms at the hospital, he turned away, holding her, completely forgetting Mona's mom was there, fussing over Mona, bringing her lipstick and something to color her cheeks for the photographs Mona's dad was taking.

Instead of all that, all the chatter and the heightened emotion, he bent and kissed Bea's tiny forehead and vowed to love her for all eternity. She smelled like a baby, a bit like sweetness so newly born there had never been another smell like it. Her eyes, when she blinked up at him, were a dark moss green, just like his own. And at the top of her head, a sprout of strawberry blond hair. She had all her fingers and toes and was perfect in his eyes.

"Mom says I have to take ballet lessons," said Bea, wiping strands of hair stuck to her face with tears. "I don't want to, Dad."

"Maybe give it a try, honeybee," he said, soft. "Those little ballet outfits look awfully pink and cute. You like pink, right?"

"Sometimes," said Bea with a little huff, uncertain, it seemed, whether she wanted to go along with him distracting her from the fact he was leaving for good and she didn't know when she'd see him again. "Not all the shades of pink, though."

Bea loved color and however hard Mona had tried to restrain her daughter in her choices of outfits, of paint for her bedroom, of notebooks and shoes, that love could never be quashed.

Where Bea had gotten her sense of style, Austin could not be sure, but he loved it on her, loved that she was brave enough to wear what she wanted to wear. Which, currently, was purple corduroy pants and a paisley patterned multi-colored shirt that might as well have come out of the hippy section of an ARC Thrift Store rather than a high-brow children's boutique in Cherry Creek.

In a very short span of time, once Austin's taxi was out of sight, Mona would likely go through Bea's closet to re-do the whole wardrobe to something more fitting for the child of a newly divorced woman who might or might not already have a new boyfriend.

"Think of the little tutu," he said, kissing her forehead. "Think of the cute little pink ballet shoes."

She made a face, as if thinking this over. He clasped her face in his hands and gently kissed her nose.

"I love you *so* much," he said, looking straight at her so she'd know he meant it with all of his heart. "I'll visit as often as I can."

"That'll be forever from now," she said, wailing, her moss green eyes filling with more tears. "I want to see you every day. *Every* day."

"Yes, I know."

"The taxi's waiting, Austin," said Mona, somewhat crisply. "And Beatrice and I have an appointment downtown."

"No ear piercing, Mona," said Austin. "We agreed Bea gets to decide if she wants them after she turns ten."

Mona merely shrugged her shoulders at this, flipped her dark hair, and shook her head. Which had been her reaction to all of his objections for the past fourteen years. In this instance, Austin wasn't budging.

"No, Mona, and I mean it." To Bea, he said, "If they come at you with the piercing gun, just start screaming, okay?"

Bea smiled, a smile she only shared with him, delighted to be given permission to rebel. He'd taught her that over the years, reinforcing with her that she got to say how long or short her hair was, whether her ears were pierced, whether she'd allow her mother to take her to a salon to get her nails done.

Bea enjoyed playing out of doors and so those nails were history within the hour after their completion. He'd always thought that if Bea wanted her ears pierced, then a nice, clean tattoo parlor, with professionals, would be the place, but he'd never convinced Mona of this, as Mona considered tattoos an abomination to her beautiful skin.

"Okay?" asked Austin. "Scream loudly. Everyone will hear, and the piercing won't happen."

"Okay, Dad," said Bea.

Her mouth trembled and her eyes grew big, and Austin knew he was just being cruel by dragging out the goodbye. He pulled himself out of her arms and gave her the best smile he could.

"See you soon, honeybee," he said. "I love you."

"I love you too, Dad," she said, tears falling down her cheeks.

The taxi driver helped him out by stepping forward.

"You want your backpack with you, Mr. Marsh?"

"Yes," said Austin, shifting his attention from a sad-shouldered Bea returning to her mother's side. "I'll carry it."

The taxi ride to the Motel Six along the highway took exactly seven minutes. Austin tipped the driver, grabbed his suitcases from where they'd been placed, and checked in at the front desk—all as if on autopilot. It was as if the years between him graduating from high school, which was when he'd really started dating Mona, and this moment had all been erased. Like the last fourteen years had never even happened. He was newly born, newly arrived on the planet, and he knew not a soul.

"Room 218," said the clerk, handing him his plastic card key. "It's around the back."

His room being around the back meant that it was on the second floor facing the highway. There, the noise from trucks and cars speeding along the cement was a constant song in his ears, along with the jackhammer blasts of repairs and construction from around the building next door that echoed off the cement barrier blocks placed on the edge of the highway.

Thornton was a busy place, a noisy place, but for now, until he secured a job and a place to live, it was home.

As he laid his suitcases on the other double bed, his phone beeped at him. He took it out to look.

Google was reminding him he had an online interview with Leland Tate of Farthingdale Ranch in fifteen minutes. The position was for an accountant and included room and board. The salary wasn't that great, but it was something.

There were plenty of accountant jobs, especially for those with a CPA certificate, but he was picky. Which had been another thing Mona had groused about, as he wouldn't take a job in downtown

Denver so they could all live in a swank high rise overlooking the Denver Botanic Gardens. And now, he wanted to move as far away from Denver as he possibly could, far away from Mona.

He didn't know whether he wanted to be so far away from Bea, but the alternative, to stay nearby on the chance of seeing her felt as though he was giving into Mona, yet again.

He had fifteen minutes to freshen up, to wash the grief from his face, to tame the cowlick along his right temple. In short, he had fifteen minutes to make himself look like he wasn't a broken man. Hopefully, the interview would be short so he didn't have to pretend for very long. But really, why was he worrying about it? A place like Farthingdale Ranch probably wouldn't want a city boy doing their books anyhow.

3

CLAY

*C*lay strolled back into the Rusty Nail, hitching up his jeans so Levi could see that Clay had gotten what he needed from Mr. Grey Suit. And if there was a trace of misty watercolor not-quite-happiness trolling around in his brain, Clay wasn't going to say anything about it. He had a reputation to uphold, even when there was only Levi to see.

"Want another beer?" asked Clay as he sat across from Levi at the table by the front door. "I'm going to have one. Maybe I'll find another guy."

Levi shrugged, then raised his hand so the waitress would see and come over for their order. When she did, Levi quietly ordered two beers and laid a five-dollar bill on her tray, even before she brought them their beers.

As always, Levi got the most amazing service anywhere he went, which Clay admired, though he didn't have money to throw around the way Levi did. Which always made him wonder, if Levi had money, why was he working at a ranch that required employees to put in 12-hour days?

"It's not craft beer," said Levi when the beers came. "But it'll do."

"It'll do," said Clay in echo, though he didn't really know what craft beer was.

He tapped his frosted beer mug against Levi's as he scanned the Rusty Nail. It was that time of night when the early crowd, made up of couples and groups of friends, were finishing their second beer or second margarita, wiping their hands free of grease from the buffalo wings or cheese fries, and packing up to go home.

The later crowd was just coming in, consisting of more hardened drinkers, truckers, sugar beet farmers, not dressed up, just coming in from the fields, it seemed like. They would want beer and whiskey and then more whiskey.

There was a little lull in the music, so Clay got up, digging into his pockets, and smiled when Levi handed three quarters over so Clay could go over to the jukebox and pick just the right songs to help the Saturday night party shift into high revel. He picked two classics, *Boot Scoot Boogie* and *Honky Tonk Badonkadonk,* and was just about to pick his third song when through the swinging louvered doors to the bar's kitchen he saw Eddie Piggot.

Of course Clay knew Eddie owned the bar, but he preferred to forget about it. Out of loyalty, Clay shouldn't be at the Rusty Nail at all, especially after what had happened with Ellis, the ex-con doing parole on the ranch. But the next closest bar was in Chugwater, or Cheyenne, and most Saturday nights that felt too far to drive. Or, if Clay got roaring drunk, it felt too far to ask Levi or Brody to drive. So here he was, holding the final quarter Levi had given him between his thumb and forefinger, about to drop it in the slot of the jukebox, when he heard Eddie shout.

Eddie always sounded on the verge of a breakdown on account of he seemed to feel like life had dealt him a handful of jokers when he wanted straight aces or kings or whatever. Clay wasn't much of a card sharp, but he knew a losing player when he saw one. No matter how much Eddie screamed about the ranch taking away business from real cattlemen, as long as he ran a second-rate bar, nothing was going to change for him.

Not that Clay minded the plywood floors and the chipped paint in the men's bathrooms. He rather liked it, liked the story the bar seemed to tell. But with Eddie at the helm, the whole outfit was a down-at-the-heels affair and just about two steps from being at the bottom of the barrel. So shouting in the kitchen was normal, only this time, as the swinging doors swung slowly on their sagging hinges, Clay saw Eddie smack some kid, smack him hard.

The kid, who couldn't have been more than nineteen, staggered back, glaring at Eddie, which seemed to earn him another hard-palmed slap. Now the kid's mouth had blood on it, and there was a gleam of sweat across his forehead. The kid looked to be just about too young to be working in a bar, anyhow, and though Clay didn't figure himself to be some kind of Superman rescuer, suddenly he couldn't stomach it.

Bounding in through the swinging doors, he grabbed Eddie by the shoulder and hauled him back.

"Knock it off, you fuckwad," said Clay, almost conversationally.

Eddie jumped back, as though shocked to see Clay there. As for the kid, at the same time he was goggling open-mouthed at his sudden rescue, he also seemed to be looking around the kitchen, as though for a good, hard implement to hit Eddie with.

"Who asked you, you piece of shit," said Eddie, shouting, spittle flying from his mouth. "This here ain't none of your concern. Get your fat ass out of here and go back to your stupid fake pony farm!"

"Fat ass?" asked Clay, though everything else Eddie had said rankled just as badly. "I'll have you know—" He paused to point his thumb at his own ass. "—that this is Grade A *Prime*, and you'd be lucky to even get a piece of this."

When Eddie swung at Clay, Clay was ready. He might not be drunk enough to blame all of this on beer, but he was loose and relaxed and his fists were plenty fast to block Eddie's arm and hit him good and hard right in his stupid mouth. Eddie, who must have been gearing up for this kind of interaction all day, punched right back. Two hard taps, one to Clay's mouth, and the other to Clay's eye.

At which point some woman in a tight capped-sleeve t-shirt and blue eyeshadow, her hair clasped in white barrettes on either side of her forehead, flew at them.

"Leave him alone, leave him alone," she screeched, battering at Clay with her manicured hands.

"Who the fuck'er you?" asked Clay, a little dumbfounded to find out that Eddie had a girlfriend, for that's exactly who she must be. As to what kind of person would want to bed Eddie Piggot, well, that was another matter.

"That's my mom," said the kid as he wiped his mouth with the back of his hand. "Better get."

"Fuck it," said Clay. "I'm out of here."

Clay slunk through the swinging doors, listening to the shouting grow dim behind him as he found Levi and jerked his head at the door.

"What did you do?" asked Levi, though he asked it in a way that suggested he was not at all surprised that Clay had gotten mixed up in something. "Was that Eddie Piggot who hit you?"

"Yes," said Clay with a grunt. His lip felt large and swollen, and he could taste blood in his teeth. Not to mention his left eye, which was puffing up and throbbing.

"Do you need ice?" asked Levi, ever polite.

"No," said Clay. He licked his lip. "Let's just go home."

That Eddie Piggot would not call the cops on Clay was almost a foregone conclusion, partly because Eddie hated anything to do with the local law and partly because the kid Clay had just rescued was surely not old enough to be working in a bar. Or maybe he was old enough to be working in the kitchens, but not in the front serving alcohol? Clay couldn't be sure, but that he and Levi could get into Levi's truck and trundle back to the ranch without red and blue bubble lights swinging up behind them said a lot.

Not that Clay was off Scott free, no, of course not. There was still the Sunday morning meeting to contend with. Leland would take note if Clay was missing from the weekly all-call that Leland held before that weeks' guests started arriving at noon.

Levi dropped Clay off in front of the path that led to the staff quarters, and Clay got to his room before anyone spotted him. His room was on the top floor at the very end, overlooking the three managers' cabins nestled among the trees. It was a simple space with only a bed, a dresser, a little desk, and a small bookshelf, but he had his own bathroom, clean sheets and clean towels delivered once a week, and it felt more like home to him than anyplace else he'd ever lived.

In the bathroom, he shrugged out of his blood-dappled shirt, tossing it on the closed toilet before examining his face in the mirror. His left eye had taken the worst of it, swollen almost shut, swiftly coloring to dark purple. The split in his mouth felt deep to his tongue, was tender, and tasted of blood, though it didn't look too bad. Still, Leland would notice right away when he saw Clay, and he would want answers.

He spent the night in the bathroom with a cold cloth pressed to his eye and another cold cloth with ice bundled inside pressed to his mouth. Every other minute, it felt like, he checked in the square mirror in his bathroom, just to see.

In the morning, the curve of his eye was still purple and dark on one side, the shape distorted. The circles under his eyes were purple-blue. There was no way Leland was going to miss the state of Clay's face, and not even Clay's best puppy dog expression was going to put Leland off from one of his famous lectures.

And indeed it did not, for as hard as Clay tried to stay inconspicuous the next morning during the daily meeting, as studiously as he stood in the back row, half-hiding behind Jasper's broad back, Leland was as sharp-eyed as a hawk on a clear day. While Leland and Maddy went through the list of special requests from the guests, and mentioned once again to keep sharp eyes out for mountain lions and, as always, went over the protocol about tips from guests and suchlike, there was no point, not one, that Clay did not imagine Leland had not seen the shape of Clay's face. Leland's gesture to Clay as all the other employees disbanded to their various tasks and routines proved it.

"A word, Clay," said Leland as he handed the clipboard back to Maddy. "In my office, if you would."

There was no way Clay was going to say no to the boss who was, and had been from the very beginning, his friend and wise advisor. From the start of their relationship, openness and honesty had been a two-way street, only now, perhaps for the first time, as Clay stood in the doorway to Leland's office, watching Leland sit and clasp his hands over his belly, he felt a bit tongue tied.

"So," said Leland in the conversational tone he used when he wanted to get straight to the point but, perhaps, also wanted to make the fellow on the other end of the line wiggle a little before confessing to everything on the planet. "I take it Saturday night was a success?"

"Sure was, boss," said Clay, smiling to make his dimples show.

Leland was unmoved by the romance of Clay's smile, his dimples, or anything else. But then, he never had been. Only curly-haired Jamie had shifted Leland from his I'll-be-forever-alone stance on life, and Clay wished them both all the best.

"And I take it there was an altercation, though whether it was before or after last call is another issue."

"Way before last call, boss," said Clay hurriedly, for while he sometimes got sloshed, he was never an embarrassment to the ranch and always would get a ride home, usually from Levi or Brody. "I'm not that kind of guy."

Leland looked at his felt cowboy hat, now resting on its wooden hook right above Leland's laptop. That Leland wanted to toss it in his hands while thinking was obvious, but that he didn't showed Clay how serious Leland was about the as-yet unremarked-upon marks on Clay's face.

"Take a seat, Clay."

Clay sighed as he saw Leland's broad gesture to the other chair in the office, a spindle backed wooden chair that creaked as he sat down in it. True to Leland's nature, he furnished the ranch with the best that could be afforded while his own office got the leftovers.

"Care to tell me what brought you to this state?" asked Leland. "That eye has got to hurt."

"It's going down some," said Clay. "I put ice on it last night."

"All of last night, it looks like, from the circles beneath your eyes."

The expression on Leland's face was one of concern, of kindness. Clay swallowed hard, absorbing the tenderness coming from Leland, kicking himself at the same time for causing Leland any worry at all.

"Did you sleep any?" asked Leland.

"No, not really," said Clay. "Look, I'm sorry. It was just Eddie Piggot was—"

"Told you not to mess with him," said Leland. "If you're going to go to the Rusty Nail, then you need to be circumspect about it and not go off half cocked when he pisses you off."

"I was, honest," said Clay, and when Leland leaned forward to rest his elbows on his knees, Clay's body responded in echo.

"So what happened?"

"The swinging doors to the kitchen, right?"

Leland nodded.

"I saw him smacking some kid around in the kitchen, some young kid. Eddie was hitting him hard. Hard enough to draw blood."

Leland's eyes narrowed, fury smoking from his eyes.

"Then he said I had a fat ass and then he called the ranch a stupid fake pony farm."

There was a smile on Leland's mouth, even as he tried to look stern about it. With a sigh, he straightened in his wooden desk chair and tipped his head back to look at the ceiling before returning his attention to Clay.

"You have a nice ass," said Leland, the smile moving from his eyes to his mouth. "As you must know."

Clay nodded. "Told him it was Grade A Prime."

With a bark of laughter that he perhaps regretted a moment later, Leland's face grew serious.

"He can say all he wants about the ranch," said Leland. "It's just talk and always will be."

"I punched him over the kid, mostly," said Clay, as earnestly as he could. "The rest of it came after, and that's when he clocked me."

"Who's the kid?" asked Leland.

"I don't know," said Clay. "The kid said the lady with Eddie was his mom, so—"

Leland lifted his hands as though an unexpected and perhaps unnerving miracle had occurred, but what he said was, "There's someone for everyone, I reckon."

"That there is," said Clay, growing quiet, for however mildly Leland was speaking to him, there was no way retribution wasn't coming.

"As for you," said Leland. "You're all marked up, so you can't be customer facing until the swelling and bruises go down."

"Bet you didn't say that to Ellis," said Clay, folding his arms around his belly. Not being customer facing meant no trail rides, no being part of riding lessons, no going to the dances or the storytelling by the fire or the chuckwagon breakfast. Clay was being shoved to the side, fit only to be tasked with hauling hay, picking up trash, raking the arena, scraping carrots in the back of the kitchen.

"Ellis got six months added to his parole," said Leland, stern. "Your punishment is to be not customer facing. You're lucky you're not fired."

The sting of that hurt worse than Eddie's fists, for while Clay would never give a rat's fart about what Eddie thought of him, he cared deeply and to his true soul what Leland thought of him.

The seriousness in Leland's eyes was steady, never wavering. When it came to the ranch, the horses, the guests, the employees, Leland was die hard all about making it work, making it perfect for guests, as well as good for the people who worked for him. He trimmed the broken and bent and unnecessary, and cultivated hard work and honesty.

Praise came to those who tried their best. That's what Leland expected from his employees, and especially from himself. And maybe he had high expectations for Clay and saw them crumbling, for Clay saw in Leland's eyes a flicker that could have been sadness or regret for having to be so harsh with Clay. And that made it worse. Made Clay's heart turn in his chest.

"I'm sorry," he said. "I hadn't had a lot to drink atall, just that Eddie always gets on my nerves and when I saw him smacking that kid— well, I shouldn't have hit him but I did, and I'm sorry."

"I know," said Leland, and he patted Clay's knee because he possibly was very aware that at that moment Clay was beating himself up more than Leland ever could. "I have something you could do for me, if you're up for it."

"Anything, just tell me," said Clay. Even as much as he might grouse about being on the B-roll for work on the ranch, he'd crawl under barbed wire to rescue a lost calf if Leland asked it of him. "What can I do?"

"Had an interview yesterday," said Leland. He stood up and grabbed his felt cowboy hat from the hook, which signaled that, at least for now, Leland was done with his lecture. Later, maybe, he might have more words of wisdom to offer, and Clay would listen with his whole heart to each and every one. But for now, he was grateful to stand up as well and follow Leland out into the front of the barn, out of the shadows and into the sweet June sunlight.

"Oh, yeah?" asked Clay, only partly interested in who Leland had hired, more interested in the fact that Leland had *hired*. The ranch had been on a tight budget all season, and that there would be someone new coming to the ranch meant that the purse strings were loosening. That things were getting better.

"New accountant," said Leland. He put on his hat and adjusted it over his forehead, and looked with long-seeing eyes at the ranch. "Needs to be picked up this afternoon. Can you do that?"

"Why can't he drive himself?" asked Clay. He wasn't trying to be obnoxious about it, just curious, and Leland seemed to know this, for he shook his head as if bemused at the vagaries of human behavior.

"Not sure, except that he just lost everything in the divorce. All flights are booked as well, so I need you to pick him up."

"Can I take your truck?" asked Clay, and though he expected to see Leland reaching into his pocket for the keys to his silver F150, he was sorely disappointed when Leland shook his head again.

"You almost got a ticket last time you drove it, so no."

4

CLAY

The more grubby type of chores were reserved for Sunday morning after the meeting, the kinds of activities that guests might not want to observe while on vacation. That meant Clay spent his morning shoveling horse shit into bins so they could be loaded into a truck and hauled away to a local composting place.

Sometimes Leland talked to Clay about doing their own composting, but then the discussion would turn to the fact that such work might make the ranch more of a farm, which wasn't what Leland had in mind. In the end, the work was sweaty and smelly and Clay hauled and lifted and scraped, going way past noon and lunchtime just to get the job finished. By the time the truck full of horse shit trundled down the road, Clay was drenched in sweat, his eye was throbbing, and manure dust was sticking to his skin.

Overhead, the sky was scudding into low grey clouds, which meant rain. Which was good for manure dust, but bad for guests who were anticipating storytelling hour around the fire pit when it got dark.

"Help Jasper set up the canopies at the fire pit," said Leland, striding past on his way to important managerial tasks. "Then go pick up the accountant. Take a shower before you leave."

"Yes, sir," said Clay with a mock salute, though a second later he regretted it. Leland didn't deserve that kind of sarcasm; Clay deserved what he was getting.

Leland saw, of course he saw, Leland saw everything, but he just shook his head at Clay, as if he'd expected better and didn't like to be disappointed.

Down at the fire pit, Clay joined Ellis and Jasper, who were already laying out the poles and cords for the canopies, which would be set over each area of seating. Though Ellis smirked at Clay's state, obviously having heard about the Saturday night fight with Eddie Piggot, he didn't say anything. But then, he never did say anything much, only pointed to the rolls of canvas as if to ask Clay's help in unrolling them.

"Sure," said Clay. "This end? Or that one?"

"That," said Ellis.

"Okay."

"Grade A Prime, huh?" asked Jasper, as they all bent at the waist to unroll the canvas.

"You better believe it," said Clay, wincing inside, wondering if he was ever going to live that down.

Jasper was big and gruff, but his low chuckle was friendly enough. Evidently everybody had heard just about every last detail as to what had happened at the Rusty Nail.

Levi had been the only one from the ranch present, but that didn't mean anything. Levi didn't gab like that. Likely the story had travelled through some line of gossip, as there was always talk in the local community about Farthingdale Ranch, and about how Leland Tate, the ranch's manager, was bringing the place back from the brink of disaster due to a guest who'd gone missing at the end of last season.

Clay didn't like to think about how close he'd come to losing his dream job, and his memories of this particular guest were dim. Had he seen him at story hour, when Bill trotted out his best ghost stories? Or had it been earlier? Brody always swore that he remembered this guest quite clearly, and sometimes the two of them got to talking about it over lunch in the dining hall, but Leland always quashed such conversations, and so the discussions were always short-lived.

At any rate, it wasn't Levi who'd been spreading the story about Clay's ass, that was for sure. Though who it had been, Clay had no idea. The story would go as the story would go and the best thing to do was to laugh it off, to pretend it didn't matter. After all, Leland himself said Clay had a nice ass, and that was good enough for him.

"Grab that pole," said Jasper, ever focused on the work at hand. Which was what Clay liked about him for despite his don't-talk-to-me nature, he always pulled his weight, was always on hand with the right tool for the right job.

"Got it," said Clay.

Together the three of them set up the beige-and-blue canopies over the hay bales and broad logs that ringed the fire pit. If there was a soft rain, then story hour could happen. If there was a hard rain, then the rain would come down furiously at a slant, and no overhead-canopy would protect the guests.

Maybe the story hour would be moved inside the dining hall, but Clay knew Bill didn't like the atmosphere, so the whole thing would likely be cancelled, to be rescheduled later in the week. Well, that wasn't his headache.

After they set up the canopies, Clay went to the dining hall, going back to the kitchens, where Levi was cleaning up from lunch.

"Got anything for me?" asked Clay. "Sandwiches? Something?"

"I've got chili and cornbread leftover from lunch," said Levi. "Would you like that? I could reheat it for you."

Levi, quiet and reserved, had the best manners at the ranch, like he'd come from a different world, which most likely he had. He was also kind of beautiful, blue eyes, broad shoulders, with glossy chestnut hair that curled behind his ears. He looked more like a magazine model than anyone Clay knew, and it was always a wonder to him why Levi didn't seem to mind being stuck in the kitchen all the time.

Sometimes, about every other week, Levi would pack up the chuckwagon to accompany a small, well-organized cattle drive that was mostly about camping under the stars and not a whole lot about driving cattle, at least as far as guests were concerned. Sometimes, since Levi wasn't an experienced driver, Clay would get to sit on the driver's side of the chuckwagon and guide the set of four horses.

He loved holding all those thick reins in his gloved hands and loved the rock-rock-rock motion of the chuckwagon. Levi's open air cooking was always a treat as well. Though, with Clay being in the doghouse, if there was a cattle drive, he would not be the one going, alas, alas.

When Levi brought Clay a tray neatly arranged with a white china bowl full of chili, topped with sour cream and decorated by green onions, he wasn't nearly as surprised as he pretended to be. What's more, the tray also held a neatly cut and quite large cube of still-warm corn bread, and there were several gold-foil wrapped cubes of butter in a small glass dish. Everything was arranged as elegantly as if Clay had been a customer in a cozy, up-scale cafe.

"You call this leftovers?" asked Clay with appreciation as he grabbed the tray and set it on a narrow wooden table along the wall where cooks and their assistants could take a break.

"Yes, I do," said Levi, dipping his chin down like he was still trying to get used to being teased about his fancy ways. "That's the last of it, though. Leland said you'd be helping me in the kitchen till your black eye goes down, so perhaps you'd like to help me make more?"

"Sure," said Clay, shoveling the food in as quick as he could. He still needed to shower and gas up the truck before heading out to pick up the accountant. "Soon as I get back, okay?"

"Where are you going?" asked Levi, using a large white cloth to wipe down his stoves.

"Leland hired an accountant," said Clay. "His name is Austin Martin or something. No, it's Austin Marsh. I have the slip of paper in my wallet."

"Well, it's about time Leland hired someone to do that for him," said Levi. He came over to Clay and stood with his arms crossed over his lean, white-aproned stomach, as though to make sure Clay was properly enjoying everything Levi had prepared for him like he should be. "That man works way into the night. I can see the light in his cabin from my window."

"So can I," said Clay, which made him feel worse about causing Leland any trouble. "Though nowadays that light might be for something other than work."

With a wink, Clay carried his empty dishes and used tray to the Hobart, and set everything in the carrying tray to be pushed through when the crate was full.

"Well, thank you for lunch," said Clay with a wave. Then he hustled to the staff quarters, raced up to his room on the third floor, and hurried through a hot shower which stung his lip and made his eye throb even harder.

After he showered, he shaved, changed into clean clothes, grabbed his cell phone, and checked for the slip of paper in his wallet. The Motel 6 where Austin was staying was located almost all the way to Denver, it seemed like, and though the drive along I-25 would be quick, Clay sighed. He did not like big cities, preferring the quiet outlands of Wyoming or places like Nebraska. Too many people all zooming around made him itch. He knew a lot of people at the ranch felt the same, but sometimes you just had to head to the Big City.

Grabbing his hat, he headed down the stairs and up the service road behind the staff quarters to the tin-roofed shed where Leland's truck was stored. Sitting next to the silvery goodness of Leland's F150 was Clay's yellow Toyota 4x4.

Clay's truck was not a beater, but it was old. It'd been old when he bought it to drive out west, when he and his dad had fixed it up together. That it was a bright lemon yellow and was developing tiny spots of rust over the wheel wells meant it wasn't likely to be stolen, so he always left the keys in the ignition, like Leland often did.

Swinging into the driver's seat, Clay buckled himself in, started the engine, and tapped the steering wheel as he listened to the engine ping as it warmed up. He would fill up near the interstate and get this errand over as quickly as possible.

"You got something loose in that engine of yours."

Clay turned his head to see Quint McKay, the ranch's trail boss, looking at him with appraising eyes from beneath a sharp-edged black felt cowboy hat.

Quint was the guy Clay never wanted to mess with, let alone ask to the Rusty Nail to be his wingman while he got his rocks off. Not that Quint was an asshole or anything, but he'd been around the block a time or two, it seemed like, and never suffered fools easily. Plus, he was older, older than Leland, and though good looking in a handsome, solid way, was not to Clay's tastes, so he'd never even considered flirting with him.

Sometimes when Quint was looking at him, Clay felt a bit like a fool. Though in reality, while Quint seemed too distant to easily be friends with, he'd never been other than polite to Clay.

"Yeah, I know," said Clay. "I looked in there and poked around last week, but couldn't see what was going on."

"You want me to take a look?"

"I would, but I've got an errand for Leland." Clay nodded his thanks. "Maybe when I get back?"

"Just let me know," said Quint. "I have the tools, so at least we can figure it out even if you have to take it to a garage. At least you'll know what to tell them so they don't overcharge you."

"Appreciate it," said Clay. "All right, I'm off."

As Clay backed up his truck carefully, so as not to run Quint, or anyone, over, Quint did not ask where Clay was headed, didn't seem the least bit interested. But that was like Quint, who, like Jasper, preferred to keep to himself. According to Leland, who had been hired by Bill when Quint didn't want to be the ranch's manager any longer, some years Quint worked year round, keeping the roads to the ranch clear during winter. Other years, Quint went off, though to where, nobody knew.

As for now, Clay trundled down the dirt and gravel road to the gate, let himself through, carefully locking the gate behind him, and zoomed as fast as he could to the interstate where he stopped at a Flying J truck stop to fill up. He also grabbed a small bag of Bugles and a large fountain drink Coke, just to tide him over while he drove to Thornton, where the accountant was.

Sucking on his straw and putting each Bugle on his pinkie before eating it helped keep him entertained for the first hour. The second hour, it started to rain. Traffic, just about the time he hit Johnson's Corner where the best cinnamon rolls known to man were to be found, got thick as it started to rain hard.

It was the kind of rain that was brisk enough to rinse the film off the roads and make everything slippery. Clay knew better than to speed, though it rankled that he had to get in the slow lane to let the idiots who didn't know any better pass him by.

He didn't stop at Johnson's Corner though he wanted to, but kept trundling along, adjusting his windshield wipers as needed, and wished he'd not drunk all of his Coke so fast. I-25 was a highway constantly under construction, especially in summer, so there were several lane changes, several close calls with the concrete highway barriers, and by the time he pulled off at Exit 219, he heaved a sigh of relief. Maybe on the way back he'd take Highway 85, which was more in the country, more to his liking.

The Motel 6 was easy to find, an L-shaped structure with metal doors painted bright blue to match the garish sign. Everything else was painted the same bland cream. Clay pulled up to the office, squinting through the rain. He should have called the number Leland had given him to let Austin Marsh know he was on the way, but even as he pulled out his cell phone to enter the number, someone stepped out of the front office, pausing beneath the small overhang.

The guy put down one of his boxy suitcases to wave at Clay, which was puzzling until it became obvious that Leland must have called to alert Austin Marsh what Clay's truck looked like. When the guy, Austin, picked up his suitcase and re-hefted his dark green backpack over his shoulder, he stepped out into the rain. Like it wasn't raining. Or, from the expression on his face, like it didn't matter that it was raining.

He was on the tall side, with dark ginger hair. He was wearing a thin windbreaker type jacket and plain beige trousers, and everything he wore was getting splatted with oblong black raindrops as he stood there.

"Hey," said Clay as he got out of the truck and hustled to the guy's side. "You're Austin Marsh, right? I'm Clay. Clay Pullman. I'm your ride. Did Leland call you?"

"Hello," said Austin as he shook Clay's hand. His voice was low and soft, not shy, but diffident, as if he felt he'd arrived at a party to which he'd not been invited. He looked at the truck, eying it up and down. "Are you from the ranch?" he asked. Then he added in a way that told Clay that Austin was only confirming this detail out of his habit of attending to details, being he was an accountant, after all. "Where will we put my luggage? It's raining."

"Yeah, I'm Clay," said Clay. "Nice to meet you. Leland sent me to pick you up, and I've got a tarp. We can store everything under that, but we better hurry before the clouds really break loose."

Austin looked at Clay with careful eyes, eyes that were a moss green shade, made darker by the color of his hair. He shrugged, moving his broad shoulders beneath the helplessly inadequate wind-breaker and nodded like he was all in, but didn't much care about what happened to him now.

Clay hurried to grab one suitcase, and together they stowed the two suitcases in the truck bed before covering them with a tarp, which Clay tied down with bungee cords.

"Your backpack?" asked Clay, holding out his hand.

"It's got my computer and backup disk. My paints," said Austin. "I'll keep it with me, if that's okay."

"Sure," said Clay. "Hop aboard."

As Clay got into the driver's seat, he didn't ask why Austin had so little with him. Of course, as Leland had mentioned, Austin's ex-wife had taken his car so maybe she'd taken a whole bunch else, as well. Or maybe Austin preferred to travel light.

Clay wanted to know all about the divorce, which sounded messy and interesting, but it wasn't polite to dig like that. Besides, Austin seemed a quiet kind of fellow who was loaded down with memories he couldn't bear thinking about.

"How long till we get there?" asked Austin as he placed his backpack between his feet and buckled himself in.

"About three hours?" said Clay. "Maybe four in this weather. It'll be just about dinnertime when we get to the ranch. You'll like it there. The food is good, and it's quiet."

Austin nodded but didn't say anything, and remained watchful the whole time Clay drove them along the road and onto I-25, which, just like every afternoon, was turning into a parking lot. By the time Clay reached Exit 221, he'd had enough of the stop-and-go traffic and so turned onto 104th Street.

"Why aren't we going on the highway the whole way?" asked Austin.

"I hate highways, especially this one," said Clay. "We're going to take a nice little backroad, it'll be great. Maybe we can pick up some coffee along the way from one of those little in-and-out coffee shops. Sound good?"

"Sure," said Austin, though again, the tone of his voice told Clay it simply didn't matter to Austin what they did.

There was a kind of hangdog air about him, a dimness to his eyes. Not quite passive, but resigned. He must have gone through the wringer with that divorce, and this was what was left of him. Sometimes, marriage seemed like a hell Clay would never willingly enter, and Austin was proof of that.

5

AUSTIN

*A*s Austin had imagined that the rain wasn't coming down very hard, and as his winter coat was stuck in the POD in a storage facility on 58th street, he'd made do with his windbreaker, the one Mona had purchased with a keen desire that he take up golfing so she could hang out at the Cherry Creek Golf Club bar.

The golf lessons Mona signed him up for had been a failure, as Austin had always been too distracted by the lush green of the course itself, and how the edges of the trees cut sharp lines into the Colorado sky.

The golf clubs were probably still in the closet in the house that was now all Mona's, and the only remainder of the golf experience was the beige windbreaker. Which was proving to be completely inadequate for a mid-June rainstorm. Which meant that by the time he'd received Leland's phone call and watched as a yellow truck pulled up at just about the same time, he was chilled through, feeling a little like he'd been standing on a rock overlooking a tumbled sea, being dashed by waves.

His life was not hard, but right then, as the truck parked right next to the office of the Motel 6, he felt hard done by. A little bit battered and a whole lot cold and tired. And not thinking straight because if he had been, then when a young man in a cowboy hat stepped out of the truck and smiled at him, he would not have felt like he'd been showered with sunlight. A lemon gold array of sunbeams and sunflowers and blue cornflowers.

In addition to all of this, the young cowboy had a black eye and a split lip, which added to this magical aura a sense of grit and danger. Should Austin actually be letting such an obvious ruffian drive him all the way to Wyoming?

Austin must be exhausted, pure and simple, to be thinking such thoughts when the remains of his life had been torn into a million pieces, flakes of ash, which were still swirling, grey and pain-tinged, all around him.

The young man came toward him and offered his hand for Austin to shake, which he did, feeling a tad unbalanced. When the young man introduced himself as Clay and that he was from the ranch, the words washed over Austin as he took in the yellow truck, thinking only about where he'd store his luggage so it'd be safe from the rugged weather as they drove.

Clay took care of the suitcases, eager and energetic, and then slipped into the driver's seat. There was nothing for it but for Austin to slip into the passenger seat, where he tucked his backpack between his legs and buckled himself. As Clay started the engine, the warmth from the truck's heaters washed over him in another way, an enveloping way, that made his muscles ache as he became warm all the way through.

Clay drove out of the parking lot and, at some speed, joined the traffic on I-25 headed north. At this time of day on a Sunday there weren't a lot of vehicles on the road, but as always, there was a melee at the junction. And while he might have been worried, remembering Mona's urging him to get in the fast lane, always, so he could show off his new Mercedes Benz, Clay drove smooth and sure, sticking to the middle lane. His hands were steady on the wheel as the windshield wipers swept back and forth across the glass, hypnotizing Austin to where all he wanted to do was cry like a baby and fall asleep, never to wake up again.

It was only when Clay took the exit onto 104th Street that Austin thought to question Clay. The answer, something about taking the back highway, lulled Austin back into his stupor where memories and regretted words swirled around the painful jagged place where lingered his sorrow and worry over Bea. She was his only child, maybe the only one he'd ever have, and though he knew, logically, that he'd not done anything wrong, he was wholly responsible for the tears in her eyes as his taxi had pulled away.

"Want some coffee?" asked Clay. "It's real good here. Or at least it was last time I came this way."

Blinking as he did his best to focus, Austin looked at Clay, and then at the storefront of a little shop called Martha Sue's Cookies. He could have sworn they'd passed at least two Starbucks along the way, and yet Clay had stopped here for the coffee he'd promised Austin earlier.

"Yes, please," said Austin.

He clambered out when Clay did, sniffing in the crisp rainy air laced with diesel fumes that built in him a sense of longing for a home he'd never had. Then, shivering again in his windbreaker, he mindlessly followed Clay inside to the small shop whose well-shined linoleum checkerboard floor glittered almost too brightly to be borne. He felt like he was wincing as he gave his order and reached too slowly for his wallet as Clay paid for both their drinks.

"Here's yours," said Clay as he handed Austin his drink. "Be careful, it's hot. Blonde mocha, no whip, huh?"

"Yes," said Austin, unable to muster the energy to explain that while he enjoyed fancy sugary coffee and had taken up this particular drink at Mona's encouragement, he didn't really know now what kind of coffee he enjoyed. Maybe at the ranch there would be something new he could try. "Thank you."

He followed Clay back outside where the rain had taken on an urgent, almost aggressive slant. He was cold by the time Clay started the engine and turned the heater on high, and sat shivering as he drank his coffee, blinking almost with astonishment as the caffeine rushed into his system.

Right about this time, had he been with Mona, and had they together stopped at such a place as Martha Sue's Cookies rather than a Starbucks, Mona would be giving him a piece of her mind. No, Mona would be giving him *several* pieces of her mind, though she'd take back every other one, wary, perhaps, of upsetting Bea in the back seat, but still going on in that way she had, shrill, strident, opinionated.

"Are you warm enough?" asked Clay as he pulled out of the parking lot and back onto Highway 85, headed north. "You're shivering."

"Thank you, I'm good," said Austin. He sipped his drink, wincing at the hot liquid, at the sugar on his tongue.

Sometimes, coffee was just too much when a nice, cold beer would have been better. He wasn't much of a drinker, though he loved the crisp coldness of a beer. Mona never liked beer, didn't like for him to drink it, either. To her, the only acceptable drinks were the expensive kind, like she saw influencers making on YouTube and Instagram. But enough about thoughts of her.

Clay drove along, steady hands on the wheel, keeping to the right-hand lane. The windshield wipers set a predictable beat that lulled Austin into a deep doze where his full-hearted attempts to talk with Mona about what was going on between them mixed in a dizzy dance with their happy times during the early years of their marriage.

Of course she'd wanted what she'd wanted, didn't everybody feel that way? Wanted what they wanted and never mind the other person? Not Austin. He'd tried to give her what she wanted and failed. Tried to be the man he saw in her directed comments, the wishful thinking he saw in her dark eyes.

He'd loved her with his whole heart, flattered by her attention to his young, nerdy, accountant-wanna-be self. Ecstatic as she'd singled him out from his friends in high school, cutting him off as easily as a trained sheepdog might. He was not immune to being wanted by her, had not been aware, back then, what her true intentions had been.

And maybe Mona hadn't known herself what she was doing but perhaps, guided by Glamour magazine articles about how to improve your man, felt she'd set her sights on a good man while wanting him to be a better man. Her kind of man. The man who would save her from a life working in a paper box factory or a sugar beet mill.

No. He did not want to think about Mona any longer. All of this was a river of regret he did not need to be headed down over and over again. He'd call Mr. Bledsoe, Mona's lawyer, first thing Monday morning, and work out a better version of his custody rights to see Bea. He had to put this behind him, but since Mona had been part of his young adult life for so long, it was hard. Still, he had to try.

Looking up, focusing on the grey-black road that stretched out in front of them, squinting to see the single white line that marked the edge of the highway, he thought he heard a small *skree-skree* sound coming from the engine. He didn't know engines, so instead of saying anything, he took a swallow of his coffee and straightened up, feeling like he was at a party he forgot he was attending.

"So where are we?" he asked, unable to think of anything more stimulating to say than that.

"We're just coming up on Platteville," said Clay, pointing with his forefinger, keeping his hands on the steering wheel. "It's about two hours from here to the ranch, give or take. Last time I drove to Denver was after I had just started at the ranch and Leland needed me to pick up a shipment that didn't make it all the way to Wyoming, I borrowed Leland's truck to do it. He's got the sweetest silver F150, but I guess I got overexcited, because I almost came home with a speeding ticket. Hence you're getting a ride in Ladybelle, rather than Leland's juicy ride."

"Ladybelle," said Austin, gazing with only half-interest at the tall, round, silver water-draped grain silos glinting by the window at speed. Who named their car? He never had, but he found it a little sweet that this young cowboy with his split lip and black eye would take the time to give his old yellow truck a nice name.

"Yeah," said Clay. "We used to have two mares, Lady and Belle, but they got too old to be ridden so regularly as they might be on the ranch. For horses like that, rather than put them down or sell them to the dog food factory like some ranches did, Leland always donates them a rehab riding school. You know, the ones where little kids in wheelchairs or kids with palsy can ride a real horse? They were the first two horses I rode at the ranch, so I named my truck after both of them."

"Really?" Austin's mind seemed to stir to life, being affected by an onslaught of ideas and images he'd not been expecting.

"The rehab ranch is south of Denver," said Clay. "Parker, I think."

A small silence filled the cabin as Clay drank his coffee, and Austin cupped his in his hands. It was his turn. Clay had just spilled out a plethora of information about himself, about Leland, about the ranch. In polite company, at least at accounting offices where Austin had worked, when a co-worker shared you had to share back.

The only thing Austin had to share was the fact that his life was in ruins, his head was still whirling from Mona's infidelity, and his heart was full of pinholes of grief and he only wanted to cry and shrink down until he became invisible. But the rest of the world wasn't like that. You had to get up and keep walking, keep acting human until you felt human again. *Act as if it's true until it becomes true*, someone had told him, though he couldn't remember who.

"So, accounting, huh?" asked Clay, not taking his eyes from the road, though Austin could feel Clay's attention shifting between him and the road, between Austin's continued silence and the whisk-whisk sound of the wipers on the windshield. "Is it hard? I only took basic stuff in college, too much in a hurry to graduate and get a job on a ranch, I guess."

It really *was* Austin's turn.

"I like the orderliness of the numbers," he said, blurting the first thing that came to his mind, regardless of how banal. "I'm not an obsessive guy, but I enjoy making sure that all the numbers in the columns balance as they should."

Clay raised his eyebrow as he looked at Austin with a half-grin. It was at this point that Mona, however much she appreciated Austin's income and could brag to her mama bear friends about her CPA husband, would wave a manicured hand and declare that it was too boring to listen to him go on about how it actually all worked.

"Not obsessive, huh?" asked Clay with a small laugh. "All those tiny details, you'd have to be obsessed, at least a little bit, to enjoy that kind of work. I mean, right?"

Taking a long, slow sip of too-sweet coffee, Austin did his best to focus on where he was. On what Clay had just said. On what he meant, which was probably miles away from what Mona would mean. Maybe he needed to trust that a new job, a new life, brought with it new expectations, new interactions. Sometimes, things stayed with you even though you wanted to let them go, though. Change was never easy. Still, he had to try.

"I guess I might be, at least a little bit." Austin took another sip of his coffee and looked out at the rain. At the passing scenery, the low fields, the silver-streaked rails of the train track that ran parallel to the road. "I like numbers. I like order."

In the back of his mind, he knew that what all of that offered to him was a kind of mental stillness. If everything was lined up, then everything would work as it should. Though, even though he thought this, felt it, even though he worked hard at that orderliness, Mona had shredded through this part of his psyche with razor-sharp efficiency, leaving Austin with nothing but emptiness.

"That's probably why Leland hired you," said Clay. "He's that kind of guy. You know, a place for everything and everything in its place. You'll like working for him, though, I think. Even though sometimes —" Clay broke off, shaking his head, and Austin seized the moment to turn the focus of the conversation back to Clay.

"Sometimes what?" asked Austin. Then, to keep the ball rolling, he added, "Sometimes bosses can be part of the problem."

"Oh, no," Clay said as he straightened up sharply, as though Austin had poked him with a straight pin. "Leland's the best, by far, of anyone I've ever worked for. It's just that I'm all full of woe an' stuff on account of I can't be customer facing, not with this black eye." Clay took his hand off the steering wheel long enough to gesture to the left side of his face. "Which means that, at least this week, I can't go on trail rides or teach riding lessons and especially I can't drive the chuckwagon for Levi."

"The chuckwagon?" asked Austin. He had a vague notion what that was, but only a vague one. He'd been so grateful for the offer of a job that would take him far, far away from Denver he'd barely glanced at the ranch's website.

"The chuckwagon is like a little food truck for the little cattle drive we take guests on," said Clay, smiling. "We only take ten head or so of cattle, and we don't go very far, but guests love it. We sleep out under the stars in canvas tents and eat Levi's good cooking in the fresh air. And I'm just pissed that I'm going to miss it, even if it is my own fault."

"And how is it your fault?" asked Austin.

"Well, Leland doesn't like any of his staff fighting. Only I got into a fight with Eddie Piggot." Clay shrugged as if amazed at his own foolishness. "He was in the kitchen of the Rusty Nail hitting some kid that works for him. Might have been his stepson, I don't know. Then he said crappy things about the ranch and stuff, and I just didn't want to put up with it anymore. You know?"

Sometimes things shifted in Austin's mind, like they were doing now, all of a sudden, sharp and unexpected. Whereas only a second before Clay had been an average two-dimensional person, albeit dressed in cowboy boots and sporting a cowboy hat, now he was someone else. Someone with depth and ideas and the heart of a knight set to rescue a boy hapless enough to be working in the back kitchen in a bar in a small town.

"That's not right," said Austin. "I mean, what you did was right, but what Eddie Piggot was doing was wrong."

"He owns the Rusty Nail, which is the closest bar to the ranch." Clay shook his head, his mouth thinning. "Looks like I can't go back there until Eddie sells up or hell freezes over. So now it's a bar in either Cheyenne or Chugwater and they're at least half an hour's drive. Not fun to drive that far late on a Saturday night."

Considering this again shifted ideas in Austin's head. He was going to Wyoming, to the middle of virtually nowhere, and now he learned that while Cheyenne and all its diversions were only half an hour away by car, the closest bar was run by someone cruel enough to smack the kitchen help around. As to what the rest of the bar was like, as to what the beer tasted like, he'd probably never get to find out now. Which might be more a blessing than not.

6

CLAY

There was a part of Clay that always loved a good road trip, even though sometimes his hands grew numb on the wheel and the windshield wipers were going so fast it was giving him a headache. Just a little one, as he wasn't prone to them, but enough to take some of the joy out of the experience. Plus, his passenger looked like he wanted to barf just about every other second, and while Lady-belle had seen worse than a little barf, he felt bad for the guy.

"Are you okay?" asked Clay. "We could stop an' take a break."

"No, thank you, I'm good," said Austin in the way he'd said it before, like he was going to say it again and again, as many times as might make it true.

For all he was holding himself so narrow, Austin Marsh took up the whole passenger area of Clay's yellow truck, and though his energy seemed low, and his beige windbreaker seemed too thin, there was something Clay couldn't quite put his finger on. Or maybe that's how he always felt when he met someone new. After all, Leland hadn't been hiring much all that season, so it'd been a while since he'd met someone new. Of course, there was Ellis, but Ellis just was, somehow becoming part of the ranch the moment he set foot on the property.

"Do you hear that?" asked Austin, sitting up, attentive, like an unexpected thought had just occurred to him.

"What?" asked Clay.

"It's coming from the engine."

As though alerted to its own plight, the engine gave a loud shriek that went round and round, and though Clay's hands were steady on the wheel, the truck yawed to the right.

Quickly, checking his rearview mirror, though it was impossible to see through the rain on the back window, Clay pulled over to the side of the road and turned the engine off. He could smell the effort the engine had given to get them that far, though that was eclipsed by the sudden realization that they'd broken down in the middle of nowhere. If Clay hadn't been in the doghouse before, he certainly was now.

Though Leland wasn't the kind of boss to throw his weight around, he was going to be more than displeased at Clay's lack of maintenance and upkeep on Ladybelle, and the delay in bringing their new employee home.

"At least there's no smoke coming up from the engine," said Austin. "What do you think it is?"

"No idea—" started Clay, but he had to stop when there came a light rapping on the driver's window from a highway patrolman dressed in rain gear who no doubt wanted Clay to move along. He rolled down his window, chest growing tight. "Hello, sir."

"Hello, young man," said the officer, whose badge indicated his name was Emmett Carvelle, badge 348. "Engine trouble?"

"Yes, sir," said Clay, reaching for his wallet while he pointed at his glove compartment. Luckily, Austin seemed to know what he needed, for he clicked it open and started digging.

When Clay handed over his license and registration and insurance card, Patrolman Carvelle looked at it, rain dripping from his plastic-wrapped hat. Then Carvelle handed back the paperwork, which Clay blindly handed to Austin, who took it.

"I appreciate your troubles, sir, but you're about three feet from the railroad tracks on one side," said Patrolman Carvelle. "You're also two inches from the edge of the road leading from the grain mill on the other. Sunday night is shipping night, so you're going to have to move your truck before the bigger trucks start coming through."

"Yes, sir," said Clay, though he couldn't think beyond this moment. He needed to move his truck. He needed to get his truck fixed. He needed to call Leland and let him know what the delay would be. And he needed to make sure the ranch's new accountant didn't end up standing in the rain, getting soaking wet.

"Who's your passenger?" asked Carvelle, leaning down to gaze into the cab of the truck.

"I'm Austin Marsh," said Austin, with a small, friendly wave, like he wasn't bothered by the patrolman's presence at all, not one bit, and all the while Clay's heart was pounding. "Do you think you could help us with a tow?"

"Certainly."

And with that one word, the patrolman was on his radio, talking to someone from R & B Auto and Diesel Repair. Within five minutes everything was arranged and the tow truck was on its way.

Clay squirreled the information away for future need, for he'd had no idea you could just ask a state cop for help like that. Maybe it had to do with their precarious position in the shipping lane of the grain mill. Or maybe it had to do with Austin's confident air when he'd asked the question.

He looked at Austin and nodded his thanks, eyes wide. Austin nodded back and seemed to reassure Clay with a glance. Some guys were like that. They knew things like Leland did, and readily shared them. Clay absorbed everything Leland taught him, but sometimes, like now, he was still a little amazed at how easily things could go if you just spoke up.

"Thank you," he said, remembering his manners. "I get a little, you know, flustered when I get pulled over."

"Does that happen often?" asked Austin.

"Not so much as you might think, me being who I am," said Clay, a bit rueful.

"Which is who?"

"You know." Clay shrugged, his hands on the wheel where the patrolman could see them as he stood there waving passing traffic, such as it was, around them. Standing guard in the rain so he and Austin could wait in the truck. "Young. Stupid. I was probably going too fast as well."

"You might be young," said Austin. "But you're not stupid. And you weren't speeding. I was watching. You know. Nervous passenger going into an undiscovered country."

"Like the poem," said Clay.

"Yes," said Austin, and he seemed pleased that Clay had gotten the reference, for he smiled, warm and low, and though the smile didn't quite reach his moss-green eyes, it was nice to see, just the same.

When the tow truck arrived, tires splashing in the mud and gravel, Clay and Austin got out into the pouring rain, standing to one side while the tow truck driver silently, and without a word, hooked up the truck to the tow truck vehicle.

"Better grab your things from the back," said the driver as he held out a clipboard for Clay to sign as he handed over the keys. "Nobody's gonna work on this till tomorrow, and it'll be outside, as the bay is locked till morning."

Handing Clay his backpack, Austin hustled to grab his boxy suit-cases, and together they stood on the side of the road as the tow truck driver got in and took off, pulling Ladybelle down the road, back into Ault. The rain wasn't quite driving itself into the ground, as it was easing up, but the clouds were getting darker.

"Can I give you gentlemen a lift?" asked Patrolman Carvelle.

Austin opened his mouth, but Clay wanted to try out what he'd just learned about state troopers.

"Is there a place in town we can stay till tomorrow?" he asked.

"Certainly," said Patrolman Carvelle. "I can carry you to the Ault Motel. It's on the old side, and it's small, but it's decent. You can check out Grey's Cafe for breakfast in the morning."

"Thank you," said Clay, shivering as the rain trickled down his neck. He'd left his cowboy hat in the truck, so he was cold and felt half naked, though Austin, in his too-thin-for-this-weather windbreaker, couldn't be faring much better. "I hope they have rooms."

"They should." Patrolman Carvelle gestured to the back door as he opened it for them. "I hope you don't mind sitting in the back, but I've got gear and a rifle in the front that needs to be kept secure. I can put your luggage up front, though, since suitcases don't tend to reach for things."

"Sure," said Clay, as he slid into the back seat, eyeing the bars that separated the back seat from the front.

Austin followed a moment later. Together the two of them sat shivering, giving each other is-this-really-happening glances as the patrol car pulled smoothly into traffic, did a U-turn with complete indifference and impunity, and drove them back into town.

Now that Clay could look, he could stare at the small town, at the brick buildings and tidy lawns, as the patrol car trundled through it, driving slowly, the engine powerful and almost silent. Within two minutes, Patrolman Carvelle pulled up in front of a U-shaped motel, the kind where the motel rooms lined the parking lot. The sign indicating that this was the Ault Motel was an old neon one, the clips holding the tubes of light rusted from years of being out in the elements.

"Here we are, gentlemen," said Patrolman Carvelle.

He unloaded Austin's suitcases beneath the overhang of the lobby entrance, then opened the back door so they could slide out into the relative dry of the overhang.

"Thank you, sir," said Clay. "I mean it. I don't know what's wrong with Ladybelle, but I hadn't realized we were in the shipping lanes there."

"Not a problem, sir," said Patrolman Carvelle. "Glad I could help. Good day."

With a tip of his plastic-wrapped state trooper hat, which dripped with rain as he tipped his head at them, Patrolman Carvelle got back into his patrol car and drove slowly around the parking lot, looking at each car or truck in turn, as if he suspected he might find information that he'd need for a future arrest.

In the meantime, realizing that the parking lot was pretty full, Clay's chest got tight. He winced at the prospect of having to call Leland to tell him why they wouldn't be arriving in time for Sunday dinner.

Together they stepped inside of the lobby, out of the rain and into the cool *shug-shug* sound of the window unit AC, which pushed out cool, stale air. A woman behind the counter looked at them in a slightly bored way, but she stepped up to the counter.

"C'n I help you gentlemen?" she asked.

"Can we get two rooms for one night?" asked Clay. He pulled his wallet out from his back pocket, trying to remember how close he was to his limit.

"Sorry, we only got the one room. It's a queen. You want it?"

"I assume this is the only hotel for miles?" asked Austin, as he stepped up to the counter.

"That it is," she said. "There's a cattlemen's convention in Greeley, so everybody in the area is all booked up."

Clay licked the split in his lower lip and considered it. He'd shared beds with other men, both platonically and otherwise, but it was likely Austin hadn't.

"That okay with you?" he asked.

"I would say we don't have much choice," said Austin with a shrug, and though his words were straightforward, the look in his eyes told Clay that Austin wasn't surprised their journey was turning out like this.

"I don't snore," said Clay. "Promise."

Austin looked at him then, a mild smile playing across his mouth. Again, like before, the smile didn't quite reach his eyes, but he laughed a little bit and said, "I've been told that I do, alas."

With an echoing laugh, Clay handed over his credit card, holding his breath as the clerk ran it through and handed him a receipt to sign. Then she handed him a slip of paper to write his make of vehicle and license plate.

When Clay handed all of this back to her, sliding it across the glass-topped counter, he let out a whoosh as he took back his credit card. She gave him an actual key on a metal ring with an orange plastic tab that said in faded gold letters: *Ault Motel - A Hideaway on the Highway.*

"I think there's twenty-five dollars left on this thing," Clay said, tucking his credit card in his wallet, which he put in his back pocket.

"The ranch will reimburse you, right?" asked Austin. When Clay nodded, he said, "I'll cover dinner then, so you won't max out your card."

"Hey, thanks." It all felt a little brighter then, despite the rain. "I need to call Leland. Better do that now and get it over with."

Together they carried the suitcases to Room Seven, where Clay looked at the double bed in the small room and shook his head.

"At least it's out of the rain," said Austin as he tucked the two suitcases in the corner. "And now I need to call Mona, as there's a message from her."

"Okay," said Clay. "I'll give you some privacy while I call Leland."

"But it's raining."

"Eh." Clay shrugged this off. "I'll stay under the walkway where I'll be pacing to ease my nerves."

"That bad?"

"Only in my head," said Clay. "It's just that Leland runs a tight ship and I hate falling short of his expectations."

Clay stepped out of the room, closing the door most of the way shut, as Austin had the key and he didn't want to get locked out. Then, taking a breath, he scrolled through his contacts to Leland's number, and thumbed the green button.

While the phone rang, he looked out through the rain, which was layering the parking lot with long shiny sheets in a slow, almost meditative way. Which helped to calm him a little. Leland wasn't the firing type of guy, anyway.

"This is Leland Tate," came Leland's voice on the other end of the line.

"Hey, it's Clay."

"Yes, Clay," said Leland. "How are the roads? It's raining hard here, so we're going to have to move story time indoors, which pleases no one, especially Bill, who is quite displeased about it."

"Uh." Clay stopped to blow out a breath, knowing it was best to be straightforward with Leland. "We're in Ault. We're kind of stuck because Ladybelle blew something in her engine and then the highway patrol came and then the tow truck driver and now Austin and I are at the Ault Motel because the garage isn't open on Sunday."

"I see." Leland's voice came across the phone as it always did, level, steady, though Clay could almost hear Leland's brain ticking as he put all the pieces together. "Is everyone safe? Anyone get hurt? Do you know what's wrong with Ladybelle?"

"Yes, no, and no," said Clay. "Look, I'm really sorry. I could hear something in her engine this past week, but figured it was just regular wear and tear, not that something was going to break."

"And I'm sorry," said Leland. "If you're on company business, I should have let you take my truck, which is the company truck, really." Then after a pause he asked, in his way, as always, putting responsibility where he felt it needed to be, "What's your plan?"

"Well, tomorrow the garage will tell us what's wrong and then we go from there," said Clay. "There wasn't any smoke, so it can't be anything too disastrous. Hopefully, we'll be able to pick it up tomorrow and be home by dinner."

"And how's Austin?" asked Leland. "This isn't the best way to introduce him to how the ranch works."

"He seems like a good guy just going along to get along," said Clay. "Listen, Leland, this is all my fault. I know it's important that we hired this accountant—"

"Clay."

Clay stopped talking.

"Sometimes things happen. All you can do is do your best, right?"

"Right."

"Now, get yourself some good dinner, and keep the receipts. Let me know in the morning how it's going."

"Okay," Clay said, feeling his shoulders come down at least four inches. "Thanks, Leland."

"Not a problem. Talk to you tomorrow."

At long last, the hard part was over. Leland knew about the disaster that had befallen them, and now all Clay had to do was his best. Except for the part where now he had to keep Austin happy enough to not simply up and go home, wherever that was now, and then share a bed with a man he'd just met.

Pushing open the door to the motel room, Clay saw Austin was sitting on the bed with his back to Clay. He held his cellphone pressed to his ear like he wanted to crawl through it. His shoulders were hunched, his elbows on his knees, body curled so tight he was like a coiled wire.

"I miss you, honeybee," said Austin, so softly and with so much love that Clay's body shivered in reaction. But who was honeybee? Surely not the ex-wife. "I know. I know. But your dad has to be away for a while until Mom isn't so angry."

A little silence fell while Austin listened to his daughter on the other end of the line. Rain started to fall a little harder, creating a curtain of grey that curved around the open doorway, as though shielding the motel room, turning it into a cave.

"Oh, I don't know about that," said Austin, straightening up a bit. "I don't think that's possible—Bea. Please don't cry. I can't—I can't see you right now. I can't be with you. You have to stay with your mom."

Austin scrubbed at his face hard, seemed to shudder and take a deep breath all at once, and Clay knew he was crying.

Here Clay had been thinking that a broken down truck and the future prospect of a lecture from Leland, as well as that slow head shake of his, which would tell Clay everything possible about how badly he'd screwed up, was the worst thing ever. He was in the doghouse already, so what was a bit more time there?

As well, what was an overnight stay in a small town motel compared with the trials of having to listen to your daughter crying on the other end of the phone without being able to comfort her? To have to tell her things she didn't want to hear?

Clay had never been divorced, but again, it had to be the worst thing ever. What he needed to do was steady himself so he could help Austin.

He was about to step out of the room again, to give Austin some space, when Austin hung up the phone with his thumb and snuffled loudly, wiping his mouth with the back of his hand. Then, as if he sensed Clay behind him, he turned, his shoulder cutting a line in the shadows of the room.

"Hey," he said, not quite looking at Clay but instead focusing his attention on some middle distance in front of him. "I apologize, it's just hard. She's only nine."

"Is Bea your daughter?" asked Clay.

"Yes, it's short for Beatrice, which Mona insisted upon."

In that short reply, Austin had spilled all kinds of beans he probably didn't even know he was spilling, like the fact that his ex-wife was sounding more and more like a royal bitch. The last thing he needed was Clay probing for more details, which would probably be painful.

"Hey," he said, drawing Austin's attention to him. "We've both had a shitty day, huh? Although I'd say yours was the shittier."

"Everything's relative," said Austin.

He stood up, scrubbing at his face with one hand as he put his cell phone in his back pocket. His expression as he faced Clay seemed to indicate that he was fully prepared for his life to keep going on like it was, that he was fully prepared for Clay to dislike having so much of someone else's emotions thrust at him.

"Well, I'd say we both deserve a treat," said Clay, putting on his brightest smile. "Why don't we check out someplace local to eat?" He paused to do a quick Google search on his phone. "Yes, this'll be perfect. It's called the Bison Breath, it's only a block or so away, *and* they have beer and cheese fries. What'd you say?"

He held out the phone and took a few steps into the room. Likewise, Austin took a few steps closer until he could read what was on Clay's phone.

"Bison Breath."

Austin looked at Clay, blinking hard, as though he was surprised to find himself in a small, slightly run-down motel in the middle of nowhere in a rainstorm with a guy he'd just met and there was only one bed. As if his life had transported him from where he'd been to where he was at that moment, on the verge of willingly going into a bar called the Bison Breath.

"Why not?" he asked with a shrug, and Clay had to smile at his bravery.

7

AUSTIN

*T*he Bison Breath was one of those bars built long to tuck between two buildings, which were, in this instance, the Ault VFW and the High Plains Harvest Church. The bar had only a few windows and those were high up, letting in sharp rays of street-lights in the rain. The upholstery for the booths was black, the bar was blood red, and the floor was an oddly splotched beige and brown.

When Austin inhaled, he could smell stale cigarettes, old beer, and a spritz of bathroom Polo that someone had applied with too liberal a hand. But he could also smell onion rings frying, and a fresh breeze from somewhere, as if one of the staff had opened the door from the kitchen to erase the funk from the place.

"Two?" asked the waitress as she stood there, eying him in his floppy and damp windbreaker and Clay in the DU sweatshirt he'd borrowed from Austin. The waitress wore a red t-shirt with an outline of a white bison and the words *A Whole Lot of Fun* with round white lines beneath, which were probably meant to look festive but which simply looked like a bad milk stain.

"Yes, please," said Clay, bright and shiny, smiling at Austin and they followed the waitress to the last booth before the bussing station. "I love bars like this."

"There's a dead stuffed bison head on the wall," said Austin as they sat down, wishing he could come up with something more scintillating to add to the evening's whirl of gaiety. "And there are bison painted everywhere. It's bisons all the way down."

Clay was busy memorizing the menu the waitress had handed him. When Austin picked his menu up, he could only imagine the implied wide variety was going to turn out to be variations on a theme, that is, burgers, any way you wanted them. Decision made, for without Mona's insistence they eat something trendy, he was going to order a cheeseburger with lots of onions, he could now let his eyes wander.

There was something comforting to be sitting still, out of the rain, with the anticipation of a good, greasy cheeseburger coming his way. And something energizing about Clay as he studied his menu, having turned it over twice now, with his blonde hair drying in dark-gold strands, his cheeks flushed, eyes bright. When he must have felt Austin look at him, he lifted his chin and smiled, showing Austin two sweet dimples.

"There's a dance floor, did you see?" asked Clay.

"Where?" asked Austin.

"In an alcove next to the bar."

Clay pointed over Austin's shoulder, though Austin didn't look, for there was something arresting about Clay's pleasure in this small fact, his smile, his brightness, drawing Austin to consider that, perhaps, the end of the day would be better than how it had started.

"I'll be your wingman if you want to ask some fine lady to dance," said Austin. Back in college, in the good old days, he and his friends would help each other bolster their courage to single out someone to dance. He'd been the recipient of such encouragement, so why not offer the same to Clay?

Clay gave him a look, an odd pull to his mouth as the waitress came up to take their orders.

"You go first," Clay said, gesturing to Austin and then to the waitress.

"I'll have a cheeseburger with extra onions and a beer, whatever you have on tap."

"You want fries with that?"

"Yes, please," said Austin.

After Clay ordered, getting pretty much the same thing, they both settled into their booth seats, and Austin found himself smiling at the picture Clay presented: a young man in a too-large sweatshirt that gaped from his neck, hair drying off, dimples showing. Pleasure radiating from him like a warm breeze.

"So, which young lady?" asked Austin. "Pick out one and I'll help."

He fully expected Clay to respond in kind, to offer Austin the same assistance, and perhaps add something about wanting to know if it was too soon after his divorce for such jocularity. Instead, Clay shook his head and looked a little rueful.

"The thing is," he said, taking a swallow of the glass of beer that the waitress had brought. "I'd be asking a gent. Not that I'm much of a dancer, although maybe I am, but I'd most definitely be dancing with a guy."

Mid-sip of the most banal beer he'd ever tasted in his life, Austin swallowed a little too quickly to give him time to think.

"Uh." Internally he winced.

"Will that be a problem?" Clay's expression, that his blue eyes went a little dim, alerted Austin to the fact that his answer was important to Clay. "If you don't want to share a bed, I can sleep on the floor, if that'll help."

The last thing Austin wanted to do was to make Clay sleep on the floor. His mind raced a bit, having never been confronted with anything like this in his life.

He'd only ever dated Mona. He'd never hung out with a gay man before, let alone slept with one. Though what did he know? Half of the guys he'd played b-ball with or went camping with could have been gay, and he was just too unaware to know it. And besides, what difference did it make?

"Well," said Austin, feeling a little like he was stepping through a doorway where one's true opinion could be expressed, where what he felt and thought would not be controlled by Mona. "I am a little concerned," he said, now grave, as though discussing world peace.

Clay looked worried for only a second, but Austin felt bad about teasing him even that much. "I am a *little* concerned. You said you don't snore, but really? Maybe you do. And maybe you're a blanket hog. Why should I trust you? Who's to say?"

To his pleasure and delight, Clay barked out a laugh, dimples rising, his eyes bright as though glittering with stars.

"Well, maybe *you* snore."

"I already told you I did, a little, so let's be clear about that. I've been upfront with you from the start about that." Finding himself laughing out loud, for it was just so silly and simple and easy, he smiled when Clay laughed again, shaking his head.

"Yes, you were." Clay lifted his glass, and Austin tapped it with his glass, and they were like that when the waitress came with their food, ample plates of greasy fried food and even greasier toppings. Fries spilling out of their grease-paper lined red plastic baskets.

They munched their way through the meal, getting second beers, though Austin winced as he tasted his.

"What's wrong?" asked Clay, polishing off his beer as though it was the finest in the world.

"It's uh—" Austin paused, wondering how much would be too much. "It's just that—"

"Out with it, my new friend," said Clay.

"It's swill," said Austin.

"Hey, that's America's finest." Clay nodded to affirm this, then stole a fry from Austin's red plastic basket. "Bud is the *best*."

Austin shook his head, glad that it seemed like Clay wasn't at all insulted, but making a game of it.

"There are better beers," he said. "Beers that taste of something other than—" He lowered his voice for effect. "Diluted cat's piss."

Clay laughed out loud, covering his mouth with his hand, swallowing the beer in his mouth, all at the same time.

"I don't know," he said. "That's all I've ever drunk."

"Well, I will show you the difference sometime," said Austin.

"I'll count on it."

When they were done eating, Austin insisted on paying for the check, folding the receipt around his credit card before slipping it into his wallet.

"You just said you only had twenty-five left on that card of yours," he said. "Besides, the ranch will reimburse the meal, right?"

"That's right," said Clay. "That's what Leland said."

Bracing themselves, they stepped out into the weather. With the clouds scudding low, it had gotten darker and it was still raining. Luckily the motel was just up the street and around the corner, but though it was only a block and a half, they were soaked through by the time Clay pulled out the key to unlock the door and let them inside.

"Oh, man."

Clay shuddered as he pulled off the sweatshirt Austin had loaned him and wiped his face and hair with it. Part of his t-shirt had been rucked up in the process, and now the curve of Clay's belly and a bit of his waist were on display, like an unintentional peep show.

As to what one gay man might see in another gay man in a moment like this, Austin had never considered, but perhaps it might be just like this, a flash of vulnerable midsection, an unobstructed gaze, just for a second, of someone's bellybutton.

Something in Austin seemed to shudder and wake up, as though pulled toward Clay for something more intense. As though Austin's body had ideas he wasn't even aware of.

Maybe his reaction to Clay was a lot like being attracted to a woman, but then what did he know about that, either? Mona had come at him a bit like a steamroller, not taking no for an answer and, in retrospect, had not really given him a chance to eye his future prospective mate before she yanked him down the aisle to the altar.

"I'm going to take a hot shower," Clay said as he draped the sweatshirt over the back of one of the room's chairs. "That'll warm me up."

"Do you want to borrow another t-shirt?" asked Austin. "I have sweatpants, as well."

"Really? That'd be great 'cause the last thing I want to do is climb back into damp clothes." The look Clay gave him was sweet and full of a sincere appreciation for the offer.

Silently, Austin opened one suitcase, then realized his extra sweatpants were in the other one, then opened that, as well. The floor was then decorated with open suitcases and pawed-through clothes. With a low, self-deprecating mock sigh, he handed Clay the dry clothes, then puttered about while Clay went into the bathroom and turned on the shower.

How strange to be here, as he was, in Ault, a pass-through, fly-over town that he'd never heard of, never been to, and would likely never visit again. How in the bathroom was another man, whom he'd only met that day, fully naked, showering.

Had this been an episode of murder TV, the voiceover would soon begin that neither of the men would be alive by morning or some such nonsense. But nothing like that happened.

Instead, Clay came out in a cloud of steam, looking strange in Austin's gym sweats, which were a tad too tight across the hips and too long on his legs, pooling around his ankles. The white t-shirt Austin had given him was also too long.

The effect was that Clay looked frumpy but comfortable in some ways, eye-catching in others, where the t-shirt shifted on his shoulders, or the way the sweatpants clung to him, snug across his backside, like he was well on his way to being in a commercial about gym membership.

"I'm going to drape my clothes here," said Clay, going about laying his clothes on the back of the chair closest to the radiator. "They'll be dry by morning, and thanks again for the loan."

"Sounds good." Austin grabbed up a dry, white t-shirt and his oldest, softest blue jeans, his belly tightening, something in his chest jumping. "My turn, I think."

Taking a shower with someone other than Mona waiting for him was just about as new and strange as it had been waiting for Clay while he'd been in the bathroom. His body tingled with the sensation of standing in the shower tub, where Clay had just been, using the soap Clay had just used.

But that wasn't right. He wasn't supposed to get worked by simply that, wasn't supposed to be having those kinds of thoughts about his new roommate. Working this through his head, he focused his mind away from that and onto the age of the grout, peeling away in places from the old, yellow bathroom tiles.

At least there was hot water. At least they weren't stranded by the roadside, standing in the pouring rain. They'd been helped by a highway patrolman and now, warm and fed, showered and safe, they'd spend the night in relative comfort. It was something to be grateful for, all of it, even if he'd be sharing his bed with another man, something he'd not done since he'd gone camping with his pals in the days before Mona, in the days of long ago.

When he'd dried off and gotten dressed, wishing he'd thought to bring in his shaving kit, he exited the bathroom amidst his own cloud of steam.

Clay was bending over to grab the remote, and the stretch of his body exposed a length of his hip, showing quite clearly that he wasn't wearing underwear. Which only made sense. The rain had soaked him all the way to his skin, so of course he'd be draping everything he'd been wearing over the back of the chair to dry.

Austin gave himself a shake, as he needed to get over any stray thoughts he might have, and just continue on as though this was the normal way of things. Which was hard, as Clay, scrolling through the channels with his thumb on the clicker, standing two feet from the TV, absently scratched his belly, exposing the same vulnerable skin he'd exposed before.

"Anything good?" asked Austin, doing his best to act as-if, which was hard because Clay was a handsome young man by anybody's standards. Good looking even in the eyes of a newly divorced straight man sharing a bed with said handsome young man. "There's always something good on the History Channel."

"There is," said Clay. He thumbed through the channels faster till he got there. "Looks like something on prairie grasses, but after that, it's pyramids and mummies. Sound good?"

Anything was better than what Mona liked them to watch together, which were shows about rich families and the one about the five guys digging deeper and deeper on an island off Nova Scotia, which could have been fun except they never found anything.

69

She also liked to watch football, but that was mostly because she enjoyed looking cute in an oversized player's jersey and posing for selfies for her Instagram account. Enough of that, enough of her. Austin turned and looked at the bed, as they might as well get this over with as soon as possible.

"Flip for the side?" he asked.

Clay turned, clutching the remote to him as though Austin had threatened to take away his control.

"I'll take whoever," said Clay. "Though I prefer—" he pointed at the side furthest from the door. "That side."

"Sure," said Austin.

He pushed the suitcases to the wall with his feet, thought about calling Bea while he plugged in his phone, and then decided against it. She was nine and resilient as all kids were, but there was no need to torture her with the fact he wasn't there to tuck her in and kiss her goodnight.

8

AUSTIN

Climbing into bed with Clay felt a little like getting ready for bed at a sleep-away camp. There was a sense of needing to be on alert, being in bed with a stranger for the first time. There was also a sense of Clay's nearness, the way the sweatpants just didn't fit quite right and exposed the length of Clay's side as he slithered beneath the sheet and single just-about-plastic motel room blanket.

"Is it too hot or too cold?" asked Austin as he figured it'd be better to get that taken care of before they settled in to watching something banal on the TV.

"No, I'm good."

Austin lay back, head on the too-flat pillow, hands laced across the folded down bedsheet, which was arrayed almost primly across his belly. He was lying there like a monk in a single cot when next to him, Clay shifted and moved this way and that, nudging Austin's leg first with his toe and then with his knee.

"Sorry," said Clay. "I might not snore, but I am what you call a sprawler."

"A sprawler."

Images, like unbidden fireflies, rose above the banality of the anonymous shades that colored everything in the room, beige and

71

white and cream and, except for the wildly overdone print of a bad watercolor, made him feel like he was sinking into a vast nothingness.

Except for Clay, vibrant and moving and alive. Austin knew wasn't likely to wake up in the middle of the night wondering who was in bed next to him, because there was no way he was going to forget it was Clay. Not with Clay's blond hair drawing faint shimmers of light on the pillowcase, not with Clay's whoosh of breath as he sighed his body into relaxing. Not with Clay's scent, warm from the day, traces of soap, traces of hard work he must have done at the ranch earlier.

All of this surrounded him, unlike any night he'd ever spent with Mona, including their wedding night. It was like a door had opened into another world, strange and new and vibrant. And most of all, when Clay must have felt Austin looking at him, he looked over at Austin, drawing the sheet up to his chest as though he was shy and not sure about Austin's intentions.

Austin had no intentions, not one. And, to some strange degree, no real thoughts about anything other than where he was, in bed with another man, a gay man, who had treated him, from the very start, with dignity and kindness and a kind of joy at meeting him.

"Should I set an alarm on my phone?" asked Austin, his mouth rather dry, like it couldn't remember how to make spit, let alone say something more interesting than that.

"I tend to wake up when the cock crows," said Clay, then he snickered under his breath. "What I mean is, I get up when I get up because I've got a full day of work ahead of me. Leland doesn't like it when I work twelve-hour days, though, so I probably could sleep in. Except you'll want to get to the ranch as soon as possible, I expect, so you can hit the books."

"Yes, I do love the books," Austin said, though that's not what his mind was focusing on at all. It was focusing on the curl of moisture that dampened a bit of Clay's hair to dark gold and stuck it to his forehead like the wayward lock of hair of a naughty child. But Clay was not a child. He was a man fully grown, and had thoughts and ideas so new, so sweet and bright, that Austin hardly knew what to do with them.

What if there was a world where people never, well hardly ever, aimed disparaging and critical remarks at one another? What if the world, the one full of Mona and bespoke suits and Cherry Creek haircuts and salons where one could have one's anus bleached, what if that world was behind him? And what if this world, full of midwestern beer that while ordinary and maybe a bit pedestrian, did its job of accompanying the taste of a cheeseburger and greasy fries, was the real one?

What if he'd stepped through a doorway into a world full of lemon yellow trucks that broke down in the rain, full of this ranch hand, this cowboy, who cared a great deal that he did the job his boss would give him the thumbs up for? A world where he, Austin Marsh, lately divorced and having survived a ten-year marriage full of sharp barbs, critical reviews and amply aimed words full of slings and arrows, had nothing more expected of him right now than to lie in a narrow motel version of a queen sized bed while watching the History Channel's version of the nine hundredth retelling of the mysteries of the Egyptian pyramids?

What if this world was the real one, and the one before, the one he walked away from, was the fake world?

Buoyed up by Mona's absence, the only thing dragging him underwater was Bea's absence. Would having Bea be worth having to live with Mona? Or would losing Bea be worth everything else?

"Hey," said Clay, rolling toward Austin with the bedclothes scrunched under his chin like he had a secret to tell that he didn't want anybody else to know about. "Are you okay?"

Startled, for when was the last time anybody asked him that, Austin looked at Clay, his mouth a little way open as his brain churned to figure out how to answer.

"I mean, you've been through a lot, and here you are—" Clay waved at the shape of both their bodies beneath the bedclothes. "Here you are sharing a bed with a stranger. A perfect gay stranger."

"I'm honestly not thinking about it like that," said Austin. "I am thinking about how this journey is taking me away from a life I knew but that didn't make me happy into a life that I don't know but that might make me happy." He smiled, thinking that maybe he shouldn't be sharing any of this. "Which is probably too much to be hoping for."

"Oh, you'll love the ranch," said Clay, wiggling like a puppy, moving closer without probably even realizing it. "I had one ranch job before this and because I was the low man on the totem pole, all I did was rake horse shit. I shoveled it, forked it, wheelbarrowed it, all day for days and days. They acted like it was a rite of passage, and while I'm fine with that because that's how it works, I figured it'd be fair that I got to do fun stuff, too."

"What's the fun stuff?" asked Austin, only mildly interested in what was happening on the TV screen where, evidently, a robot with a camera taped to it was trundling along one of the largest pyramid's many mysterious shafts.

"All the good stuff is with guests," said Clay. "Riding lessons, the trail rides, the dances. All that stuff. I'm good with guests, Leland says, so it's really killing me right now—"

Clay broke off as though talking about his own woes was some kind of bad manners.

"Anyway, after a month of shoveling horse shit at that first job, I answered an online ad at the ranch job website. I had an interview with Leland and Bill almost right away—"

"Who's Bill?" Austin stopped. "You mean Bill Wainwright, who owns the place, right?"

"Yeah," said Clay. "He's old, older than Leland, even, but he's always working, always around, and he tells the best stories around the campfire."

"I look forward to meeting him," said Austin, though what he really wanted, what made him feel an odd eagerness, was to hear more about what Clay did all day and what he found more fun than slinging horse shit.

"You will," said Clay. "He's always around, but he's not always where you expect him to be, you know? He has an office next to Maddy's, but he's hardly ever in it."

"Maddy is the ranch's admin, right?"

"Right. You'll meet her, too." Clay yawned, his mouth wide, red against white teeth. "Oh, look," he said, pointing to the screen. "This is the part where they mention ancient aliens only to debunk them. What do you think, Austin? Do they exist?"

"Ancient aliens?" asked Austin. He'd heard about them, of course, but never had given it much thought. "I don't know, but have you ever heard of the Drake Equation?"

When Clay shook his head, Austin explained how the percent of possibility showed there was nearly a one hundred percent chance aliens existed somewhere in the galaxy.

"And I'm not talking microbes either," said Austin with a yawn of his own. "I'm talking fully realized alien life."

"Cool," said Clay with an echoing yawn and a sweet, sleepy smile as he slunk low on the pillow, his eyes already half closing. As if sleeping with another man, one he did not intend to have sex with, was a simple everyday occurrence. And maybe it was. This was a new world, after all, where saying goodnight was not also accompanied by bitten back words of rage or, usually, not so bitten back ones.

Austin had held his tongue for a good many years, thinking that what he was experiencing was how married life was. It was only when he'd unearthed the fact that the neighbor had spent the night with Bea in the house that he realized it had all been a sham.

In fact, it had been Bea who had told him, innocent, unwittingly spilling the beans about Mom's new friend who'd had a sleepover with Mom. Mona's fury over Bea's telling tales had alerted Austin to so much more than the sleepover, which might have happened more than once, though he didn't care to ask as once was enough.

He also saw at that moment, and with some clarity as though he was viewing everything their marriage had been through objective eyes, how she'd cornered him in his own life. How she'd made him into an image suitable to stand at her side, but not suitable to stand on his own. For in a beige suit and tasseled loafers and a Cherry Creek haircut, he was no better than a Ken doll who was constantly being threatened with being locked out of Barbie's Dream House.

And now here he found himself in a motel in the middle of nowhere, reaching for the light switch on the lamp on the nightstand, flicking the room into darkness while he turned down the sound on the TV to let it drone on a bit before turning it off as well.

The next morning it wasn't quite raining, though with the skies scudding low, soapy grey clouds, it certainly was thinking about raining. And, as they waited in the small lobby of the garage, Austin could look through the small window to where Ladybelle, yellow and bright in the low gloom of the repair bay, shone like a sunbeam that refused to fail.

"Fan belt replacement and new spark plugs," said Clay. "I'm going to have to call Leland and get his credit card number." The sad pull along his eyes told Austin how Clay felt about this.

"I could cover it with mine," said Austin. As Clay shook his head, phone already out, finger ready to press the number to alert Leland what they needed, he hurried to add, "I work at the ranch now. I have the room on my credit card. The ranch will reimburse me. Let Leland know, by all means, but we don't need his card."

"Okay, I guess," said Clay, though the glum tone in his voice might be more about an anticipated lecture from Leland in his future.

As Clay called Leland and updated him as to their situation, Austin signed for the bill, handed the keys to Ladybelle to Clay, and within half an hour they were on the road again, the tires splashing through flat muddy puddles as they pulled out of the gravel parking lot and onto Highway 85 just where two lanes turned into one.

"We're only two hours from home," said Clay.

Austin nodded, happy to be moving with a delicious breakfast burrito from Grey's Cafe in his belly. When they reached Greeley, he pointed at the roadside coffee stand and silently, as if in full agreement, they stopped for coffee and were back on the road inside of a heartbeat.

It was only when they finally were trundling through the quiet town of Farthing that Austin's heart speed up. Farthing didn't look like much, just a sleepy podunk town like all the other flyover places he'd never been. By the horizon that spread out before them when they exited Farthing, he knew he was well and truly in the middle of nowhere.

Though there were still clouds drifting in the sky above, they were thin and puffy, showing blue sky behind, like a promise of something newly washed, wholesome, and somehow more delightful than any sky he'd seen before. Which was just his overworked brain trying to focus on something other than how his morning had begun. Which had been with him on his side, facing Clay, who had curled himself in the shape of Austin's body, as though, with just a little effort, he might push himself neatly into Austin's arms.

The sun had, just for a second, poked a brilliant ray of gold and blue between the parting in the curtains, shone on Clay's face, the curve of his cheek, the lay of his lashes like tiny lines of thought. Then the room had gone back into a state of semi-gloom, Clay snuffling awake, doing what men did when they woke up, which was to tame their morning erections with a sleepy gesture, like they were petting their cocks back into restfulness, like someone might soothe their dog, absently.

Austin didn't have that issue and, in fact, had not been overly troubled by erections it for the last six months or so. It might have taken years of Mona's criticism, or it might have been the end of a tail of comments along the lines of *Don't do that, it's so messy.* And *no, not in the morning, it's gross.*

The end result had been that his *thing*, as Mona had often called it, refused to waken as other men's things did, at least not around Mona, and not a heck of a lot other times.

He'd gone to a doctor who, after some testing, told him it was psychological and offered him Viagra, which he refused. He visited a therapist a few times, without Mona's knowledge, and was told the same thing and offered Ativan, which he also refused. From his research on the internet, he'd gleaned that his erection as well as his interest in sex would come back if he let it, which was no more than his doctor or therapist had told him and completely frustrating to boot.

Not that that was anything he needed to share with Clay who, as he petted and stilled and shifted and finally sat up, obviously had no problems whatsoever. He was a healthy young man with all the energy of youth, all the drive, and a perfectly normal morning erection. All of this was sweetened by his smile, which Austin found himself the focus of, found himself absorbing almost without realizing it.

Clay stopped Ladybelle at the gate to Farthingdale Ranch, a rustic sign with the name glinting with bits of iron twisted into rustic shapes.

"That's new this season," said Clay. "Jasper, our blacksmith, made it. He's a whiz at stuff like that." Then, after a second's pause, Clay added, "Could you get the gate? I mean, I could get it, but usually the passenger gets it."

"Oh," said Austin, though he knew he really shouldn't be surprised that this was how it worked. He was in the world of gates and cows and horses and hay and each day, each moment, really, would be full of unfamiliar sights and smells and things that needed doing. Which was exactly what he needed at this moment in his life, for as his life, or what he'd figured had been his life but had really been Mona's, had been taken away, the ranch would give him a new one.

9

AUSTIN

*C*lay drove Ladybelle into the ranch, over a stone bridge, through a small glade, and across the round circle of the parking lot where the trees seemed to step back to reveal a wide sky-blue vista over glades of green trees. The air was sweet and fresh, and he took a deep breath of it.

The truck trundled along a dirt and gravel road that seemed to lead to the very heart of the ranch. There, as Clay parked in front of a large red barn whose double doors were swung wide open, stood Leland Tate, whom Austin instantly recognized from the Zoom interview.

Leland, the ranch's manager and his new boss, was even more vibrant and commanding a presence in real life as he shook Austin's hand. He even looked the part of a cowboy, with legs a mile long. And he was dressed much like Clay, except his snap button shirt looked as though someone had taken an iron to it before putting it on.

"I've got a quick meeting with the folks from BLM, so I hope it'll be all right if Clay shows you around. Then you and I can meet here in my office after lunch. Sound good?"

"Sounds great," said Austin because of course it sounded better than good. He would not be thrust into ranch life all on his own, and he would have Clay as his companion. Clay smiled, lifting himself up on his toes as if he'd been anticipating this moment for a good long while.

"That okay with you, Clay?" asked Leland.

"You bet," said Clay. "Otherwise, it's all chores, chores, chores. Right, Leland?"

"That's just about right," said Leland.

When Austin saw the smile they exchanged with each other, it wasn't as boss and employee, it was as friend to friend, only one of them happened to be in charge of the other. The fondness in Leland's expression, his warm gaze at Clay, spelled out such a difference. Showed how it could be not just between two men, but between two people who worked together and shared the ups and downs of each other's world. Which was how marriage was supposed to be. How his marriage should have been but never was.

"Great," said Austin, though as he knew he sounded a little less than enthusiastic, he dug deep to pull out how he really felt, though it was a little like trying on a new hat. "I'm just overwhelmed by how pretty it is up here. I honestly didn't know Wyoming could be so pretty."

"It is pretty," said Leland, though his expression wasn't one of simple agreement, but almost that he appreciated Austin's recognition of it.

Austin looked out over the green trees that ringed the gravel parking lot in a way that framed the view of a small grassy dip, beyond which a smooth river flowed. Beyond that was the bluebell-blue sky, and beyond that were the humps and round shapes that made up the foothills.

It was as though someone had painted a very large canvas and plopped it down for all to admire. The only thing keeping the view from being static and formal like a painting was the way the clouds raced across the sky dragging fleecy tails behind them, leaving swaths of shadow that moved across the landscape as the wind blew, rippling the tops of the green prairie grasses.

"Stella gave me the keys to your room, Austin," said Leland. He dug in his pocket and handed a set of keys to Austin. The phone in his back pocket rang, and Leland answered it while striding away. "See you," he said with a wave before going behind the barn.

"He's a busy man," said Austin.

"Well, he's got a lot to do," said Clay, looking at Austin from beneath the brim of his straw cowboy hat with some earnestness. "And if I'd gotten you here yesterday, like I was supposed to, he could have shown you around himself. He usually meets with the BLM folks about once a month, so he had to go."

"BLM?" asked Austin.

"That's the Bureau of Land Management," said Clay. "Their land abuts ours and since we graze our cattle there sometimes and take trail rides and cattle drives on it, it pays to have a good relationship with them."

"Ah." Austin nodded. "I guess I have to get used to living in flyover country where things are different from what I'm used to."

"Flyover country?" asked Clay as he hauled Austin's two boxy suitcases from the bed of the truck and hefted them one in each hand.

"That's places in the country that aren't on the coast, aren't full of beaches and nightlife that everybody wants."

"Well, I don't want that."

Sensing that he might have ruffled Clay's feathers, which he most certainly did not want to do, Austin took one of the suitcases from Clay, hefted his backpack on his shoulder and slapped on a smile. Clay deserved better than to have his lovely ranch maligned as being worthy only of being passed over.

"I'm sorry," said Austin, and he meant it. "I'm still ragged from the divorce—" He stopped, uncertain if Clay even knew he was divorced, or if it was common knowledge. "There's just been a lot of change in my life lately. I don't mean to be rude, though."

"Oh, you're not," said Clay with a shrug, his smile returning. "I know you'll like it here once you settle in. As for now, let me show you where you'll be living."

Now that they were going at a walking pace, Austin felt his body slow down and his eyes open to what was around him. He and Clay went along a dirt path beneath a tunnel of green leaves that granted sweet-scented shade while offering tidbits of blue sky, along the side of a large structure that looked like it was made of wooden logs. Up ahead was a set of stairs that led to a long shaded porch. He followed Clay up the stairs and then, once inside, up two more flights, until they were on the top floor.

"I'm at this end," said Clay, pointing to the left with his elbow as he turned right to go along the wood-paneled passage. "And you're at this end. The rooms are small, but you'll have everything you need and all the privacy, too. Most employees don't like to come up all this way, but when Leland asked me about it, I told him I thought you might enjoy the view."

Putting down the suitcase, Clay opened the door, which wasn't locked, and stepped back. It wasn't quite noon, so the room was in shadow, but beyond the small, white painted walls and the single bed with the white-painted iron bedstead, and through the open curtains, lurked the promised view.

Putting his suitcase down next to the tall dresser, Austin went to the window with a kind of wonder and leaned to look through the thin window-screen. To the left were more leafy green trees that might be cottonwoods, though he couldn't be certain, and long-trunked pines growing out of the hillside. To the right, through an opening in the trees, circled the glimmer of a blue river along a green bank, wending its way into the hills. And beyond that, open space, without a single building or structure or fence or power wires.

The view seemed to curve over a low plateau and disappeared into the distance of blue sky. In Thornton, or anywhere in the outskirts of Denver, such a view would have taken an entire lifetime to buy. But here, in the middle of nowhere, the view was being given to him, the ranch's newest employee. As a gift, a kind of bonus, maybe, though to think in those terms seemed to imply that he was trying to measure a view like it was money. Like it could be bought. Which it couldn't.

"Nice, huh?"

Clay came up close, pressing his shoulder to Austin's shoulder, looking out as though he'd not seen the view a hundred times before.

"I used to have this view before I moved to the other end of the hallway where it's a little shadier in the afternoon. That sun can get fierce in the afternoon, but the sunsets are gorgeous."

"I don't mind," said Austin, and he meant it. "That view is marvelous."

"All the views are like that," said Clay. He stepped back, and Austin turned to look at him, to absorb that smile, the pride that lifted his chin, the starlike sparkle in his eyes. "Every single one."

A thought flickered in Austin's head about the view he was seeing now. About the energy coming from Clay that he probably didn't even realize he was giving out, and that Austin was absorbing as though he was a battery that'd run all the way down to empty and feared he could never be recharged again.

Then Clay took the suitcase from the doorway and plunked it next to the other suitcase.

"If we leave these for now, I can show you around, and then we can get lunch." Clay nodded as Austin placed his backpack on the bed and shuffled the suitcases closer to each other. "You don't want to miss Levi's good cooking. He's the cook for the ranch, but I think he's had real training or something because he's just that good."

Having doubts that the cooking on a ranch was any better than a common cafeteria, Austin kept his thoughts to himself. He was used to a different life, different ways, but he'd left that behind him, willingly or not, and now he needed to get used to a new life. Which meant not voicing a negative opinion on every little thing like Mona always did simply because that's what all her friends did. Raise yourself up by taking the other fellow down a peg or two at any opportunity. He didn't want to be like that. Not here.

Together he and Clay clomped down the stairs to the long porch, where Clay took a moment to point out where they were to orient Austin. Then he led Austin through the small glade to the road, where he showed him the bunkhouses, the main lodge with the dining hall and rooms for guests above that, and the select cabins, the roofs of which could just be seen peeking up above a small rise.

"Those are pretty special cabins," said Clay. "They're very private and have amazing views. Let me show you the barn."

At the barn was a small gathering of horses in a group being led into a sandy arena. Along the wooden fence stood people dressed in cowboyesque outfits too new and too crisp to be real.

"That's the riding lesson, or one of them," said Clay. "Let's go this way. My face is still too banged up to be customer facing."

They walked for a good hour, up to the ridge where the fence between ranch property and BLM land was, beyond which loomed the foothills and a taller ridge of mountains, rugged and dark against the bright blue sky.

"That's Iron Mountain," said Clay, pointing. "That's where our storms come from, and our fresh breezes, too."

At the bottom of the road that led beneath the trees, they arrived at the gravel parking lot, where two flag poles stood between two wooden buildings. One was the ranch's store, and the other was Maddy's office.

"You'll meet her later," said Clay. "She's pretty busy on a Monday, with new guests and a whole lot of paperwork, so I hate to bother her. Ready for lunch?"

"Yes," said Austin, slumping with gratitude, for even though he'd worked out three times a week for ten years, there was a big difference between being able to do two sets of fifteen for every part of his body and actually using every part of his body to walk up and down stairs, up and down slopes, and all of this at a higher altitude than he was used to.

"We'll stop in the restrooms to wash up," said Clay, leading them around to the dining hall and into the gents in the entryway. There, Clay took off his straw cowboy hat and sighed at his reflection, at the blue and purple bruises around his eye. Then he put his hat back on and looked at Austin in the mirror as he washed his hands. "That's the last time I get into it with Eddie Piggot, I tell you what."

"He sounds like a real piece of work," said Austin, washing his own hands.

"He is," said Clay. "C'mon, let's eat."

Together they stood in a briskly moving line that took them through a buffet where, instead of the regular, ordinary cafeteria buffet dishes, there was an array of crisp fried chicken, and mac and cheese that looked homemade rather than coming from a box. There were also three different salads, an array of sandwiches cut into triangles with the crusts cut off, and three different desserts: chocolate cake, carrot cake, and something that looked like key lime pie.

"Holy cow," said Austin, sliding his tray along, unable to decide.

"Get used to it, my friend," said Clay, piling a healthy helping onto his plate. "You're about to enter the world of instantly gaining ten pounds. Though I think I gained twenty, but I hope it's all muscle."

By the time Austin joined Clay at a long table, across from two young men, he was on the verge of shaking as though he'd run a good long while.

"You okay?" asked Clay, spreading cloth napkin in his lap. "I should have been getting water for you. Around all the buildings there are coolers with ice and bottles of water. You should drink more up here, on account of it's dryer than where you come from."

"I will do that," said Austin. He gulped down his glass of water and gasped a breath as the good coolness slid into him.

"And this is Brody, our horse wrangler," said Clay, pointing across the table at a reedy young man who looked like he'd be filling out his shoulders in a few years. "And that's Ellis. He works with our blacksmith."

"Hey," said Brody, not quite meeting Austin's gaze.

"Nice to meet you," said Austin, nodding at Brody. Then he nodded at the other young man, whose dark hair fell across a unique-looking tattoo on his neck of a circle of blue water and a grey stone. Not having imagined that Leland would allow his employees to display body art that way, Austin kept his opinion to himself. "And nice to meet you, as well."

Ellis nodded, but didn't say anything. Austin was on the verge of thinking he'd made some sort of huge faux pax when Clay looked at him and shook his head, a slight quick movement that seemed to tell Austin not to worry about it and that Clay would fill him in later.

Which was sometimes how it went during meetings at his old job, where a subject might come up that bordered on being taboo, and a co-worker would shrug to dismiss the subject and the meeting would move forward without a word being said about it. That the same sort of thing would happen on a guest ranch in the middle of nowhere had never occurred to him, but it did happen, and he would just have to be patient.

"Is Jasper joining us?" asked Clay as he dug into his fried chicken, holding a thigh with his fingers, chomping into the crisp skin with sharp teeth.

Ellis nodded, and in that moment, his grey eyes shone like a beacon, and he was almost smiling. Then the smile turned real as a large, broad-shouldered man swung into the seat beside Ellis, flush-faced, and gruff around the eyes till he looked at Ellis and they shared a secret smile between them.

"How do," said the man. He reached an arm across the table in a genial way, offering his calloused hand for Austin to shake. Austin shook it, not quite wincing at the man's strength. "I'm Jasper and you're the new accountant Leland told me about and boy, am I glad you're here. That man was working himself half to death, and that's not an exaggeration, is it, Clay?"

"Nope." Clay shook his head and kept eating, licking his lips. "Fourteen-hour days, near as I could figure it. He was doing all the books himself, though I don't know if he told you that."

"He mentioned—" Austin paused, trying to figure out how best to put it that wouldn't betray any confidence Leland had shared with him. Though, seeing as how everyone seemed to be aware of the situation, it might be okay to be straightforward about it. "He mentioned having to let the last accountant go to save money, seeing as how the ranch wasn't doing so well last year?"

"Oh, the ranch was doing fine," said Jasper, seemingly carrying the conversation for everybody at the table. "One of our guests disappeared at the end of last season and the ranch took a hit, what with the police investigations and all and the FBI stopping by on more than one occasion."

"The mountain took him, that's what Bill said," said Brody, though he clamped his mouth shut as though surprised he'd spoken.

"The mountain?" asked Austin, a little surprised at the variety of ways the same story could be told.

"That's Iron Mountain," said Jasper. "And no, the mountain didn't take him."

Brody, his mouth a thin line, didn't say anything, though it looked like he wanted to.

As for Clay, his expression told Austin he didn't really know which side of the story he wanted to stand on, whether the disappearance was something mundane or more attached to the shadowy side of things.

"At any rate," said Clay, digging into his mac and cheese, "Leland doesn't like us talking about it."

"That's because it riles the guests, should they chance to overhear us," said Jasper.

"I see."

Austin let the idea of the missing guest swirl around inside of him to settle at the bottom of a distant place in his mind. What might or might not have happened the year before only mattered in that the ranch had let its previous accountant go and had now hired him. He was going to do right by the ranch and move on from the mess his life had developed into.

Whether that mess had started from the first moment Mona laid eyes on him, or whether he'd caused it to happen by not pushing back against the man she'd wanted him to be, he would find out in time. In the meantime, he wanted to move on, so he needed to make himself move on.

10

AUSTIN

*A*ustin concentrated on his meal, on the conversation that eased its way between his table companions, on the general hubbub of the dining hall, sounds of voices rising and falling, chinked in between by sounds of cutlery against china. A laugh. A louder voice. A softer one.

"You okay?" asked Clay.

Austin looked up, feeling bleary-eyed. "I'm okay," he said, though he wished he could feel more conviction at the thought. "Maybe it's the altitude."

"It might be," said Jasper. "Drink more water, that'll settle you."

The meal finished and everyone shuffled out, except for Clay, who'd been relegated to the back kitchen to help prep food for dinner. Austin responded to Clay's mock-sad wave goodbye with a small smile, pleased that Clay could keep his sense of humor, even as he was still being sent to the back of the room.

Leland met Austin at the doorway to the dining hall and took him to meet Maddy in her office by the gravel parking lot. He liked her straight away, liked her firm handshake and the no-nonsense way she greeted him, though the overstuffed filing cabinets behind her desk gave him some pause.

"I'm glad to have the help," she said, flipping her grey-and-white braid over her shoulder. "Leland here had it in his mind we needed an accountant, and if it'll save him staying up till midnight, then I'll agree." As she paused, the screen door opened and in walked Ellis, who went behind the desk to stand beside her, looking at Austin as though he suspected Austin might set fire to the place if he, Ellis, weren't there to stop him. "I expect you'll want to change everything, even though I prefer real paper folders to fake ones."

In any other circumstance, a corporate meeting, or following a lecture from the CEO, Austin would have presented his best smile, his mildest patter and, talking in accountant-speak, said anything necessary to detract from the fact that he was, essentially, about to poke into financial records that were, very likely, in a disarray and whose investigation might reveal less-than-sterling accounting efforts.

During his interview, Leland had alluded to there currently being three bookkeeping efforts: Leland's, on behalf of the ranch, the store's accounts, and Maddy's office and petty cash account. That all three should be straightened out and probably combined in some way would have typically been his automatic response.

But in this case, perhaps something else, some other answer, was needed. This kind of guest ranch was a million dollar a year business, to be sure, and while this one had fallen on some hard times, they'd kept it going, so they'd all been doing something right.

"Well," said Austin, realizing that the three of them were waiting for an answer. "I figure I might want to check Leland's math and straighten out the books, but mostly, I just want to streamline every-thing to make it easier to keep track—"

"You'll probably want to put everything on the cloud, too," said Maddy. Her scowl, fierce and sudden, told Austin a great deal about how she felt about that. "I do know what the cloud is, by the way," she added.

"I'm sure that you do," said Austin. "And while the cloud is a marvelous tool, not everything belongs there. Your computer looks new, and it looks like you have a good backup system—"

"That's Ellis' doing," said Maddy, pointing at Ellis with her thumb, over her shoulder, as though the two of them were good pals from way back "He set me up this way and I like the way he did it."

"I've no doubt about that," said Austin. "My goal here is to set up the accounting for the ranch in a way that is workable. Some things might need to be accessed by you, Maddy, and Leland, and the store. Other accounts might just be for your office, or the store, or Leland's office. I won't be making any changes, large or small, without consulting you. Does that sound like something you can work with?"

It was important that he win her over, and his irritation at Leland not alerting him to this fact warred with his desperate hope he'd done it right, that he'd addressed her concerns so she'd be willing to work with him. Sometimes office admins were hard wins indeed, and Maddy did not seem at all like an easy win.

"Yes," said Maddy with a lift of her chin.

Maybe she'd been worried that he'd steamroll right over her, and in any other circumstance, maybe he would have. But the ranch was already, in his mind, its own world and seemed to demand from him a different way of looking at things.

"Reckon you and Maddy can set up a time to meet," said Leland. "Meanwhile, why don't you and I walk to my office and start going over the ledgers."

"Ledgers?" asked Austin as they walked out of Maddy's office, down the wooden steps, and into the sunshine. "You mean hand-written ledgers?"

"The very same," said Leland. "That's how accountants have always kept the books around here."

Austin didn't let himself shudder at this, or at the idea of what a brisk office fire might have done to years of records. He hadn't been there then, but he was here now. As they walked up the road to the barn where Leland's office was, he took a deep breath of the clear, Wyoming mountain air, and reminded himself he was in a different place, a different world.

The ranch ran on its own timeline, had its own rules. What's more, when they got to Leland's office and Leland pulled out a small pile of ledgers, he flipped the top one open to reveal tidy, square lettering, row after row of accounts and amounts.

The next ledger, which Leland placed in Austin's hands, contained more of the same, only with different handwriting, a different style of writing the numbers. Each ledger was like that, and though some were a little messier than others, each displayed an earnest desire to track how the money flowed.

"We go back all the way to right after WWII," said Leland. He pulled out a ledger whose binding was still holding on, but only by dint of some powerful glue and duct tape. "Bill's grandad started this place as a guest ranch, and he kept the books himself."

Austin thumbed through the ledger with some reverence, as the entries were all done in blue ink that was so strong it had faded only slightly. Row after row displayed an impeccable sense of neatness, of good mathematics and, amazingly enough, few mistakes.

"Despite what Maddy might be worried about—" Leland took off his hat to toss it in his hands before hanging it on a wooden hook above his desk. "All of this needs to be transcribed into a digital record. All of this—" Leland waved his hand at the pile of ledgers now sitting on his desk. "When I started, I only wanted to keep up with the money and how it was going, but even then, as green as I was at it, I knew there needed to be a change. I started two spreadsheets and messed 'em both up, but then my skill set is horses rather than spreadsheets."

"I'm sure you made a good start," said Austin, nodding.

Part of him itched to dig right in, to bury the unsettled feelings inside of him in a pile of numbers, in the chatter of a good, solid calculator, to create order out of chaos.

The other part of him knew he wasn't at his best. Maybe it was the altitude, or the dryness. Maybe it was, again, that the ranch was not yet home. That he was still packed. That he wanted to plant roots, his own roots, as much as he could, the sooner the better.

"I'd like to get a fresh start in the morning, if I could," said Austin. "And where would I work? Here or—?"

He left the question hanging open so Leland could move him

where he liked, which might be, he thought with a small, silent but crazed laugh, in a horse's stall.

"Bill doesn't use his office all that much, so I reckon you could use that. It's just off Maddy's office." Leland let that sink in. "But with a laptop, which the ranch will provide, you can work just about anywhere you like."

"Oh."

He couldn't quite explain, even to himself, what the idea of that did to him. Of being able to move anywhere he wanted. Of course, in a corporate office, he'd had a laptop also, but the options were his desk, the break room, or the boardroom, all of which were closed off spaces where the air was slightly stale, smelling of badly made coffee.

"I like the idea of that," Austin said. "Now, show me your files, and we'll start there."

They discussed the ledgers together, and Austin looked over Leland's spreadsheets, and they talked about how best to organize the transfer of information to being online. And though Austin did his best to focus, all the while he thought about Clay and his sunny face, his kindness. When they got to a good stopping point, Austin folded his notebook shut.

"I think I've got enough to be starting on for now," he said, standing up. "I'll work on the basic accounting for the ranch, then tackle the petty cash and Maddy's records."

"It'll work itself out," said Leland. "I think it'll work itself out just fine."

He remembered Leland handing him a satchel with a new laptop in it, remembered tucking the most recent ledger beneath his arm. Remembered the long flight of stairs to his room. The door opening. The care with which he placed the satchel on the small desk along the wall. And after that? It was all a blank, a long, black place from which he awoke with a start, his feet on the bed, one loafer off and the other one on. His mouth was as dry as a slate and his head ached.

When he woke up, outside the window, grey-edged clouds laced the sky with a purple-tinged dusk. There was a low sound, a skittering sound, a shh-shh-shh sound he could not identify, and beyond it, a low moan. Blinking, he stumbled to his bathroom to sluice his mouth with water, then hopping into his other loafer, went down the stairs to the front door of the employees lodge to stand on the front porch blinking.

It was not quite dark. The air was perfumed with the warm scent of pine needles cooling as the sun went down. And as for the sound? It was the leaves in the trees, unhindered by city noise and traffic and movement, all on its own, a natural sound, unbridled, unfettered. Free.

Along the path, through the trees, came a small group, dressed like Clay had been, in jeans and cowboy boots, some with straw cowboy hats, others without. They seemed to be ambling rather than rushing, which, at the end of a long working day, only made sense. He must have missed dinner, though his stomach never felt less like eating than it did at that minute.

At the back end of the group, walking with his head down, his hands in his pockets, came Clay. Austin made a sound, reacting, grateful to see somebody he knew with the purple twilight coming down, the fresh breeze from the mountains stirring his hair in a very uncitylike way.

"Clay."

Clay lifted his head and from beneath his straw hat came that smile that, as he came closer, reflected like starlight in his eyes.

"Hey, Austin," said Clay in greeting. "You missed Bill's story hour. He was in fine form."

Standing to one side, Austin let all the other staff go past him while he waited on the porch for Clay.

"I'm sorry I missed it," said Austin, meaning it in a way he couldn't quite understand.

He had yet to meet Bill. Had no idea what stories he might tell. Yet, deep inside, he wanted to have been there, especially with Clay, who would have made a comment or two to clarify, or would have smiled at Austin when the story grew amusing.

In the growing dark, in the breeze, in such company, the ranch seemed full of possibilities he'd not even begun to imagine. And all of this seemed encapsulated in Clay's smile.

"You'll catch the next one," said Clay with a nod. "Bill does it just about every week, sometimes twice a week, depending on the weather and his mood."

"I'm glad to hear it." Austin wiped his mouth with his hand. "I think I missed dinner, but I'm not sure my stomach cares all that much."

"Have you been drinking water?" asked Clay.

"No," said Austin, feeling very much like he was about to be scolded by someone years younger than him.

"Well, I know just the thing. Follow me."

Clay led Austin along the path beneath the trees to the dining hall. There on the porch, from a cooler full of ice that had melted during the day, Clay pulled out two plastic bottles of water, then led Austin to some wooden bench seats along the wall.

"Sit down and drink," said Clay. "There's nothing going on, and no need to rush. Just drink."

Austin did as he was told, glad, in that moment, to have someone else lead the way. He unscrewed the lid, his hand shaking a little bit, spilling cool water across his fingers, onto his canvas trousers, leaving spots behind. Then he drank and sat back, drank some more, and smiled at Clay, who smiled back.

In that moment, with the twilight coming down in dark waves of purple black, he felt good. Felt like maybe this time he'd made the exact right decision. There was no telling if he'd feel the same way come morning, but now, the cool water soothing him from the inside, the fresh breeze tenderly curling around him, Clay nearby, all seemed well. All seemed like it could get better, which starting from zero, as it had, looked like it could get a great deal better indeed.

11

CLAY

*T*uesday morning, Clay had nothing to look forward to except shoveling horse shit, picking up trash, washing dishes for Levi, and other out-of-sight chores. He also had nothing to look forward to for many days to come, as in the morning meeting Leland had announced that Brody would drive the chuckwagon for that week's cattle drive, even though Clay's black eye was going down, and his split lip was well on its way to healing. When he licked it, it barely tasted like salt, but he was still off the roster.

Unable to fault Brody, for he was as good a driver as Clay was, probably even better, Clay still felt hard done by as he made his way from the barn to the main lodge for breakfast. There, he climbed up the stairs to stand in line, bowing to guests while letting them go ahead of him, when he spotted Austin.

Austin had not been at the morning's meeting, but then, being the accountant, he would not have to be kept abreast of current goings on or be alerted to special needs of particular guests nor even the weather, which promised to be hot and dry for the next few days.

Fully prepared to stand at the end of the line, Clay looked up and saw that Austin was looking at him rather like he'd found a long-lost friend. And, potentially unaware of buffet line protocol, he waved to Clay to join him.

This was definitely not something Leland would have encouraged, but the expression on Austin's face, the light in his eyes, seemed expectant and hopeful all at once. Maybe because Clay was probably the only one he knew at the ranch? Except he'd met most everybody, so that couldn't be it.

At Austin's second wave, Clay gave in and scooted forward in line. Guests and employees merely smiled at him for, as everyone knew by this time, there was plenty of food and all of it was good.

"Hey," said Clay when he reached Austin's side. "You're looking better than when I saw you last."

"Thanks to you," said Austin. He might not have been smiling, but there was a smile in his eyes. "After that water, I went straight to bed and slept like a baby."

"A baby who snores," said Clay, snickering as the line shuffled forward. Behind the easy laugh, his mind caught up with him, reminding him how they'd shared a bed that night. How the warmth of Austin's body had drawn Clay to him. How sweet Austin's smile was, even though Clay had ended up way too close to him, them being strangers and all.

"Those were baby snores," said Austin with a laugh. "Very tiny snores, as you recall."

They might be getting looks from guests who were listening and watching this exchange, but in that moment, Clay didn't want to worry about that. He wanted to enjoy the morning, the anticipation of a good breakfast. And really, the idea of sharing the meal with Austin, who was looking at him now and frowning.

"I think I need to get different clothes, though," said Austin.

"What?"

"Everybody here is wearing—" Austin pointed at the dining hall in general and then at Clay specifically. "Cowboy boots. Blue jeans. Shirt with snap buttons."

"You mean these?" asked Clay as he reached down to unsnap the first three buttons on his cotton shirt, giving his wrist a risqué flip as he did this. He was not flirting with the new accountant, no, he was not. "All the cool kids wear them, doncha know. You want to be a cool kid, right?"

"Yes, I want to be a cool kid," said Austin with perfect seriousness. "How do I do that? Will I need to drive to the nearest cowboy store or something?"

"All the way to the ranch's store, next to Maddy's office," said Clay. "We have everything you need there. I pointed it out yesterday, remember?"

"Yesterday was a blur," said Austin with a shake of his head. "I feel like I stumbled through most of it."

"The altitude will get you every time." Clay grabbed a tray and stuck close to Austin, maybe to see what he was getting, and maybe to just be close. "And look, you don't want to miss out on the biscuits and gravy, for sure."

After they got their breakfasts, Clay led the way to a long table beneath the windows.

"Usually Leland likes us to mingle," said Clay as he put his tray down and sat. "But I figure you're still new, so might like some company."

"I would, and thank you," said Austin. He went around the table to sit across from Clay, which was a bit of a surprise, as the view was from this side. But it turned into a treat, as now Austin was sitting with his back to the windows, his dark ginger hair lit up by sunshine, like a halo, his eyes solemn as he looked at Clay.

"You can get those clothes on account," said Clay.

"Clothes?"

"Cowboy clothes," said Clay, smiling as he ate. "At the store. Just tell the clerk you're an employee and he'll fix you up with a discount. They can take it out of your pay."

Austin nodded, concentrating on his food, on looking around him as if still trying to get his bearings.

"So how do the accounts look?" asked Clay.

When Austin looked up, it was as though Clay had startled him.

"I'm sorry," said Austin. "Sometimes I'm in my own head so much I fail to realize that it's polite to pay attention. Mona always said—"

"I don't mean to be blunt," said Clay, feeling a push of anger at the brittle way Austin said his ex-wife's name. At the hangdog expression that sagged Austin's shoulders. Nobody should be made to feel bad like that, and especially not someone who'd figured they'd be better off without Austin. "Though sometimes I am. Truth is, your ex isn't here. Do you really want to keep inviting her to the ranch?"

"No."

The answer came without thought, though the expression in Austin's eyes seemed to indicate that he was surprised at how fast he'd said it.

"It's an old habit, I guess," said Austin. He pushed away his plate as if about to get up, as if the whole conversation was just too much for him. "I don't mean to be boring about it."

"You're not." Clay nodded, scrubbing at his mouth with his napkin. "Habits can be broken, if you want them to be."

"I do, I think."

"Well, look at it this way. If a horse has a habit you don't like, you don't punish it, you don't break him. You coax him. Guide him."

"Is this from the horse expert?" asked Austin, smiling, a tease in his eyes.

"One of 'em," said Clay, smiling back. "Brody is our real expert. Him and Quint. And Leland, of course."

"I don't know much about horses, I'm afraid." With a small sigh, Austin returned to eating, to looking around, like he was anticipating being on the verge of discovering something new. "I guess I should learn. How to ride. How to dress."

"Those are easy," said Clay. "Go down to the store right after breakfast. They'll fix you up. Then I'll check with Leland, but I bet you can sign up for our beginner lessons. They're not extended lessons, right? They're just to orient you to the horse. It's what we do for our guests. We put them on gentle horses who know they've got a beginner on their back."

"You make it all sound so easy."

"What?"

"Fitting in."

Clay turned this over in his mind. He'd been on the ranch a whole season, and now was on his second. From the beginning, everyone he'd interacted with was in the business of ranching, of horses, of cattle, or whatever. If they weren't, then they were guests and needed to be handled a different way.

Now here was Austin, somewhere in the middle of all of that. Not a guest. Not a ranch hand either. Yet at the same time, he seemed to be turning himself inside out, figuring where he fit in. Nothing needed to be that hard. Nothing.

"You don't have to change who you are to do your job," said Clay. "Though you might feel more comfortable in blue jeans and boots, it's because of the weather, the terrain. Not because you have to become somebody else."

Austin's expression, with those solemn green eyes, the lines of his face, seemed to open up what he was thinking to Clay. Divorce always sounded so messy, but it seemed like the ex had left behind a trail of damage Austin was still recovering from.

At some point, Clay was going to ask about it, get Austin to talk about it, like lancing a wound. In the meantime, he was going to do what he did best, and that was making the other person feel comfortable and at home. He did it with guests, when they felt out of their elements, and he did it with guys at the bar, so they'd fuck him nice and slow and proper.

"Thank you for that," said Austin. He shook his head as though Clay were arguing with him, and put down his silverware to gesture with his hands, like he was gathering his thoughts. "Everybody at the ranch has been very nice, though I'm still looking for a smile from Maddy."

"You were in her office, right?" asked Clay. "That's her territory. Don't mess with Maddy."

"I won't." Now Austin's smile grew. "But I just wanted to say—" Austin blew out a breath, his forehead wrinkled like he had just learned something new, only he didn't know how to prove it. "Meeting you first? Put a whole tone to everything."

"A tone?" Clay knew what he meant, of course, but it was rather pleasant watching Austin work his way through his own words. Watching the light in his eyes become warm, watching the smile curve his mouth.

"You had a smile and a way about you," said Austin. "You know how if you drive into a city along the parkway where it's all green and lovely, then your impression of the city is that it's green and lovely."

"So I'm green and lovely now?" asked Clay, his palm splayed across his chest, pretending to be affronted, though that was instantly ruined when he laughed out loud.

"Golden and lovely," said Austin and the words must have come without thought, for he flushed a rather delightful shade of red, and though he looked abashed, he did not take the words back.

"Aw, shucks," said Clay, laughing it off, though his mind did a few backflips of joy because nobody had ever described him that way.

After they finished their breakfast and bussed their trays, as they were going out, Brody was coming in. He had his hat in one hand and a pair of leather driver's gloves in the other.

"I'm looking for Leland," said Brody. "Is he in there?"

"I didn't see him," said Clay, trying to keep his voice even. He knew Brody was going to be the one driving the chuckwagon this week, but it was hard not to be jealous about it.

"I'll check at the barn," said Brody, and then, at a trot, he was off, going down the wooden steps and up the road.

"What's that all about?" asked Austin. When Clay didn't answer right away, Austin pointed to Clay's forehead. "You've got this little, almost invisible frown going on."

"I do." Clay didn't even pretend he didn't. "I love driving the chuckwagon—no, I mean I really *love* driving the chuckwagon, but I can't this week. Brody usually works with horses, so he's great at it, only—Leland said no."

"Does he know how much you enjoy it?" asked Austin.

"I'm sure he does," said Clay, grabbing his hat from the peg on the wall before they walked out into the breezy morning.

"Maybe he doesn't," said Austin. "Your face lights up when you talk about it—"

"It does?" Nobody had ever talked about him the way Austin did, like Austin was taking notes, and had been the whole time.

"Yes, it does." Austin nodded, perfectly serious. "You love your job, I can tell. And all the different parts of your job, well. Your face glows when you talk about it. Like driving the chuckwagon. Or giving lessons to guests. I think you should tell Leland, truly tell him, so he'll know."

"It won't change anything."

"It doesn't need to. He'll know for next time." Austin reached out like he meant to pat Clay on the shoulder to give him courage, but at the last minute, he pulled back. To fix that, Clay took Austin's hand and patted his own shoulder with it, as Austin had meant to do.

"I feel very encouraged right about now," said Clay, with a low laugh.

"I'm glad to hear it," said Austin, smiling, like he could hardly believe it was that easy to just be friends with someone. If Clay ever met Mona, he was going to give her a piece of his mind. "Well, I'm off to my meeting with Maddy. See you at lunch?"

"Sounds like a deal," said Clay and, with a whistle in his heart, he headed up to the barn, taking his time.

When he reached it, the chuckwagon had indeed been pulled out of the service shed, with the tongue laid out, while Leland and Brody stretched the canvas over the round, iron wagon bows. Someone, another ranch hand, was inside the tack room oiling the four-horse harness, checking the reins, making sure of the buckles.

Feeling about as left out as ever he had, Clay took a breath and sauntered over to the chuckwagon.

"Anything I can help with?" he asked in his brightest voice.

Leland looked up, his eyes lighting up the way they did when he was glad to see you.

"There are four matched bays in box stalls in the barn that need brushing, need their hooves cleaned and oiled. Can you manage? We're due to head out by ten o'clock. Quint's already got horses just about ready to go in the arena."

"Sure thing, boss," said Clay, glad to even be this close to the proceedings.

The weeks that there was a cattle drive or even a little horse drive were always exciting. Guests paid extra for such events, so everything had to be perfect. Of course, Leland would trust Clay with grooming, just like he would anybody else who worked for him. If only he would let Clay drive the team.

While Clay groomed each bay, tended to their hooves, combed their manes and tails, he thought about what Austin had said, and what Austin had done in the past. He'd spoken to that highway patrolman like it was nothing, like the guy didn't scare him at all.

Of course, Clay wasn't afraid of the local law, not exactly, but he had a few speeding tickets under his belt, so it always made his heart rush when he encountered one. As for Leland, Austin had suggested Clay speak his mind and let his boss know how he felt, even if he thought Leland already knew. Austin had been rather handsome as he'd shared his wisdom, all green-eyed and solemn, strong shouldered and sure of himself.

When the horses were groomed, the image of Austin stayed with Clay as he helped put the harness on each one, and then led the team out to the chuckwagon to carefully put them in place before asking them to back up. Brody helped with that, and between the two of them, the team was harnessed and Brody was slipping on those thick leather gloves.

"We're ready to go, boss," said Clay, looking for Leland. Seeing him by the arena, where guests were excitedly mounting their horses, and Quint was steady and quiet as he helped them, Clay went up to Leland.

"You got a minute, boss?" he asked.

"Sure thing, Clay," said Leland. "What's up?"

"I just wanted to say—" Clay had to stop to gather his thoughts, to make sure the words were lined up just right so it didn't come out like he was whining, which he wasn't. "I'm missing out on driving the team this time around, and it's because I punched Eddie Piggot and I know that. But I wanted you to know—" Another hitching breath. "—that I'm *really* missing out. I love driving the team. I love everything about it and I hope you will put me on the roster for next time."

"Of course I will," said Leland. He even took off his hat and twirled it around his hand, so Clay knew he was really listening, really thinking about what Clay had just said. "I knew you enjoyed it, but not how much. Thank you for letting me know."

With that, Leland hurried off to help Quint, and Clay walked back into the barn to clean up horse shit and old hay and to make the barn spick-and-span for when the next round of horses would need to be groomed, or if any guests happened to wander in.

As he picked up a pitchfork and opened the first box stall, he shook his head in some amazement. Austin had done him a solid favor. Of course, Clay had always known how to speak his mind. The trick was to get him to shut up sometimes. But to be honest in the way he'd just been? Had taken a nudge from a friend. Which he hoped Austin was, he really did.

12

AUSTIN

*A*ustin had to talk himself into buying blue jeans and cowboy boots, had to really work around the idea, as the clothes he had were perfectly serviceable and he didn't need more clothes. And maybe he'd feel foolish wearing the boots when he really didn't know the first thing about horses or how to ride. But after he'd met with Maddy and spent a good part of the day going over her books with her, he felt he might deserve a treat, as working with her had not been as easy as working with Leland.

"I like having physical receipts," she said, showing him the various shoeboxes and accordion files where she kept them, stacked on top of the three black filing cabinets, which were stuffed to the brim with file folders, more receipts, and a shoebox of telephone pole glass insulators. "I can find anything I need to find and that's a fact."

"I realize you can, Maddy," said Austin, keeping his tone reasonable. Wasn't there a saying about leading a horse to water but being unable to make it drink? "But there's more to it than that. What if the IRS wants to do an audit? How quickly could you hand over those records?"

"Quickly," she said with a flip of her braid. "Very quickly, in fact."

"And what if you were to win a million dollars and move to France—?"

"I wouldn't move to France," said Maddy in a way that told Austin she was being stubborn just to be stubborn. And maybe when she saw he knew this, she smiled. "Anyway, if I won the lottery, I'd move to Iceland or maybe Spain, not France."

"The point is, Maddy," he said, moving the catalog of office equipment toward her, which she'd closed only moments before. He flipped the catalog open to the page with the scanners. "We need to streamline so information can be quickly accessed by me, or by Leland, or by the IRS. You know where everything is, sure, but does Leland? Does Bill?"

"Bill couldn't care less how I handle it," said Maddy.

"Where is Bill?" asked Austin. "I've yet to meet him."

"He's doing the rounds with the hay and alfalfa dealers," said Maddy. "It's going to ruin your perfect record keeping because he does handshake deals, no contracts, no receipts, and only works with cash."

"Ah."

"Don't mess with Bill, I'm telling you."

"And I was told not to mess with you," said Austin, throwing up his hands, frustrated. "Yet here I am."

"And yet here you are," said Maddy with a laugh, but somehow his offhand comment broke the ice between them and he could have a serious discussion with her about scanning receipts to store them in the cloud, while keeping only the previous month's receipts in physical form.

"You'll have much more room in your office without all these filing cabinets," said Austin. "And more room to increase your display. This ranch goes all the way back to 1945, so there's a lot of history to share. Wouldn't you like more than a single glass-topped table, and a single wall of photos? You could display those telephone pole insulators, too. We could fill the entire half of this office with artifacts and photos, not to mention we could get you another leather chair and make it so guests could come in and put their feet up."

"I guess I would," said Maddy, looking at him as though she finally was listening. "I've got boxes in that closet that haven't seen the light of day in years. It'd be nice to unpack them and show them off. I've even got a buffalo hide coat in there, packed in mothballs, did you know that?"

"No, I did not," he said. "But I'm sure it'd make a fine addition. So let's pick out a scanner, and get you set up. You'll be in charge of the project, and I'll only check in once in a while."

"And go over my files," she said. "Everything's in order."

"I'm sure it is," he said. He pointed at the row of images of scanners in the catalog. "Now, how about this one? It looks pretty sturdy and the ratings are good."

The meeting went on for another hour, and when he was done, he packed up his laptop and trundled over to the ranch's store. There he told the clerk what he needed, what Clay had suggested he get. In about an hour's time, he walked out into the sunshine with new, stiff-feeling blue jeans, a sturdy pair of brown cowboy boots, a straw cowboy hat, and his first ever pearl-snap button shirt. Mona would have had a *fit*—

But who cared what Mona would have thought? All he wanted to know was what Clay thought, whether Clay would approve of his choices. He used to have to check in with Mona about what he wore to the office, donning bespoke suits she'd picked out for him, wearing tassel loafers she'd approved of. But this felt different.

He didn't need Clay's approval, but he wanted it just the same. Only Clay would be different than Mona, or at least Austin hoped so. Maybe Clay would give Austin the thumbs up and say *Nice job* and that would be it. Or maybe he would suggest a different type of shirt, and that the hat was all wrong—and why was Austin so worked up about what Clay might think?

Because he was, and that was the truth of it.

He put his regular clothes and his laptop in his room, leaving the straw hat on the dresser, and hustled down the steps to the dining hall. It was different walking in cowboy boots, as the stacked heel seemed to lift him up in one long, straight line. Getting used to them would take practice, as would the fit of the jeans, which, as they had five buttons instead of a button and a zipper, seemed to tuck awfully close around his hips. But as he walked along the path between the trees and joined the throng in front of the steps of the main lodge, nobody seemed to pay him any particular attention. Except then, he heard a long low whistle and turned.

It was Clay. He'd obviously stopped to wash up, as moisture glinted in his hair, and there were water stains around the neckline of his cotton shirt.

"Whoo-wee, sweet daddy!" said Clay, clapping his hands to his face as though astonished by the sight of Austin. "Just *look* at you."

"Is it too much?" asked Austin, overwhelmed at this response.

"Oh, no," said Clay, shaking his head, tipping his head to the side like he wanted to take in the view and not miss a thing. "It's perfect. Don't change a thing. You're going to start a new trend with those—" Clay pointed at the shiny row of buttons marching up the front of Austin's jeans. "Buttons."

The innuendo was there, as plain as daylight, but the smile Clay gave him told Austin there was no malice there, nor any actual push for something sexual. Rather it was playful and fun and the idea of it, this kind of gentle teasing, rose inside of Austin, and he wanted to keep this feeling forever.

"Thank you," he said, then pointed to his shirt. "It's just a color, just pale blue, not the plaid that everyone's wearing, but they didn't have one in my size. I put in an order for one, though."

"Brings out the color of your eyes, I'd say," said Clay. "Besides, you stand out better this way. Anybody claps eyes on you, they'll say *There goes the accountant.*" Clay smiled and patted Austin's shoulder and didn't move away as they mounted the wooden steps of the main lodge to stand in line. "We'll get you something to rough up the soles of those new boots so they're not so slippery."

"Thank you," said Austin, flustered and flushed by Clay's compliments. Also, he'd not thought of how his boots tended to slip around like he was walking on glass. "Did the wagon train leave okay?"

"Wagon train?" Clay laughed as he helped himself to chili and cornbread. "It's a cattle drive, but yeah, they left late, around eleven thirty. I told Leland how I felt, by the way."

"How did it go?" Austin grabbed probably more chili than any one man needed to eat and with a contented sigh, followed Clay to the table beneath the window. They settled in, sitting side by side, facing the dining hall rather than the view out of the window because, as Clay had pointed out, there were great views everywhere and it might be fun to people watch.

"It went good. He said he hadn't realized how much I loved it and promised to put me on the roster for the next drive."

"Excellent," said Austin, more pleased about it than could be accounted for.

Last week, he'd not realized a place like this existed, still reeling from all the papers he'd had to sign, the way it felt to hand over the keys to the Mercedes to Mona. Now, though, it was a different story. A different world. And eating with Clay was becoming, quite quickly, his favorite part of the day.

Clay never remarked that Austin shouldn't have two helpings, didn't chastise him for getting an extra Fudgsicle from the white freezer. Didn't say a word about it, but just got one for himself and joined Austin and the general gathering on the front porch as everyone chatted and ate their Otter Pops and Drumsticks and other icy delights that evidently Levi kept well-stocked in the freezer.

Austin spotted Jasper and Ellis at the edge of the small crowd, but though the two didn't come over, they waved.

"There's Ellis and Jasper," said Austin, waving back, licking the side of his thumb where the Fudgsicle was quickly melting.

"He's in our ex-con program," said Clay, apropos of nothing. "Just so you know. He had a tough time in prison, which is why he doesn't have a lot to say, except to Jasper. I mean, he can talk, but just to Jasper mostly."

"Ex-con?" asked Austin, remembering what Leland had told him, but wanting to hear what Clay had to say about it. "Why do you have an ex-con program?"

"We needed the money," said Clay, quite blunt. "It got us some tax dollars or something, and it worked well with Ellis, as he fit in right away." Clay waved the air in front of him as if dismissing Austin's concerns. "He was selling and dealing in drugs, which, okay, is bad, but his mom was dying of cancer, I think, and so he was trying to raise money."

"Oh." Austin didn't quite know what to say to that, but at least now he better understood why Ellis hadn't spoken to him.

"I heard Bill say he wants to do another one, but Leland thinks there's a lot of what he calls unknown risks, so—well, they'll figure it out between them and the rest of us will adapt."

With a nod, Clay finished his Fudgsicle and licked the wooden stick before grabbing his and Austin's trash to throw away. When he came back, he was smiling.

"Jasper is not one to be soft, you know?" said Clay. "But Ellis has him eating out of his hand."

"So—they're together?" Austin looked over at the two men, who were standing quite close in a little bubble all their own. While that wouldn't have meant anything to him in his old life, now, in his new life, maybe it did.

"That they are," said Clay. Then he laughed, a small bark of amusement. "Leland used to have this pretty stringent anti-fraternization rule, you know? But then along came Jamie, and that rule went right down the shitter."

"The shitter?" asked Austin with a laugh, looking at Clay, open-mouthed, wondering when was the last time he'd laughed so much.

"Yeah." Clay shook his head, snickering under his breath. "He had these two rules, right? No drifters and no fraternizing. But then Jamie, who was a drifter, by the way, showed up without an appointment? Leland took one look at that cute face an' that was all she wrote."

"Oh, my."

"Yeah, oh my." Clay folded his arms across his chest and nodded, as though satisfied by this. "Sometimes love holds sway."

"I guess it does," said Austin, feeling the pull of his body to fold his arms across his chest as well. "I've not met Jamie yet, I think."

"He's around," said Clay. "He used to do grounds maintenance, and he still does that most of the time, but Leland's been sending him off with Bill to buy stuff for the ranch like molasses-laced grain for the horses for treats. Maddy said something about getting receipts, so Jamie's along to make sure that happens."

"I was just talking to her about that."

"Yeah, I know." Clay smiled up at Austin. "I was in Leland's office when Maddy called to tell him about it. Not to tell tales out of school, but that woman is one of the good ones, only she's worried she'll come up with mistakes, since she and Bill have been somewhat loose about it."

"My only concern is to get it set up so we can keep good records moving forward." Austin shook his head. "I'm not out to penalize anyone."

"That's good to know."

Feeling a sense of camaraderie, of belonging, which had not happened in a good long time, Austin tipped his head at Clay.

"Listen, I'll say goodnight and see you in the morning?"

"See you in the morning," said Clay.

Pleasantly exhausted, Austin returned to his room, made notes about his ideas on how to streamline the ranch's accounting. Did some laundry, put away his new clothes, all the while wondering why he'd said goodnight so early.

Despite this, he had one of the best night's sleep he could remember in a long time, and in the morning, he awoke to a bright, sunshine-filled sky filled with warm pine scent, a soft breeze, and the pleasant chatter of the guests. The best part was waiting on the steps of the main lodge for Clay to show up. And when he did, they stood together in line, amiably shuffling forward, loading up with pancakes and bacon and coffee before grabbing spaces at the long table beneath the window.

"I've got to unload sacks of grain today," said Clay. "Around ten. You should come up to the barn then, you can meet Jamie and Bill and admire my manly muscles."

"Your manly—"

Austin stopped, not sure how to respond to this or even how to think about it. Except he could instantly picture it, Clay in his snap button shirt, the top snaps undone as they always seemed to be, as if once he'd unsnapped them he could not bear to do them up again. Clay with his blue eyes and his fair hair curling around his ears. Clay, whose jeans were tight around his hips and thighs and who strode in his cowboy boots like he was walking the earth looking for adventure.

"Are you *flirting* with me?" he asked, finding his voice.

"Maybe I am," said Clay, his smile broadening as he took a sip of coffee. "Is that okay?"

"I'm—"

Austin looked down at his nearly empty plate, which once held delicious pancakes that he'd eaten without counting a single calorie. That he'd slathered with butter and real maple syrup, which later he'd dipped bacon in.

Breakfast with Clay came easy, wasn't hard. Wasn't a struggle to deal with while being mindful of Mona's needs, what mood Mona was in that day. Being with Clay was like breathing. Was exactly like taking a breath of the fresh air that scurried around the trees and across the sky. Easy. Natural. Nice. *Very* nice.

"I'm not sure, actually."

"Oh." Clay's eyes grew a little dim, his mouth tightening. "I'm sorry. I'm like that. Moving too fast. Wanting what I want without thinking about the other person. Too excitable, that's me."

"You—" Again Austin stopped, his brain mixing up all kinds of ideas his tongue simply couldn't translate into words.

"You'll hear about me through the grapevine soon enough," said Clay. He began assembling his knife and fork on his plate, folded his napkin and placed it on top of everything else. "I am known as a flirt. A big, easy flirt. I tried it on Leland and he was not interested. I went out with Brody once, and that was all she wrote. Jasper was always too grumpy, and now he's taken. Levi's always waiting for someone who will never come, and I'd ask Quint out but I do not have a death wish."

Clay stopped talking and stood up, looking at Austin with a resolute expression in his eyes.

"Now I go to bars," said Clay. "I cruise there. Sometimes I leave alone and sometimes I don't. Maybe I try too hard, I don't know."

"You don't try too hard." Austin stood up, as well, and touched Clay's arm, marveling at his own foolishness that he thought he could stop someone that way. "I'm usually better with words than this. Much better. Except—" Austin took a breath and let it out slowly. "Nobody's flirted with me since I was in college. I don't even know how it goes anymore."

"Do you want it to go?"

"Like I said, I'm not sure, but it's definitely not you—"

"Did you just give me the *it's not you, it's me* line?" asked Clay, his smile making a familiar appearance.

"I think so," said Austin, pretending that he could go along with the flirting, while deep below, he was bestirred in a way he'd not thought ever to be again.

They were having a disagreement, a misunderstanding that back in the days of Mona would have ended in him apologizing over and over, giving Mona whatever she said she wanted or needed, just for a little peace. Only now, he and Clay—it was different. He didn't want to hurt Clay's feelings and, it seemed, Clay didn't want to hurt his, either. It was all so new, behaving this way, he wanted desperately to keep it going.

"Only I forgot my script, so I'm not sure."

"Leland would not approve," said Clay with a shake of his head. "You need to have the script with you at all times." He picked up his tray and took a step back, as if he wanted to give Austin the room he needed to make his choices. "Will I see you at the barn at ten?"

"Yes," said Austin, nodding extra hard so there was no mistake.

He didn't have anything on his schedule that couldn't be shoved aside, and hard. Even if he didn't know what he was doing, even if he didn't quite know how to handle the fact that a young man wanted to flirt with him, wanted to show off for him, the way he felt when he was with Clay was miles away from the way Mona always made him feel. And that, in and of itself, was reason to continue, wasn't it?

"You'll see me," he said, wanting to make a small joke to ease things between them. "And I'll see you."

"Great." Clay's smile was broad, and the lights were back in his eyes. He seemed to relax his shoulders as he and Austin bussed their trays and walked together through the open double doors. "I gotta hustle. See you then."

"See you," said Austin, the words faint in his ears as he gestured with an unseen wave at Clay's departing back.

He only had around two hours of work to occupy him till he met Clay at the barn, so he raced to his room to grab his laptop, then went down to the office to make himself a space on Bill's unused desk. For the most part, as he sorted through a stack of receipts to break down the categories for future tax filings, Maddy seemed busy with her own work, though at one point, she brought him a can of Endust and a dust rag.

"You may as well have at it and make yourself at home," said Maddy. "Seeing as how you're going to be here every day."

Which maybe meant Maddy had been a little lonely and didn't mind his company. It was only when she brought him a cup of coffee at ten that he realized he had somewhere he needed to be.

Being late was offset by the realization that he'd kept himself so busy, he'd not had time to question what the hell he was doing or how he felt about it. But could only bid Maddy good morning and walk as fast as he could up the hill and under the trees to the barn. There, he found a battered truck hauling a flatbed trailer, upon which was stacked many, many white sacks, rather than the burlap ones he'd been expecting.

A young man with curly hair was hefting one of the sacks on his shoulder, while nearby Leland looked like he was desperately trying not to help. Next to him, an older man tossed a sack on his shoulder like it weighed nothing.

And then there was Clay who, while he was carrying only one sack, looked sturdy and strong enough to be carrying two. His hat was off and he'd rolled up his shirt sleeves, and he went striding into the barn, into the shadows, vanishing from view.

"Hey there," said Leland, coming up to him. "This is Jamie, our groundskeeper. Jamie, this is Austin Marsh, our new accountant."

"Nice to meet you," said Jamie, pert and wide eyed and so very young as he held out his hand.

"Nice to meet you as well," said Austin, shaking Jamie's hand, thinking how subtle it was between Leland and Jamie, and how they might be taken for just friends, just employer and employee. That is, if it weren't for the gentle way Leland touched the middle of Jamie's back during the encounter.

"Here to help or just to watch?" asked Leland.

"Here to help," said Austin, though that had not been his intention. His intention had been to hide in the shadow the roofline of the barn created, watching and thinking about what had happened between him and Clay that morning while he waited for Clay to come back out again. "I need a break from numbers anyway."

"How's it going with Maddy?" asked Leland. "Here're some gloves. You'll need them, as the sacks can be kind of slick to the hand."

"It's going good," said Austin, slipping the gloves on. "I think she's past the point where she feels her job was slipping out of her control, which I can totally sympathize with. We're scanning receipts as soon as the scanner arrives."

"How much did that set us back?" asked Leland.

"Around two hundred, but it's a sturdy model and will last you for years."

"Sounds good," said Leland, then he jerked his chin, and when Austin looked, there came Clay, all sweaty and golden and, somehow, marvelous. "Just follow Clay, he'll show you where we're storing some of these. The rest will go in the supply shed behind the barn."

"Got it," said Austin, smiling at Clay when Clay smiled at him like they were sharing a secret, only it didn't need to be hidden.

"About time you showed up," said Clay with a mock frown, which was replaced quickly with a smile and a small laugh. "Actually, I'm glad you're here because I need to get this finished and set up the canopies by the fire pit on account of Bill said it's going to rain later."

Austin looked up at the cloudless sky.

"It's going to rain on account of I say it will, you young fool," said the older man as he took off his felt hat and wiped his forehead with the back of his forearm.

"That's Bill," said Clay, smiling.

"And who's this fancy city fellow?" asked Bill with an almost half-roar.

"I'm—I'm Austin," said Austin, a bit taken aback at Bill's abrupt question. He looked down at himself, sensibly dressed for being on a ranch. "How can you tell I'm from the city?"

"Jeans are so new they've still got a crease in 'em," said Bill. He held out his hand for Austin to take, and as they shook hands, Austin marveled at Bill's strong grip. "You're the new bean counter, right?"

"That is correct, sir," said Austin.

"Just call me Bill," said Bill in a gruff way, as though he'd been reminding Austin of this for years. "We don't stand on ceremony here. Ain't that right, Clay?"

"Sure enough, sir," said Clay, smiling and Bill, seeming to enjoy the sass, smiled right back. "C'mon, Austin, grab a sack and let us put you to work."

Walking up to the flatbed trailer, Austin grabbed a sack of grain, which was heavier than it looked, and was made up of some kind of plastic mesh that slipped off his shoulder every other step. He leaned to one side as he saw Clay doing, then followed him into the barn, into the shadows where it was just him and Clay side by side as they put the sacks on the pallets.

If he'd not been occupied figuring out how to set the sack down in a tidy fashion on top of the other sacks currently stacked on pallets, then he'd be flustered about what to say around Clay. What to do. What to think.

But Clay, rather than attempting more flirting, was all work and no play. He'd go out of the barn as soon as the sack he'd been carrying had been put settled on top of the growing stack.

Austin followed, like a well-trained dog, or a hapless fool who has succumbed to the first bit of kindness he'd experienced in years. Was he this easy? Was it all going to blow up in his face? Had he always been into men, or was it just Clay who'd tipped the balance?

They spent a good hour unloading sacks and putting them in neat rows on the two pallets inside the barn. Then Bill revved up his truck and pulled the flatbed trailer behind the barn, where they unloaded most of the sacks onto pallets inside of a steel-sided supply shed. By the time they were done, Austin was dripping sweat down his neck, his new blue jeans were covered with flecks of molasses-laced grain, and his new boots were properly broken in, or just about.

When they stopped for lunch, Austin realized he'd not been stressed or worried about anything, not even the fact that no accounting work had gotten done other than the two hours he'd spent that morning. It was like Clay had said the other night, that there was nothing going on and no need to rush. Just the work that would get done in its own time.

And then there was Clay. He was a hard worker, steady, always moving, carrying fifty-pound sacks with ease. Sweating beneath his armpits, pulling the tails of his shirt out when he wiped his forehead, exposing his belly, not tucking the shirt back afterwards. Sweat dripped down his temples, sticking his hair in dark gold streaks to his head.

Clay was moving, always moving. Slowing down to wait for Austin who, while he had ten years in the gym three times a week under his belt, was not used to the physical labor. But nobody chided him, nobody yelled at him to go faster, to work harder.

The smile Clay gave to Austin lit up the shadows of the barn, made the work seem easier. Made Austin's heart beat a little faster.

But there was no way this gentle flirtation between them could go any further, right? He was only recently divorced, couldn't get it up, and wasn't into men. Though, as he watched Clay heft yet another plastic sack onto his shoulder, Austin thought he might be rethinking that last one.

"Want to get lunch?" asked Clay. "After I put up the canopies?"

"Yes," said Austin, without any hesitation. "I look forward to it."

13

AUSTIN

*A*ustin made a point to call Bea every day. Well, he had to call Mona first, and get into a strident, heated conversation with her. After which, she wasn't always willing to hand over the phone to Bea, but on Friday he got lucky.

"Don't take too long, she's got ballet lessons," said Mona, in a short tone as though he'd taken up too much of her time already.

"How are those going?" asked Austin.

"She loves them. Here she is."

The phone changed hands, and there were a few muffled words from Mona, and a *Yes, Mom* from Bea.

Then he heard his daughter's voice.

"Dad, Dad, Dad!"

All the energy in Bea's voice flowed into him, all the love and affection like a balm after speaking to Mona for even just five minutes.

"How are you doing, honeybee?" he asked, cupping his hands around the phone, as though someone might overhear him, but also to focus his love for her through the phone. Through the airwaves, through the air, to where she was.

"I have a new tutu," she said. "And a leotard and tights and those cute little shoes. All pink. I hate pink!"

"I bet you look sweet in them," he said. "Look, get your mom to take a picture of you in them and send it to me so I can show you off at work."

"You work on a farm?" asked Bea. "Mom said you did."

"It's more like a ranch," said Austin. On the one hand, he was glad Mona hadn't said outright where he actually was, because Bea was likely to want to come visit him even more than she already did. Then, when she got there, she was likely to want a pony all her own. "With cows and stuff."

"Mom said it was a dirty place to work."

"It can get dirty," said Austin, thinking of Wednesday morning stacking sacks of grain, which had left him with sticky molasses on his hands, on his new blue jeans. "But it's fun, too. Like playing in the mud."

"Mom says—"

"Bea," said Austin, interrupting her. "Tell me how you are doing. You're not in school, but you're taking ballet. Does mom take you to play with your school friends?"

"Sometimes, but not always." At the other end of the line, Bea sighed. "I miss you, Dad. I want to come see you."

"Well, you can't now, Bea. We talked about this. You have to stay with Mom."

"I don't *want* to—"

Bea cut herself off, it seemed like, and when she spoke again it was as if she'd pushed the phone against her ear in order to talk close and low.

"Mom takes me to Miss Minchin's a lot. A lot. Then she goes out with Uncle Roger."

"Uncle Roger?" It was really soon for Mona's new beau to require that kind of title, but while he wanted to believe Mona had told Bea to call Roger Colchet her uncle for the best of reasons, he knew that wasn't true. "And who is Miss Minchin again?"

"She's the lady who has a daycare at her house, Dad," said Bea with all the exasperation of a nine-year-old who can't believe that an adult could be so forgetful. "The one with the plastic chairs and the yard full of rocks."

"You mean Mrs. Delgado?"

"Yes, but I call her Miss Minchin. You know, Dad, from the story about the little girl who lost her dad. 'Cause I'm kind of like that, I lost my dad."

"*The Little Princess*," said Austin, his racing mind grateful to have landed on the right book.

Mrs. Delgado was a middle-aged woman with a big heart, strict rules, and a large yard with a small playground and, yes, rocks. She had a rock garden, and the kids weren't supposed to play in it, but they did and usually got hurt in the process.

Austin didn't like Bea going there and had put his foot down about it last summer, but Mrs. Delgado's was close and the price was right. But if Mona didn't want to look after Bea, and wanted only to go out with Roger, why had she insisted on keeping Bea all to herself?

"And what would Sara Crewe do? Wouldn't she pretend to have a good time?"

"I tried, Dad, but I'm not Sara and it makes me sad—"

Now Bea was crying, being quiet about it, but making that little hitching noise in her throat like she couldn't breathe. Mrs. Delgado's had been fine when Bea had been a little younger, but now she was nine and needed something else. Only it wasn't up to him, it was up to Mona, only Mona couldn't be bothered—Austin stopped this train of thought, on the verge of tears himself.

"I'm sorry, honeybee," he said, swallowing hard over the fist in his throat. "I miss you so so so much—"

"I miss you, Dad," she said, the sob breaking through her voice.

Then there was a muffled thump and Mona was on the line.

"You're only upsetting her when you let her go on like that, you know." Mona's voice was icy and pointed. "And I'm the one who has to deal with her."

"Her life is upside-down right now, Mona, so why don't you—why don't you think about what Bea needs for a change, instead of what's easiest for you? She doesn't like being at Mrs. Delgado's house, for starters."

"Are you telling me what to do?" Mona snapped. "I'm doing the best I can here, and all you can do is complain. Why are you always like this? Why can't you be more sympathetic to what I'm going through?"

As always, Mona worried about Mona. Only Austin had not realized it until the last six months of their marriage.

In the background, he thought he could hear Bea crying to herself, but if he asked Mona to give the phone back to Bea, she'd only say no, and then after the phone call she'd be cold and snippy to Bea, even if Bea was her only daughter and needed her.

Bea needed her dad, too. But that wasn't going to happen, though Austin could try to manage that a little better, regretting the fact that he'd let Mona have her way about the visitation rights. He needed to change that, needed to figure out a way to make it happen.

"I would like to be able to speak to her more than once a week," said Austin. "That's fair. Even the judge would say so."

"I suppose," said Mona, in that way she had, like giving in would break her. "She has to use my cell phone for that, and I am a busy woman, very busy."

"Please, Mona?" asked Austin, hating the begging sound beneath the words, hated the way he felt like he was crawling on broken glass, afraid that at any moment, Mona would really explode on him and maybe take it out on Bea. "Do it for Bea. Besides," he added, angry that he imagined he could hear Bea crying in the background. "We do have joint custody. The judge said so."

"I'll think about it," she said. There was no warmth in her voice, but then there hadn't been for a good long while now.

Still, if Mona had to allow Bea to talk to him more than once a week, it was yet another thing she could complain to the other Mama Bears about, her stupid ex-husband who *insisted* on talking to his daughter, can you imagine?

"Thank you, Mona," he said. "Kiss Bea for me, will you?"

"Goodbye," she said, and the line clicked and the phone was silent.

With the cellphone an inert piece of metal in his hands, Austin looked out the window of his small room where the view was transformed by silver rain against the window.

What he wanted to do was borrow Leland's truck and race down to Thornton so he could give Bea a giant hug. Then he'd get her to tell him about her day, and share with her funny things that had happened in the office, like they used to do together.

Thornton wasn't a far drive away, but at that moment it was light years. Even if he had left that moment, when he arrived it would be late, Bea would be in bed.

Mona would be at the door, her arms crossed, manicured fingernails making tapping motions on her sleeve. Probably Uncle Roger would be standing close behind her, marking his territory, waggling his eyebrows at Austin as if to say, *Yes, I've seen the bleached anus that you've never seen.*

He had to shake himself hard to dispel the image, to rid himself of how it felt to be so disconnected from a life that he'd lived with his full heart. Missing Bea was a big part of it. Missing who he thought he'd been was the other.

His cellphone chirped. He looked down at his hand and thumbed the most recent text open, thinking it was Mona with a last-minute request of him. But it was Clay.

Dinner's almost over. You coming?

Austin found himself looking forward to meals more than he thought he would. And though Clay, who worked hard, often showed up well after the dinner hour had begun, Austin would wait as long as it took. This time, Austin was making Clay wait, which he didn't want to do.

Quickly he typed: *Yes.*

It was like Clay to check up on him. It was like Clay to care. And it was like Austin to wonder if Clay might consider their friendship, and whatever else it seemed to be, too much trouble to bother.

He typed again: *Coming.*

No, there was no innuendo there, not a bit of one. But after he plugged in his phone to charge it, he checked himself in the mirror.

In his eyes there was that hangdog look Mona always complained about and would probably keep complaining about till the universe ended. There was nothing to be done about it. He looked like he looked.

Only—he had a second snap-button shirt he'd bought, a green plaid one that had arrived at the store that morning. Maybe he could put it on—*for Clay*—and act as if. Maybe Clay would say he looked nice, and even if the tone in his voice was teasing, it wouldn't be mocking. Rather, it would be encouraging.

And what on earth was he supposed to do with the fact that he very much would like more teasing from Clay? What was he supposed to do with the idea that he was terrified if that teasing should lead to something more?

Except this wasn't a horror movie. He wouldn't die from it. Nothing bad would happen if it all should go wrong, except maybe some discomfort between co-workers whose fling didn't quite work out.

And it really wouldn't work out the second Clay found out that Austin could not, as Joe Public might say, *manage*. Austin couldn't get it up. While the sweetness of being on the ranch had made a bit of difference in how he was feeling, he'd long since taken himself in hand, so it was almost like he'd forgotten how.

Mona liked him to do all the work. Mona liked—but to hell with what Mona liked. Mona had given him up for Uncle Roger, and Austin was on his own. And why should he worry? Anyway, he wasn't Clay's type, however friendly Clay was, however sweet the teasing. Not to mention, he had no idea how gay men went about things.

Giving his shirt collar one last tug, Austin grabbed his windbreaker and his room key and made his way downstairs. Out on the front porch of the staff quarters, the rain made a steady pattern on the roof, coming down in silver strings from the overhang. There would be puddles on the path, but his cowboy boots could take it, they were made for rough weather.

He hustled between the raindrops to arrive at a dining hall that was just being cleared from dinner. Fine, he wasn't hungry, anyway. He just wanted to see Clay and to thank him for everything.

"Hey," said Clay, coming through the guests as they clomped onto the porch. "Here, I grabbed you a bowl of mac and cheese, which, I know, is not good for your girlish figure, but hey. We can wash the bowl afterward. And besides, we're setting up for game night on account of the rain."

"Thank you," said Austin, taking the offered bowl and spoon, eating as he stood there while the idea that Clay thought he had a girlish figure raced around in his head. "Does it rain like this all the time?"

"Depends," said Clay. "End of August is our monsoon season, but if we've had mild winters like we did this year, then it rains on and off all summer. Drives Bill crazy when he can't tell his ghost stories beneath the stars, but then sometimes we get thunderstorms and those are always pretty."

Polishing off the mac and cheese, Austin wiped his mouth with the back of his hand like he was five years old.

"That was excellent," he said, and meant it. "Now, how can I help set up?" He shimmied out of his windbreaker, and was somewhat astonished when Clay took it to hang up for him.

"You need a Carhartt," said Clay, mildly scolding. "This thing is fine normally, but it can get chilly when it rains."

"What's a Carhartt?" asked Austin as the two of them helped wipe down the tables.

"It's a kind of ranch coat," said Clay. He grabbed a broom and handed one to Austin. "We don't sell them at the store, as there's not much of a demand by guests who are only here in the summer months, or who have brought their own coats. They're kind of pricey, too, but the ranch'll cover the cost. Just ask Leland."

"I'll do that," said Austin.

When the dining hall had been wiped down, swept, and set up, guests started coming back in, laughing as they shook off the rain and grabbed boxes that contained table-top games or puzzles. Austin had been expecting that when they were done, Clay would say goodnight and goodbye, having already put in a full day's work. But, as always, Clay surprised him.

"Want to do a puzzle together?" asked Clay, leaning close, as though the question was a secret. "I should sit with guests and be jolly and stuff, but, well, honestly, I'd rather just sit with you."

"Clay—" Austin stopped himself, unable and unwilling to blurt out that he had no idea what he was doing and even if he did, Clay was bound to end up disappointed. What did gay guys do in these situations? More to the point, what did anyone do? Again, he had no idea.

"Don't worry about it," said Clay. "I just like your company and I bet you're a whiz with puzzles."

"I am, as a matter of fact," said Austin with mock gravity, as if it was the highest, most prized skill in the land.

If this—whatever it was between them—went any further, he was going to have to tell Clay that he couldn't get it up. Right? He'd have to say it out loud, rather than make Clay discover the fact at the last minute.

And, thinking about all of this, about maybe being naked with another human being other than Mona, a *man*, made his chest tighten. He needed to calm down, needed to be in the moment. Needed, no, wanted to enjoy his evening with Clay.

"How about this one?" Clay stood up from where he'd been bent over to select a puzzle. The one he held showed a group of wild cowboys running from a herd of cattle, shooting in the air for no apparent reason. There were one thousand pieces and the puzzle was rated for age fourteen and up. Perfect.

They grabbed a table near the windows, not the long table, but a smaller one, where the box and the lid, propped up to show them what they were working toward, took up all the room. There was only room for the two of them, making them a couple.

The lights were dimmed and staff brought out kerosene lamps to give the dining hall a festive air. From the kitchen, Austin could smell hot chocolate being made, and the noise descended to a low, comfortable hum as people bent to their puzzles, or rolled their dice, or moved their checkers across a black and red board while freshets of rain-scented air breezed in through the propped-open double doors.

It was hard to concentrate on the puzzle, as much as he tried, for his eyes kept going across the pieces to stare at Clay. Whose hair turned golden in the kerosene lamps, his face flushed in the warmth of the room. Absently, he rolled up his sleeves, and picked at the puzzle pieces with his fingers. He tried a lopsided join here, a zig-zag connection there, turning each piece this way and that before planting it into place with a happy sigh.

"You know you're staring, right?" asked Clay, without looking up.

"I don't mean to," said Austin. His mouth was dry.

"And you don't look so good around the eyes." Now Clay looked up, making a circle with his finger around his own face. "You look sad, and it's not just because you missed my company at dinner. So what happened? And don't tell me nothing."

"Nothing," said Austin, trying for a small joke, but though Clay smiled, he shook his head.

"Friends tell," said Clay. "And yes, we're friends."

"Okay, so—" Austin reached up to scrape his short hair back from his suddenly warm forehead. "I call Bea almost every day. Most days Mona won't let me talk to her."

"Well, that sucks," said Clay, frowning, his dark brows drawing together.

"It does, and today I got to talk to her, and she was crying within five minutes. She misses me, she says, and she doesn't like it at Miss Minchin's."

"With a name like that, I wouldn't like it there either."

"She's a character in a book. The real name of the lady who watches Bea is Mrs. Delgado, but the result is the same. Mona and I share custody, but right now, Mona's trying to override my visitation rights. Except, instead of spending time with Bea, she's palming her off to someone else. She was so insistent so why is she doing that?"

"Why indeed?" Clay looked down at the partially finished puzzle as though it could tell him what he needed to know. "It's a funny world," he said, looking up at Austin, his eyes very blue in the lamplight.

"Sometimes you get what you want, only you don't want it anymore. And sometimes, you don't even know what you want."

They might have been talking about Mona and her full custody, or maybe they were talking about something else. Austin didn't feel brave enough to ask, so he didn't, instead saying, "I suppose it'll hurt less with time."

"You miss Bea," said Clay. "You miss your honeybee."

"How do you know I call her that?" asked Austin, feeling like a bit of his heart had been flayed open and laid bare for anyone to see.

"You were on the phone with her at the motel," said Clay. "I wasn't trying to overhear, but I heard, so I know you miss her."

"Yes, I do," said Austin, and he had to swallow hard to erase the shake in his voice. "Anyway, what about you? You have family, do you not?"

"I do," said Clay, and he told Austin about them, about his five older sisters, and his parents, both farmers, and the farm where they grew corn, and the humidity that was never-ending in summer.

His face lit up as he talked, and it was easy to see that while he cared about them, he didn't miss them, for he seemed happy to be on the ranch, and his talk soon turned to where they were, in Wyoming, on a ranch, putting together a puzzle while it rained.

Through the open doors came a flicker of lightning and the faraway thud of thunder. Austin was glad, in that moment, to be where he was, was glad to simply be with Clay, who looked at him with affection and seemed glad to be with him. And who, in the end, if it came to that, might not mind about all of Austin's flaws, the ones Mona had been ever so diligent about pointing out to him.

14

CLAY

*I*n the morning, as Clay showered and shaved and examined his face in the small bathroom mirror, he figured his bruises and black eye had gone down enough to be almost unnoticeable. He'd be brave then and march into Leland's office after the morning's meeting and ask to be put back on the regular roster, the no-longer-in-the-dog-house roster.

As he scraped his damp hair back from his face and figured out what shirt to wear, he thought about Austin and how he'd looked in the lamplight the night before. How his eyes had been so dark and sad and, when he'd finally told Clay what was up, Clay had felt sad right along with him, determined to sympathize and cheer Austin up as best he could.

The best way had been by distracting him with funny stories about his older sisters, and mentioning the Carhartt jacket once more, clarifying which color might look best on Austin. Which made him blush a hard red.

Austin probably didn't know his face was flushed, that he got flustered when Clay said nice things to him, which made Clay want to find Mona and give her a good talking to. A man as good looking, as tall as Austin was, as clean as he was, who smelled as good as Austin did, should not be flustered by compliments.

Austin was *so* good looking, with his manly jaw and ginger coloring, he should be so used to compliments that they were almost boring to him. Though, of course, Austin was a polite kind of guy, so he'd never act bored about it, but would always say thank you in that warm voice of his. Whiskey warm, pleasant and slow, like Tupelo honey on a warm day.

Which was not how Clay should be thinking about Austin, not at all. He'd made his little pass, almost unconsciously, like he did with a lot of men he'd met. It went along with his handshake, and was tucked inside the way he said *hello* and *how do you do*. It was like he was always searching, not just for somebody to go to bed with or to do harum-scarum things in the alley outside the Rusty Nail with, but for more, though he'd never been quite able to define what that more was made of.

Undoing his top snap buttons, he grabbed his cell phone to unplug it and quickly searched for the Carhartt he'd been telling Austin about. Should he send the link for the moss green one? Or should he pick the brownish tan one, so Austin's green eyes would stand out?

The green one was awfully nice, so he clicked on that one and texted the link to Austin, then sauntered down the stairs to the morning meeting in front of the barn. A glance up the hallway showed him that Austin's door was closed, as he was lucky enough to not have to come to morning meetings at the freaking break of dawn. Later, though, he'd catch up to Austin for sure so they could have breakfast together.

The meeting, run by Leland and Maddy, as it usually was, went quickly, with the regular announcements about Saturday leaving times, and how they were staggered so as not to create a melee among the guests in the parking lot. And then there was Maddy's usual request to help the housekeeping staff with baskets of laundry.

Of course, Clay raised his hand. Volunteering for this task put him in good standing with Stella and her mighty band of cleaners, which was a good thing when he accidentally needed new towels on account of he'd neglected to hang up his damp ones to dry on the rack rather than leaving them on the bathroom floor where they'd grow moldy.

Maybe Austin wouldn't like to be with a guy who had messy habits, though, so maybe it was time he stepped up to the plate. Still, he held his hand up to volunteer and got the nod from Leland, which really made his day. As did the fact that he was on tap for helping with the riding lessons for new riders come Monday. Which meant he was really out of the doghouse at last.

"I think I've learned my lesson, boss," said Clay as he went up to Leland after the meeting.

"I'm glad to hear it," said Leland with a smile. He'd no more enjoyed disciplining Clay than Clay had. Clay knew that in his heart, but the smile was the topper. "Just you keep downwind of Eddie Piggot in future, yes? He'll call the cops for sure the next time one of mine gets into it with him."

"You got it, boss," said Clay. "Well, I'm off to breakfast."

He trotted all the way from the barn to the main lodge, though the morning was muggy and hot after last night's heavy rain and any sensible person would have walked. But seeing Austin at mealtimes had become the bright part of his day, so it was hard to slow down.

Though, when he climbed the steps and looked along the line, he saw Austin had already gotten his breakfast and was sitting with Quint and Bill.

Maybe they'd met up with Austin in line, and it wasn't like he could say no to them. Plus, it looked like they were having a serious chat, probably about money issues, so he waved until Austin saw him, his face brightening as he waved back.

Both Bill and Quint turned in their chairs, probably to see what had distracted Austin from listening to them. When they saw it was Clay, he waved like the shy, delicate flower that he was, and flashed his dimples at them. Bill made a grousing motion with his hand and turned away, and Clay laughed under his breath and got in line for breakfast.

The rest of the day seemed to go like that, with him keeping an eye out for Austin, but missing him all day long. He texted to see if Austin liked the color of jacket he picked out.

It goes with your eyes, he texted.

It does?

Just messing with you...but yes.

He probably shouldn't be messing with Austin, who while fully grown was quite reserved, sometimes withdrawn. Clay had to work at the friendship, maybe harder than he'd worked at any other friendship. But then, nobody else on the ranch, let alone in any bar, drew him the way Austin did. Being with him while hauling sacks of molasses-laced grain or putting together a puzzle with way too many cowboys on it, it did not matter.

Especially last night. Everything had seemed to slow down to a walking pace, rather than the brisk way Clay went about things, flirting at the first hello, getting fucked at the Rusty Nail by the first guy who showed any interest.

Maybe the slowing had come from the fact that Austin was an accountant, and had looked so nerdy and glum standing in the rain at the Motel 6. Austin, who even after he'd started wearing that pale blue pearl-snap button shirt buttoned up to the neck, looked like he was hiding beneath his clothes, not wanting anyone to see.

Surely there were freckles on those shoulders to go with that hair. Surely those muscles in his arms and legs were as long as they seemed to be because when Clay had bumped into Austin, more than once and yes on purpose, those muscles had been hard as iron, in contrast to his scholarly air. Kind of like a monk who'd trained to fight any Vikings that might raid his village.

Which made Clay the Viking in this scenario, which wasn't right. He wasn't tall enough, for one thing, didn't have that regal air Austin did, didn't hold his chin high enough or walk so tall, like Austin did. Even taller now that he'd taken to wearing cowboy boots all the dang time, which tilted his hips and made his butt a sharp blue denim-covered curve.

Gah. He needed to stop torturing himself like this. And probably he needed to figure out whether he wanted to keep flirting with

Austin to see where it led, or back off and just have a good friend in his life, without worrying about which of them was the monk and which the Viking.

He was late to lunch and so missed Austin yet again, and groused to himself as he ate Levi's terrific BBQ meatloaf and mashed potatoes, and smiled as Brody came up to his table, tray in hand.

"Hey," said Brody as he sat down. "Levi and I are going to Chugwater, to the Stampede Saloon, tonight. You in?"

"Sure," said Clay with a nod, his mouth full of meatloaf. "Mind if I ask Austin along?"

"No problem," said Brody. "Levi's Volvo will fit four easy. Austin doesn't look like that kind of guy, though."

"What kind of guy?" asked Clay, ready to defend the object of his flirtatious affection.

"The kind of guy who'd step into the alley for a quickie first chance he got." Brody laughed under his breath as Clay bristled like he was affronted.

"Well, he's not," said Clay, absolutely sure of this. "I just figured maybe he'd like a night out."

"Well, you're welcome to ask him," said Brody. "Levi figures we'll leave at seven."

"What's he all antsy about?" asked Clay, for Levi usually was more casual about their Saturday night rendezvous.

"Oh, I don't know," said Brody as he stirred the BBQ sauce into his mashed potatoes. "Something he saw on the news, I think. Something about Terrytown."

"Oh." Clay nodded. Terrytown was where Levi hailed from, but other than that, he was a closed book, at least to Clay. "Well, seven it is then."

Finally, at the end of the day, after grooming horses, shoveling horse shit, and carrying baskets and bags of laundry, he caught up with Austin at the dining hall.

"Hey, stranger," said Austin as he stepped to the side, making room for Clay in line. "I'd almost forgotten what you looked like."

"How could you forget this face?" Clay gestured to his own face, putting on an expression of woe to be so forgotten. "How could you forget these dimples?"

"I couldn't. I didn't," said Austin brightly, though his mouth closed over the words like he was surprised he'd said them.

"Hey, listen," said Clay, his hand on Austin's arm to draw him close as they shuffled forward in line for the buffet. And yes, those muscles beneath the white button-down shirt he was wearing again were solid as marble. Solid enough to lift a truck or maybe just be *firm* with Clay — "The guys are going to Chugwater for some Saturday night fun. Do you want to come?"

"Tonight?" asked Austin, his eyebrows arching, as though Clay had asked him to fly to the moon. "I was going to get out my paint box and get reacquainted with it."

"A paint box?" Clay picked up a tray and silverware and moved along to where he could see the warming dish of lasagna. "What're you going to do with that?"

"Paint," said Austin, giving Clay a little nudge with his elbow so he could get at the lasagna too. "It's a promise I made to myself. That I would pick it up again after Mona—that is, I'm not very good. Mostly landscapes and suchlike."

"Well, a promise is a promise," said Clay. "Wouldn't want you to go back on something like that. Maybe you'll show your stuff to me sometime."

"Maybe."

The word came to Clay low and cautious, like Austin had either never shown his paintings to anyone or had never been asked. Either way, as they went to the long table and settled in to eat, it was pleasant to think about. Austin in a room with an easel, paint smudges on his fingertips, his hair wild from all that creativity, like Clay had seen in the movies. He'd smell like paint and dark French coffee, and maybe he'd let Clay kiss him, just once, for luck.

As they'd sat at the long table, Brody sat with them, and Levi, and even Quint, though he didn't have much to say, and so Clay couldn't get a private moment to ask Austin to talk more about his paintings. To see that faint glow in his eyes, like when he'd mentioned the paint box, grow into something stronger and brighter.

Nobody deserved to have to hide away something they enjoyed, and again Clay wanted to find Mona and give her another piece of his mind, for who did that to someone they'd promised to love and cherish? Who?

After dinner, Brody grabbed Clay and wouldn't let go, and while he was given an opportunity to go to his room and spruce up for the evening out, he didn't have another chance to ask Austin if he wanted to go. With his best hat on, and his cowboy boots polished, he took out his phone as he slid into the back seat of Levi's Volvo.

Then, in the darkness, as Levi drove along the two-lane road to Chugwater and he and Brody chatted about the rainy weather and the condition of the roads, Clay texted, half-blind, squinting: *Hope the painting's good.*

Within a second came the response, in glowing letters: *Everything's dry. Will order more.*

And then, from Austin came the question: *Will you dance at the saloon?*

Clay texted: *Am terrible dancer. Mostly there for smex.*

He thumbed the send button before thinking that might be too much to share, and would Austin know what smex meant anyhow? But then, Austin was on the internet and might know, except at the same time, was that how he wanted Austin to think about him?

After a long five minutes, during which he imagined Austin scowling at the screen of his phone, holding it in both hands while he decided how to respond to that, Clay finally got his answer.

Be good to yourself.

Now, what the heckfire was that supposed to mean? He was always good to himself, with sturdy boots on his feet, a new straw cowboy hat every season, and a job he loved. He had people he enjoyed working with pretty much most every day, and the food in the dining hall was terrific. He lacked for nothing, outside of an engine rebuild for Ladybelle.

All the way to Chugwater he thought about Austin's text, silent beneath the conversation between Levi and Brody. Blinking at the brightness of the streetlights of Chugwater as they came up the rise and drove under the highway. From there it was a quick zip through the town to the Stampede Saloon, which sat along the railroad tracks next to the grain towers.

The parking lot was huge and gravel, and Levi sped to a parking place at the furthest point so his ancient Volvo station wagon wouldn't get dinged.

Then they sauntered across the parking lot with the throng of people who'd also decided to hang out in a bar with plywood floors and dancing cowboy and cowgirl decals plastered everywhere, and which had more kinds of beer than the Rusty Nail offered. But then, The Stampede Saloon was on a major highway, and so they were more visible, and ordered more in.

With a happy sigh, Clay walked up to the bar, taking in the tables with their red and white checked tablecloths at one end, and the band on the carpeted stage on the other. The band was just tuning up, so the night had yet to start hopping.

As he inhaled the scent of beer and whiskey slopped on the bar just before the bartender wiped it clean with a cloth, he figured maybe it was a good thing that he couldn't ever go back to the Rusty Nail, at least not until Eddie Piggot sold up. But he never would, alas, so that was one watering hole forever closed to him.

"What c'n I get you, young sir?" asked the bartender, an older man with dark Brylcreemed hair and a bolero tie with a chunk of turquoise in it.

"Sure, hang on," said Clay, pulling out his wallet.

"Oh, no, young sir." The bartender pointed to the end of the bar. "The drink is on the man, there, with the denim jacket."

Clay looked along the bar.

The man in the denim jacket was handsome, had a hard jaw, and looked a little on the tough side, like a trucker who drove an eighteen-wheeled rig and did the long hauls over mountain passes in the winter. Like he liked it rough, like he had a special place outside the back door of the Stampede Saloon where he liked to do what Clay liked to do, which was to fuck, messy and fast, and then go their separate ways. Like he had condoms and packets of lube in his pocket, just ready to go.

Clay was ready to go, of course he was. He always was. It was why he came out on Saturday nights to blow off a little steam, to have some fun, to feel the touch of a hand on his hip, and maybe a tender kiss on his shoulder before the other guy pulled out.

Only.

Except.

Be good to yourself, Austin's text had read.

"I'll have a Bud," he told the bartender, not really understanding why he was going to do what he was about to do. "In a glass, if I could."

The bartender poured him a beer in a frosted glass and handed it over. Clay took it and went around the bar to nestle up to Mr. Truck Driver, settling in, his elbows on the bar, before he took his first sip.

"You're mighty kind," said Clay. "But I have to tell you, there's this guy I kind of like, and though you look like you'd be miles of fun—"

"You're saving yourself, eh?" Mr. Truck Driver took a long slug of his own beer, and smiled at Clay with white teeth, his nose all perfect in his face, dark hair curling across his forehead like some kind of dreamy contestant on a gay Dating Game. "Well, it was nice for you to come and tell me, instead of being a tease with that nice, round ass of yours. What about your friends?"

Clay looked where Mr. Truck Driver was gesturing, which was at Levi and Brody at the far end of the bar, chatting with the bartender, discussing their beverage options.

"The taller one? With the chestnut hair like he's out of a magazine?" Clay pointed with his glass of beer.

"Yeah?"

"Nope." Clay shook his head. "I don't know what his deal is, but he never goes home with anybody. He's a nice guy, but kind of a loner."

"And the other one?"

The conversation wasn't quite on the verge of him pimping out his friends, but it was awfully close.

Mr. Truck Driver might be fun for a quickie, and sometimes Brody was up for that, the way he sometimes told it. But sometimes Brody was like a skittish mare whose previous owners had been cruel.

Clay didn't know all of Brody's story, only that he'd been a trick rider, a trick roper, on the circuit from the age of five. And that, though he would put on a show for guests at Leland's urging, he never really talked about it, never seemed to want to brag about how good he was, and he was mighty good.

"I think you're more my style, my speed, than his," said Clay. "You get me?"

"I get you." Mr. Truck Driver flashed Clay a bright smile, and with a jerk of his chin, moved toward the crowd around the bar, on the prowl, like a denim-jacketed wolf. "Well, thanks anyway. Enjoy your beer."

Which left Clay with a half-drunk beer in his hand and his ass absolutely un-fucked. But if he wasn't gonna go with Mr. Truck Driver, then why the heck was he at the bar?

Mr. Truck Driver had been exactly what Clay always looked for. Exactly the type he liked to go with, the type he liked to do the shimmy-shimmy with in back alleys. And while it was likely, if he stood up straight and looked around and showed his dimples, that he'd get another offer, just exactly what was it he'd been thinking about, turning this one down?

Only, he knew the answer to that without having to spell it out to himself. Here Clay was in the Stampede Saloon, a nice place with a pretty decent band, a cold beer in his hand. He'd just been left on his own at the bar and didn't actually straighten up or smile. And that was because thoughts of Austin, all alone in his room, kept pulling at him. He could so easily imagine Austin digging through his room for his painting stuff because he was going to try living a secret dream of his, only to find out that the paints had dried and now he'd have to order new ones from Amazon.

Clay could just see the sorrowful face Austin would make as he looked at his dried out paint box, his expression quite still, eyes grave, green like ancient moss. And from what Clay had noticed about

Austin, he'd just take his disappointment and absorb it. Maybe he'd not even order those new paints, maybe he'd just settle into his ranch life with no speck of creativity.

Well, if Austin had told him to be good to himself, then he needed to make sure Austin was good to himself, too.

Clay pulled out his phone and, holding it close to his chest, brought up Amazon and searched for paint boxes. Amazon displayed a long list, showing all sizes, all prices.

He didn't really know what kind of paint Austin used, come to think of it, and Amazon was showing him oil paints, and acrylic, and watercolor, and something called gouache. To be funny, he found the most enormous, most expensive one, didn't matter what kind of paint. The box was made of wood, and it had tubes of paint, an easel, along with paper and about a dozen paint brushes.

Copying the link, he pasted it into a text message and wrote: *Found your new paint set! Arriving in two days! Have fun!*

Within two seconds, he got his response: *I hope you're kidding.*

Clay laughed while texted: *Heh*, then added a bunch of smiling faces, including a poop emoji, just to be amusing. *Just get the paint*, he texted, and scrolled and scrolled till he found the right icon, a tiny little artist's palette complete with circles of color.

It was the most fun he'd ever had at a bar, which said a lot right there.

15

AUSTIN

*H*alfway through Monday morning, Austin was in Leland's office, going over notes he'd made about bank balances and what he'd found in a box of scribbled information on the backs of envelopes. Bill Wainwright did handshake deals, Maddy had told him, and not all the love or money in the world would make him get a receipt. The most he would do was leave a note with Maddy that hay, alfalfa, or straw was on its way and could she schedule somebody to unload it all?

"I'm afraid you're not going to change Bill," said Leland, with a solemn shake of his head. "It's his ranch, after all."

"Look, I get that part," said Austin, struggling to balance good accounting practices against the fact that this was a living, breathing business, and not just a cold corporation in a high-rise in downtown Denver. "And I appreciate that he sometimes leaves those notes for Maddy, but what needs to happen when the deliveries arrive is that they need to be recorded. Not only will it fix the problem of the fact that, somehow, somewhere, someone is overcharging Bill, it will help streamline future orders. If you know how much hay you ordered in June, for example, this year, then next year, you have an estimate to start with. Do you see?"

"Yes, I see," said Leland slowly as he sat back in his office chair, probably doing his best to look like he didn't long to be in the fresh open air, on horseback, or directing one of his ranch hands. Anywhere but where he was, which was with Austin telling him that Bill Wainwright needed to do a better job of tracking his spending.

A fresh breeze came in through the open double doors of the barn, swirling around the open door to Leland's office. All around him Austin could smell straw and horse sweat and leather oil, and all the scents that marked the space as a barn. Beyond those open doors, a blue sky beckoned, like a patient mistress.

He'd not realized before how much time he used to spend indoors when he'd been married to Mona. Now, being out in the open so much, walking from Maddy's office to Leland's office and then back and forth from his room in the staff quarters to the dining hall, the contrast was stark. He could never go back to a cubicle or even an office after this job, and his hope was that he never would have to.

"Hey, Jamie." Leland stood up, moving forward on his toes, and Austin turned to see Jamie come through the door, bright eyed, full of energy, his eyes focused on Leland, though his face was serious as though he had news to tell. "Either of you want a root beer?"

"No thanks," said Austin, never having been fond of soft drinks.

"I'll have one."

Leland pulled two brown glass bottles out of his little fridge and opened them with some ceremony. Both men drank and then sighed as they clinked their bottles together, a little laugh shared between them.

"What brings you in?" asked Leland. "Or is the trail ride back already?"

"It is, just in," said Jamie. "Quint told me he saw a mountain lion, and so we brought the ride back early."

"How close was it?"

"Close enough to see, not close enough to see if it had tags." Jamie pushed his curls back from his forehead. "If Quint had his rifle with him, I think he would have shot it."

"Well, we better go take care of it," said Leland. He polished off his root beer, recycled the bottle, and reached for his hat. "Get Clay, would you? Then get my rifle and scope from the storeroom."

Austin watched as Jamie dashed off, and stood up, as Leland's energy seemed to pull him to his feet.

"You're not going to shoot it are you?" asked Austin, even as he considered he didn't know very much about wildlife, let alone rifles and bullets. Didn't know whether a mountain lion was a threat to cattle or horses, though it might be scary for someone to encounter one on a trail ride.

"No," said Leland, shaking his head as he reached into his desk to pull out two pairs of binoculars.

"Then why the rifle?"

"To scare it," said Leland. "That's why I'm bringing Clay for this. If I brought Quint, he'd want to shoot it. We'll find it, and then Clay will scare it by shooting *around* it. And if we see it has tags, we'll alert Wildlife Management. Or maybe alert BLM and let them deal with it. Want to come?"

"Yes," said Austin, his mind automatically going to the fact that he'd get to spend time with Clay. As to what kind of time that might be, he didn't know, but still. The day turned brighter inside of a heartbeat, and he pushed thoughts of Bill's sloppy record keeping aside.

Jamie soon came back with a rifle in a rifle-bag, a box of bullets, or whatever it was that the rifle used, and Clay in tow.

Clay was flushed from his work, cheeks pink and warm, eyes bright. A single line of sweat trailed behind his ear and down his neck, and from the damp circles beneath his arms, to the hay speckling his blue jeans, he looked exactly like what he was: a ranch hand, bursting with muscles to do the work, and to keep doing it, sunup to sundown. Energy radiated from him like a pulse from a heartbeat, reaching Austin and echoing inside of him.

"Hey," said Clay, smiling at Austin, and it was like being gobsmacked with pleasure and joy and energy, all at once. "I hear we're off on a hunting trip."

"That we are," said Leland.

"Well, it beats the heck out of shoveling horse shit." Clay's voice curled around the words in a twang and he crooked his mouth, like he must have thought a good Southern boy would do, and then laughed, bringing up the laughter in Austin's chest like a gift.

"I hear you're a good shot," said Austin, doing his best to rein in his galloping emotions racing around inside of him as he watched Clay take the rifle bag and the bullets from Jamie, hefting them as though he'd done it many times before.

"Well," said Clay, with a shrug, wiping the sweat from his jawline with the heel of his palm. "I'm good, but Quint's better."

"Don't be fooled by his modesty, Austin," said Leland, giving Clay a hearty clap on his shoulder. "I've never seen such steady hands. Besides, Quint might be better overall, but Clay is top-notch in long-distance shooting."

This Austin was about to see, making him quite glad he'd said yes when Leland had asked him. Watching accountants at work was the most boring thing ever. Watching Clay do pretty much anything had been, from the beginning, quite the opposite. Watching him on the hunt was completely out of Austin's realm of experience and despite doing his best to stay calm, his heartbeat had picked up, even as he borrowed a spare hat from the barn and followed the other men out to Leland's truck.

For a moment the four of them stood there beneath the bright sun to discuss how their efforts would go. Austin did his best not to stare, but if he tipped his hat low, he could look at Clay from beneath the brim of his hat, and maybe Clay wouldn't notice him staring. And it was hard not to stare as Clay adjusted the long canvas strap over his shoulder, muscles bunching beneath his cotton shirt.

"We'll drive out, following the ridge," said Leland. "Isn't that where the trail ride went?"

"Yes," said Jamie. "I can direct us to where we saw the cat."

Leland nodded and handed one pair of binoculars to Jamie and the other to Austin.

"You two ride in the back. Jamie will be with me."

Feeling rather like a kid on his way to a drive-in movie on a summer's evening, Austin climbed into the truck bed of Leland's silver F150 and was very glad of the hat inside of one second, as the sun poured into the truck bed like hot gold. It was better when the truck started moving, as the breeze moved over them like a cooling blanket.

The truck bed had a liner, but it was still bumpy going till Clay showed him how to prop himself on the wheel well. Clay kept the rifle tucked behind his boot heels so it wouldn't slide around, and held the box in his hands, which, now that Austin could read the label, contained some kind of cartridges.

They rode like that, hunched on wheel humps opposite each other. Clay smiled as Leland drove, looking pleased to be where he was, and Austin found himself smiling back for the pure joy of joining in.

Leland drove them up the road to the ridge, pausing to let Jamie jump out to open and close the gate behind them, and then trundled the truck on a bumpy dirt road along the high ridge.

"Fun, huh?" asked Clay, smiling, his elbows resting on his knees, grime-traced hands loosely hooked together.

"Yes," said Austin, enjoying the breezy air, the blue sky, the way he could lean back just a little bit and take in the view of grass and more grass that went on along the foothills as far as he could see, and the line of the horizon, where blue sky met green grass, triggered a painting urge, faint and faraway, but there.

When he leaned forward again, Clay was watching him, his eyes serious, as though he'd been studying Austin when Austin had been studying their surroundings.

"Get those binoculars out," said Clay. "Leland is slowing down, so this must be where Jamie said Quint saw the mountain lion."

"What do they look like?" Austin did as he was told and took out the binoculars, then stood up to hold them to his eyes.

"You will know it when you see it," said Clay. "They're tawny brown and long in the body."

Even though Leland was going slow, it was bumpy going and hard to keep steady, so he had to pull the binoculars away. Then Austin heard Jamie tell Leland to stop.

When the truck became still, Austin braced himself against the truck cab, and started scanning toward the foothills, for even if he knew little about wild animals, it made more sense than to look along the grasses of the high prairie. Clay was at his side, holding the rifle in his other hand, close enough to bump against Austin, maybe by accident, maybe on purpose, and Austin knew he didn't mind.

As Austin scanned the foothills, something came into sharp focus, moving, shifting against the rocks, leaping up and then down. The animal's coat was tawny, just like Clay said, but there had been no way he could have prepared for the power of the animal, the shift of its body when it moved. The look in its brown eyes, as if it was fully aware it was being looked at but was too busy hunting, too busy being a mountain lion, to give over any of its energy to Austin.

"That's it," said Austin, taking the binoculars away from his face. He pointed to where he'd been looking. "I'm not sure how far away the animal is, but it's in that direction."

"Got it."

If Austin expected that Clay would hold up the rifle, load it with bullets and start shooting, he was wrong, so very wrong.

"Turn the truck to the west," said Clay, leaning to talk to Leland through the sliding window to the truck's interior.

They both steadied themselves against the cab of the truck while Leland moved to point them in the right direction. Then he turned off the engine, and while the tick tick of cooling metal grew silent, the hush of the wind lifted, the scratch of grasses against each other, the low moan of the breeze through the crags in the rocks.

Clay rolled up his shirtsleeves, exposing his tanned, corded forearms, and tipped his hat back on his head. Then he handed the box of cartridges to Austin, who held them with some trepidation, having never been this close to bullets before.

The box was a serious weight in Austin's hand, unexpectedly dense, feeling lethal. As Clay withdrew the rifle from the canvas bag, he let the bag drop to the truck bed. Never once did he move quickly or shift the gun around like a toy. The entire while he handled it like what it was, a deadly weapon that could kill.

"Cartridge please," said Clay, holding out his hand.

His eyes were intent, and the way he looked at Austin, it was not as if he was a stranger, but it made him look like Austin had never seen him before. So focused, his body drawn tight. He lifted his chin to relax his neck muscles, shrugged his shoulders, moved beneath his clothes like a lithe animal, readying himself to do battle.

Austin carefully placed the binoculars on the roof of the truck's cab, then opened the box and withdrew a cartridge that was pointed at one end and round on the other and looked like it was made of brass and copper. As he watched Clay shift something on the rifle to reveal a space where the cartridge would go, Clay looked up at him from beneath the brim of his straw cowboy hat, his blue eyes perfectly serious, his face drawn and still.

"Put the box down—carefully—and check one more time for me, would you?"

"Sure," said Austin, more excited, more worked up, than he had an explanation for. Putting the box down was like putting down an explosive collection of little bombs, and it was a pleasure to pick up the binoculars once more to scan the foothills.

"He's still where he was," said Austin.

"Point for me."

Austin lifted his hand and, doing the best he could, moved his finger to just below his view in the binoculars, and then straightened his arm in the direction of the mountain lion.

"Okay." Clay shifted, his weight moving the truck bed liner slightly. "Stand over there."

Austin moved where Clay indicated, at the passenger side of the truck bed, while Clay was at the driver's side of the truck bed. Slowly, though with the confident air of someone who had done this type of thing before, Clay braced his elbows on top of the truck cab and moved the scope on the rifle.

Now Austin had a perfect view, though it was strange to call it perfect because while they were dealing with a wild animal who might or might not have taken the risk to kill cattle or attack guests and horses, he was looking at Clay. At Clay's profile beneath the shade of the brim of his straw cowboy hat. The way he relaxed his shoulders, took a breath, moved his neck to relax it, as well.

The stillness of Clay's body created a stark outline against the rugged contours of the brown and green foothills. Some wind picked up the blond hairs that curled around Clay's ear. The warmth of the sunlight flushed his cheeks. Overhead, a bird, maybe a hawk, though Austin didn't know, swirled around on the warm updrafts.

Nothing distracted Clay from looking down that scope, and when he lifted his chin just a fraction, Austin's whole body tightened, for he somehow knew the shot was coming. He heard a faint click and saw Clay tense into stillness at the same time. The bang of the rifle came after a hesitation of silence, and Clay's body absorbed the blow of the butt of the rifle as the small, hard bang popped in Austin's ears. A second later, metal twanged against rock. Clay's ribs moved as he took a hard breath and lowered the rifle.

"Check for me, would you?"

Austin scanned the landscape, searching for the brown shadow of the mountain lion.

"He's going up into that space between the rocks there," said Austin.

"That's a canyon," said Clay. "It doesn't look like much from this angle, but sometimes we take trail rides up there. If he's going that way, he's gone. At least for now."

"Oh." Shivering, Austin was glad for the warmth of the sun, glad that he could just stand and be, the binoculars in his hand as he watched Clay wipe down and check the rifle before putting it back in its canvas bag, which felt much safer to Austin.

"You are an excellent shot," said Austin, when Clay laid the rifle bag down and stood next to him.

"Oh, I don't know." Clay shrugged, then leaned down to say something to Leland, who started the truck's engine. "Leland says so, but Quint is much better."

Clay stood up and took the binoculars from Austin's hand to scan the landscape. When he handed them back, the truck began to trundle down the road, and they both grabbed the rail on the truck's cab to steady themselves. They were quite close. Close enough for Austin to see the flecks in Clay's eyes, lit to gold in the sunlight. See the curve of his mouth, smell the sweat on his skin.

"I'd say—" Austin swallowed hard, not sure what he wanted to say, or even what to do with the energy that seemed to shift between them. He dipped his chin and pretended he was checking his footing as the truck bumped along and tried again. "I don't think—"

He looked up, made himself look up. Made himself brave the waters of his racing emotions. He liked looking at Clay, enjoyed his smile, those dimples. Liked that looking at Clay like he was at that moment never felt like he was about to be slammed for saying or doing the wrong thing. Clay was a safe place, a respite from the last ten, no, fourteen years of his life.

"I don't think Leland would lie about a thing like that," he said, finally getting the words out, even if he hadn't ended up saying what he wanted to say, which was this: *I like you, Clay. I like the way I feel when I am with you.* "Leland knows talent when he sees it, don't you think? After all," he joked. "He hired me, didn't he?"

"That he did," said Clay, laughing, reaching out to give Austin's shoulder a few solid pats and if his hand lingered, Austin was glad to let it.

16

CLAY

*B*usiness and guest bookings were picking up on the ranch. The reason Clay knew that was because he'd not a moment to spare and got to meals late or had to run errands for Leland, the result of which being he didn't see Austin for what seemed like an eternity.

It wasn't an eternity, of course not, but it was the rest of Monday, all day Tuesday, and no, he wasn't counting the hours, but it was a lot. A lot more time to feel like he was missing out by not being with Austin and a lot more time to kick himself, yet again, for flirting too hard. Especially when they'd been in the truck together.

He was not blind and had seen Austin watching him while pretending not to watch and so yes, he'd flexed his muscles a bit and rolled up his shirt sleeves to bunch the fold right at the curve of his bicep. This was a little maneuver he'd used a hundred times over at the Rusty Nail and other places. It acted like a fishhook with really good bait and got him excellent results.

As for the result with Austin, yes, he wanted that, wanted to be closer, even though he'd promised himself they'd just be friends. So he shouldn't have moved his shoulders, or showed his dimples, or posed himself so that when Austin looked, he might enjoy the view all the more.

The only time he'd not been strutting his stuff was when he'd actually been handling the rifle while shooting it, as Leland had been very serious about this when he trained Clay. A rifle could easily kill or hurt someone if mishandled, and Clay had taken the lesson to heart from the very first.

He'd wanted to laugh, at least a little bit, at the way Austin had held the box of cartridges, like it was a snake that might bite him, but at least he'd not been all casual about it, like a fool with a bomb in his hand. He treated the box with respect, just the way Clay had treated the rifle. And he'd been attentive the whole time, helping Clay find the mountain lion.

If there'd ever been any idea in Clay's mind of what kind of guy would become an accountant, it vanished in that moment, at least regarding Austin, who, the whole way back, hanging onto the rail, seemed a little overwhelmed, and talked about the vista view and the mountain lion and, in a way, tried to express, it seemed, what was inside of him. Hesitant, pausing, like he was worried that Clay was going to laugh at him for being moved by what they'd been doing, that he thought Clay would think him foolish for getting worked up over an animal almost a thousand yards away.

Clay respected him all the more for it, but couldn't say it in a way that would make sense and not come across as him acting all superior about it. He had, many times, mentioned to Leland a guest who really seemed to appreciate what the ranch had to offer, and Leland would reflect back that he'd thought the same thing.

The ranch was a special place, and while some people got full enjoyment out of their week-long vacation there, some people, a certain few, actually seemed to feel some vibration of pleasure coming up from the ground, or in the cooling breezes from Iron Mountain, and one guest, Clay couldn't remember exactly who, had described the feeling as magical.

Being with Austin felt a little like that, though he felt foolish thinking that way. And maybe he was feeling it because, like long-lost lovers or something, he was straining at the harness of work, wanting to skive off and find Austin.

Luck was with him, though, during the lesson on Wednesday morning, for who should show up looking just-about-ready-but-not-quite to ride but Austin. He'd put on his new green and blue plaid snap button shirt, and his by-now broken-in boots. His legs looked so long in his new blue jeans that Clay wanted to whistle and tease Austin into a smile. But with nine other guests all lined up and ready to mount up, it would be inappropriate and might make Austin feel uncomfortable, and he didn't want that.

"You here for the lesson?" asked Clay, just as polite as could be.

"Yes," said Austin, slipping between the wooden rails to enter the arena. "I'm sorry I'm late, but Leland had told me about it after break-fast and then I got caught up—"

"It's all right," said Clay. "We've got Gwen saddled and ready for you. She's a very gentle mare. Here."

Clay guided Austin to the mare, not reaching out to touch Austin in the small of his back, even though he wanted to. There were people watching his every move, even though Brody was in charge of the lesson.

"Say hello to Gwen," said Clay. He petted Gwen's broad, flat cheek to show Austin how it was done. "We've already done the safety part of the lesson but basically follow Brody's instructions, and if you need help, just ask. Ready?"

"Yes," said Austin. His eyes were bright with the challenge of putting his booted foot in Gwen's stirrup to pull himself up and into the saddle. Then he sat there, almost shocked that he'd done it, and grabbed the saddle horn when Gwen stomped her foot to adjust herself beneath his weight. "Man, it's a long way to the ground from here."

"It's shorter than you might think," said Clay smiling, and then he allowed himself to pat Austin's leg. Though he meant to pat his knee, Gwen moved, shifting again, and he ended up patting Austin's thigh, which was long and muscled and just right at eye level, making it very hard not to stare. "We neck rein here, so to go right, you pull the reins across her neck to the right. To go left, pull the reins across her neck to go left. And to stop? Pull back gently. To go? Nudge her with your heels. Okay?"

"Okay." Seeming delighted with both the pat and the easy instructions, Austin drew his whole body up into a single line, like he was ready to march through whatever fears he might have.

Brody led the lesson, giving instructions for the guests to walk their horses around the arena, then picking up the pace a bit to a trot. His instructions were in a calm tone of voice, the one he used when working with any horse, any person, and it made the lesson go smoothly.

The riders were confident enough to even do a bit of a canter, then a trot, and then a canter. It was when Brody instructed them to slow to a walk and turn their horses to go the other direction that the trouble started.

Most guests were just happy to be on a horse, happy to follow instructions, happy just to be riding. But one rider, a young man who, as Clay suspected from the get-go, was extremely bored with the whole thing, had leaned forward to unbuckle his horse's bridle. Like a kid who is messing around to see how much he can get away with.

The young man was astride Beltaine, a sweet, dark mare who adored her friend Gwen. Sensing her bridle was off, Beltaine must have figured the lesson was over, for she gave a slight hop and bucked her rider to the ground, then trotted briskly over to where Austin was dutifully trying to turn Gwen to go the other way.

"Hey," the young man shouted. "She fucking bucked me off! My dad's going to hear about this, you wait and see. I'm going to call him."

Aroused by the shouting, the horses grew a little anxious and their riders with them. As Brody worked to settle everyone down, Clay hurried to Austin who didn't know how to back his horse up to untangle himself from the situation he found himself in, which was with Beltaine sidling up to Gwen, who was now pressed to the fence line.

There wasn't enough time to grab Beltaine's bridle from the ground, so Clay scooted over and shouldered his way in between the two horses. Not the smartest thing, as each weighed enough to smash him, should they so choose. Austin's face was white, though he sensibly did not yank on Gwen's reins, but held onto the saddle horn. He needed rescuing, and Clay was going to be the one to do it.

"Just sit tight," said Clay. "Here, girl, here." He reached under Beltaine's jaw and cupped his hand around her soft chin and gave a little tug. "C'mon then, Beltaine, there's a good girl. Walk this way, okay?"

All the horses on the ranch were treated with kindness and slow hands, so inside of a minute, Clay was escorting Beltaine over to where Quint had entered the arena and had picked up the unbuckled bridle to hand it to Brody.

"It wasn't her fault," said Brody, quickly.

"I know it," said Quint. He seemed to tower over everyone and everything as he pointed at the miscreant. "You. Get out of the arena."

"I want my lesson," said the young man. "I paid for a lesson and riding and stuff and I'm going to get it."

Quint moved close, so close that only Clay could have heard what he was saying.

"You will get out of this arena or I will pick you up and carry you out, understand?" Quint's glare was enough to shock the young man into stillness. "You disrupted the lesson and scared these good people, not to mention distracting Beltaine from her job, so if I hear one more word, you will pack up your stuff and go home. No refund. Got it?"

There was a long, still moment, and then the young man, looking a little pale beneath the dust on his face, nodded and followed Quint's instructions to the letter. When the arena was quiet, Quint half-bowed to Brody and then to Clay, and slipped between the wooden rails to walk back to where he'd come from.

"Well, then," said Brody. "Y'all want to try that again? Just take it slow, and gently pull your reins against the horse's neck until they are facing the other way. No rush. We've got time."

To Clay he said as he patted Beltaine's neck, "Just take her back to the barn and give her a good brushing and carrots or something, for a treat. She deserves it for being so patient."

"You got it," said Clay, and though he really wanted to stay and help Austin learn to ride a horse, he slipped the reins around Beltaine's neck. Then he opened the gate and led her back to the barn, sighing the whole while, feeling like the fates must be furiously trying to keep him from Austin.

Except maybe the fates wanted to reward him for sticking to his work, for just after dinner, when he was clomping down the wooden stairs of the main lodge, head swiveling to catch sight of Austin, he actually saw him just beyond the small green glade in front of the staff quarters. His head was down, he had something tucked beneath his arm, and he was headed at a fast clip to the barn.

"Where are you headed?" Clay called out as he hustled to catch up. "I didn't see you at dinner. Where are you going?"

"Oh." Austin stopped, gripping what looked like a small box that might or might not contain paints, and a pad of paper to his chest. "I was going to ask Leland if I could borrow his truck, as I wanted to find a view to paint. You know, to pick it up now that I don't have to justify it to—"

Clay knew that Austin was thinking about Mona and had just revealed she didn't think much of his painting, but he kept his ongoing negative opinion to himself.

"Can I come?" he asked in a hopeful voice. "I mean, I know some great views. I could take you in Ladybelle, if you'd like. Leland would probably lend you his truck, sure, but I'd be happy to take you." When Austin paused, hesitating like Clay had asked him if he wanted company while jumping off a cliff, Clay added, "I won't pester you or anything, but I could show you this view I'm thinking of and next time you could take yourself." He had to let this go if Austin truly didn't want him along, even though it would be hard.

"Sure, okay." Austin still looked like he would rather go alone, a nervous light in his eyes and the way he held his supplies tight, like he thought Clay might try to take them away from him.

"Really?" asked Clay. "I can get you there in ten minutes and then wait in the truck or walk along the ridge, whatever you need."

"Thank you," said Austin. "I don't mean to be a heel about it, I'm just used to—I'm just used to it being more difficult than this."

"Well, I'll make it as easy as pie, just you wait."

Together they walked to Ladybelle and got in. Clay started the truck, glad to know recent repairs had been done on her so they wouldn't get stuck on the road and have to call for help. He drove past the barn and up the ridge where they'd seen the mountain lion, then down along Horse Creek to just beyond where it met Sand Creek.

There, the river had carved a space long ago, a flat, oblong hollow. Along the edge of the hollow, if you stood in just the right place, the land sloped long and gently, stretching out in what seemed like endless miles of green grass beneath a cloud-dotted blue sky.

Clay parked Ladybelle just at the sandbar, where the gravel was thick and sturdy.

"We can walk out to that little hill there," said Clay, pointing through the windshield. "On that side of the river, the view is unobstructed and pretty wonderful."

"How did you find this place?" asked Austin, unbuckling his seatbelt.

"We sometimes take trail rides this far, and sometimes overnight rides, for more experienced riders." Clay turned to Austin, his hands on the wheel like he meant to demonstrate that he wasn't going to interfere with whatever it was Austin needed to do. "You go that way, and I'll walk across the river to the other side. You'll have all the privacy you need."

"Thank you."

Clay waited until Austin had picked his direction. Then, leaving the keys in the ignition, he crunched across the gravel to the sandbar, hopping over the rocks to the other side of the slow, season-low river. When the rains came in early August, the river would come out of the canyon in a torrent and it wouldn't be a safe place to be, but for now, the river was pretty tame and easy to cross.

He made his way along the grassy bank to where the narrow leaf willows tucked their roots in the sandy soil and made a shady place, where he settled his hat on his head before heading up a small slope to a groundswell that allowed a view of the large area where Sand Creek and Horse Creek merged into one before heading south.

In the winter, geese would land and spend the night, and in the summer, the river fed the land. The smell was damp and green and Clay stood there, inhaling deeply, hands in his pockets, and watched the low water swirl in eddies across the sand.

Across the way, Austin had stopped, and was facing north, the dappled sunlight on his shoulders. In his hand he held his pad of paper, and what looked like a paintbrush, which he seemed to dip to the side, and then stroke across the paper.

Clay hadn't asked what kind of paint, but he would once they got back in the truck. It was nice that Austin could trust him with this, so he would be careful not to be too nosy, though he did want Austin to know he was interested. He would figure it out as he went, wanting, at the very least, Austin's friendship. And as for everything else? That was up to Austin, though Clay could hardly hope that a straight guy would be the least interested in him.

Sunlight dipped in and out from behind the clouds until the shadows were long and the light between the shadows was a velvety violet and blue. When Austin lifted his head and lowered his pad of paper, Clay headed across the river in the growing twilight, splashing the toes of his cowboy boots in the water, then scrambled up the bank to where the truck was.

Neither of them said a word as they got into Ladybelle's cab. Clay drove them back along the ridge road to the ranch and dropped Austin off in front of the glade before the staff quarters with as much dignity as if they'd been on a proper date, which he very much would have liked.

He parked Ladybelle, then nodded at a few people he knew on his way back to the staff quarters. In short order, he was in his own room, stripped to the skin, stepping into a very hot shower. There, he scrubbed off the sweat from the day, the grime along the back of his neck.

Even all the soap in the world couldn't wash away the look in Austin's eyes as they'd sat in the low-lit interior of Ladybelle just before heading back. Austin's eyes had been dark, warm with grati-tude, and maybe a little surprised at how easily it had all gone.

Nobody deserved to have their dreams squashed as Austin seemed to have experienced, and while Clay would have been willing to drive Austin to various views in the local area, he knew, or thought he knew, that Austin would need to go by himself.

Not that Clay knew what it was like to be an artist, as he'd not a creative bone in his body. But he thought he'd read it somewhere, that some artists needed chunks of time and miles of space before they could create. Then again, some could do it in a broom cupboard, it all depended. He just knew he wanted Austin to get what he needed, wanted it more than he could have thought possible upon meeting Austin on that rainy Sunday.

Stepping out of the shower, he dried himself off, and brushed his teeth and basically got ready for bed. It'd been a long day, but his mind was still racing and his body felt keyed up, like he had unfinished business to tend to.

Normally, in this circumstance, he would find a bar and make his availability known, offer lube and condoms, if the other fellow didn't happen to have any, and pretty much enjoy himself. Now, though, it felt more intricate than that, like a dance he didn't quite know the steps to, and he was pretty much a terrible dancer, in spite of pretending that he knew what he was doing on the dance floor.

Inside of a minute, he pulled on his blue jeans and a clean t-shirt and, barefoot, padded down to the other end of the hall where Austin's room was. And stood there for a full three minutes, his hand raised to knock, before he realized what a dumb move it was.

Austin had just gotten a divorce. He was not in the market, for sure, and in no way was interested in getting it on with a guy who had a hard-on for getting it on at a moment's notice.

The two of them were as different as city and country, as much a contrast as light and shadow. His was a desire that had no place to go or, if it did know the direction, the surrounding country was so new he needed a map that had not yet been drawn. Maybe Austin could paint him a map? Maybe, but then Clay would have to describe it to him.

Dropping his hand, Clay made his silent way back to his room, finished getting ready for bed, and forced himself to think of practical matters. Like taking himself in hand first thing in the morning, so he didn't walk around having to adjust himself for an hour and a half.

When he awoke, he shaved and brushed his teeth, his mind still busy with the questions as to how he might move forward. All of this was new to him because before Austin Clay would not be thinking about it like this, wouldn't be thinking beyond the first good fuck. Austin was different. He was careful and still and smart, not Clay's usual at all.

He slid on his boots and put on a long-sleeved shirt, then grabbed his hat. Just as he took his keys from the top of the dresser, he saw a white piece of paper that someone had slid beneath his door. It must have been there for a while, for there was a bit of cottonwood seed fluff in the middle of the paper.

Bending to pick it up, he couldn't for a minute figure out what it was. There was a wash of color, a large patch of blue that he realized was the sky. Below that were streaks of blue amidst the green, and it made him think of the place where Sand Creek and Horse Creek met, and all at once he knew what it was, the painting Austin had done the day before.

Taking a closer look, he saw there was a ghostly image of a cowboy on the other side of the river. There was a smudge for his straw cowboy hat, a dapple of colors for his shirt. A stripe of dark blue for his jeans. It was him; he knew it was him. Austin was supposed to be painting the landscape but instead painted *him*.

For a moment, all he could do was hold the painting to him as though to absorb it into his very soul. Nobody had ever sketched him before, let alone painted him. That Austin had taken the time to include him in the wonderful vista view, to use his newly bought paints—

With a sigh, Clay laid the painting carefully on the bed. He'd get a frame from the local hardware store, or maybe he'd have to drive into Cheyenne.

Or maybe—he could ask Austin what kind of frame he should get and together, with their shoulders pressed each to the other and their heads close, they could muse over whatever Amazon had to offer and that way the frame would mean more, and when he hung it up on the wall, it would always remind him of Austin, no matter what happened.

17

AUSTIN

*I*n most of his adult life, business meetings were either tedious or they were boring. Sometimes, no, usually, they were both. But his meeting with Bill Wainwright, owner of Farthing-dale Ranch, turned out to be neither of those, partly because Bill simply wasn't interested in by-the-book accounting practices. So the meeting was interesting as Austin did his best to keep Bill on track, to instill in Bill a desire to keep good accounting records, which Bill wasn't terribly interested in.

Austin's biggest distraction was because he ached all over from his recent riding lesson, the inside of his thighs feeling as though they'd been run through some kind of meat press. The instructions Brody had given, along with Clay's steady presence in the ring, made the lesson an easy one to follow. At least until the point that one of the riders had started messing around and Austin had ended up with one leg pressed against the wooden fence as another horse, frisky without its bridle, had pressed against his horse, Gwen.

Inside of a heartbeat, Clay had moved between the horses, as calm as could be, pushing those huge animals apart, completely without fear, like he did it every day. Sweat had continued to cool along the back of Austin's neck as he watched Clay go, leading the horse away with only the reins around its neck, as if he wasn't worried about the horse racing off without the bit in its teeth.

There was a lot about horses and horsemanship that Austin had yet to learn, but he knew a pro when he saw one, and Clay, with the patch of sweat darkening the back of his shirt, was definitely a pro. Austin couldn't understand what was drawing him more, the sturdy set of Clay's shoulders, or the way he'd gone about rescuing Austin, serious and focused, not missing a beat.

Austin needed to focus on the meeting between him and Bill, rather than letting his mind follow a line of memory that took him from one encounter with Clay to the next and then to the next. Clay was a distraction, pure and simple, and certainly not what Leland was paying him for. So, back to work.

Leland had warned him that Bill followed his own rules, liked to do handshake deals, and never liked to write things down. He especially didn't like to get receipts, which had resulted, as far as Austin could tell, in a nearly thirty-thousand dollar deficit in the feed and supplies category on his spreadsheet.

In no way did he think Bill had pocketed the money, nor did he imagine Bill had frittered it away on snakeskin boots or anything like that. Bill's outfit was, as always, time-worn jeans, thin at the knee, cowboy boots broken in so far the sole of the right boot was flapping off, and a felt cowboy hat that was ragged at the edges.

No, it was quite easy to imagine how this had happened. After a handshake deal and the hay or feed or whatever had been delivered, Bill would pay them but neglect to record the expenditure, which resulted in an ongoing incorrect balance.

Austin had gotten the majority, or so he hoped, of the paper receipts, he had to deal with the ghost receipts. Now had come the time to get Bill not only indoors, but sitting down in a wooden chair in front of the desk that had once been his. Austin had encouraged him to move the chair around behind the desk so he could see the spreadsheet on Austin's computer, but Bill had shaken his head no.

"Don't need to see it," said Bill. "I trust you. Hired you, didn't I?"

"That is true, Bill," said Austin. "I just think it's important that we both understand why we should have a better record of this kind of spending moving forward."

"I tell Maddy or Leland when a delivery is expected," said Bill. "I don't have time for more than that, and I don't like using computers and suchlike. I'm not good with 'em. I'm usually driving around, making sure folks know this ranch is a part of the community and not just a tourist destination. We give back, you know. There's the ex-con program, which we hope to do more of, and the Frontier Girls are always coming by to earn badges, and I've got this young fellow wants to interview everybody and make a little documentary for his tube."

"You mean his YouTube channel?"

"The very one. Quite popular, so I'm told."

"How did he—" Austin could see a short film about the ranch might be good promotion, but he didn't know enough about video to even know what questions to ask.

"Friend of my nephew's is a budding filmmaker and historian. Heckfire, even if it turns out crap, it'll get the word out."

"Is there a licensing fee?" asked Austin, figuring it would go in the ad category of deductions.

"Heck if I know," said Bill. "Besides, what's a few bucks if it works?"

A few bucks could make the difference between balancing the books and running in the red, but Bill obviously had different views about the importance of tracking any of that, so would it make any difference?

Austin made some notes in a text file, then added a name and date and put it in his To Do folder. Then, suddenly, he had an idea.

"How about this, Bill." Austin reached down to pull out a slim but sturdy ledger and a pencil, which he'd found earlier that morning in the back of the desk. "Take this and write it down when you order the hay, how much it costs, and when the delivery is expected. Then Maddy or I can transcribe it into the online account. That way, you'll be doing your bit, and we can track the demand of grain and hay. Are you willing?"

He pushed the ledger across the desk and watched as Bill picked it up. Austin had yet to meet a human being who could resist the pull of a new notebook with crisp blank pages just waiting to be filled. Plus, this was low-tech enough that even Bill could use it.

"I reckon I could give it a try," said Bill as he stroked the surface of the ledger with calloused fingertips. "Leland asked me to be willing, so I'm willing."

"Thank you, Bill," said Austin. He stood up and Bill stood up and they shook hands.

"You could do me a favor," said Bill.

"Sure, name it."

"Come to the dance tonight." Bill nodded as he straightened his ragged-edged hat. "You've been doing nothing but work and I promise you, the numbers will be there in the morning."

"Sure," said Austin.

He might remember something Clay had mentioned about going to the dance, but surely he was going because Bill asked him to and not because Clay was going to be there? Clay had mentioned the dance and how he didn't know how.

Austin could just imagine how it might go, Clay, fresh faced and smiling, looking at the dancers with hope and trepidation about how he might perform up to snuff. Had not enough people told Clay he was fine just the way he was? Or, more to the point, had Clay never had anyone tell him he was not just fine, he was marvelous?

And he was, he truly was, in ways that Austin couldn't explain. The day before, when he'd held his paint and paper close to his body in an effort not just to hide what he was about to do to the world, but also from himself, he'd thought to borrow Leland's truck. Then he'd been going to check out Google maps to find a good view to paint, even if just for a little while.

He wasn't much good at people, and maybe he was okay at land-scapes, but most of his paintings were like watercolors verging on abstracts, with shapes and lines of color. And that was fine, since he never showed his paintings to anyone, except Mona, that one time, and that had been enough. At any rate, he'd go out, then come home and go to bed, hoping he'd gotten it out of his system.

But as usual with these things, at least since he'd arrived at the ranch, it wasn't turning out like he'd expected it would—it had turned out better.

Clay had come along and just about swept him off his feet, driven him to the most beautiful ridge and then—left him alone. Walked off so Austin could paint. Didn't pry and ask questions afterwards, just drove them to the ranch and said goodnight. Sweet and unassuming and kind. Not judgmental. Not anything bad.

When Clay had flirted with him before, more than once it seemed, the words and actions added up to something nice that Austin struggled to define. It was hard not to compare Clay to Mona, but when he did, it was light and dark, day and night.

Clay made him feel all the good things he'd forgotten, the pleasure of a new day, a job well done, the anticipation of seeing how a painting would turn out. This, it seemed, was spilling over into anticipation of seeing Clay each day. Stopping with Clay in the dining hall. Following Clay's every move while he loaded and shot a long distance rifle, eyes focused and serious, intent on his task.

Clay was worth waiting for and worth catching up to. But dance with? And of course Austin was thinking about it, thinking extra hard. Overthinking it, very definitely, the way he usually did.

Gay guys danced with other gay guys, right? They held each other in their arms and danced. But at a guest ranch?

Perhaps all Austin could do was watch Clay dance with the guests. Perhaps that would be enough.

The idea of it, though, as he stood on the front porch of Maddy's office while she locked up for the day, stirred in his minds' eye visions of himself racing back to his little room after dinner to shower and shave. Put on extra cologne, and his newest shirt. Polish his boots. Use hair gel, for crying out loud.

He wanted to look nice so that if Clay glanced his way, maybe the glance would linger. Maybe the feelings Austin was feeling now as he climbed the stairs to the staff quarters would linger and grow. Maybe the staticky jolts of energy in his belly, thimblefuls of liquid lightning, would expand until that jittery something's-about-to-happen feeling would come back, would feel the way it used to before he met Mona.

Before Mona, life had been full of the expectation of something good. Then life *had been*, simply, good. Mona had stripped all of that from him, without him being aware it was happening. But being on the ranch, having Clay as a friend? Was bringing that feeling back and then some.

Not waiting to determine if any of this was a good idea, he did go to his room and shower, put on his newest shirt, and ran the edge of a towel across the toes of his cowboy boots. He did put on cologne after he shaved, but not too much.

As he strode back to the main lodge, where he could see people gathering in the warm dusk, the little fairy lights strung between poles, the air seemed full of expectation, charged with something as though from a faraway and much anticipated storm. Along the porch was a small band with, a lead singer and other members playing instruments.

He'd seen the bills for the band, and there seemed to be some sort of handshake deal between the band and the ranch, for they were quite inexpensive, given the band's reputation. He'd checked their website, and they were quite good and could go anywhere and play for anyone. Most weeks, they stopped by Farthingdale Ranch to play for the home team, getting people on their feet, getting people to dance and have fun.

Festive chatter from the guests rose and fell, dispersing into the trees, into the night, purple and black-blue, like a mystic cape surrounding them, giving them just the right amount of shelter from the cool breeze from the mountains.

Austin stood at the edge of the dance floor furthest from the porch, where the band was. He saw Leland and Jamie across the way, at the edge of the porch, and waved. Both men lifted brown bottles of what was probably root beer.

To keep in good with the boss, he was going to have to try some one day. Not that Leland would hold it against him if he never did have any root beer, but it would be a nice gesture to a man who was turning out to be a very good boss.

18

AUSTIN

*A*t the other end of the porch from Austin, looking like he was about to head off into the trees and go back to his room, was Clay. He was without his straw cowboy hat for once, and had spruced himself up. Even from this distance, Austin could see his curved smile, his freshly shaved face. Could imagine he smelled the cologne that Clay might have put on, evocative as it warmed against his skin—

These were not new thoughts, they weren't. But they were coming all at once, like a spiral of energy pushing into him, creating more thoughts and more ideas, all of which were about Clay.

Had he liked the painting Austin had given him? Or was he embarrassed by Austin's lack of talent? Would Clay figure out how much courage it had taken Austin to try his hand at painting another human being?

Would he pick someone to dance with and make his way across the dance floor so Austin could see him in action up close? Maybe Clay would take a break from dancing and he and Austin could grab a bottle of water from the cooler by the porch and—and then what? What did one do in these situations? He'd forgotten, if he ever even knew, and a hardy sense of nerves began to squash all the expectations that had been rising in him like bubbles.

Then Clay saw him and, in that brief second, before Clay figured Austin could see him, he saw Clay wasn't smiling. The normal happy-go-lucky mien was gone and in its place was something withdrawn and quiet. Clay wasn't dancing, he was merely watching.

Clay raised his hand to catch Leland's eye, perhaps so he could then assume he'd been counted on the roster as having attended the dance. Leland waved back. Then, dipping one shoulder, Clay began to slide into the trees.

Without thought, Austin raced along the edge of the dance floor just as the band began to play something that might have been *Stand By Your Man* or might have been something far more obscure. Either way, Clay, all shaved and sweet, was headed back to his room like the last kid to be selected for a side of dodgeball.

Which wasn't right. Clay worked too hard not to have at least a little fun and besides—Austin had a brief flash in his head of him and Clay dancing together. Dancing was a prelude to kissing and kissing was a prelude to everything else, much of which felt like a mystery to him at that very moment, when he stepped into the shadowy dusk of the trees.

"Clay, wait." Austin reached out and tugged on Clay's sleeve, only to have the sleeve tugged out of his grasp as Clay turned around. "Are you not staying for the dance?"

"Well, Leland saw me there, so—" Clay looked up at him, shadows of branches flitting across his face, the fairy lights flickering in his blue eyes. "And I'm not much good. It's not as critical that staff attend, now that our numbers are going up."

Austin felt himself being swallowed up by the distance in Clay's expression, the low tone of his voice. The way his shoulders sagged. He was so good at everything he did, except, it seemed, for this one thing, dancing.

On the other hand, Austin was quite good, having taken lessons at Mona's request. He knew all the moves, from waltz to tango and yes, to the cowboy two step. Even if he couldn't paint very well, he could dance.

Mona used to like it when he twirled and dipped her, to show off her long dark hair and skinny waist, so he was very good at dancing, knew how to lead, knew how to place his hand in the small of the back and with the pads of his fingers, guide the other dancer. Who, in this case, might be Clay. If Austin asked in the right way, and if Clay said yes—

"We still need more numbers," said Austin, having spent days poring over the finances of the ranch.

The ex-con program brought in extra dollars, but despite Ellis having turned out to be a very good fit, there was such a risk in doing that more than the one time. And while a thirty thousand dollar deficit, courtesy of Bill, wasn't huge, in the grand scheme of things, this was a million dollar business, and as such, it needed large amounts of energy and time and money.

None of which seemed to make any difference at all as Clay looked at him, a puzzled draw beneath his eyebrows. Austin needed to make up his mind, that's what it was. Needed to figure out whether he should jump left or right—and what was he thinking? That he and Clay would dance and then would follow everything he feared? Everything about his body that had forgotten what pleasure was?

Clay would surely laugh, perhaps even point, when he found out Austin couldn't get it up and surely he would have no patience or time for a guy who wasn't even gay—

"Would you like to dance with me?" asked Austin, almost without realizing it. The words echoed in the soft darkness, spiked through with the small gold and silver lights from the dance floor, coming in through the dust-darkness like arrows.

"With *you*?" asked Clay.

Austin could sense Clay working all of this through. Then his sense of humor seemed to surface. He smiled, then laid his palm on his chest as though quite shocked at the suggestion. "Are you—are you *flirting* with me?"

It was decision time. Austin could pivot with the ball and pass to another player. Or he could try the shot.

"Yes." His breath choked in his throat, but the word came out clear as a bell. "I don't know what I'm doing, I just know—being with you makes me feel good. I'm happier than I've ever been and if I could just be with you, just be brave—"

If Clay said yes, he would know what it felt like to put his hand on Clay's waist, which from what he had seen was solid muscle. So different from Mona, whose waist always felt like he could snap her in two.

Or maybe Clay would put his hand on Austin's waist. After all, the only reason Austin might lead the dance was because he knew how. Maybe at some point they would switch, and Clay would quickly find out that while Austin wasn't a wilting flower, he simply wasn't able to have sex right now and Clay wouldn't want to be with someone like that.

"Never mind," said Austin, trying to smile, his heart banging so hard it made him shiver. "There's probably some rule against two gays —I mean two guys dancing together—"

What was he doing? Why was he doing this? He wasn't even gay.

"I would love to dance with you," said Clay, his voice soft, his expression kind and behind that, the light came back into his eyes, the one Austin was so used to seeing. The one that made him feel like his life was full of possibilities, full of potential joy. Full of promise. "We could dance here in the trees, beyond the pines, and nobody would see us."

Clay was not a secretive person, as far as Austin could tell. Yet he was willing to stay in the shadows to make it easier for Austin. That alone was a gift of trust he'd not been used to for a good long while. And certainly not what he'd been expecting.

Strains of music floated along in the darkness, tender ribbons of sound amidst the pine-scented night.

Clay stepped close. Austin, almost on instinct, took Clay in his arms the way he used to take Mona in his arms, the soft sloping twang of a country western song he didn't recognize instilling in him the familiar nostalgia of a faraway time, when he was a young man on the verge of his own life.

Clay wasn't Mona, not even by a little bit. His waist was solid beneath Austin's hand, his shoulder a line of ironwood, wrought through daily hard work, honest and true and trustworthy all the way to the bone, it felt like.

"I'll lead, for now," Austin said, tipping his head down, looking into blue eyes that seemed to have absorbed the Wyoming sky into them and were now shining just for Austin.

Their hips were close enough to brush. Clay was hard in his jeans and Austin felt his belly tumble as though some long lost, forgotten part of him was suddenly paying attention in a way it never had before.

The lyrics to the song were about happy accidents and stars and moonlight shining down. The pace was slow and rhythmic enough for a two-step just for two, and together they danced in the arms of the glade of cottonwoods ringed by ponderosa pine, a perfume lingering in the air as the night grew cool.

Austin led Clay around their tiny dance floor of dirt and tree roots. Most steps they stumbled, laughing, always swirling amidst sighs, and inside all of that it suddenly felt okay that he couldn't get hard for Clay, couldn't get an erection. But it didn't matter that it couldn't happen between them, not for all the money in the world, because maybe it would be nice just to *be* with Clay.

It was a rare Sunday morning when sex wasn't on the agenda between him and Mona, when they'd just have coffee in bed, and cuddle in the sheets, pretending all the while they'd get up soon and be productive. That had been before Bea had been born, as he recalled, in a long ago time when Mona hadn't been simmering with silent anger every other minute, because Austin refused to move to a high-rise apartment overlooking the Botanical Garden in Denver, from there to commute to Lo-Do and a swank accounting job she could brag to her friends about—

He needed to stop thinking about Mona. Needed to stop comparing his relationship with Mona to what was happening between him and Clay.

"Austin?" asked Clay.

Austin had stopped, and the music had stopped, and somehow the magic seemed to have melted away, like a promise of a cool breeze on

177

a hot day, remembered, mourned, missed. He wanted to cry. But men didn't cry. Did gay men cry?

What would Clay think if Austin told him all the aches in his heart, the lost and broken promises. The unfelt, unexpressed love because Mona suddenly decided that Austin was simply, in the end, not good enough for her.

The shiver was back, his body reacting, reaching for something solid when all around him his world was shifting. The ground was moving beneath his feet.

"I don't know," he said, being as honest as he could. "I don't know if I'm okay."

Another song had started up, one he thought he knew that felt more familiar. The words like old friends, the melody a gentle rush of energy with ideas about following someone you loved to the ends of the earth, to the edge of the sea, of riding the cloud and finding the dream.

It was a faster-paced song than the one before it, and one tiny part of his mind wondered what the band must be paying for royalties to cover such a well-known song? Then he squashed that as Clay took Austin's hand and tucked it firmly about his own waist.

Clay moved closer and linked his fingers with Austin's so their palms snugged together and their hips met. And when Clay breathed, his chest pushed against Austin's chest.

"Show me how to dance to this one," said Clay, his voice breathy and low, eyes shining as though he believed Austin could show him the way. As though he didn't know the way already.

Which he did, of course he did. Didn't he? Or was there something Austin could share with Clay that he didn't already know? That he could give Clay something he wanted and needed. Something only Austin could give him? It was too much to hope for. Too much of a faraway dream—or was it?

"It goes like this," said Austin, clearing his throat, it seemed, in the middle of every word. "And we move a little bit faster, you see, to follow the music."

Clay was not a natural. For all he was so adept at lifting and moving and guiding and shooting, his progress to follow Austin in a simple two-step with a brisk pace was accompanied by stumbles and stepping on Austin's toes.

The music folded itself around Austin's heartbeat, and he was able to follow the rhythm. Clay was not, and after the first chorus, he stumbled into Austin's arms, all elbows and tangled legs.

"I suck at this," said Clay, righting himself, holding onto Austin's forearms with hard fingers. "I suck so hard, only nobody knows. I hide it. Been hiding it." He looked up at Austin, shadows pulling across his face, traces of sweat and frustration beneath his eyes. "You probably want to be dancing with someone else. It's okay. I'll just head back—"

"No," said Austin, his throat closing up hard as he took Clay's hands in his and laid them on his heart, which was beating fast. "We don't have to dance. We can do anything. We can hold hands and walk up the road to the ridge and look at the stars—and maybe take dance lessons someplace."

He meant everything beyond those words, but the words to explain what he really meant simply wouldn't come.

"Leland used to take dance lessons with his mom," said Clay, though he too seemed to be trying to express something beyond the words. "He's going to take them with Jamie this winter, he told me. Maybe we could go with them."

"Maybe," said Austin. "As for now—"

Never in his life had he felt so tongue tied, the words sticking like pitch in his throat, his mind grappling with the enormity of the step he was about to take, the height from which he would step off into a vast and untried, undiscovered country. Into the new.

Gently, Clay pulled one of his hands from Austin's trembling grip and curled his fingers, warm pads, around the back of Austin's neck.

"Can I kiss you?" asked Clay, seemingly unaware that he'd just assisted Austin in jumping off a cliff. "I'm not flirting. I mean it."

There was a simple truth in these words, echoing in Austin's heart. It felt different from the time that Clay had flirted with him before, like a playful pup who only wants to have a bit of fun. Now it felt more serious and, at the same time, more heart-true, more honest. More real.

"Yes," said Austin. His mind raced at the thought of it, mouth suddenly dry, heart beating fast, sweat breaking out in unexpected places. He knew Clay wasn't messing with him, but he had no idea. Did men kiss each other differently than a man and woman kissed?

"How do we—?" He paused, then girded his nerves to continue. "How do men kiss?"

"Let's find out," said Clay with a smile, the smile reaching his blue eyes.

It felt newly born. It had a feeling all its own as he bent forward, half closing his eyes, mouth tense but expectant, and when he felt Clay's lips on his, electric and firm and new, he almost jumped back. But Clay's fingers tugged on his neck, tender and gentle but not letting go, pulling Austin close, joining them.

It was a sweet kiss, warm and close and soft, but beneath it pounded waves of potential connection, where they could each reveal themselves to the other, bare to the skin—

"I can't get it up," said Austin with a gasp, pulling back. "I didn't know how to tell you, don't know how to tell you—" He panted hard, struggling against Clay's hold. His connection. His closeness.

"It's okay," said Clay, tender and close, brushing Austin's chin with his own, like another kind of kiss.

"No, it's *not* okay." Fear rippled through Austin like a snake. "Mona always made fun of me and finally—"

"Fuck Mona," said Clay. "No, seriously. She was shitty to you from the beginning, it sounds like. I'd be happy to let you list all the ways she didn't deserve you, any time, right? But now? Fuck Mona. And just kiss me another time. Let me take it with me."

The sad sound of those words, the hope in Clay's eyes. He could hardly believe it. Clay went to bars, cruised for fast sex, and sometimes came home happy, or at least that's the way Clay told it. Only now, the truth had a different face, gave a different slant to Clay's eyes, a hushed tone to his voice that spoke of unanswered dreams, and false starts, fake joy. Clay didn't deserve any of that, and Austin knew he wanted to give him what he had been searching for.

"Yes," he said. "If you'll be patient with me, yes."

He pulled Clay in his arms, pressed their bodies together, the heat licking up and down his front, the scent of Clay's cologne, now warmed into his skin, full in his lungs. And then he kissed Clay, a little like he might have kissed Mona, back in the day, a full on kiss, full of sweep and daring and all of his heart, while flickers raced up his back, between his legs.

The difference between then and now was that Clay met him full on, moist mouth, tender inside of his lip, the taste of him, sweet and salt all at once. Clay hummed, blood pounding beneath his skin as Austin reached up and cupped Clay's strong jaw in his hands. Something Mona would never let him do on account of it might mess with her makeup.

"I'm going to stop thinking about her," said Austin. "I swear it."

"I'll help you," said Clay, whisper-low as he reached up and hooked his arm around Austin's neck, kissing him back hard, kissing away all the sadness and anger and sharp memories that kept slicing at him. "I'll help you if you'll let me."

"Yes," said Austin, heart-felt, the trembling feeling replaced by a firm longing that surged through him, tugging at his groin, zipping through his belly.

This was what it should feel like, new love, new hope. This, this, this.

19

CLAY

The last thing Clay would ever have expected to do was to walk away from a kiss like that. A kiss that rocked him from the bottom of his toes to the top of his head. A kiss that wrapped itself around him, and that felt good and warm, rather than a prelude to something else. Not a tease or a come-on, with condoms and lube standing at the ready, no.

When his arm had gone around Austin's neck to pull him into the kiss, Austin had responded, hesitant at first, but then it was as if he'd let off the brakes and leaned into Clay like Clay was his last refuge. Like Clay was something lost that had been found, which made it different from pretty much every other guy that Clay had ever kissed so he could get fucked in an alley outside of a bar.

Not that fucking was going to happen. Even if Austin's confession, gasped out, hadn't alerted Clay to the fact that Austin couldn't get it up, the lack of Austin's erection spoke volumes.

Then again, without that warm hardness, Clay might have assumed that Austin simply wasn't into him and that the kiss was a lie. But with such a truth, probably something Austin hadn't wanted to reveal, the kiss was more than honest, it was soul felt. And different. And sweet.

But Clay was out of his depth, at least a little bit. Usually the other guy was as experienced as he was, at least that, and probably more. Each, he and the stranger, knew what they wanted and how to get it.

As for Austin, he was straight, as far as Clay knew, and maybe even as far as Austin knew himself. But something had awakened him to Clay, made him switch gears. This, along with everything else to do with Austin, what was going on with him, made Clay realize he needed to go slow. Slower than he ever had in his life.

"Hey," he said, drawing back, holding Austin's face in both of his hands. "We should take it slow, you know?"

Austin's eyes were wide and dark in the shadows, and he was still beneath Clay's touch.

"I've already jumped off the cliff," said Austin slowly, as though tasting the weight of each word, one by one.

"Yeah, but you don't want to crash land, you know?" Clay moved his thumb across Austin's bottom lip, like he was sealing the kiss in so Austin could taste it later. "I want this to keep going. Us."

"You do?"

The question, the two words, held an armful of hurt, of doubt, of simply not knowing. Clay didn't know either, not really, not having taken this long with any man before. It felt more serious in a way, but in a good way, going deep inside of him.

"Yes, I do," said Clay. "This is the courting part, I think. The dating part."

"Are we dating?"

"Yes," said Clay, stoutly. "We are. If you want to. We'll take it slow."

"And you don't mind about—you know."

"I don't know." Clay chewed on his lower lip, thinking it over. "I've never encountered this before, you know? But I'm willing to wait, if you are. Till you're ready."

"You make me sound like a virgin." Austin's voice fell a little flat, just then, as if his ongoing problem and his lack of experience with other men was a deficit, a drawback.

"You are." Clay rose on his toes to kiss Austin's nose and then his mouth, gently, lightly. "To me, at least."

He let go of Austin's face and slid his hands down Austin's neck to his shoulders and then to his upper arms, never letting go, never losing touch.

"We'll just go slow," said Clay, now. "It's all new to me, too, right? Being with someone with no experience."

"I have experience," said Austin, affronted.

"Of course you do. Just not with guys." Clay pointed to himself and nodded, pretending to be quite wise in these matters. "Maybe I can't dance, but I'm a rock star at everything else."

"That you are," said Austin, his voice low, making Clay shiver.

Austin bent close, tipping his head down like an offering, and came close enough to press his forehead against Clay's. They stayed like that for a moment, in stillness, connected as the cool air of the glade swirled around them, scenting the air with pine and earth and dampness.

When Clay realized that the music had stopped and laughter and chatter had risen, he knew the dance was over. And if he was going to be a good boyfriend, the best, really, he needed to make sure of Austin and stop them both before he gave into his desire to take Austin to bed, remove all of his clothes, and tumble them both between the sheets.

"We should get to bed," said Austin, as though reading his mind.

"We should," said Clay. "And we will. I've never—I've never gone this slow, but I want to go slow. For you."

Sweeping his hand along Clay's face, Austin kissed him again, sending that same charge of energy through Clay, the same thrill of desire, warmth pooling in his groin, the back of his neck heating up.

In a flickering part of his mind, Clay knew Mona was an idiot and was missing out, and then he shoved that away, because he never wanted to think about her again. Or at least not until Austin needed to talk about her, which Clay imagined he would, one day.

"Goodnight," said Austin, with one last kiss, a tuck of Clay's hair behind his ear. A smile, those dark eyes pulling Clay into them. It took all of his will to resist. "See you at breakfast?"

"Yes, please," said Clay, giddy as a kid at the prospect. "Bright and early, right?"

"Yes."

Austin dropped his hands, turned, and walked in the direction of the staff quarters. Which, thank goodness, he had more willpower than Clay did.

Clay was all for doing it now—but Austin deserved more. Deserved his patience and his care. Austin made him feel different from any fast fuck, any chance encounter, made him feel good all over, inside and out. And if waiting would help Austin? Then Clay would wait till the ends of the earth and that was the truth, plain and simple.

He waited a good five minutes, saying hello to the staff who passed him on the path, directing guests who'd wandered into the glade when they meant to go past the fire pit to their cabins over-looking the river. Went back, even, to help clean up after the dance, anything to keep him occupied so he could give Austin a chance to get to his room without Clay jumping him and folding him in an embrace, which would surely lead to more than Austin was ready for.

After Leland thanked them all, and he and Jamie headed off to their cabin, Clay made his way upstairs to his room, took the hottest shower ever. He thought about rinsing off cold to stave off any last lingering desire, then decided against that.

Then, dressed in nothing, squeaky clean from his shower, opened the windows wide, pulled back the sheets, and lay in the bed, body pulled tight, the breeze sweeping across his skin, cooling him. Goose-bumps prickled on his body as he curled and uncurled his toes, still amazed at how it had gone between him and Austin.

His cock pressed against his belly, hard and ready to go. With one hand, he caressed it and thought about how quickly he might jerk off so he could go to sleep. He gripped himself, silky skin over muscle and blood pumping just below the surface. Swiped his thumb across the top of his cock, felt the moisture there, drew the scent of his own excitement into his lungs. And then paused—

Should he wait like a bridegroom might wait for his wedding night? Or, more to the point, should he wait until Austin was ready?

It would be like a kind of gift, wouldn't it, to do that? Of course he wouldn't tell Austin, even though Austin might feel less alone if he did because Austin being Austin might feel obligated to rush himself, push himself. And that wouldn't be good for either of them, that type of pressure.

Maybe, since he was already worked up, he would go just this one time, and then, come morning, he would work it out with cold showers and hard work and the promise he'd made to Austin to take it slow.

Clay's chest rose and fell, like small gasps at the idea of it. That he'd made a promise to another man, one that he knew, and continued to know. Someone he shared meals with, who seemed to like, simply, to be with him.

No one had ever done that for Clay, or wanted that from Clay. Having quick fucks all over the place meant *being* a quick fuck, meant being less than nothing to anyone. But not to Austin. He'd made the leap for Clay. Wanted to be with him. Sought him out. Over and over and over.

He petted his cock with one long, soft stroke.

"Easy, little man," said Clay, whispering. "You'll get your turn soon. And it'll be better with someone you care about. I promise you."

He easily fell asleep, but in the morning, his cock woke up before he did and as he swung his legs over the side of the bed and ground the heel of his palm against his forehead, he struggled. Took a cold shower, and then turned it to hot, as punishing himself wasn't going to work.

Then, standing there in the shower, dripping, water in his eyes, he slid his hands down, grasped his cock, and tried to make it stand down, which it wouldn't do. Quickly, one hand braced against the shower wall, he jerked himself off, body swimming in pleasure when he came, thoughts of Austin standing in a field of green grass, painting Clay with his precious watercolors. Tiptoeing down the hall to slip the painting beneath Clay's door.

Slick semen slid down his leg. He wiped himself down with the used washcloth, then stepped out of the shower to shave and dress and get ready for Friday. And for Austin, whom he spotted as he got in line for the breakfast buffet.

Austin waved him up in the line as usual, but Clay waved back and shook his head. Insistent and with a smile, Austin moved down the line to join Clay.

Austin looked newly shaven and bright-eyed, like he'd gotten a good sleep and was ready for anything. His hair shone like dark copper and when he looked at Clay, his eyes were a deep green, like the greenest valley in springtime after a hard rain.

"What's with this?" asked Austin.

"What's with what?"

Austin touched the space between Clay's eyebrows with a gentle thumb. "This. A worry line. I'm not used to seeing it on you."

"Oh," said Clay. He grabbed a tray, a plate, and a knife and a fork, shuffling his way down the line, taking a stack of pancakes, which was what his mouth wanted. "I'll tell you when we sit down. Alone, you know?"

"Sure," said Austin, obliging, as he ever was.

When they sat down, it was side by side at the end of a long table along the wall. Not a prime spot for the view, so it was spare of people. Plenty of privacy.

"Okay, now," said Austin, digging into his eggs and bacon with a sigh, like he'd been starving. "Tell me what's going on?"

"Okay, so." Clay swallowed a mouthful of pancake, then swallowed some black coffee to get that down and realized he was stalling. "I thought to make you a gift of—uh—not jerking off until you were ready to go—"

"You did what?" Austin's fork paused halfway to his mouth. "Why would you do that?"

"For you," said Clay. "I would wait for you, only I was all worked up last night after that kiss, and then again this morning, I finally gave in."

"Don't do that." Austin shook his head and seemed to be arranging things on his tray to give his energy somewhere to go. "Don't do that for me. I'm touched that you would think of it, but you don't need to do that. Not for me—"

"But for you—"

"Not for *anyone*, okay?" Austin shook his head again, like they'd been arguing for hours over this. "I appreciate you being patient with me, but I don't want you to deny yourself, well, something like that."

There was flash and passion in those moss green eyes, and color on Austin's cheeks. His jaw was firm as he looked at Clay, and Clay knew he meant it. Every word. That it was okay if he took himself in hand, that he didn't need to wait for Austin. Which was a gift.

"I don't know what I'm doing," said Clay. He shoveled in more pancake, loaded with butter and real maple syrup because, really, what problem couldn't be solved with more pancake?

"I don't either," said Austin.

While Austin's voice was solemn, his smile was sweet. Clay's heart curled around itself, all heat and the roll of desire, and the promise to himself that he would find any way possible to see that smile on Austin's face all of the time instead of some of the time.

When they finished their breakfast and bussed their table, Austin headed off to his day. Clay headed off to his, which involved, among other things, cleaning stalls in the barn. After which, he went to help Jamie repair a line of wooden fencing at the top end of the service road that went behind the barn.

He was already sweaty and tired and not paying much attention when he heard a high-pitched rattle and saw a movement of brown and darker brown diamonds, a thick, sage-dusted body and a diamond-shaped head, all curled around the fencepost just one foot away.

In that second, the snake lunged at him, hissing, rattles shaking to show Clay the snake meant business. The snake lunged again, postponing up on its coils, the rattle sound sharp the dry air.

Clay fell back, scrambling away from the snake, his hands and heels pushing against the dirt as the snake hissed and lunged at him again. Clay was out of reach now, but only barely.

"Shit."

Because of the rain, the grass was damp and the rattlesnake probably only wanted to warm itself. All God's creatures and all that. But to have a venomous snake on the ranch where guests from the city might not understand how dangerous the animal was, was another thing entirely.

"Jamie." Shaking, Clay barked out Jamie's name so Jamie would know it was serious.

When Jamie, two fence posts along, stopped his pounding of nails and looked up, Clay pointed at the fence post with his chin, sweating the whole while.

"We need to get in the truck and call snake control."

"Got it."

As Jamie made a wide circle to the truck, Clay kept his eye on the snake. It was big and healthy and if Clay had a gun, he would have shot it, despite Leland's rule about snakes.

Snakes were part of the ecosystem and should be given a wide berth, left alone. But this snake was too close to the ranch and was, in fact, on ranch property. Removal was the next best thing. Not to mention where there was one, there might be others.

Standing up slowly, backing away even more slowly, Clay didn't hardly take a breath till he was in the truck, next to Jamie, who'd picked up his cellphone to call the nearest snake control company. It was only then Clay could take a breath, wipe the sweat from his neck with his palm.

"You did good," he said to Jamie, who was white.

"You did, too," said Jamie. His mouth barely moved as he spoke. Then he dialed Leland's number, and when Leland answered, he explained the situation.

"Leland wants us to wait here, so we don't startle the snake," said Jamie when he clicked his phone off. "He wants the snake to be where we saw it, so snake control can get it easily."

"Got it."

Rubbing his mouth, Clay thought about how there was a cooler in the truck bed full of several plastic bottles of ice cold water. But if he opened the door, he might startle the snake, so the two of them would just have to sit tight. Which they did for a good half hour, in the rising heat.

Jamie had left the windows down when he'd parked the truck, so at least they had a breeze. And if Clay squinted, he could see the snake, still wrapped around the fence post, basking in the sun.

Soon after that, a man came walking up the hill, carrying a dark cloth bag and a metal snake hook to capture the snake with. He nodded at them as he came up to the truck.

"You boys are smart," he said beneath the shade of his cowboy hat. "Where is it?"

"There."

Clay pointed at the fence post where he could still see the snake, napping, and he was very glad that it wasn't him who had to approach the snake and grapple with it using the snake hook. The rattles started going, and the snake spun around, but the handler captured it neatly and tucked it in a bag. A bag that shifted around, like the snake was trying to find a way out.

"Tell Leland I'll send him the bill," said the man as he walked back down the hill.

Clay wanted a cold drink of water and then he wanted a beer and maybe a shot of whiskey, though maybe not in that order.

"Should we go back?" asked Jamie. "Pick up our tools and go? Or stay and work?"

"I think we should stay and finish," said Clay, though it made his skin itchy to think of what a close call they'd had.

Jamie nodded, and they got out of the truck, grabbed a bottle of cold water for each of them to drink, and sauntered over to the fence line like they both weren't about to jump out of their skins.

Clay had just picked up his hammer and was kicking dust over the spot where the rattler had curled around the bottom of the fence post when Leland came driving up the hill, parking his truck next to the other one. He got out in one smooth motion and walked right up to Jamie to take him in his arms. Kissed him hard. Carded his fingers through Jamie's hair.

Clay looked away and let them have their moment, thinking maybe that if Austin had known, he might have come up and kissed Clay. Not like Leland had kissed Jamie, but in his own way, passionate and deep. Then Austin might have hugged him, a full body hug, like Clay was somebody he really cared about. Which he did, actually.

Ducking his head, hiding his smile, Clay kicked a tuft of grass and waited for the boss and the hired hand to end their kiss. When they did, Leland looked at Clay, face flushed, his smile tilted up at one end.

"Let me help you boys finish up," he said. "I've got the snake wrangler coming up again on Saturday, after the guests have gone, to check for a nest."

Together, under the cloudless blue sky, they fixed the fence, tightened the boards so they wouldn't come loose in the wind and weather. They made short work of it, though it left sweat drying everywhere Clay could think of.

He itched for a shower, but there wasn't time if he wanted to get back to the main lodge to have lunch with Austin. Which he missed, since he was late, and Austin had eaten early, according to Brody when he asked him.

"Why you wondering about him for?" asked Brody. Then, after a minute, as he tucked into the strawberry shortcake Levi had made for dessert, he said, "Oh, man. Have you fallen for the *accountant*? What will Leland say when he finds out."

"And he will," said Clay. He stirred around the bits of strawberry left on his plate, knowing it was likely that the non-fraternization rule would apply to him, even if it didn't apply to Leland. He had made a joke about it to Austin, but it was only a joke. Rules were rules.

"I won't say anything." Brody shrugged and went back to his dessert, drinking large gulps of milk between bites. Hardly any grown person Clay knew drank milk, but Brody did, every chance he got, and Clay had it on good authority that Levi made sure to order organic milk, just for Brody.

"Thanks."

As Clay finished his lunch, he didn't say anything to Brody about the snake. Snakes were a part of the landscape, though the ranch was pretty active, and the snakes liked it quiet. He couldn't admit that he'd been scared, that even now he could imagine how it might have gone if he'd not backed away and been safe in the truck. Prairie rattlesnakes were deadly, especially when startled.

What he wanted, what he really wanted, was to tell Austin, and have Austin hug and kiss him, comfort him. Let him be scared for a little bit, unlike everywhere else, where Clay needed to put on a brave face.

Which, come to think of it would be the second time Austin knew something about him that nobody knew. First that he couldn't dance, and second that he was afraid of snakes. Being so open about himself wasn't his first nature, normally, but it was becoming so with Austin. The accountant.

Smiling, Clay got up, bussed his tray, and strode out of the main lodge, rolling up his shirtsleeves in case Austin was close by and watching.

20

AUSTIN

*A*ustin kept his tone even as he pointed to where the menu was on the computer screen for what felt like the hundredth time. Maddy was smart in her own way, but the new technology involved in using the document scanner was throwing her.

Both of them were on their last nerve and Austin longed to give up for the day, wash up for dinner, and find Clay so they could eat together. He'd gotten no texts from Clay all day, so he took out his phone.

Dinner in a bit? he texted, along with *Have you eaten?*

"Oh, I get it." Maddy put her hands flat on the desk as if she meant to keep it from floating off. "It's like a folder within a folder within a folder. Like you stuffed it in there to save space."

"That's right." Austin whooshed out a breath. "You've got it. Always go to the menu if you get stuck. There's a help file there to point you in the right direction, and if that doesn't work, I'm nearby. But I think you've got it just fine."

Beyond the open door, the blue sky over the ranch beckoned. It hadn't rained in days and the weather was warming up.

Maybe he'd go painting again, seeing that so many wildflowers were in bloom, Indian paintbrush, red windflower, lemon sage wort, and on it went. He'd looked them up on his phone so he'd be sure to use the right term, find the right colors. He'd paint a span of grass dotted with flowers, and maybe he'd add a ghostly cowboy off to the side, one with blond hair and sturdy shoulders—

"Go along now," said Maddy, waving him off. "You're making me nervous staring into the air like that. Go have your dinner."

Without waiting, Austin strode out of the office and up the dirt and gravel road to the main lodge. Passing beneath the shade of cottonwood and pine trees was a blessing of coolness, tinged with the scent of damp, of green things growing. Every day he got to walk around like this, either taking a break from his work or going to the main lodge, was like a gift. He never would have thought, in his old life, that something so simple would become so necessary.

As he approached the steps, moving to the side so that guests could get in line first, he saw Clay coming along the path from the staff quarters. He looked cool and freshly showered, but when they got closer to each other, he saw that Clay looked a little white around his jawline.

"Hey there," said Austin. "You got my text okay then?"

Clay shook his head as they got in line, and while he shuffled forward when Austin did, his heart didn't seem in it.

"Is everything all right?"

The question sounded reasonable enough, but other thoughts began to crowd that out, like did Clay regret saying he was okay with Austin's inability to get it up? Did he want someone whole? Someone more gay? Or nobody at all? He could have kicked himself when Clay looked at him and moved closer, curving his fingers around Austin's forearm before letting him go.

"There was a snake." Clay looked white around his eyes now as he spoke. "A big prairie rattler right under my feet. I almost stepped on it. It almost got me."

"But you're okay?" Austin stopped himself from grabbing Clay and looking him over to make sure. Obviously, if he'd been bitten, he wouldn't be standing with Austin now. "You're okay."

"Yes, but—" As Clay looked at him, his blue eyes enormous circles, his jaw working, sweat dappling his upper lip. "Cowboys aren't supposed to be afraid of snakes, right? I am. Just about pissed myself today. Don't tell anyone, okay?"

"I won't," said Austin, restraining himself yet again from taking Clay and holding him close, like he seemed to want, for he moved close, and closer still till his body was an echo of Austin's. "I never will."

He held back an earnest and heartfelt speech about how many people were afraid of snakes, and how a rattler would be extra scary, and Clay had no cause to be ashamed of that fact.

But words didn't seem like they would help, just then, so Austin kept close to Clay in return as they got their trays and food and settled down at one of the long tables, since the smaller tables were all taken. He let Clay eat his baked spaghetti, let him drink his iced tea, eating his own food at the same pace, in sympathy.

"This is stupid, but—"

"But what?"

"I'm going to have nightmares, I just know it." Clay scraped his blond hair back from his forehead, tugging at the roots of his hair. "I dealt with it today, you know? Did everything right. But it gave me the creeps to see that snake handler walking off with a bag full of rattler. He's going to be back on Saturday, did you know? To find a nest, if there is one, or a cave of 'em. Then he's going to bag 'em up and take them into the hills where they'll make new homes. It's the right thing to do for the ecosystem and all but it's giving me the creeps just thinking about it."

Brody came up to the table, with a tray of dirty plates, empty milk glass in hand.

"Hey, guys," he said. "There's a meteor shower that's bright just after sunset. Want to come? Quint's going to drive a few of us up to the ridge."

From behind Brody came Quint, whom Austin had met only briefly. Austin had come across a few receipts signed by Quint, each one balanced to the penny as to what was on record. This was not a guy who messed around or, probably, let anyone else mess around.

"It's the Bootid shower," said Quint in a voice that could be heard even though it was quite low and the dining hall was rather noisy. "It can best be seen after dusk, so I thought we'd head on up a little before nine. Are you in?"

Clay looked at Austin and nodded, moving only a fraction. Austin nodded back and smiled at Quint.

"Sure, where shall we meet?"

"At the service shed," said Quint. "I'll take whoever up there in my truck."

Quint and Brody went off, and Clay shuddered, putting his fork down.

"We were fixing the fence along the service road behind that shed when we came across that snake." He shut his mouth as if trying to keep from saying anymore that might mark him for life as being afraid.

"We don't have to go," said Austin.

He leaned forward, fingers reaching out across the table. Clay reached out his fingers in return.

"Better get it over with, going out there," said Clay. "Well, anyway, we'll be making too much noise, and it'll get cool that time of night so—"

Being brave, Austin curled his fingers around the edge of Clay's palm so they were almost holding hands.

"Will you protect me?" asked Clay as he let Austin's hand cover his.

"You don't have to joke."

"It's what everybody expects of me," said Clay. "To make a joke of things. Ha ha ha, Clay's afraid of snakes. Funny, no?"

"No."

He wished he could kiss Clay then and there, right in front of everybody. But he couldn't, he wasn't brave enough, and maybe it would upset the guests. And maybe Leland would see, and the anti-fraternization rule would be paraded with some force in front of them. So he left it, with his feelings suspended in mid-air, and Clay's self-recrimination rising from him in waves.

They went their separate ways after dinner, as Clay seemed to want to be alone, and as much as Austin wanted to go with him, he knew what it was like to feel the way Clay was feeling. Like everything you believed about yourself was wrong, and you couldn't bear for the world to see your mistake.

He took the time to freshen up in his room, to dab on cologne, to change his shirt three times. What was he thinking, that this was a kind of a date? Would they ride in the back of the truck again and, in the darkness, would they chance a kiss?

He met Clay after he got the text *Front porch*, and hurried down the stairs to meet him.

Clay, he discovered, had shaved, and changed into a clean white-t-shirt, so not dressed for a date. Except he was, maybe. The t-shirt was tight, clinging to every muscle, the line of Clay's ribs, the bulk of his shoulders.

He'd combed his hair, like a little kid getting ready for a class picture, only his hair had a mind of its own and stuck up in blond waves. As well, his blue jeans looked old and snug, like they'd been washed to the point of softness.

Clay looked better than he had at dinner and when he saw Austin coming out the door into the shadow of the porch at dusk, his eyes widened, and his smile grew.

"Hey," said Clay, opening his arms like he wanted Austin to walk into them. "You clean up good, I'd say."

"So do you," said Austin. "More than good."

"So, is this a date?" asked Clay as they walked up the service road to where Quint's truck was parked.

"I think it is, at least it feels like one." Austin focused his attention on where they were headed, keeping his eye out for snakes, which was hard as the dusk grew darker. "But then, being with you always feels —" He whooshed out a breath. "I'm not good at this. Mona was my first. She picked me out of a herd of local boys in high school, and it's only been her ever since, so I don't really have any idea—"

"There's no idea." Clay shook his head and walked close at Austin's side as if there was no place he'd rather be. "No idea atall. Just you as you are. It's fine. I like it."

There wasn't a chance to respond to this as they arrived at Quint's truck, an older Ford, white with a blue hood. Only Brody was waiting for them, so Brody got into the truck's cab with Quint, which left the truck bed for him and Clay.

Kindly, Quint had provided a pile of blankets, so the ride in the near dark up to the ridge where they could see the meteor shower was more comfortable than the ride to tend to the mountain lion had been. This time, the two of them sat close on the pile of blankets, bracing themselves by holding onto each side of the truck bed, and smiled each time the bumpy road jostled them together.

"It's like a private outing," said Austin, raising his voice above the noise from the truck's engine as it growled its way up a hill.

"It is." Clay nodded. "Quint likes to do weird stuff like this. Sometimes he invites people and sometimes he doesn't. Mostly he doesn't, so we lucked out. I mean, we could have come on our own, right? But Quint knows the best spots."

"You do too," said Austin. "For painting, which I hope we can do again."

This last was added hastily, for he was pretty sure he'd rather go painting with Clay than without. But when was Clay going to run out of patience with him? They'd kissed once, and while it had been a pretty knee-weakening kiss, a young man like Clay was hardly likely to stick around if that's all that was on offer.

When Quint parked the truck, Austin looked over the side of the truck bed and saw that they were on the edge of what looked like a small cliff of rock, where the drop-off looked sheer and disappeared into darkness.

Above them was the dark outline of the shoulders of the mountains, and beyond a flat expanse of dark green grass melting into grey. The sky was clear and moonless, darker to the east, still pinked with sunset to the west.

Quint got out and walked around to the truck bed.

"Hand me some blankets, if you would," said Quint. "You fellows c'n stretch out in the truck bed or join us on the ground. I didn't bring chairs, on account of there's no point craning your neck for a good hour waiting for the stars to fall."

"Thank you," said Austin as he felt Clay stiffen beside him. "I appreciate the offer, but being a city boy, I'm terrified of snakes and would rather stay in the truck, if that's okay with you."

"Suit yourself," said Quint. He took the armful of blankets that Austin held out. "Frankly, it's a smart man who's wary rather than foolish around wildlife."

As Quint walked off into the gathering darkness, Austin smiled at Clay and bumped Clay's shoulder with his own.

"You covered my ass there," said Clay, smiling back.

"I got you, bruh," said Austin in the way he imagined the cool kids would say it, which just made Clay snicker.

Together they laid out the layers of blankets, using one that they rolled into a long pillow for their heads. Austin arranged himself in a comfortable position, and just after Clay arranged himself at his side, a slow, sweet silence fell.

There was no sound but the wind whispering past the edges of the truck. No sensation but the curl of woolen blanket beneath them. No sight except the sky above them, dark and purple-hued, clear all the way up to forever as the stars, one by one, came out.

With a sigh, Austin moved his head to one side, and Clay's head gently moved against his, and they stayed that way for a good long while, waiting and watching. When Austin clasped his hands over his belly, Clay did the same. When Clay stretched his neck, Austin did likewise.

When the first shooting star pierced across the midnight-blue sky, Austin pointed, silent, open-mouthed. Clay, without a word, reached up and took Austin's hand so they were pointing together. And when Austin dropped his hand to his side, Clay did not let go, but held onto Austin's hand. And they stayed that way, holding hands like young lovers newly met, filling Austin with bubbles of expectation, zipping energy in his belly.

"Hey," said Clay, whisper-soft in his ear. "There's one. Did you see it?"

"Yes," said Austin, though the sight that filled his heart was the glimmer of light in Clay's blue eyes, a reflection of starlight in a cloudless and clear dark sky.

Clay, perhaps sensing that Austin was looking at him with as much awe as he viewed a shooting star, turned his head, and ducked his chin so they were close, foreheads almost touching, mouths only inches apart.

The warm whisper of Clay's breath drew him close till they were kissing like young lovers at a drive-in movie, completely forgetting why they'd come, the movie unwatched as their lips met and tendrils of energy moved between them. Kissing Mona had never been like this, sweet and kind, though behind that kindness stirred something more, more energy, a drive, a heartfelt swirling that he wanted to let swallow him whole.

"You okay?" asked Clay, drawing back, the words moving his lips against Austin's lips. "You're shivering all over. Ought to have bought that Carhartt jacket I sent you the link for."

"I will," said Austin in response, though the words meant nothing in light of the warmth they shared between them, covered from overhead by a dark, nighttime blanket.

"Green to match your eyes," said Clay, planting a soft kiss on Austin's nose, so tender, full of affection and playfulness that Austin wanted to weep for all the lost years, the wasted years.

Why had he stayed with Mona when he could have gone out into the world and found Clay? But the last ten years, at least, had been filled with a responsibility for Bea, the bright, energetic bundle that had been placed in his arms only moments after her birth.

He'd borne that responsibility gladly, and would continue to do so. And maybe he should be grateful that he had this between him and Clay. The way Clay held his hand and kissed him on the mouth, full and proper, taking Austin with him into a swirl of delight that tingled across his skin and raced down his spine and circled him with warmth and energy, Clay's scent, the perfume of him all around like a balm, a tender blanket of love and acceptance.

Clay drew back, took a breath. "Wow," he said low, a whisper like poetry. "Nobody ever kissed me the way you do."

"Nobody ever—" Austin couldn't finish what he meant to say, as it overwhelmed him to think of it, that nobody had ever made him feel the way Clay did.

Instead of speaking, he rolled toward Clay, and tugged on Clay's bejeaned hip to get him to roll towards him.

While overhead the stars streamed across the sky, he kissed Clay and held him close and closed his eyes and made a wish, that this could last. That he could find this kind of happiness in the morning. That he could be together with Clay, fully, and love him every way possible.

"You okay?" asked Clay, and if his words trembled, there was nobody to know it but the two of them, curled together in the truck bed beneath a nighttime of shooting stars.

"Yes," said Austin, kissing Clay once more. He wasn't entirely okay, but he would be, if they could be together like this always.

21

AUSTIN

*T*hat they ended up in Clay's bed to sleep together didn't surprise him as much as it might have only weeks before. They'd gotten back late from the star watching party, as Quint and Brody had gotten to talking, while Austin and Clay had become entwined in the truck bed, too caught up to note the passage of time.

When the night-sky show had slowed down, Quint had trundled the truck slowly back over the dirt road to the ranch and bid them goodnight to head back to his little cabin next to Leland and Jamie's cabin.

They'd walked to the staff quarters with Brody, quietly, so as not to disturb anyone, and bid him goodnight on the second floor. Then up on the third floor, completely silent and still, they said goodnight, kissed, and said goodnight again.

Only Austin had followed Clay to his room, as though Clay had something to show him, and indeed he had: the painting Austin had done of the place where the rivers met and of Clay, a shadowy, watercolor cowboy drawn from life, had been carefully thumb-tacked to the wall.

"Will you stay?" asked Clay. His eyebrows went up, like the question mattered to him very much.

"Yes," said Austin without hesitation. "I can't—you know—but I'll stay."

"We'll just cuddle," said Clay, the words muffled as he pulled his white t-shirt, now streaked with dirt that came from somewhere, over his head. His chest was bare, with only a small swirl of dark gold hair along his breastbone.

Somewhere in Austin's mind was a bit of shock that he was looking at another man getting undressed and he wasn't running away. He was moving close, reaching up a hand, though he did not dare touch.

"Here," said Clay. He took Austin's hand and gently placed it across his heart, and kept his hand on top of Austin's hand so he'd know it was okay. "How's that?"

Austin could only nod wordlessly as Clay guided his hand to trace over the swell of muscle, the curve of shoulder. Clay was sturdy, the muscles dense from everyday work, but his skin was soft and warm beneath Austin's touch.

"Okay?" asked Clay, and the question seemed to encompass so many questions behind it, in particular whether Austin was comfortable and behind that, perhaps, if Austin liked what he saw.

That took Austin right out of his own concerns inside of a heartbeat.

I saw you looking, Clay had said to him once. And maybe people did look at Clay, for he was pretty to behold, shapely and strong, dense thighs, broad shoulders. But maybe nobody ever told him, thinking he already knew?

"You're more than okay," said Austin, dipping his head to brush a kiss across Clay's cheek. "You make me want to paint you, even if I don't know how to paint people. At all."

"You can practice on me," said Clay, grinning now, as he undid his belt buckle. "Every day, if you like. But for now, you're not going to sleep in your clothes, are you? You can if you need to, though. You can borrow my toothbrush or just let it go till morning."

There were a lot of things Austin was prepared to let go of, past ideas about gay men, his marriage to Mona, his apprehension about how all of this should go and, yes, brushing his teeth. All for the pleasure of stripping down to his boxer briefs, though he kept the t-shirt he'd worn under his cowboy shirt on, tugging it low over his hips.

His legs felt too gangly and long, the red-gold hair on his legs to stark against his pale skin. His cock lay nestled in the curve of his boxer-briefs, and beneath that his balls, cupped together, seemed surprised at the draft that felt like it was shooting up between his legs, like everything in the room was focused on his flaccid cock, his nasty bits, as Mona called them. His arms and hands felt like they had nowhere to go.

Though when Clay smiled at him, all of this seemed unimportant including his lack of any kind of erection which, yes, he could plainly see Clay had. Like he had so much energy to spare, his cock inside of his white briefs wanted to make the most of this moment.

"Later, little man," said Clay, petting himself, laughing as he lifted his head to look at Austin while he stood there, naked except for his briefs, bare feet curling and uncurling on the wooden floor, his sturdy thighs flecked with dark gold hair that thickened as it made its way up to his groin. "Dicks got a mind of their own, am I right?"

"You're right," said Austin, breathing a sigh that Clay could make light of this, but in the nicest way.

"Dibs on the wall," said Clay. He clicked off the light and padded to the bed, swinging the curtain closed as he went. Then as he got under the sheet and light blanket, holding them open for Austin, he laughed again. "Remind me to tell you my little fantasy about the monk and the Viking."

"The monk and the *Viking?*" It was a joke, surely it was, but it made getting in that bed harder, now that all of him was awake for some reason. But when Clay patted the bed, Austin took a breath and got in next to Clay and shivered as Clay drew up the sheet and half the blanket.

"Okay," Austin said, his voice definitely not squeaking. "Tell me about the monk and the Viking."

"Well," said Clay, in a serious way. "I had this idea that underneath your clothes, you had long, tight muscles, which I know you do because I can feel how dense you are. Do you work out?"

"I used to," said Austin, mulling the idea of this over in his mind, deciding not to mention that he'd worked out because Mona wanted him to.

"Well, see, that makes sense." Clay turned on his side, bumping his knees against Austin's thigh. "Don't forget, I'm a sprawler."

"I won't." How could he forget anything about Clay when he was only inches away, inches that kept getting smaller with each heartbeat?

"But back to the monk and the Viking." Clay yawned and stretched and flopped one arm over Austin's belly, like Austin was his giant sleep toy and this was just how they were when they shared a bed at night. "In my mind, I figured you were as fit as a Viking. But then with your red hair, and if the Vikings raided Irish villages, that made *you* the monk, which meant I'd have to be the Viking. For which I'm a little short, though I do have blond hair."

Austin laughed, low in his belly, as he waded through all of this. "You can be the Viking, as you are not that short."

"And you'll be the monk, all naked beneath your brown habit, ready to be raided?"

Something inside of his body did a little jig at the thought of being raided by Clay. A wash of energy was entering him, which must be how dry earth felt after the rains finally came. The only sound he could make in response to this was a low gurgle, which made Clay laugh a little bit as he snuggled closer.

"I'm not going to touch you anywhere, except like this."

Tucking his head beneath Austin's chin, Clay made a contented sound, like someone who has come home at long last. Which sent Austin's heart leaping, and he dipped down and kissed the top of Clay's head, inhaling his scent, reveling in the feel of another's touch, another human body. Soaking in the idea that Clay didn't seem to want him to do anything or be anything other than what he was, and simply wanted to be with him.

"Goodnight," he said in the darkness, thinking he might remember this moment for a very long time.

"'Night," said Clay with a huge yawn, a shift of movement against Austin's body.

The darkness was quiet and took care of them till morning, though Austin was surprised to awaken with the room bright with sunlight.

Clay was wrapped around him like a starfish, sporting an erection that pressed against Austin's bare thigh. Meanwhile, Austin's phone ringing in his jeans' pocket on the floor. It was Mona's ring, which meant it could be about Bea, which meant he needed to answer it.

"Hey," he said, lifting Clay's arm to shift him a bit. "I have to get that."

"Okay," said Clay, his voice warm from sleep.

He blinked as Austin got up, seeming to accept that this was the way between them, like maybe it'd been this way for a very long time. Enough for Austin to feel quite comfortable in his boxer-briefs, unashamed for the first time since the whole lousy business had started that he didn't have a morning erection.

Under the sheet, he sensed Clay was stroking himself, not to get off, but to get his cock to settle down, out of politeness.

"Hello?" asked Austin as he thumbed the call open. "Mona?"

"It's me," she said, in that pert way she had when she had news to deliver. Usually this was gossip about the neighbors or about something scandalous that had happened at the spa, but Austin didn't care about any of that anymore.

"Is everything all right with Bea?" he asked to make her come to the point.

"Well, that's the thing," she said. By her tone, Austin sensed she was not alone. "Roger and I are going to take a quick trip to New Orleans for a long weekend."

"What?"

"I would send Bea to Mrs. Delgado's, but she's full up, so I'm looking around for another full-time sitter for a few days."

"*What?*" he asked again, more forcefully this time, though it didn't make any difference. Mona's plans were already in place while Bea's needs were getting trampled underfoot. "She hates Mrs. Delgado's as it is, but why would you send her to a stranger? That's not right for Bea—"

"Well," Mona said now, drawing out the word. "That's all I got right now."

Behind him, Clay had gotten up from the bed and was standing close, looking at Austin with that worried wrinkle between his eyes. He was adorable in all kinds of ways as he stood there in his white briefs, his body tanned in the way a farmer's body is tan, from the shoulders down, and from the mid-thigh on down. Everywhere else was pale, dusted with gold and—Austin jerked his mind back to the conversation.

He didn't know what he'd do to arrange everything, but he knew that he did not want Bea staying with a stranger, not even for a minute. She was plenty flexible for a nine-year-old, but this would be taking it beyond her ability to cope, beyond what was right for her.

And although he realized, with some kind of clarity that came from being on the ranch, and from being with Clay, that Mona had led the conversation exactly where she wanted it to go, he knew what he needed, no, *wanted* to do.

"I'll take her," he said. "I'll come get her. Today. I'll be there in a few hours, so make sure she's ready to go."

Without waiting for Mona's response, he hung up. Maybe that was a dangerous thing to do, worthy in Mona's mind of the fiercest retaliation, but at that moment, he was beyond caring. And, thanks to Clay, beyond thinking that all of this was his fault.

Maybe he was to blame for his bad choices, but Mona had taken advantage of a green high school kid, and was now willing to sacrifice Bea to tend to her own needs above those of her daughter's. Which, in his mind, was the worst, shittiest thing she'd ever done.

"Mona's going on a trip," he said to Clay, holding his phone out like he'd be willing to sacrifice it if need be. "I can't let Bea go with strangers—"

"Of course not." Clay took the phone from Austin's hands and took those hands, shaking slightly in his own, his skin warm to the touch, calming Austin. "We'll get dressed. We'll borrow Leland's truck, of course. And then—"

"I'll have to take days off to look after her, when I've only just started." Austin's mouth felt numb and except where Clay was holding him, he was cold, chilled beneath his skin. "Surely, Leland, as nice as he is, won't like that."

"Why don't we ask him?" Clay nodded. "He always tells me it's better to ask and get a real answer than imagine what might be."

That steadied Austin in all the right ways, clearing his mind to make decisions.

"Okay."

"It's Sunday so he'll be having an early breakfast." Clay began pulling on his socks and then his blue jeans, hopping around like he was late for an appointment. "We should grab breakfast too, though we can always get snacks along the way, and I do like a good fountain drink and some Bugles."

All of this was said as if the entire problem was, for Clay, solved because they were going to talk to Leland about it. Borrowing the truck was one thing. Asking Leland to make concessions to a new employee with a young daughter was another.

Maybe he could get the days off. Maybe he could work remote from wherever while looking after Bea. Or maybe this was another disaster Mona created while living her selfish life.

He got dressed, thinking that he should shave, should charge his phone, but all of that didn't seem to matter with his whole energy intent on rescue. Once dressed, he grabbed his phone and tucked it in his back pocket, still worried, but buoyed up by the fact that he'd get to see Bea, whom he missed every minute of every day.

Along the path to the main lodge, Clay bumped shoulders with him, smiling.

"We don't need to tell everyone we've had a sleepover if you don't want to," he said.

"A sleepover?" This made Austin laugh in spite of himself. "What are we, ten?"

"Might as well be," said Clay. "Or maybe we're older, seeing as we're going on a road trip in Dad's truck." He made quote marks around the word *Dad*, and snickered, and Austin envied him that sense of adventure, of innocence. "Maybe he'll even give us money for candy."

Now laughing full on, Austin mounted the steps to the main lodge and entered the dining hall, looking for Leland, who was to be found at a long table, along with Quint and Bill, all three deep in the throes of conversation.

"What's up?" asked Leland, as they came up to the table. He scrubbed his hands with his paper napkin and looked prepared to jump into action, then and there.

"Well," said Clay. He shuffled his feet and shrugged, as though signaling that he was willing to wait for a private moment with his boss.

"Ah." Leland nodded at Quint and Bill, in turn. "Are we done?"

"Adventure rides are moneymakers," said Quint. "But I've said my piece. Decide how you want."

"Thank you." Leland got up and took his tray. "And Bill, it's not a deal breaker, but it would help the ranch."

"Heard you the first time," said Bill, burying his frown beneath a sip of black coffee.

Without responding to that, Leland nodded they should follow him, and Austin girded his loins as he watched Leland bus his tray.

"The situation is," said Austin, beginning in the same way he would have were Leland a CEO of a huge corporation, getting right to the point. "My ex-wife, Mona, has decided to take a sudden vacation, and would leave my daughter Bea in the hands of strangers. I'm going to go get her and then I would need a few days off to look after her until Mona comes back. Which, at this point, is an indeterminate number of days. I'll need to find a hotel or something—"

"Bring her here."

"What?"

Leland wiped his hands on his napkin before throwing it away, and then he faced Austin full on, his shoulders broad enough to shield

Austin from anything bad happening to him. Austin had to blink in the face of this, uncertain where the feeling had come from.

"Bring her here. We'll fix up the other manager's cabin, on the other side of Quint's place. It's only got the one bathroom, but it has two bedrooms. A small living room. A front and back porch to watch the sun rise and set."

"What are you saying?"

"Bring her to the ranch. She can have riding lessons, she can hang out with the Frontier Girls, and Sue Mitchell runs an excellent day camp. Maybe we'll cut back your hours, but you can work from anywhere and watch her, right? We'll help you."

"I'll help," said Clay, though he looked astonished to have volunteered. "And we need to borrow your truck to go get her."

"We?" asked Leland, seemingly oblivious that Austin's voice had been stolen, overcome that people he only barely knew, his boss, for one, would respond with such kindness and generosity.

"Sure," said Clay with a shrug. "You always say, don't go alone."

"That I do." Leland nodded. "Keys are in the truck." He reached into his wallet to pull out a credit card, which he handed to Clay. "Ask for receipts. I'll get Stella to give the cabin a good going over, and maybe Jasper can come up to put some curtain rods in." He smiled as he looked at Austin. "A staff member had a party in that cabin some years back. They stripped the place and now that person doesn't work here anymore."

"I'll be careful with it." Austin nodded, swallowing. "Thank you for this, seriously."

"You've got some driving ahead of you," said Leland, and though the words seemed serious, he was smiling. "Better get started."

"Thank you." He shook Leland's hand, then paused. "Is it okay if Clay comes with me?"

"Never go alone, I always say."

"Thank you."

He strode out of the dining hall, Clay at his side, hurrying to catch up.

"He knows," said Clay, half-moaning.

"What does he know? Which way is the truck?"

"This way." Clay pointed ahead of them and to the left. "We cut across here and he knows we slept together."

"How do you know that?"

"Because he knows everything."

"It's nothing to be afraid of, I guess," said Austin as they climbed into Leland's F150. "Unless you're thinking of the non-fraternization rule."

"I am."

Inside the truck's cab, Clay's words rested heavily, but he started the engine and carefully pulled through the parking spot on the gravel, and headed slowly down the main road to the front gate. There, Austin knew enough to get out and open the gate and close it behind Clay after he'd driven through.

"I need coffee and I imagine you do, too."

"We'll stop at Ranchette's," said Clay, putting on the gas as he headed south out of Farthing, down the 211. "They've got Bugles and fountain drinks, which is what we really need, on account of this is a road trip and all."

After a brisk twenty minutes while the green and brown hills flashed past the window, Clay barreled into Ranchette's Stop-n-Go, skidding to a stop in front of one of the pumps.

"Hey," said Austin, holding out a hand to touch Clay's arm. "You can't drive that way with Bea in the truck."

"Oh, no," said Clay. "I would never. I just want to get us there as fast as possible so you look happy again."

That was Clay's worry. Not that his Sunday would be taken up on this errand that belonged solely to Austin. Not that he missed breakfast, or that his sleep had been affected by the fact that there was another person in his bed. No, he was worried about Austin and a child he'd never met. Even if they never shared more than friendship, Austin knew it was something to treasure.

He filled up the tank, paying for it with his own credit card, while Clay grabbed snacks for the road. Perhaps knowing somehow that Austin didn't like soft drinks, he'd gotten a giant bottle of raspberry flavored iced tea, along with his own fountain drink, a bag of Bugles, and a box of peanut butter crackers. Then they were on the road, with soft pop rock on the radio station, and I-25 taking them further and further into civilization, with big eighteen wheelers crowding along the lanes with Mercedes and Jeeps, all going as fast as they possibly could toward downtown Denver and beyond that, to unknown destinations.

At the Thornton exit, which he pointed out that Clay should take, his heart beat faster, and with each inch closer to his old house, his old life, he thought it was going to come out of his chest. And then, when Clay turned the truck into the slanted driveway of the beige and tan split-level house where he used to live, he could almost have cried. For there on the front step, with her little Sleeping Beauty rolling suitcase and her Batman backpack, stood Bea.

The door was closed behind her. God knows how long she'd been waiting with expectation.

His Bea. The magical thing, the only good thing, that had happened to him amidst years of misery and misunderstandings and self-doubt that crawled across his skin every waking moment. When she saw him as he stepped out of the truck, seconds after Clay parked it, she jumped on her toes, but didn't race into the driveway, only waited, impatiently hopping.

"Dad, Dad, Dad," she shouted, excited, arms wide open, eyes shining.

He reached her inside of a moment, his eyes hot with unshed tears, his heart tearing itself asunder for having not fought harder to keep her closer to him. Being Mona's husband had been an exhausting prospect. Being Bea's dad was the best gift in the world.

"Hey, honeybee," he said, hunkering down to take her in his arms and hug her tight, tighter than tight. She hugged him back, and shuddered a sigh, as though it'd been ages since she'd seen him rather than a mere two weeks.

"Mom says you're taking me to a dirty old farm," said Bea, pulling back, scraping flyaway hair out of her mouth.

"I'm taking you to a ranch, Bea," said Austin.

He stood up, fuming inside that Mona made it seem like Bea was going to a place where she couldn't have any fun. Of course, early on, hadn't wanted to bring her to the ranch either, only now he wanted to take Bea around the ranch, arrange for her to ride a real horse, show her a purple-dappled sunset. Paint her in a field of tall grass along the banks of a slow, glassy river.

"Who's that?" asked Bea. "Dad, do you know a cowboy drove you?"

Bea was looking over his shoulder with serious eyes. When he turned his head, Austin saw that Clay had stepped out of the truck, perhaps with the intent of helping Bea with her luggage like the gentleman he was.

Clay had put on his straw cowboy hat and so, along with his stance, a little diffident, and his cowboy boots, the large buckle, he looked exactly like what he was. A cowboy. A ranch hand. Austin's friend, and maybe something more than that. All worthwhile, good things to be, and he was lucky to have Clay in his life.

"Yes," he said. "A cowboy drove me. His name is Clay, and he's going to take us to the ranch. Are you ready?"

"Does he have a horse?" asked Bea, looking up at him with shining eyes.

"He has—" Austin paused, bending close, and beckoned to her, like he had a secret to share, and then mock-whispered, "He has a whole *herd* of them."

Her smile was as bright as a sunrise, and joy filled her, seemed to stream from her hair and her fingertips and everywhere.

"Can I ride one?"

"Yes," he said. "We'll pick out the perfect one for you to ride. Sound good?"

"Yes."

He held out his hand to her, and she took it, and together they turned to look at Clay, still patiently waiting.

"Excuse me, sir," said Austin in a teasing voice. "Might you be headed anywhere near Farthingdale Ranch?"

"Why, yessir," said Clay in his best cowboy voice, tipping the edge of his cowboy hat with his fingers. "I'm going there today, if you've a mind to come with me."

Bea giggled behind her hand, and when Clay came close to grab her suitcase, she smiled up at him, and jumped a little.

"Hi," she said, looking up at him.

"Hi, yourself," he said in return. "And welcome to your accommodations for the next few hours."

As though she was a lady, he half bowed and gestured at the truck. Bea laughed and hopped up and down, still holding Austin's hand. Even if their time together would be short, at least he had this. At least he could show Bea the ranch, and he would not think about having to bring her back inside of a week, no he would not.

2 2

CLAY

*T*he rain started up the second they hit the highway, grey clouds scudding overhead, the roads slick with foam. Clay drove carefully, for they had precious cargo in the truck.

Bea was buckled in behind Austin, in the passenger seat. When Clay looked in the rearview mirror, he found she was looking at him, studying him, her eyes round and expectant, like she thought he was taking her to Christmas morning.

It was an odd feeling to have someone look at him like that. Of course, many a stranger in the alley behind the Rusty Nail had kind of looked like that when they saw him, but this was different. Way different. Bea was depending on him to get her safely to her destination, where he hoped she would have such a good time she would never want to leave.

As for Austin, he was buckled in securely, staring straight out through the windshield like he meant to keep track of the balanced rhythm the windshield wipers made as they zoomed back and forth, pushing puddles of rain away.

"It's a steady rain," said Clay. "But I think I'll stick to I-25 anyhow, as it'll get us home faster."

"Good idea," said Austin. "But we should stop for a treat, right? Bea?"

When he turned his head so she could hear him clearly, Clay was able to get a good hard look at how drawn Austin's expression was. Of course he was overjoyed to have time to spend with his daughter, but it must be weighing on him that he'd have to give her back in the end.

Mona was a piece of work doing this to him, this push-me-pull-you kiss-kick bullshit. Maybe it was better the door to the house had been closed. Maybe it would be better if he never met her.

"Dairy Queen," she said. "Cherry dipped cone!"

"Oh, honey, I don't know if they have those anymore," said Austin.

"They do," said Clay. "Harlin has a Dairy Queen that still has those on the menu. We can swing off the highway easy. Won't add but ten minutes to our drive and by then, maybe the rain will calm down."

Austin nodded to this, still buried in his own thoughts it seemed.

Clay turned the radio to an easy pop station and settled in, his hands always at the ten and two, keeping his eyes on the road, his heart focused on Austin. He took Highway 52 and drove up to Harlin, slowing down along Main Street, the cute part of town that somehow was modern and, at the same time, looked like it was out of an old black-and-white TV episode of *Leave It to Beaver* or something.

Clay parked on a side street, and ran inside the Dairy Queen. Dodging raindrops, he returned with a cherry dipped cone for Bea, a vanilla shake for Austin, and a chocolate shake for himself. Of course he was soaked by the time he got back into the truck, but he shook himself like a dog, making Bea laugh and bringing a smile, finally, to Austin's face.

"Don't get it everywhere, Bea," said Austin, handing her the cherry dipped cone and a pile of napkins.

"The truck'll wash," said Clay as he trundled through North Harlin, looking at the old houses in the rain, the mom n' pop shops, the no-name taco shop in a strip mall that Brody had assured him on more than one occasion served the best tacos on the planet. "It's seen everything from dirt to horse shit, so—"

"Dad," said Bea, leaning forward, poking her head between the seats. "He just said a bad word."

"Sorry," said Clay, at the same time Austin asked, "Is your seatbelt on?"

Somehow this relaxed the energy inside the truck, and Clay whistled along with the radio as he drove north and further north, going through Wyoming, taking the exit at the Ranchette's Stop-n-Go to drive along the low green hills to the west. Going to the ranch. Going home.

The feeling as he drove slowly through Farthing to the road that led to the ranch was the same as it always was. A sense of heading west, near the foothills, into the good country on the edge of the world.

It was still raining steadily as Austin got out to open and close the gate to the ranch, and mud slopped up beneath them as he crossed the bridge over the churning water below.

Clay was quickly able to finish his chocolate shake with one hearty suck of the straw along the paper bottom of the cup, and pull behind the main lodge along the service road, where he parked in front of the staff quarters and the short path that led to the managers' cottages.

Leland was waiting, wearing his long canvas slicker and a cover for his straw hat.

"Here we are," Clay said. He turned off the engine, looked at Austin and smiled. "Bet you never thought we'd do this, eh? Bring Bea to the ranch?"

"No," said Austin. He seemed to consider the question. "I guess I never thought I'd do a lot of things." He paused again, and when he looked at Clay, his expression was steady, his eyes such a deep green that it made Clay gasp. "But I'm glad I have."

"Where are the horses?" asked Bea, unbuckling herself and slithering through the gap between the seats to see out the front window.

"Some are in the barn," said Clay, undoing his own buckle, telling himself to simmer down his excitement at her excitement. "And some are in the fields." .

"Can we see them now?" she asked, clasping her hands together.

"Once we get you settled, we can go see them." Austin got out and opened the door to the rear passenger seat, and hauled Bea out gently, giving her a hug before setting her on the ground. "Once it stops raining so hard."

"I'll get the bags," said Clay, feeling a little left out by the gesture. Of course Austin would want to look after his kid. Of course, Clay should carry bags and follow behind like some kind of bellhop. It was his job, after all.

The rain pattered the leaves overhead, scented with damp pine. The path was scurried with water, which made it slick going. Maybe they should put down flagstones instead of just having bare dirt? Maybe Clay could suggest that he be the one to do that so he could have an excuse to hang around the cabin.

Up ahead, the door to the third manager's cabin was open. Jasper was on the tiny porch, out of the rain, while he packed up his toolbox. Ellis came out, dusting his hands, but when he saw Austin come up, hand in hand with Bea, he stopped, a little wide eyed, and hurried to go down the wooden steps so he'd be out of their way.

"Welcome home," said Jasper with a smile. He was quite tall, and filled the space in front of the door, and Bea looked up at him as though awestruck. "We've got everything in order, curtain rods in place, curtains hung. Stella's great team just came by to tidy the place up, and they left fresh linens and made the beds. All you need to do is unpack."

"Thank you," said Austin, a sigh filling his words with gratitude. "Bea, this is Jasper, our blacksmith. He's the one who puts shoes on all the horses. And Jasper, this is my daughter Bea."

Jasper came down the stairs and shook Bea's hand, his hand swallowing hers.

"It's nice to meet you, young lady." Jasper smiled as he straightened up, errant drops of rain dripping from his dark hair. "And this is Ellis, my foolish assistant."

"Hi," said Bea, almost unable to draw her eyes away from Jasper.

Ellis, unseen, waved at her and mouthed *Hi*.

"We'll let you get settled," said Leland. "Then we can meet you at the dining hall, as you're just in time for dinner. And Clay?" Leland shook the rain off his shoulders and gestured to Clay as he headed to the stairs, as he meant to take the luggage all the way inside and maybe get a small moment with Austin. "Put those on the porch for a minute."

That meant Leland wanted to talk to him, so fine. He followed Austin and Bea up the stairs, placed Bea's Sleeping Beauty rolling suitcase and her Batman backpack out of the rain, and walked back down, hurrying, rainwater dripping from the brim of his straw cowboy hat.

"What is it, boss?" asked Clay as he handed over Leland's credit card and the receipt for the gas and road trip treats.

"Thank you for doing that, bringing them," said Leland. He took his hat off, shook it free of rain, then put it back on again, nodding as Jasper and Ellis headed down the path, back to Jasper's cabin. "I think Austin was a little shook by his ex-wife's behavior, so your company did him good. Now, regarding the cattle drive."

"Yeah, sure," said Clay, sticking his hands in his back pockets, shivering a little as the back of his snap button shirt grew damp. "What's up?"

"You're on the roster this week to drive the chuckwagon for Levi for the cattle drive."

"Oh, good." Clay had to pretend to be more excited than he actually was, for if he went away on a cattle drive he'd not have the chance to talk to Austin for two whole days, which was two days too many. Now that he'd gotten the chance to drive, he didn't want it.

"However, this rain." Leland shook his head as he looked at the cabins, and the sigh of raindrops on the trees, the shift of wind. "It's too much. The trail will be rutted and it'd be too easy for the chuckwagon to get stuck. I've got guests expecting it, as that's what we advertised for this week. Since we can't go, I'm offering partial refunds, if they want it, or full, if they'd rather go home. We might do a daytime trail ride if it clears up, but it might not, so we're going to have to shift and be flexible. Okay?"

"Yeah, boss," said Clay. "You can count on me, for sure."

"Thanks." Leland touched his finger to the brim of his hat. "See you at dinner."

As Leland headed through the trees, Clay watched him go, then turned to look at the cabin, streaked with rain, looking quite cozy and sheltered beneath the green trees.

He was not a member of the family. He worked at the ranch, and wasn't allowed to go gallivanting off to knock on the door and ask to be welcomed. He had a job to do, and though he knew it was true, it made him ache inside to turn away and head to the barn to see if he could help with anything last minute.

Brody had everything in hand at the barn, and only needed help shifting some bales of hay, so after he took care of that, Clay went to his room to dry his hair and change his shirt. Only too late did he think he might have offered to help Austin pack up stuff to move from his room to the cabin, but by then it was dinnertime.

He hurried down the stairs, racing in the rain to the main lodge to mount the steps to the dining hall. The room was already packed with guests, the chatter reaching the wooden beams overhead. The line moved swiftly and Clay could have gotten into it and gotten his dinner quickly, but where was Austin?

Clay quickly spotted Austin and Bea with their dinner trays at the long table in front of the window. They were surrounded by Leland and Bill and Quint and Maddy.

There were smiles all around, as who didn't want to get to know a cute little girl like Bea? Which meant there was no room for Clay, so he would have to make do with his own company or, if he followed Leland's oft-given advice, go and find a lonely-looking guest to entertain with his dimpled presence.

He shuffled along to keep his place in line, loaded his plate with BBQ ribs and cornbread, got a glass of iced tea and surveyed the dining hall. Maybe he'd sit with the older couple over there, or the middle-aged ladies who already looked like they were well on their way to having a good time. Or maybe—

Across the room, Austin stood up and waved him over, and Clay felt foolish and pleased all at once. He and Austin shared a friendship, a good one, and Austin wasn't the kind of guy who would just abandon him, as Clay thought he had.

"Coming," he said to no one as he hurried through the crowded dining hall to the long table. There, he found himself a spot on the other side of Bill, only two down from Austin. Austin gave him a smile, which seemed like he was saying thank you, even if they couldn't sit side by side, the way they had been doing.

But then there was Bea.

"Clay!" she shouted when she saw him. "Leland says I can have horse lessons and Bill says I need cowboy boots all my own."

"That's excellent," said Clay, raising his voice over the din. "I'll bet you want pink cowboy boots, huh?"

"No," she shouted in full voice, causing a few heads to turn her way. "I want boots like *you* have. Real cowboy boots, not little girl ones."

"Oh." Ducking his head to hide his sudden grin of pleasure at having been singled out, Clay then looked up and saw Austin's smiling eyes. "I will be more than happy to help you pick out a good pair. A real pair."

He watched as Austin and Bea ducked their heads together, sharing a moment, words, their hearts.

He found himself wishing he was part of that conversation, his heart aching even as he was glad Austin had this time with his kid. At the same time, they surely would want to do things by themselves, and who was he to them? Just a ranch hand who liked to have sex with strangers, and surely Austin wouldn't want him hanging around.

What did he know about kids, anyhow? He didn't, not a thing, except what he'd learned by helping with riding lessons. That, he was good at. The ranch normally had a cutoff age, nobody under twelve was allowed, but he supposed Bea would be the exception to that while she was here.

Maybe he'd make sure he was signed up for any lessons she would have, and maybe Austin would watch from the fence rail, and maybe he'd notice—what? That Clay was good with kids and that Bea liked him? But why? So he could become part of their little family?

Maybe that was it. He had a family of his own, for sure. But they were all in Iowa and not much interested in cows or guest ranches or anything like it.

Who was he, though, to want to be a part of what Austin had? Who was he to think he might go up to Austin and ask to be part of his family? That would make him a dad, in a way, and Bea would be like his daughter, and that added a whole lot of responsibility to a lifestyle he might not be ready for. Who was he to dream or want or seek? Nobody, that's who.

With a glum feeling running through him, Clay finished his dinner, flashed some fake smiles, took his tray to bus his dishes, and didn't look back to see if Austin was watching him go.

23

AUSTIN

*O*nce they were back in the cabin after dinner, Bea was too wired to settle, and upset that she'd not been able to visit the horses on the account of rain. He managed to get her to take a shower, and when she came out, dressed in her pink-and-blue Lilo and Stitch pajamas, he set her in a chair and gently combed out her long, damp hair.

"I get a room all my own," she said, wiggling a bit. "Not pink, like at home. I'm tired of pink."

"The pajamas you have on are pink," he teased, using the towel to wipe away some of the water from the ends of her hair.

"I know, but it's different. Stitch is a cartoon, and he's blue, so he looks good against the pink."

"I'd say he does," Austin said, admiring her sense of color, something Mona hadn't been able to train out of her.

"Will I get my boots in the morning?" she asked, suddenly turning in the chair, her fingers on the edge of the back as she looked up at him, hopeful, expectant. "And horse lessons?"

"Yes," he said, nodding quickly as he moved a strand of hair away from her forehead. "We'll get that all set up for you, but only if you go to bed at a reasonable hour."

"Is the cabin haunted?" Bea asked.

She almost looked like she wanted it to be, but he knew it was a bad idea to encourage this. Austin looked around at the tabletop lamp on the end-table next to the short couch.

Beneath the ruby glass, the light was low and soft. In the bedrooms there were lights in the ceiling, but out here in the small living room, it was different, more cozy than efficient. And maybe a little spooky.

"No," said Austin. He nodded to show he meant it. "Leland wouldn't allow it."

"That's the tall man, right Dad?"

"Yes, honeybee, the tall man is the boss of the whole ranch. He's my boss, too."

"And Clay's boss?" she asked. "Is he Clay's boss?"

"Yes," he said. "Now sit still a minute while I finish. Then you can read to me your favorite part of *The Little Princess* before I tuck you in. You brought it with you, right?"

"Duh." Bea turned around and straightened up, an exaggerated posture to show how still she was sitting.

As Austin combed her hair, he went extra slow, enjoying this moment between them, when she was still little enough to need help with her hair. He could remember her being born as if it had happened only days ago, and now she was demanding her independence from pink, thinking about buildings being haunted, and doing her best to memorize all the names of the people she'd been introduced to.

And then there was Clay, who'd sat only feet away from Austin at dinner, but who barely looked at him. Who'd had that wrinkle between his eyes, and who'd left quite quickly after eating.

He'd much rather Clay had sat closer, like on the other side of Bea, who'd been a tad overwhelmed by the interest of his co-workers, who kind of acted like they'd not seen a nine-year-old before. The ranch had an age limit, and Bea was well below that, but she was, it seemed, being given the exception. But then, she *was* exceptional, and he wasn't ashamed to say that to anyone.

Clay and Bea would get along great, at least he thought so, given

Clay's ready smile and easy manner when he met Bea. That he'd been so patient with Austin's issues spoke of a kind heart, and he felt it, deep inside, that he needed to make sure Clay knew he was welcome around them.

He'd make a point of texting Clay before meals so they could all sit and eat together, and he'd count on Clay to help him find a pair of cowboy boots for little girls that weren't pink. He didn't know anything about cowboy boots other than how to put them on, and Clay knew—well, Clay seemed to know everything to put Austin at his ease and make Austin feel welcome, and now he wanted to do the same for Clay.

"You ready to read to me, honeybee?" he asked, giving Bea's hair a gentle tug before he wiped the comb on the towel.

"Yep."

Bea raced to her room, half slipping on the wooden floor, and came back with her e-reader, throwing herself into the only easy chair in the room. That was fine with Austin. He sprawled on the couch, put his feet up on the coffee table, and waited with expectation.

When he'd left the house and moved to the Motel 6, he'd never thought he'd get to experience this kind of evening again. His daughter was reading to him from her favorite book, her voice smoothing out after a few minutes of reading, as she relaxed into her task, relaxed from showing off a little to her dad into something more enjoyable for her. Plus, she loved the story of Sara Crewe and read it over and over.

"I like Becky, Dad," said Bea, stopping to look up at him.

"I like Becky, too," he said.

"She's had it much harder than Sara, right, Dad?"

"Yes," he said. "And I think Sara knows that."

What he didn't know, what he wanted to know, was whether Clay understood how Austin felt about him. Which he almost didn't know himself, but he knew that being with Clay was a good thing, and that they seemed to click in a way he'd not experienced before.

That Clay was a man was fast on its way to becoming unimportant, a category that was of no consequence. That Clay was patient with Austin was another thing that he cherished, and he refused to let himself dwell on how Mona had taken it that first evening when he couldn't get it up.

Which had been badly, as she'd slapped his thigh in her frustration, then pushed him off her. He'd slept on the couch that night and many nights afterward, until she'd let him back in their bed because heaven forbid, what if the neighbors found out! Enough about Mona. He'd rather think about how sweet Clay was, how he made Austin feel good about himself. And of course, he'd rather think about Bea, who was holding her e-reader in both hands, totally focused on reading aloud to him.

"Is this the part where Becky leaves the pin cushion covered with old flannel?" he asked, having lost the train of the story.

"That's right," said Bea. "With the words *Menny hapy returns* written with straight pins in the flannel."

Bea continued reading until Austin heard her voice get tired. Then he told her to close her e-reader, tucked her into bed, and left the light on in the bathroom, in case she got anxious about being in a new place.

In the morning, he'd see if the store had nightlights. And he'd make sure of Clay, make sure he was okay. That was as important, it seemed, as anything else.

All during the night, the wind moaned around the eaves of the small cabin, but it seemed to have done a good job of blowing the clouds away, for in the morning the sun was streaming through his newly curtained window, and beyond the sky shone like polished sapphires.

It might still be too wet to actually ride, but he'd show Bea around, make sure to acquire cowboy boots for a little girl, somehow. He also wanted to meet up with Clay, for he'd never said thank you for making the drive to and from Thornton with him. And then when he had to take Bea home again? He'd want Clay with him, for he didn't know how he'd manage that journey without him.

They got ready, Bea laughing as she brushed her teeth, spraying toothpaste everywhere, him pretending he'd forgotten how to shave.

All of this was feeling very much like the time Mona had gone for a girls' weekend that had turned into a girls' week, with Mona and her pals ending up in Vegas, and the credit card bill through the roof.

But he'd not minded, for he'd taken time off work and just spent time with Bea, at the park, taking her to the Denver Art Museum *and* Elitch Gardens. He'd held her hand as they discussed whether she was tall enough for Twister II, the ten-story high wooden roller coaster. When he'd sensed her fear, he shook his head sadly and told her she wasn't, and that she should wait another year till she was taller. Her casual response that it was okay told him he'd done the very right thing.

In that regard, it would be likely that Bea's first ride on the roller coaster would be with her friends. In the meantime, they had gone on the Blazin' Buckaroo mini roller coaster, and rode the horses on the Carousel, and braved the DragonWing flyer, a kind of Harry Potter knockoff, and ate much more cotton candy and funnel cake than was good for either of them.

Now, though, as he took her hand and together they walked along the muddy path beneath the still-dripping trees to the main lodge, he felt this was going to be even better than that, for with nothing to distract them, he could show her all the reasons he'd fallen in love with the ranch.

A small breeze stirred around, bringing the scent of some kind of sweet flower, and she giggled a little bit, holding her hand over her head as if to block getting wet, without minding that it felt like it was still raining.

"Will they have pancakes, Dad?" she asked, half-skipping, pulling on him to hurry, in case someone else ate all the food before they got there.

"I do believe so," he said with all the seriousness the question deserved. When you were nine, pancakes were of utmost importance. "They might, and I say *might*, have chocolate chips in them."

She squealed with delight and tugged even harder and by the time they reached the steps of the main lodge, she was pulling so hard she was at an angle, and he was leaning back to support her weight, so he was at an angle, and it was all so deliriously joyful that he laughed out loud.

"There's Clay!" With an excited shriek, Bea let go of Austin and raced to the steps. "Clay, Clay, Clay!" she shouted to Clay, jumping on the step as he stood up with a box in his hands.

"Hey," said Clay. He held out a box, which Austin could easily see held a small pair of cowboy boots of just the right size, or close enough, for a little girl of nine. "I went down to the store and made 'em open up early, 'cause I knew just the pair. They're dark brown, an' I think—" Clay paused and leaned down to hold the box out to Bea. "I think you'll like them. They're definitely not pink."

Sensing perhaps Bea's hesitation at taking the offering, he opened the lid and slid it beneath to reveal a pair of glossy brown boots with a diamond pattern in lighter brown stamped out, with red outlining each diamond.

"Oh!" Bea clasped her hands to her face.

"Everything all right, honeybee?" asked Austin, warm all through at the thought of Clay's generosity, not just in the gift but in the act of it. Clay worked long hours and for him to get up even earlier than he already did to fetch a pair of boots for a little girl he'd only just met was beyond kind.

"They're perfect," she said with a sigh, reaching out to touch the pointed toe of one. "Can I put them on now, Dad? Can I?"

Clay looked at Austin, his eyes bright as new stars, and half-shrugged, smiling as if he meant to off-set any scolding Austin might deliver at having done all this without checking with him first.

"Yes, of course," said Austin. "Quick as you can so we don't keep Clay from his breakfast."

That, of course, wasn't the point, but he had to focus on helping Bea sit down to pull her sneakers off, tucking them in the box to hold them at his side while she tugged on the boots, the cuffs of her jeans all lopsided, and hopped up and down on the wooden step with great force.

"Lookit!" she said, her face flushed in her excitement and pleasure as she balanced on her heels and clicked her toes together exactly three times. "They're so perfect, so pretty."

Austin opened his mouth to remind her to say thank you, but Bea beat him to it, clung to Clay's hand and as she hopped up and down, said, "Thank you, thank you so much!"

On the top step, she turned and held out her right booted foot for Austin to admire.

"I'm ready for my riding lesson now," she said, smiling wide.

"We won't forget," said Austin. "I promise."

"Shall we go to breakfast?" asked Clay as Austin climbed the steps and took Bea's other hand. "I mean, can I eat with you?"

A little stunned that Clay even felt the need to ask, Austin moved close, not quite close enough to hold hands, but close enough so that Clay would know the words were meant only for him.

"Of course," he said low. "Had we not met this way, I would have texted you. Held you a spot."

He wanted to add *next to me*, so to make sure Clay understood, but maybe that wasn't necessary, for Clay smiled and those stars in his eyes brightened.

"Thank you for the boots," Austin said.

"Happy to do it," said Clay.

Together they got in line for chocolate chip pancakes and whatever other delicacies were in store for them. They were able to get a spot at the long table beneath the window and Austin made sure Bea was facing out, or tried to, as Bea preferred facing in so she could watch all the people, her eyes wide at all the activity and chatter and movement.

Other people sat near them so Austin, his heart filled with gratitude for what Clay had done, could not say all the things he wanted to but kept his conversation neutral.

It felt like he was almost having to put a lid on his feelings, the way he'd always done with Mona, to keep the peace, to go along to get along. But in this instance, he knew, underneath it all, that he just needed an opportunity to speak to Clay. To be with him in a quick private moment, so he could share all that was whirling around inside of him.

At the end of breakfast, Ellis came in, carrying another box, this one a bit bigger than the one Clay had brought. He came up to the table and, standing on the far side of Austin, laid the box in the middle of the table.

"Is this what I think it is?" asked Clay, pointing at the box as he scrubbed his hands on his napkin.

"Delivery," said Ellis, nodding, then he moved away quickly and went back out of the dining hall.

"Why does he do that?" asked Austin quickly, unable to restrain himself.

"Do what?" Clay picked up the box and held it in his hands and grinned at Bea, who grinned back.

"Always moving away, keeping his distance." Austin waved a circle in the air to indicate the distance he meant.

"Well, he's our ex-con, right?" Clay shrugged. "He thinks he's scary, so he does his best not to scare anyone."

"Oh." Ellis didn't seem all that scary, not to him, anyhow, but he appreciated Ellis' thoughtfulness. "So what's in the box?"

"Well," said Clay. He shook the box and held it up to his ear as though to hear what was inside. Bea giggled and held her hands over her mouth, that is, until Clay handed her the box. "It's a special delivery for the ranch's very most special guest."

Slowly, as though the contents might jump out and bite her, Bea slid the lid open. Inside, nestled in gold and pink-toned tissue paper, was a perfect little straw cowboy hat with a brown leather hat band and a very small fake blue flower in the front.

With a heartfelt sigh, Bea lifted the hat out, letting the box fall to her lap, the lid to the table, and put the hat on. Then she tried to jump up, but got tangled in the legs of the chair and it was only Clay's quick action that saved her from tumbling to the floor.

"It's my hat!" she shouted, causing heads to turn their way, smiles following from those who could see a little girl overjoyed as she plonked it on her head. "I'm a cowgirl, Dad, a *real* cowgirl!"

"I arranged it with Leland for her to join the beginner session at ten o'clock this morning," said Clay. "Is that okay? I figured she wouldn't want to wait any longer, and that you wouldn't mind."

"You've done so much," said Austin, knowing he'd not had any idea how to go about arranging the riding lesson, let alone acquiring boots and a hat for Bea. "I don't know how to repay—"

"Uh-uh." Clay shook his finger at Austin in a scolding manner. "What I did is what friends do. And you're my friend, right?"

"Right."

Austin wanted to say more, on account of all the words and feelings piling up inside of him, like they wanted to burst through some kind of invisible dam. But there were people around, and Leland came up to say good morning, and to admire Bea's hat and her boots as she pirouetted around, pleasure blazing from her as she danced and then curtsied. Everyone clapped.

Had Bea been any other little girl, he might have been worried about her ego at all the attention, but she giggled as she sat down to finish her breakfast, shining so brightly, he couldn't remember the last time he'd seen her so happy. She deserved to be spoiled and admired and loved and to be like this always.

Then his throat grew thick and his eyes were hot and he had to turn away and pretend he had something in them so he could scrub at them and collect himself, and tuck away the feelings that rose up. Of Bea, a happy little girl and how he was going to have to give her up in a week if not sooner, and how she hated it at Mrs. Delgado's—

He stood up and cleared his throat.

"Are we ready, Bea?" he asked her as he grabbed the box with her sneakers. "Let's go for a little walk and maybe I'll braid your hair before we go to the arena for the lesson."

"I'll see you there," said Clay.

"Yeah!" said Bea, grabbing her tray so she could follow Austin up to the bussing counter. "See you there!"

Once outside the main lodge, he paused at the top of the steps, and took Bea's hand, and looked at her.

"Yeah, Dad?" she asked, as though he'd asked her a question.

"You know the scene where Dorothy is in the house that has been set down in Oz?"

"Yeah."

"And you know when she opens the door and suddenly the world turns to color?"

"Yeah."

"Well, I want you to think about it like that. Like you're about to step through a doorway into another world. You've seen the cabin where we slept last night, and you've seen the dining hall—"

"And ate chocolate chip pancakes."

"Right." He nodded at her and clasped her hand tightly for a second. "And now, we're going to walk around and look at the river, and the birds overhead, and the green grass that stretches to the horizon."

"Like looking a painting, right, Dad?"

"Right, honeybee." He had to swallow hard at her earnest expression, at the curve of her nose, the flush in her cheeks, and thought about how beautiful she was, how happy she was, just to be where they were, standing on the top step of the dining hall, about to step into the day.

"I want you to point out all the colors to me as we go," he told her. "So I can paint them."

"Okay, Dad."

They stepped down the wooden steps and slowly walked along the road above where the valley spread out beyond the river, the blue sky meeting the far horizon. And as they headed even more slowly up the road, and through the trees, she pointed out the red of Indian paintbrush, the sage green of sage, the purple and red windflower, and long petals of yellow arnica nodding among the high grass.

The barn drew both of them like a magnet, him because Clay would probably be there, and her because horses would most definitely be there. As they walked into the cool, shadowy barn, Leland came out of his office to meet them.

"Excellent," he said, smiling, pleased. "You're just in time to meet some horses, and maybe help groom them for the lesson."

"Oh," said Austin, thinking this through. "I need to get her hair braided before then, so maybe we ought to head back for a bit before we get into all of that."

"Oh, no," said Bea, tugging on his hand. "Please, Dad? Can't we stay. Can't I pet the horses an' help groom them? My hair will be okay."

What was he doing? He was acting like Mona, taking all the fun out of everything before it'd even begun. So what if her hair flew around and got tangled? So what if he'd have to take extra time to help her comb it out before bedtime? So what?

"Got a horse comb here," said Leland. "Brand new. And there's string to make a braid, like we do with the horses."

"*Dad.*" Bea practically breathed the word. "I can be like a *horse.*"

Which was how, after all of everything, Bea was propped on two hay bales, holding her hat in her hand while Austin used a new horse comb to neaten her hair. Which was how Clay found them when he came into the barn, whistling.

"I can braid that," said Clay. "We'll do it just like we do for trail rides when it's windy. A fishtail braid."

After Clay braided her hair with deft strokes, and Bea was ready, she got to lead each horse out of its stall, with Clay helping her. When the horses were all assembled in the arena, the guests who were also signed up for the lesson came to help, and someone found Bea a box to stand on, while Clay showed her how to be gentle as she brushed.

Leland came out of the barn to help, holding a tail comb and walking behind horses like he'd not a care in the world that they'd kick him.

"I'll make up the hours later," said Austin to Leland as he passed by him.

"Never mind that," said Leland. "It's your day off, as far as I'm concerned."

When the horses were groomed and saddled, Bea could almost not contain herself as she waited for her turn for help getting astride.

"This here's Travelle," said Brody, bringing a quiet-looking bay mare over to the mounting block. "She's perfect for a nice little girl like you."

"You have to move slowly around horses," said Clay, leaning down as Bea began to dance, kicking up dust. "Horses like calm, slow people. See? Look at her eyes. She's still waking up a bit."

"Okay," said Bea with a solemn nod.

Austin stood outside the arena, leaning against the wooden fence as he watched Clay assist Bea into the saddle. Clay was saying something to her, her nodding in response as he adjusted her stirrups and gave her one-on-one instructions how to hold the reins in one hand. The look on her face was something he folded into his heart to keep for later, when he couldn't see her every day. When he had to beg Mona for a chance to talk with her on the phone.

The only thing that gave him comfort, then, was the gentle way Clay talked to her. The way, even attending to all the guests, he kept coming back to Bea as the horses went around the arena at a quiet walk.

Then, when Brody called for everybody to trot, Clay was at her side, not touching the reins, but just being there so Bea could be brave, straighten her back and go with the trot.

She bounced a bit, but she was concentrating on her form, face flushed, eyes wide, and pleasure in her smile when she spotted Austin and waved at him. And in that moment, one hand on the reins, one hand in the air, not hanging on to the saddle horn like many of the other guests were, he was so proud of her, he could have exploded into a million pieces and not minded one bit.

24

CLAY

*T*he riding lesson went well, and Clay was pleased at how much Bea had enjoyed herself. Seemed natural and not afraid. He knew Austin was watching from the sidelines, leaning against the fence, doing his best not to shout out instructions like some kind of soccer mom. He let Clay do his job, let Bea find her own way, but stayed nearby in case she needed him.

After the lesson, as Clay hurried to help guests dismount, then brought out brushes and chamois cloths and sweat combs, taking away saddles to the barn to be wiped down. He lost track of Austin, but then saw him and Bea headed away, hand in hand, Bea looking up at her dad as she chattered and half-skipped in her new boots.

Maybe they were going to the fire pit and then through the long grasses down the hill to the river. Or maybe they were headed to the shade of the trees on their way to the river rock bridge. Wherever it was they were going, Clay longed to go with them.

The feelings were so new, that kind of longing, like a lost thing coming home, felt so uncertain he didn't quite know what to do with himself. He was the guy who could have sex with pretty much anyone he wanted to, just by crooking his finger at a handsome stranger and flashing his dimples. His ass had many admirers, as did his thighs, his smile.

Having sex in the alley behind the Rusty Nail used to be the culmination of his hard-working week. Only now, looking ahead to the weekend, that was the last thing he wanted to do. He wanted to be part of the father-daughter walk. Wanted to be part of simple events, like braiding hair, and horse lessons with Austin watching. Wanted to think a different way as to what was important and what was not.

Was he ready for that? If he and Austin truly started dating, he'd be dating a guy with a kid, which sounded so homey and sweet but also serious and maybe something he wasn't ready for.

He didn't know, so he threw himself into work, always checking his phone for text messages from Austin, which came, but which only told him what Austin and Bea were doing, rather than asking Clay to join them. Which was fine, really, it was. He needed to get his head on straight, and quit pining for a guy who had his daughter with him for only a short time.

Plus he had a job to do, a job that he loved and wanted to keep, so he volunteered for extra barn duty. Went with Jamie to pick up trash along the riverside. Helped Quint when the engine of his old blue and white truck started pinging, and they adjusted the fan belt and added some good oil, and didn't snicker when Quint patted his truck's hood and told Blue Jean that she was a good girl.

All of this was his everyday world, what he loved. And now there was Austin and Bea and maybe a new kind of world he could share with someone.

At dinner, he scrambled to clean up from where a cow had slobbered all over him as he untangled her hoof from a bit of barbed wire. He had helped Quint clean the wound, and watched the cow walk off like nothing had happened, and was late to clean up, late to dinner.

When he got to the dining hall, Bea and Austin were once again surrounded by people, the older couple, the three fun-loving middle-aged ladies.

Clay had to go sit with a couple with two teenagers who looked bored enough, like they wished they were somewhere else, but who, in the end, were well behaved enough to at least pretend to have a good time. Some people, well, the ranch wasn't for them, and that was okay by Clay because for some people, the ranch was everything.

The evening was clear and the air was dry, and Clay was happy to help set up the fire pit for Bill's story time. He wished he could plop down on a hay bale next to Austin and Bea and just listen to Bill draw out the ghost stories and hustle through the funny ones, but he was on tap to bring out supplies for making s'mores, and he was on tap for cleaning up after.

When he was done with that task, he discovered Austin and Bea had gone back to the cabin. And then realized it was simply too late to go knocking on that door to ask if Austin would like to stand beneath the light of the quarter moon and hold hands and kiss while night owls hooted and scolded and faraway coyotes sang to each other.

The next few days went like that, with Austin busy and occupied with Bea and his own job, leaving Clay in a state that felt like dust was settling on him, a drought with no rain in sight.

"Everything okay?" asked Leland on Thursday afternoon when the two of them were in Leland's office with Brody, going over the rotation for horses so the vet could come out and give them each a quick checkup.

"Everything's fine," said Clay, not waiting for a private moment with Leland, the way he would have done, had he wanted to share.

Normally he would have drawn Leland aside and asked him for advice, but that would be tantamount to asking Leland who Clay should become. Leland would, no doubt, tell Clay to be himself, and then ask why it was an issue. Then Clay would have to spill the beans and explain that he was steadily and inexorably falling in love with a tall, red-headed monk wannabe accountant with long muscles over pale skin Clay could not stop thinking about.

"You got your head on backwards," said Brody on Friday afternoon, when Clay moved too quickly with a saddle in his arms, tripped over the girth, and landed flat on his ass, looking up at Big Red's belly. "What's wrong with you lately?"

Standing up, pulling the saddle from the dirt, brushing it off, putting it to rights, Clay didn't want to say.

Brody was who Brody was. He didn't need anyone or anything and wouldn't understand how Clay could be so affected by the presence of a nerdy accountant. How a recently divorced straight guy, how that simple thing could make him feel like he needed to turn his life around. Needed to change who he was. He was so out of his depth he was drowning.

"It's the accountant, isn't it." It was not a question, and Clay pushed past Brody as he carried the saddle to the tack room. "I seen you looking."

"You have, huh?" Clay put the saddle on the rack and fiddled with the stirrups as he figured out what to say. "Well, maybe I am. So what."

"So nothin'," said Brody with a shrug. "Does he know?"

"Maybe."

"Maybe is not good enough." Brody shook his head and looked over Clay's shoulder to the main part of the barn, and took a deep breath. "You should always tell because maybe they don't know and you'll have missed your chance."

"I know."

"You want that?"

"No."

"Well, then."

Clay twisted himself up hard until he couldn't be any more tightly wound. Hating the feeling he tried to work it off by carrying more luggage to the parking lot than anyone else, hurrying so everyone was off the ranch, there'd be no guests to worry about, and he could find the gumption to tell Austin what he needed to tell him. Which was what? He didn't rightly know, but he had to get how he felt off his chest before he imploded.

Pulling out his phone, head down, he texted as fast as he could before he lost his nerve.

Where are you?

Within minutes, came the answer from Austin: *At Jasper's forge.*

Can I come? Talk to you?

Yes!

He rushed down the path, thinking only too late that he should have changed his shirt and combed his hair, gotten himself ready. But then he would have sweated through his shirt anyway by the time he got there, and Austin already knew what he looked like covered with hay, so what did it matter?

He arrived at the forge inside of five minutes, and hung back as he realized Jasper was giving a demo for Bea and Austin, just a private event for two.

Jasper loved to show what he could do with an iron rod and that hammer of his. Clay had to admit that the sight of sparks flying, the smell of hot metal, the deep rasp of metal on metal, was invigorating in a way that always surprised him.

Standing close by, pulling on the old-fashioned leather and wood bellows, was Ellis. He wasn't dressed in his foolish apprentice outfit, the one Clay liked to tease him about, but he was totally focused on what he was doing, on what Jasper was doing. Despite that, when he saw Clay, he lifted his chin in welcome.

"Hey." Clay moved to stand beside Austin, who was holding Bea's hand.

The heat from the forge wafted out at them, carried off by the vagaries of a cool breeze, and the scent of charcoal burning in the forge sifted over the scent of pine, drawing back, moving forward, drawing back again.

"And this is how we finish the metal," said Jasper. He nodded at Clay as he moved a now-flat bit of metal into a large rubber bucket of water, where it hissed and steamed. "We'll start again with the other side to make a butterfly that you can put in your garden."

Clay's heart was beating fast, but he was going to ask his question just as soon as he could draw Austin away from the forge. At the point when Jasper turned to get another rod of metal, Clay took a breath.

"Hey," he said. "I wanted to talk to you, but not here. Someplace. Out."

"Out?" asked Austin, totally focused on Clay now. "Like on a date?"

His eyebrows rose, but he didn't seem at all surprised, only expectant, and maybe a little hopeful, which gave Clay courage.

"Yeah." Clay felt warm through his chest, across his skin, energy racing inside of him. "Maybe we could go to a place that has good beer, like you told me about."

Saturday night was usually the night he went out and got laid, and here he was in the yard of Jasper's forge, beneath the dappled, sweet-scented shade, asking for something completely different. He was in the midst of sunshine and fresh air, miles away from a dank, urine-puddled alley.

Thinking of this contrast, doubts crowded in. Maybe this wasn't right for him. Maybe he didn't deserve this. Maybe Austin only wanted friendship. Maybe he had no idea and should just go ahead like he knew what he was doing.

"When would you like to go?" asked Austin, ever practical.

"Well, I have tonight off," said Clay. He shifted on his feet, put his hands in his pockets, then took them out again. "Saturday *is* my only night off."

"What about Bea?" Austin tugged on Bea's hand and looked down at her, and that was when Clay realized how selfish it was of him to ask Austin out when he only had a few days with his daughter before he had to give her back. "She can't go to a bar, which is where they serve beers."

"I don't like beer, Dad," said Bea. She bumped her head against his arm, then did it again just for fun, and smiled at Clay. "Grownups do, though."

"I could watch her," said Jasper. He came up to them, wiping his hands on a cloth, tugged on the edge of his apron to straighten it. "I've got a pony coming by for a set of new shoes, and plenty of ice cream and root beer in the fridge. It'll be fun. After all." Jasper smiled as he looked at Bea. "Someone's got to ride the pony to make sure the shoes fit, eh?"

"Uh—" Austin frowned, tugging on Bea's hand, and looked like he was doing his best not to look at Ellis.

Ellis scraped his hair out of his eyes and seemed like he wanted to back up until he was far, far away. Clay felt bad for him, but understood Austin's hesitation.

"We can do it another time," said Clay, rushing the words. "After Bea goes back to her mom."

Austin opened his mouth, probably to agree, but Bea let go of Austin's hand. She crossed her arms over her chest, stuck out her chin, and looked like she was about to stand her ground till the end of time.

"I want to stay at the forge," she said, stoutly. "I want to ride the pony and eat ice cream." Then her face softened, as if she realized that being a brat about it wasn't going to get her way. "Please, Dad? You and Clay can drink beer, and I just want—" With solemn green eyes, Bea looked at the forge, her chin wobbling.

Maybe she didn't know what she wanted at that moment, and Clay only wanted to break the tension. He'd asked the wrong question at the wrong time, and he needed to fix it.

"I want to stay, too," he said, in the same way Bea had just spoken, crossing his arms over his chest, in echo. "I want ice cream and to ride a pony. Can I?"

Ellis barked a laugh under his breath, and Jasper reached to pat him on the shoulder, and all at once, Austin relaxed.

"I keep forgetting I'm not with Mona anymore." He sighed and rubbed at his eyes and nodded at Bea. "Yes, honeybee, but promise me not to overdo on the ice cream, and with the pony—" He looked at Ellis and Jasper each in turn. "Be sure to follow their guidance, okay? We'll come back for you after we've had beers."

"Yeah!" Bea jumped up and down, tugging on Austin's hand with both of hers, jerking him down until he was close. "Thank you, Dad."

"You bet, honeybee." He kissed the top of her head and held out her hand to Jasper. "Well, I guess I'll go get ready for my date." He turned to Clay, his eyes soft, like Clay had given him a gift. "It is a date, right?"

"Yep." Clay shrugged, easing the tingling of his skin, the force with which his heart was beating.

He wanted somebody to tell him he was being brave, or to tell him he was being foolish, but until he spelled out what was in his heart to

Austin, there was nobody to tell him anything. He just had to move forward, to continue on like he started, and say what he felt. Otherwise, he would go on longing till the end of time.

"Now, Bea," said Jasper as he took her hand. "We need a new bucket of water, and sometimes Ellis, well, he's foolish, and doesn't always know how full to fill it. Will you help him?"

Giggling, Bea went with him into the shade of the forge, Ellis following behind, and Clay looked at Austin.

"Okay?"

"Okay."

Together Clay and Austin walked up the dirt road beneath the trees, going to the side as a truck pulling a small horse trailer came down the road. At the top of the hill, in the sunshine, the glassy river tumbling into white ribbons alongside them, Austin reached out to stop Clay.

"You wanted to talk to me?"

"I do," said Clay. "But I wanted it to be special, not like this. Not with me covered in hay and sweat."

"But I *like* you covered in hay and sweat." Austin moved close, as though they were in a crowded room, and what he had to say was meant only for Clay. "I like *you*, Clay."

He could tell Austin meant it, and his heart jumped in his chest. People normally enjoyed being with him, of course they did. He was tons of fun and cute as a cut button

As for Austin—he seemed to see inside of Clay, right to the heart of him, and didn't seem to expect him to be anything other than what he was. A ranch hand. A guy who was good with a long-distance scope rifle. A young man who worked hard.

If Austin could see into Clay's past, he'd know all the details about all the men, all the alleys, and maybe Clay would have to fill him in one day. But not today. Today was meant for something special.

"I'll tell you now, then," said Clay, taking his hands out of his pockets to touch Austin's face, gentle strokes from his fingers. "To spare you the suspense. I—" Now he had to take a breath and, in the bright sunshine, get it out, tell the truth. "I like you. A lot. And I don't care if you can't get it up. I just want to *be* with you. That's what I wanted to say."

"I wish I wasn't like this, I wish—" Austin's voice broke and to Clay's horror, his eyes shone with tears. Inside of a heartbeat, Clay slid his arms around Austin's neck and pulled him close, kissed his cheek. Listened to Austin's heartbeat thudding in his chest, felt the way he shook.

Austin gasped and pulled back, still holding onto Clay, with Clay's arms still around his neck.

"I never thought anyone would want me like this," Austin whispered.

"I want you." Clay swallowed and kissed Austin gently on the mouth, then on his nose. "And I'm willing to wait. For sure. For my tall, red-headed monk? I can wait."

Austin scrubbed at his eyes and huffed out a laugh and shook his head, as though at Clay's foolishness.

"Aren't you a little short for a Viking?" asked Austin, with a final wipe to his eyes with the edge of his sleeve.

"I have it on good authority that Vikings come in all sizes." Clay made a scoffing sound, then tugged on Austin's hand. "C'mon, let's go clean up for our date."

"Do they even have good beer in this state?" asked Austin, as if that was all that concerned him.

"We'll google it, my friend," said Clay. "And we'll drive as far as we need to to find it."

As they walked toward the staff quarters and the managers' cabins, Clay felt light-headed, buoyed up by bubbles of joy. He didn't know how they might manage, but he'd told the truth, and that was a very good start.

25

AUSTIN

*I*n the end, after sprucing up for their date, and Austin knew he'd put on way too much cologne, they searched on his phone for a decent place with good beer. They ended up going to Uncle Charlie's Tavern on the edge of Cheyenne.

They had to take Ladybelle on a good forty-minute drive down the highway, but well worth it, as the tavern was cozy and warm, with enough trendy beer to make anyone happy. They got a high-top just for two at the far end from the band, which was currently taking a break, and the cheeseburgers were so good, they ordered another one to split between them.

"Gah, this is good," said Clay. "I really like Levi's cooking, but sometimes, bar food just hits the spot. You know?"

"I do know," said Austin, taking another swallow of beer from a local brewery called Highgrass, and eased into his seat, relaxing further with each moment like this spent in Clay's company.

They'd gotten the hard part out of the way when Clay had told him his honest truth, that he just wanted to be with Austin, in spite of his troubles, in spite of everything.

And, looking at Clay now, at his dimples, that smile, the way his fair hair curled behind his ears, Austin wanted to wish on the stars in

Clay's blue eyes for a way to get over all of Mona's harsh words and looks of disgust. Wished he could leap into a future time, where he and Clay could just be together, like he imagined two men might be together. Which couldn't be too different from the way a man and a woman were together, could it?

There was so much he didn't know, but what he did know was that he wanted to be with Clay, and wake up with him in the mornings, and share late night pizza and Netflix at night. All of this drifted in and around ideas of sliding his hand down Clay's bare side, onto his hip, to feel the pulse and warmth of Clay's skin. To take him in hand and then do—what?

His only experience of anything sexy below the waist was Mona looking up at him from between his legs with a hard twist to her mouth, letting him pulse in her hand, always unhappy about it, always worried that his semen would get in her hair.

"Hey," said Clay. He reached to curl his fingers around Austin's arm. "Such a serious look. What are you thinking about?"

"Truth?" asked Austin.

"Of course."

"I don't know what I'm doing," said Austin. "I just know that, yeah, being with you makes me feel good. But as for everything else— maybe I should watch some gay porn, or something—"

To his astonishment, Clay laughed out loud, leaning back, his eyes sparkling.

"Oh, my friend," he said. "Sweet Austin. Porn is fine, but it's such an exaggeration of how it really is. Besides—" Clay leaned close, close enough to kiss Austin's cheek, close enough to lower his hand to Austin's thigh and cup his fingers tight for a brief second. "Maybe we should just fool around sometime, see how it goes. No pressure. No porn movies. Just you an' me. Right?"

That sounded better, much better. Easier. Austin nodded, the muscles on his neck feeling jerky and stiff. Then Clay kissed him soundly in front of everybody, and nobody seemed to care, so he took a deep breath and turned his head and kissed Clay right back.

They finished up the meal, genially arguing over who should pay.

In the end, Austin won, though this made Clay pout in such an adorable way that Austin kissed him in the doorway of the restaurant, and then again inside of Ladybelle. Inside of that kiss, their tongues met, warm, almost innocent, and Clay sighed, eyes half lidded as he cupped Austin's cheek.

"You're a good kisser for a straight guy," he teased.

"Well, you're a good kisser for a gay guy," said Austin before he thought. "Wait, I don't even know what that means."

"I don't either," said Clay, laughing as he started the truck. "Let's go pick up Bea before Jasper puts a leather apron on her and teaches her how to get that forge hot enough to melt iron."

Clay drove the truck along the dark, two-lane road that went parallel to the foothills, while overhead the stars twinkled and pulsed and made their presence known.

At one point, Clay slowed down at the top of a low rise, and turned onto a side road made of dirt that didn't have any name. There, he turned off the engine and they got out to crane their necks and take in the soft furrow of the Milky Way, streaming across the sky.

Austin took Clay's hand and kissed his fingers and knew that he was glad he'd said yes to Clay, yes to the job. Yes, to a new life. If only he didn't have to lose Bea when Mona wanted her back, then he might have been happy all the way through instead of hitting a wall of anticipated grief.

Clay, perhaps sensing these dark thoughts, made himself the little spoon, pulling Austin's arms around him, leaning back against Austin's chest. As they looked up, Austin kissed the side of Clay's neck, lightly, because he didn't quite have permission, but could't help himself.

Clay pressed back and back until Austin was against the truck, then turned around, pressing his front to Austin's front. Their hips met, snug and close, and while Austin started with surprise, he didn't move or push Clay away.

"Romantic, no?" asked Clay, sounding suave and silly all at once. "Two guys making out beneath the stars—"

"Like teenagers," said Austin, half gasping, half laughing as he looped his arms around Clay's waist. "What's our age, again?"

"I think we're, like, eighteen," said Clay, smiling as he kissed Austin, then frowned as though working the image through. "We're horny as hell and shouldn't be out this late."

"I remember." Austin pulled Clay close, tipping his head back to rest against a panel of Laydbelle's truck cab.

Clay let him and sighed, as if revealing in this closeness, in the warmth of Austin's chest and thighs and yes, the growing heat of his groin, which Austin could feel, even if it wouldn't amount to much.

Clay tipped his chin to let Austin kiss him along his neck and when Austin did, steady and sure of himself, Clay shivered and leaned into Austin's shoulder. He looked up at Austin, his etched against the darker night, his blue eyes lit with starlight, a curve to his mouth.

"Eighteen year olds also do a lot of groping," said Clay, nudging Austin's chin with his forehead. "I'll start, if that's okay."

"I remember that, too," said Austin. "But standing?"

"Yeah," said Clay, nodding as he pulled Austin's arm from around his waist. "And fully dressed. You grab me, an' I grab you. It'll be hot. Hot like the sun."

Austin tensed against Clay and then he took a breath and let it out in a whoosh. The sound faded into the dark, into the whir of the night breeze across the grasses, the rustle of trees along the low bank of a slow moving river at the bottom of the slope where they'd parked.

"If I start?" asked Austin, quietly. "Will you follow?"

"Yes," said Clay, his heart in his voice.

Clay held himself quite still, inhaling slowly as Austin held Clay against his chest like a damsel and kissed him. As Austin kissed him, he trailed his fingers down Clay's front, tugging at Clay's belt buckle, playing, teasing, before reaching down between Clay's thighs.

The touch felt hesitant to Austin, but Clay stayed still for a minute before barking out a laugh.

"Did I tickle you?" asked Austin, kissing Clay's ear.

"Nope," said Clay, smiling, turning his head so Austin could kiss him on the mouth. "I was just thinking I'd give you a helping hand an' it made me laugh. Just keep going, an' then I'll go."

Austin pressed his hand against Clay's cock and rubbed, gently, then a little harder, then gently again, which got Clay hard inside of a heartbeat or two. When he returned the favor, swirling his fingers along Austin's cock, trying to find his way through the layers of denim and cotton, Austin could feel a twitch, feel some warmth, and Clay kept going, doing what Austin was doing, gentle then hard, gentle than hard.

It was almost too much to be able to concentrate, what with Clay's sturdy fingers doing what they were doing, and the little sounds Clay made as Austin tugged and pulled on him.

"Something there," said Austin, the words muffled as he gasped for breath.

"Soft or hard?" asked Clay, to clarify the situation, kissing the corners of Austin's mouth, licking Austin's lower lip, sighing when Austin sighed.

"Hard," said Austin, his body shuddering at Clay's insistent touches. "I like it hard."

A breeze came up, chilly and full of the scent of faraway rain. It seemed to push Clay against Austin's body, then Clay reached between them, pressing with his fingers, halfway gripping the base of Austin's cock—mock squeezing before letting go to cup his hands between Austin's thighs and push up with his fingertips to surround Austin's balls with a pulsing grip-and-let-go motion.

Austin shuddered a groan, hardly believing that what they were doing was so simple but seemed to be putting them on the right track. Clay it again, trying to stay in a standing position as Austin copied the gesture and used it right back. Their rhythm, on again, off again, was in sync, their bodies warm against each other, the breeze cool on their warm skins.

When Austin felt Clay's body, Clay's cock hard against his belly, Clay seemed to hesitate, as though he was deciding whether it was okay for him to come if Austin couldn't—then it was too late, so Clay held the flat of Austin's palm against his pulsing cock, letting him feel it, letting the rhythm of it soak into Austin's body.

"Oh." Austin sighed into Clay's mouth, a tender flick of his tongue against Clay's tongue. "Oh."

"Good, huh?" asked Clay, tugging at his pants as Austin wrapped both of his arms around Clay's waist, pulling Clay to him once more. "Except now I got more laundry to do."

"I have quarters," said Austin. He took Clay's face in his and kissed him soundly, then softly. "Thank you. That helped."

"It'll work out," said Clay in the darkness, low so as not to disturb the nighttime sounds of wind rushing over the tall grasses. "It has to."

The world didn't work that way, so the idea of everything working out brought together the bitter and the sweet, the memory of Clay's touch mingling with Austin's lack of response. Still, he'd rather they stood beneath the stars and shared the intimacy, rather than do without being with Clay like this.

They straightened their clothes and got back into Ladybelle and drove to the ranch and down the road to Jasper's cabin. Where, like a small herd of deer, Jasper, Ellis, and Bea were standing in front of the forge as the truck's headlights passed over them.

Bea raced to the truck before it was even parked, and Clay jerked the truck to a stop as Bea hung on the open window.

"Dad, Dad, Dad," she cried, her voice full of blissful joy. "I got to ride a pony. I got to ride it over and *over* and make it trot up and down the road."

"Ellis was there every minute," said Jasper, coming up. "Holding onto the halter."

"Good," said Ellis on the other side of Jasper, and though whether he meant they'd all had a good time or that Bea had been a good girl, Austin didn't know. The word seemed to encompass the whole evening in a host of ways he couldn't even begin to sort out. But what did that matter, when a blanket of joy curled around all of them.

"Climb on in, Bea," said Clay.

Austin opened the door, and Bea clambered in to sit between them, like she'd been doing it that way all of her life.

"Thank you both," said Austin, waving out the open window as Clay turned the truck around and drove up the dirt road.

"That was fun," said Clay, smiling in the semi-gloom of the truck's cab, lit only by the dials on the dashboard.

"It was."

"We'll figure out a way to do it again, huh?"

"Is that you asking me for a second date?" asked Austin, teasing, smiling, his arm around Bea's shoulders, her head heavy in the curve of his arm.

"Yes," said Clay, his voice warm and soft. "If you'll have me."

"I'll have you," said Austin, almost automatically. Then he laughed and realized what he said. "I mean, as soon as I am able, you realize."

"We'll get there, my friend," said Clay. "We'll get there."

When Clay pulled the truck up in front of the glade of trees and the little dirt path that led to the managers' cabins, Austin kissed him, quickly, lightly, over Bea's head, then slid out, taking Bea with him, happy all the way through. With a small honk, Clay drove Ladybelle away, leaving the two of them in the dark shadows beneath the pine and aspen trees.

"I had a good time, Dad," said Bea. "You should go with Clay for beer all the time, and I'll stay with Jasper and Ellis."

"I'd like to," he said, and he meant it. "Now, let's get you to bed so we're fresh for the morning."

Once in the cabin, he turned on the ruby glass-topped table lamps, and monitored while Bea washed her face and brushed her teeth, chattering all the while about the forge and the pony and the ice cream float they'd had after dinner.

Once she was in her pajamas, he undid her braid and gently combed out all the tangles and waves. By the time she climbed into bed, he was able to turn off her bedroom light without any requests for water, or any announcement that Bea was going to read from her e-reader.

It had been a wonderful day, all the way around, and Austin found himself humming as he got himself ready for bed. In bed, dressed in his boxer-briefs, he tried an experimental sweep with his hand between his legs.

There was no response, none, though he felt a twinge in his belly, like it anticipated that there might be something, and sooner rather than later.

He rolled over, stretched out his legs beneath the single sheet, curled the pillow in his arms, and sighed. Applying for that accounting job at a faraway ranch and meeting Clay was the best thing, next to Bea, to ever happen to him in his life.

2 6

AUSTIN

*M*orning came quickly, with his phone ringing, which was odd for a Sunday. As he reached for his phone on his nightstand, he swung his legs over the edge of the bed, toes curling on the cool wooden floor.

The ID of the caller was Mona, but as it was only an hour later in New Orleans, he couldn't understand why she was up so early. Mona liked to sleep in. While on vacation? Mona liked to sleep in till noon, at least, especially if she'd been drinking the night before.

"Hey, Mona," he said as casually as he could after he'd thumbed the phone to answer it.

"Austin," said Mona, by way of greeting. "I guess I forgot the time difference, but whatever. I have news. Roger proposed to me last night."

Austin blinked at the streams of sunlight coming in through the open curtains, dappled with tree-shade, scented with early morning damp.

"Did you hear me?" she asked, irritation already lacing her voice. "We're getting married so I won't be getting alimony any more. I could use some help with the wedding, which is going to be this week in New Orleans, so I need you to still send me some money."

"Uh—"

"You're not saying anything," said Mona, the words accompanied by that hesitant laugh, like she wanted to make a joke of everything so she could get her way without hardly trying.

"I just got up, Mona," he said. "And I'm still trying to wrap my mind around all of this. What about Bea?"

He found he couldn't imagine sending Bea off in a plane by herself to New Orleans, or anywhere for that matter. It wasn't just the flight, it was the destination and the reason for it.

"What about her?"

Austin could almost imagine Mona rolling her eyes as she examined her manicured nails, looking for any flaw, concentrating on that because she already knew all of Austin's flaws. Her mind was probably full of wedding plans, as well, without the least bit of interest in Bea or her welfare.

"So can you send me the money or what?"

There was a sound in the background, and maybe it was from a high energy, never-ending party in the street. Or maybe it was Roger Colchet, telling Mona he wanted to fuck her in the next five minutes or else. At any rate, only half of Mona's attention was on her conversation with her ex-husband.

Mona's alimony and child support costs were high, but then, as an accountant, he made a lot of money. Or he used to, since while the ranch paid pretty well, it wasn't as much as his old job. But sure, he could send her a month's worth of alimony as a parting gift to help her with the wedding.

That would leave him with the responsibility of child support costs, which—

Like a runaway truck, came the idea of it—if he could get Mona to agree, Bea could be *his*. He could take care of her, make her smile, make sure she never had to wear pink, unless she wanted it, and when, *if* she wanted her ears pierced, he'd make sure it was done right at a nice, clean tattoo parlor, which Mona had always objected to.

On the heels of *that*, like a blow to his chest, came the realization that he had no idea where they would live. Surely he'd have to get a different job, rent an apartment somewhere, find a good school for Bea, all the things he wanted to do as a responsible parent.

But still—Mona might go for it, if he phrased it right—and hell, didn't he have an awful lot of experience doing that? And wouldn't Bea, his honeybee, his magical daughter, be better off with him than with Mona and Roger?

"Say, Mona," he said as casually as he could, given that his heart was thumping. "I have an idea."

"What's that?" she asked. "Does it involve you sending me a check overnight? Or a bank wire?"

"It's even better," said Austin. "I would think that maybe you want to be alone with your new husband for a few months, maybe a year. Does that sound about right?"

"Roger did say—" Mona broke off, making that humming sound she did when figuring out what might benefit her. "He did say he'd rather start with a new family, rather than somebody's leftovers—"

"Did he say that?" asked Austin, moved to reach through the phone to shove Mona aside so he could punch Roger over and over.

"Well, maybe not that." Mona laughed that laugh again, and Austin clamped hard on his anger. The trick to getting Mona to doing what he wanted was to make it seem like he was thinking of her needs, thinking of what Mona wanted.

"At any rate," he said, then took a breath. "If you send her to me and hand over total custody, I'll wire you that money first thing after I get the papers to sign."

"Are you saying you want her?" asked Mona. "But we have joint custody. I'm her mother, you know."

Affronted, Mona was speaking faster and faster, and Austin knew he had to say something, say the *right* thing, to settle her down, and get her to send those papers. Now that the idea was in his heart, he wanted Bea, and he would do anything to keep her.

"Yes, I want her," he said, as calmly as he could, given that his heart was beating so hard. "Send the papers. I'll sign and send them back with a bank wire. Then you can hire a jazz band and get married beneath trees draped with Spanish moss and everything. Think about it—bet you no one in Thornton will have a wild wedding like that, right?"

There was silence on the other end of the line, as if Mona was thinking this over, like she suddenly wasn't sure she wanted to give Bea up, even though it was obvious to Austin that Mona hadn't the slightest interest in being a real mother to Bea. And, as always, Mona was probably thinking of how this would benefit her before anybody else.

Austin knew to go on almost as if everything was settled, like it was just about a done deal. Almost like the papers were already signed, and a copy was in the lawyer's office.

"What do you think, Mona, my dear?" he asked in his brightest everything-is-perfect voice. "It sounds great to me, except for the fact that buying a wedding dress in New Orleans will be very expensive, so I don't know—"

"Wire the money," said Mona, like he knew she would because, as it usually had been in their married life, if Austin complained about the cost of anything, Mona wanted it all the more.

"I'll wire the money when I get the paperwork for full custody of Bea and not before," said Austin, a little shook at the coldness in his own voice.

Austin clutched the phone in both hands and waited. The trick was to stand your ground with Mona, at least when it was most important. If he could be brave during the next few seconds, Bea would be his daughter, his and his alone, and Mona's neglect and disapproval of Bea would be a thing of the past.

On the other end of the line he heard Mona talking and a low voice responding to her. Then with a huff, Mona was on the line.

"Roger says we're going to do that but you need to send *two* month's alimony."

Together, Mona and Roger were making him pay for his own daughter, like she was an object to be traded, bought and sold. But

love was more important than money, so Austin swallowed his stran-
gled reply, along with a half-hysterical laugh.

"Do you want half up front?" he asked, politely.

Austin heard more sounds of conversation, as though Roger and
Mona were discussing the issue.

Then Mona came back.

"Roger says he trusts you."

"All right, then," said Austin, not having any idea what to make of
Roger except that he was a money-grubbing asshole who deserved
Mona and then some. "It is Sunday, but I bet you could get Mr.
Bledsoe on the line and have him get the papers together, along with
your e-signature. Then you can send everything by overnight, to
arrive tomorrow."

"Fine." Mona's response was clipped, but it was obvious she didn't
care how he felt about it, or how Bea might feel about it. She only
cared that she'd gotten what she'd wanted, and what she'd probably
not realized she'd wanted, which was to have no daughter at all.

"That sounds great, Mona," he said, being his boldest self. "We'll
figure out the details of Bea visiting you, but anyway, bye for now."

He hung up, his thumb on the phone as he clutched the phone in
both hands. And decided he wouldn't say anything to Bea until the
papers were signed, just in case Mona pulled a fast one. Then he
slumped as he clunked the phone on the nightstand.

Dealing with Mona was exhausting, trying to figure her next
move, impossible. He just had to move forward like it was going to be
smooth sailing.

And he needed to talk to Clay. Needed to figure out where he and
Bea would live, because surely the idyl that was the ranch couldn't
continue forever. How far away he'd have to move to find a good
school for her, he didn't know, but it might be too far to continue
what he had with Clay, even as it was just starting. But then, he'd have
Bea to look after, and surely that was the most important thing. His
own needs would have to be sacrificed.

"Bea," he called, standing up, reaching for yesterday's blue jeans, scrambling into his shirt and his boots. "Time to get up. Time to go to breakfast. Are you awake?"

As though from a distance came a sleepy affirmation. But like the good girl she was, Bea got dressed while he shaved and then he helped her get ready and brushed her hair into a ponytail, which, after yesterday, seemed quite appropriate. She insisted on wearing her cowboy boots and hat, even though there wouldn't be any riding that day, and hand in hand they marched up to the main lodge, meeting Leland along the way.

"Hey there," said Leland, with a wave. "It's a beautiful morning, prettiest of the season."

"That it sure is," said Austin, agreeing, stomach sinking at the fact he'd soon have to give his notice and move on from the ranch, and mornings like this one would only be a memory.

The gathering in the dining hall was thin, occupied only by staff, as it was Sunday with no guests due till at least noon. Austin helped Bea get her pancakes and bacon, urged her to take a little bowl of honeydew melon, got himself the same, and a huge mug of coffee, black, so he had enough energy to face the day. To face Leland, and more importantly, to face Clay and tell him how everything was going to change.

Just as he put his tray down next to Bea's at the long table, he spotted Clay going out.

"Bea," he said to her. "Stay here and eat with Leland, okay? Leland, I'll be right outside the door but I need to—"

"Not a problem," said Leland. "You all right staying with me, young miss?"

Bea covered her mouth and giggled and Austin hurried out of the dining hall and down the wooden steps of the main lodge, there to catch up to Clay halfway to the barn.

"Hey," said Clay, turning at the sound of Austin's footsteps. "I'm sorry I couldn't wait breakfast, but a bunch of cows and horses broke through the barbed wire early this morning, and Quint, Brody, and I are going to round up the animals and patch it up."

"I wanted to tell you—" Austin's breath caught in his throat at the way the sunlight lit up Clay's fair hair and the warmth of the morning flushed his cheeks, and how he stood there, sturdy and strong and just about ready for anything the day might throw at him—except what Austin was about to tell him.

"What's up?" asked Clay. "Do you mind walking? I have to be at the barn about five minutes ago."

"I'll tell you quick," said Austin. He reached out and tugged on Clay's arm, not wanting to share this news with anyone else but Clay.

"Okay." Clay stopped, looking at Austin full on, rather than having half his mind on the task ahead of him. "What is it? You look funny. Is Bea okay?"

"She's fine; she's with Leland." Austin shook his head, and looked at the young man he cared about very deeply and found he couldn't imagine being with anyone else. But all of that was at risk. "The thing is, Mona is going to marry Roger. That's the guy she's in New Orleans with. And he doesn't want Bea, so Mona is giving Bea to me. I'll have full custody once she sends those papers. All I have to do is sign them and send them back."

"That's amazing." Clay's smile was bright, his eyes full of pleasure, and he moved close, as though for a celebratory kiss.

"The only thing is, I can't stay here. I can't raise Bea here."

"What do you mean?"

Austin shook his head, thinking of everything Bea had had in Thornton, including one of the best elementary schools in the Denver area, and ballet lessons, and art classes, and libraries, and all the culture a little girl needed.

"It's nice of Leland to lend me the cabin for a little while, but it's not a full-time option. Bea needs something more stable than this. It's fun in the summer, but this isn't something that will work in the fall, when she needs to go to school. I need to move us back to Denver. There's nothing for her here."

"What do you mean there's nothing for her here?" Clay lifted his arms expansively, as though to gather all of Farthingdale Ranch in his arms to show it to Austin.

"It's the middle of nowhere, Clay," said Austin, on the verge of thinking he was saying it all wrong, only it was too late, it was already out there. "It's flyover country. I can't raise her here. I need to get her set up for a new school in the fall. Please understand—"

"It was good enough for you yesterday," said Clay, a huff in his voice, a hard flush to his cheeks. "You liked it plenty fine *yesterday*."

"I *do* like it fine." Scrubbing at his mouth with his hand, Austin tried to explain it another way. "Those stars last night, with *you*, were amazing."

"But you're saying this life is no good, that's what you're saying." Clay blinked hard, frowning, the lines between his eyebrows fierce. "Or you're saying it's only good if it's temporary, like a summer guest who stays a week and then goes. Guess I was a summer fling to you, then. Good enough for yesterday, right?"

"That's not what I mean at all," said Austin, desperation rising inside of him. "I'm just trying to do what's right for Bea."

"Move to the city, then," said Clay, toneless. "Meanwhile, I live *here*, and I have work to do."

Clay turned and started walking to the barn, passing beneath the trees. He glanced at Austin over his shoulder, and Austin couldn't believe how badly it had gone. He'd said all the wrong things, hurt Clay's feelings when he'd not meant to. But what else was he supposed to do? The ranch was like summer camp. It was fun while it lasted, and then you went home. Right?

Slowly he made his way back to the dining hall, all appetite gone, shoulders tight, all the stresses of his old life coming down on top of him. Back at the table, he sat down and drank some coffee, now half cold, and watched Bea chatter happily to Leland, who mostly nodded as he ate his breakfast, as if a fast-talking little girl was part of his everyday world.

"Meant to tell you," said Leland, as Austin poked at his breakfast. "Sue Mitchell's bringing the Frontier Girls up today to Jasper's forge. They're going to build a fire without matches and then bake bread in an old coffee tin. Sue wants to know if Bea would like to join them."

"Today?"

"Later this morning, I think." Leland looked at Bea, tipping his head down. "You interested, young miss?"

"Yes, please," said Bea, lighting up, sitting up straight.

After that, there was nothing for it but to finish breakfast, bus their trays, and head on down to the forge, holding hands, Bea skipping in the bright morning sunshine while dark clouds oozed through Austin's heart.

27

AUSTIN

*A*fter Austin walked Bea to the forge, he went slowly back up the hill in the dappled shade, going even more slowly than he ever had, as though fearful of what he might find at the top. There, he looked across the road to the dirt track that Leland had mentioned led to a replica of a cabin that had once stood there. To the right was the parking lot, empty of cars.

The office was locked up for Sunday morning. If he wanted, he could wait until Maddy showed up at noon to get the keys, and or he could get them right now from Leland and get straight to work, even if it was a Sunday. Which would be a shame, as the day was quite beautiful with a soft breeze coming off the river, the grasses green and lush from all the recent rain, the trees bursting with energy.

Wind stirred his hair. He should have brought his hat. Should have stayed with Bea and the Frontier Girls and joined in the fun, as he'd been invited. But most of all, he knew he should have done better by Clay. Who was no doubt still working hard, fixing barbed wire fences, herding animals to other locations while repairs were going on.

A new set of guests would be arriving today, so Clay would be extra busy, as he was every day. The time he'd taken out of his own work days for Austin's sake, for Bea's, was amazingly kind. The thought of Clay's smiles, those sweet dimples, ruined into a frown by Austin's carelessness, what had he been thinking? On the other hand, it was the truth. The ranch was no place to raise a little girl.

He headed up to the barn where Leland would surely be. Then he'd get the keys, go to his office, and get some work done. He was behind anyway, and the slog of catching up would keep his mind occupied, which was the best thing, really.

The barn was quiet except for Brody, who was doing something in the tack room across from Leland's office, where the door was open, as it usually was. Leland was at his desk, typing on his computer, looking out of place with his rolled-up shirtsleeves and sweat along his jaw, mud on his boots. No doubt he'd been in the field helping with the fence repairs and was now writing about it or ordering more barbed wire without taking time to clean up.

"Hey, Leland," said Austin as he came to the door.

"Morning," said Leland, not taking his eyes off the computer. "BLM and the ranch split fencing costs, so I'm sending them a short email." He finished his email, then leaned back in his squeaky wooden chair with a smile. "What brings you to me, sir?"

"If I could get the keys to the office," said Austin. "I thought I'd catch up on some work I missed this week."

"Surely." Leland reached to the row of hooks behind him and grabbed the keys. Then he paused, still gripping the keys in his fist. "You look a mite troubled," he said. "What's up?"

Austin thought to ask how Leland knew, but then Austin already knew the answer to that. He was holding himself like a stiff board, the way he did when having confrontations with Mona, as though he figured that doing that might help him resist her barbs, her hard-flung words. But Mona wasn't here and wasn't likely to ever be anywhere near the ranch, so why was he holding on to old habits that were no longer of use?

When Leland waved to the other chair, Austin sat down.

"Everything all right with Bea?" asked Leland, as he laid the keys on the desk like a promise. "She's a sweet little gal, for certain."

"That she is," said Austin. "She's at the forge right now, lighting fires with her bare hands and sifting flour to make some kind of can bread."

"That's campfire bread," said Leland. Then he shook his head and smiled as if at some inner memory. "It always burns on one side, somehow." He straightened up and focused on Austin once more. "So Bea is well. What about you? Liking your job? Happy at the ranch?"

"I love it here," said Austin, and he meant it.

Not used to having someone to talk to about these things, he didn't quite know how to proceed, or how much to share. But Leland had been good to him, and really seemed to care about the well-being of people on his ranch. Clay sang his praises almost every day, and Austin knew Clay well enough to know that couldn't be faked. Leland was a good guy. Austin should just tell him.

"My wife, I mean my ex-wife, called this morning," he said, settling into the chair, then leaned forward to rest his elbows on his knees. "She wants to give me full custody of Bea. I agreed. The papers are coming this week."

"Well, that's wonderful."

Austin looked up. Leland's smile was broad and seemed to encompass all the good this would mean for Bea.

"Only it means changes." Austin straightened up, rubbed his bejeaned thighs with his hands, and took a deep breath. "I've got to get a job in the city, get an apartment, get Bea ready for a new school in the fall—"

"Why a new job?" asked Leland. "Seems to me you already got one right here. Working for me."

"I do have a job and I love it, but—" He sighed. "I'm a single parent now. I need to do what's best for Bea. There are no close schools, no close hospitals, or libraries. No—" He stopped himself from saying *no culture* because that would be out and out rude, not to mention judgmental. He wanted to kick himself for thinking like that, but wasn't he looking out for Bea? Trying to do his best by her?

"Well, there's an elementary school in Chugwater," said Leland, slowly. "Or if you'd rather, there are several good ones in Cheyenne. Junior high and high schools there, too."

"But that's an hour commute each way."

"No more'n people drive in the city," said Leland, quietly, as if to counter Austin's agitated state. "There're ways around that such as long distance learning and such. At any rate, let's stop right here and look at this more sensibly before you go running off to Denver or some such place."

"Okay."

"The ranch shuts down in the winter, did you know that?" asked Leland.

"Yes," said Austin. "I've seen the records."

"Sometimes Quint stays over the winter, but mostly it's Brody, looking after the animals, keeping an eye on things." Leland ran his hand through his hair, making it stick up behind his ears. "With that laptop, you can work for me from anywhere, or maybe stay at the ranch in the winter. And in the summer, why, it's working out fine for you and Bea to live in that cabin. And we can put her to work, too, keep her busy and out of trouble."

"Work?" asked Austin, half sputtering at the thought of Bea digging fence post holes or lifting hay bales like a man. "She can't do that kind of work."

"Easy now," said Leland with a laugh. "Not grown up work, mind. Something a kid can do. She'll have plenty of fresh air and good food, and she'll grow up straight and tall with the wind in her hair. Ride all the horses she wants. She'll learn more and have more fun than any classroom, any day care you'd like to think of."

Austin found his eyes growing hot with tears at the thought of such a life for Bea, and scrubbed at them hard while Leland, rather than pretending he didn't notice, looked at Austin straight on.

"You can't always know what tomorrow will bring," said Leland, quite gently. "So just think about today. Think about what you want, and what Bea might want. Come back tomorrow. You still want to leave? That's fine. I'd pay you for the entire month, on account o' you did such fine work so far. But think about it, will you? Now, get. I have to go help the boys with those fences."

Taking his hat and putting it on firmly, Leland got up and strode out of the office. Which left Austin sitting there looking at an empty chair that rotated slightly with the energy of its former occupant still in the wood.

Across the way, Brody clomped around in the tack room, whistling tunelessly under his breath while in the box stalls horses stomped their hooves and blew out breath and genially ate their high quality alfalfa hay. The smell of leather oil mixed with horse sweat and hay dust, stirred together by the fine, light breeze in the open double doors of the barn.

Austin could see out to the blue sky and the grasses waving and the thin layer of white clouds along the horizon. He got up and walked out of the barn, out of the shade, standing in full sun while Leland's words worked their way into him. And thought about Bea as a young woman, riding up on horseback, the wind in her hair, her eyes full of joy, and how maybe she'd lean down to him to tell him about her day and how maybe she'd not be too old to say *Dad, Dad, Dad,* full of excitement to see him.

If he took that opportunity away from her, he'd be thinking very small indeed. If he limited them both to a life in the city, simply because it was what they were used to, then he'd be cutting her off from the grand adventure that life could be, that is, if he didn't make her afraid simply because he was afraid.

And that was the truth of it. He had always been on edge, walking on eggshells around Mona, perhaps from the very beginning, even without realizing it. But now, at the ranch, he'd begun to turn into a different person, one who wasn't afraid all the time, realizing that life was bigger than a beige-painted split-level house in a suburb with green lawns, each lawn just like the one next to it.

And it was bigger than trips to the museum, although those were fun, and they could always visit one—they could always order books, and paint, and watch movies on his laptop. And after, they could hold hands, while she was still little enough to do that with, and walk down to the river and watch the barn swallows wheeling above the water, diving in for a drink before sailing up into the sky again.

And then there was Clay. Maybe out of his own fear, his own troubles, Austin had used his sudden custody of Bea to shove Clay away, to abandon even trying what they'd just begun, like some kind of coward. He'd faced Mona in her worst moods, her most demanding moods, and come away scarred forever, but that was no reason to have done what he'd done to Clay. Tossed him aside like he didn't matter, which was the worst wrong, because he *did* matter. Mattered so much that Austin laid his hand over his heart, trying to soothe the pounding there. The ache in his gut, the twist in his belly.

But he couldn't just fling himself at Clay's feet, could he? Clay was hardly going to forgive him and besides, even if he did, he wanted Bea to know—couldn't imagine telling her, *hey, honeybee, your Dad's got a boyfriend, is that okay?*

Her approval was equally as important as his own desire to be with Clay. Sure, if she'd been an older teenager, it might not be as important, but she was only nine, and had been through enough upheaval with the divorce, traveling to Wyoming, leaving all her friends and familiar things behind, for him to continue on without her consent.

He needed to think about this and he needed to talk to Bea and he needed to keep himself busy until she was done at the forge. And then, maybe—no, more than maybe. He needed to apologize to Clay.

Whether Clay would forgive him was another matter, but in the meantime, he needed to keep busy, so he went back into Leland's office, grabbed the keys, and headed down to the office. There, he unlocked the door and settled at his desk, opening his laptop and sharpening his pencil so he could make notes if he needed to.

Then he worked, going through receipts, finally opening the top banker box in a pile of banker boxes to straighten out the last five years of accounting, sloppy and sketchy, though the ranch had done well for itself since the day it had opened. Except for last year, of course; they were still recovering from last year.

Work took him till late afternoon, as he'd skipped lunch, not wanting to run into Clay until he'd talked to Bea. As for Bea, he went down to the forge to fetch her for dinner, and found that the Frontier Girls had all gone home. Bea was at the side of the river, soaked up to her knees, stuffing small piles of weeds and trash into a black plastic bag. Close by, Ellis and Jasper, wearing waders from the waist down, moved in the river, laughing and splashing each other and Bea in the process.

It looked all so simple, the two of them watching his little girl for him while they carried on with their regular life. And maybe it *was* that simple. Maybe he'd been making it more complicated to avoid committing himself to this new life, which was foolish, since it was obvious, at least it was now, that his new life had already been long underway, from the point when Clay had picked him up in the rain at that Motel 6.

Ellis saw him first and waved, a soundless greeting curving his mouth to a smile. Bea saw him next and, still carrying the bag, dragged it over to him. Her shirt was damp in large splotches, and there was a weed in her hair and a smudge of what looked like chocolate on her cheek, and she was as happy as he'd ever seen her. *Ever.*

"Dad, Dad, Dad," she said, coming up to hug him, hard, and he almost cried, right in front of everybody.

"We tried to call you," said Jasper, climbing onto the bank of the river, a dangerous-looking pitchfork in his hand. "Figured you were busy, so we just kept her."

"Thank you," said Austin, heartfelt. "I must have left my phone at the cabin." He looked down at Bea, sweeping her hair back from her flushed face. "Did you have a good time, honeybee?"

"Yeah!" She jumped up and down, bumping against him, almost spilling open the black plastic bag of trash. "We had campfire bread, and then, for lunch, guess what we had, Dad. Guess!"

"Uh—" He scrunched his face and pretended to think very hard. "Roasted tennis balls?"

"No!" Her laugh raced through her body and she leaned against him, looking up, shaking her head as though he was the silliest dad on the planet. "We had tomato spaghetti, that's what we had. And milk."

"How did you get her to eat tomatoes?" Austin looked at Jasper in wonderment.

"I don't know," said Jasper with a shrug. "Ellis fixed 'em with a bit of garlic, 'cause he likes 'em that way. He's learning to like tomatoes, too."

The smile the two men shared between them made Austin's heart ache all over again.

"Thank you," he said again. "I'll take her to dinner now. You ready, Bea?"

He held out his hand, and as Jasper took the black plastic bag, Bea let go of that and held on to his hand. He squeezed her fingers gently, and the two of them ambled up the road to the main road that would lead to the lodge. All along, absently pulling the weed out of Bea's hair, licking his thumb to remove the smudge of chocolate, he kept his eyes out for Clay.

At the steps of the lodge, he paused, looking around, but no Clay. Inside, the dining hall was bustling with the excitement of guests newly arrived, ready to dive into their vacation experience, which left Austin feeling a little bit like an old, experienced staff member, which was fine with him and what he was, really.

After he and Bea got their dinners, hearty helpings of meatloaf and gravy, he sat at the long table across from Brody, who was halfway done with his meal.

"Where's Clay?" he asked, helping Bea with her utensils, her napkin.

"Don't know." Brody shrugged, his eyes looking elsewhere. "Think he took Ladybelle for a drive. Don't know when he'll be back."

That told Austin everything that he already knew, that he'd hurt Clay, enough to make him drive off on a Sunday night, when the ranch was at its most frenetic. Clay prided himself on being there when Leland needed him, or when a guest needed him. That he'd driven off was Austin's fault, pure and simple.

After dinner, as they left the dining hall, Austin kept looking, though he knew Clay would not be there. Beside him, dragging her feet, head down, Bea hung on his arm.

"You had a big day, huh?" he asked her. "What do you say we get you home, and you hop in the shower, and I'll braid your hair wet so it'll be all curly in the morning?"

"Like a horse's mane," she said, smiling, tugging on his hand even harder. "And if nail polish is like hoof oil, I have some."

"What do you mean?" he asked, squawking. "Did your mom get you nail polish?"

"It's only pink, Dad," she said, rolling her eyes at his foolishness. "Bubble bath pink, it's called."

"I thought you didn't like pink," he said.

"This is different."

A lot of things were going to quickly become different, and he sensed, somehow, that he needed to make the most of this moment, and all the moments to come, as best he could. So he squared his shoulders and tugged on her hand.

"Can I put some on me, too?" he asked, raising his eyebrows in hope.

"Sure!" She tugged on his hand right back and pulled on him to hurry.

When they reached the cabin, they carried on as they usually did, with Bea in the shower, and him looking at his paints and his brushes and paper, all piled on his dresser in his room, wondering if he and Clay would ever go out in search of a view again.

When Bea came out, dressed in her pink and blue Lilo and Stitch pajamas, he dragged one of the kitchen chairs out onto the porch, where she sat facing the sunset while he carefully combed her hair and braided it. Unbraided it, then combed it again, and braided it again. All the while Bea relaxed and sighed and the kick of her heels became slower and slower.

He finished, and she hopped up to bring back a little bottle of pink nail polish, some tissue paper, and a bottle of purple nail polish remover. She sat in the chair and handed everything to him, and he did his best to apply the polish. When it was his turn, he sat in the chair, and she put polish on his nails, doing a better job than he did, far tidier.

"It's okay, Dad," she said as she came out after putting the nail things away. "It takes practice, at least that's what Mom says."

"Bea," he said, getting up to push the kitchen chair aside. "About that. Come sit with me on the steps for a minute."

"Okay," she said, plopping down next to him, flinging her still-wet braid over her shoulder.

She was his daughter. She was fearless and happy and strong, and he was going to do everything in his power to make sure she stayed that way.

"So, about your mom," he began. "We've decided that you're going to live with me now. And I'm thinking that we should stay on the ranch for the summer, and, I don't know, maybe the winter, and you'll go to school in Chugwater, or Cheyenne, depending. What do you think about that?"

"In the cabin?" she asked. "What about my friends? I'm going to be in the fourth grade, Dad, which is the year all the kids in Mrs. Harr's class get to put on a play. It was going to be *Alice in Wonderland* an' I was going to be the caterpillar."

"There will be other chances to be in a play, right?" Of course he wasn't certain about that, but there would also be chances for her to do things she'd not yet dreamed of. "And," he added, slowly, playing his ace card, grateful none of her questions had been about Mona. "You'll get horse riding lessons all summer. Every week. Every day if you want."

"Oh." Bea looked up at him, eyes wide in the slowly building dusk, and sighed with happiness. "I'll be a real cowgirl then."

"You're a real one now, you know." He hugged her close and kissed the top of her head, and drew a breath, for he had one last thing to talk to her about. "And then there's Clay. I wanted to ask you about him—"

"He wasn't at dinner, Dad," she said. "Did he go somewhere in his yellow truck without us?"

"He did, honeybee, and that's your dad's fault. We had a disagreement over a lot of things, things that are important to Clay. And they are to me too, only, when he and I were talking, I said stupid things, and that's why Clay is keeping his distance. I hurt his feelings."

"You can always say you're sorry, Dad," she said, leaning against him, playing with the damp end of her braid. "That's what you always tell me, right? You say it *all* the time. Talk to the other person. Straighten it out. That's what you say."

"I do say that," he said. "And I'm going to talk to Clay as soon as I can find him tomorrow. But what I also wanted to add and to check with you about is—" He took another deep breath. "Clay and I are friends. *Good* friends. Friends like Mom and I used to be. Close. Maybe kissing close. I want to spend time with him like I used to with your mom."

He wrinkled his brow and hunched up his shoulders, waiting for her to respond to this.

"Kissing is gross," she said, biting on the edge of a finger, cleaning his sloppy polish application with her teeth. "But I like Clay. You smile when he's here. He makes me laugh. I like his truck, too. It's yellow. Maybe yellow is my new favorite color."

"Already?" he asked, struck by how quickly she moved on from what he considered a very sensitive subject. But maybe to her, he'd said he liked Clay, and that was all she wrote. "I thought purple was your favorite color."

"I'm tired of purple," she said. "I think I need a yellow t-shirt to match Clay's truck. Ladybelle, that's her name, right?"

"Yes," he said, thinking of Bea's love for color and her passion for new things, and the calm way she sat there at his side after he'd announced to her he and Clay were kissing close. "Why don't we go in and you can read to me. Anything you like."

"Even *Black Beauty?*" she asked. "I'm just kidding. I know it makes you sad. It makes me sad, too, so how about *The Secret Garden?*"

"Perfect," he said, standing up, holding out his hand so he could gently pull her to her feet.

They went inside. He turned on the ruby-glass lamp while Bea grabbed her e-reader and plopped down on the small couch. He plopped down on the armchair, putting his feet up on the small coffee table and, with his hands over his stomach, nodded that he was ready. And he was, more ready than he thought he would be, to talk to Clay in the morning. If only Clay would forgive him, then Austin would do his best to become more than the half-man that he was.

28

CLAY

$\mathcal{T}$he drive to Chugwater, no matter that he drove as fast as he could, spitting up dirt, fishtailing on the curves, did him no good at all. Neither did the single beer he grabbed at the Stampede Saloon, which he downed while eyeing the clientele, wondering whether the space between the saloon and the railroad tracks was dark enough for a special meet-and-greet between him and whoever caught his eye.

He'd been on the verge of a relationship so sweet he could hardly believe it was happening to him. Austin had been all the things Clay had never thought he'd want. A tall, red-haired, clean living, recently divorced nerdy accountant. Not to mention *straight,* with a nine-year-old daughter.

He'd thought his days of fucking in back alleys were over for good. That he'd found love. Found someone who was easy and fun to be with, and who looked at him like he was something special, more than cute and blond and dimpled, like he was someone whom Austin could count on. Could trust.

And Clay had been those things—*was* those things, all of them. He'd been willing to wait until Austin felt comfortable being in bed with him. He'd even been willing to forgo *sex*, an impossible thing to imagine only a month ago, willing to just mess around and make out like a teenager and be with Austin until they were both ready. Until Austin wanted more.

Except, it seemed, Austin wanted a different kind of life altogether. One that didn't include any of the things Clay found important. Austin wanted big city life, like the wife on that old *Green Acres* program, and all Clay had to offer him was blue jeans, horse shit, and fresh air. Which was not enough, it seemed, for Austin, which meant Clay wasn't enough for him either.

Oh, Clay'd been enough when it was hand-holding time, something Austin wasn't afraid to do. Hadn't seemed afraid to try other things as well, had responded to Clay's suggestion of fooling around to see what would happen like it was a good idea.

Now that Austin had Bea with him, all of that had changed.

"Get you another'n, young man?" asked the bartender, wiping the bar down with a damp cloth that smelled like old beer and Pine Sol.

Clay paused as he sucked off the last of his beer. It was cheap beer. It was Budweiser. The dregs were bitter on his tongue. The tap needed cleaning.

All of this felt more familiar than he wanted to admit. Familiar enough to slip into like an old trap he'd built himself out of one-night-stand encounters, a pocket full of condoms, and a belief, way down deep in his heart, that that was the way to find true love.

Only to find out, in the end, that true love could be found beneath the overhang of a Motel 6 in a downpour. Could be found in a cheap, small-town motel with only one bed. In a drive to see a vista view while he walked off to give the other fellow his space. In a painting of him, slipped beneath his door in the wee hours of the morning. In a red-haired, green-eyed accountant who'd survived a divorce so miserable, his shoulders were in a perpetually locked position.

None of which involved lube or pulling his dick out of his briefs or bending over so some guy, some stranger, could get his rocks off. All of this was like night and day. Like city to country.

Was it so wrong to ask Austin to pick Clay and the ranch over his old life?

He lowered his glass, looked at the suds settling and drying along the inside of it.

"Well?" asked the bartender. When Clay didn't say anything, the bartender kept moving in the direction he'd been going, wiping down the bar, gathering up used coasters, putting everything to rights.

Which was what Clay needed to do, put everything in his life to rights. He only needed to be brave enough to do it. Only he didn't know *what* to do.

"No, thank you," said Clay, but it was to the air, as the bar was too loud and the bartender was too far away to hear him.

He laid a five-dollar bill on the counter and sauntered out to his truck. Ladybelle waited by the railroad tracks beneath the single light over the back parking lot.

He got in, cranked her engine, and drove slowly home. Along the way, one elbow resting on the windowsill, driving with one hand, he looked up at the stars, not hardly looking at the road at all, which was fine. Ladybelle knew the way as well as he did.

It was late when he parked behind the barn, next to the supply shed, the last spot in a neat row of trucks that got used for what trucks were meant for. Hauling hay bales, barbed wire, boots, and shovels. Sometimes, though, a truck bed could carry two men, and blankets for pillows so they could look up at the stars together.

It was a night he'd remember for a good long time, in spite of everything.

As he stepped out of the shadows of the roofline of the supply shed, the auto-light sprang on when the sensors detected him. He saw Leland waiting by the barn, leaning against an old, dark-ribbed cottonwood tree, whose branches spread in a wide circle and covered Leland with shadows, whose spicy scent filled the night air.

"You're back late," said Leland, casually, pushing himself up off the tree and into the light. "And you scooted out early, which isn't like you."

"Sorry, boss," said Clay. He'd left his hat behind so he didn't even have that to take off and resettle on his head to give him something to do while he rustled up an explanation. Sunday nights were busy, and he knew that. "Just needed some thinking time."

"About anything in particular?" asked Leland, falling into step beside Clay, like they were headed to Leland's office in the barn. "Or about *anyone* in particular?"

The auto-light at the corner of the barn snapped on, bathing them both in electric white, cutting the darkness around them in a hard-edged circle. Clay had known the lights were a good idea when Leland had them installed at the beginning of the prior season, but at a moment like this, when he needed silence and darkness before he confessed his sins, he rather hated them.

"I'm not blind, Clay."

Leland let the silence fall around them, which Clay knew full and well this was to give the other fellow a chance to confess. He scuffed the toe of his boot into the dirt, stuffing his hands into his pockets like a kid who got caught taking more than his fair share of candy.

"I know you're not," said Clay, low. "I just don't know what to tell you."

"How about the truth," said Leland, equally low. "That's always worked well between us before this."

There had been a time when Clay had confronted his boss about his attraction to a certain drifter. He'd spoken man-to-man with Leland and then told Leland to pull that stick out of his ass so the happiness he'd found in Jamie's company could be a permanent thing. Which made it too late for Clay to dance away from this particular conversation, as Leland would only follow and eventually, being Leland, find out the truth.

"It's Austin, like you probably already guessed." Clay nodded when Leland nodded, glad to have that much out of the way. "It was fine. We were going slow and all and I know that there's that non-fraternization rule you got going—"

"Hardly my place to hold you to that rule when I broke it myself." Leland's smile was small, but the warmth in his eyes told Clay a lot.

"Anyway." Clay shrugged, his hands still in his pockets. "It was going good. We were holding hands, looking at shooting stars, and he even—" Clay's voice broke. He had to stop and swallow before he could go on. "He even painted a picture of me. Said he could only do landscapes and there it was beneath my door—"

"I didn't know he could paint," said Leland. "But what happened between the two of you?"

"Bea." Clay snapped his mouth shut over the word. He liked Bea, liked her just fine, and it wasn't her fault her dad was using her as an excuse to move away from what he'd shared with Clay.

"That's rough," said Leland. "He's probably feeling the weight of being a single parent just now. And after that divorce—"

"I know *all* about that." Clay tried to move away, go to his room, where he could work out his sadness alone. But Leland stopped him, putting a warm hand on Clay's shoulder, leaning close to look Clay right in the eye.

"Like you told me once, Clay," said Leland. "Tell him how you feel. Don't let this chance at happiness pass you by being stubborn."

"I also told you to pull that stick out of your ass," said Clay, trying for the joke, failing when it fell flat in the night air because Leland wasn't laughing.

"That I did," said Leland. "And in this case, I'll tell you this advice. Shake off your pride. Find out the truth. Then move forward. Don't live your life with regret. Okay?"

"Okay," said Clay.

He didn't have a single useful idea how he was supposed to do any of that, but when Leland started along the path through the small glade toward his manager's cabin, Clay followed him. Leland had been his mentor and guide from the moment he'd stepped foot on the ranch.

He knew Leland was right, he truly did. But as he looked beyond Leland's cabin, nestled against the hillside next to the staff quarters, he saw that the third cabin along, Austin and Bea's cabin, had its lights off. They were already in bed.

Austin wasn't waiting for Clay, hadn't stayed up to greet him. Didn't care that Clay had gone out with the intention of getting rip-roaring drunk.

"He has a nine-year-old daughter, Clay," said Leland, pausing. "Nine-year-olds need to go to bed earlier than you or I. Keep that in mind as you think this over."

That was a new thought, all fresh and springtime different. He'd worked with a lot of kids, from the bratty to the sweet. He knew how to talk to them without talking down to them. Knew how to coax the bravery out of the shy ones, how to keep rascals and their shenanigans down to a dull roar.

But he'd never put a kid to bed or taken them to the dentist or worried about their grades. He'd never been a dad, and here he was, grousing because Austin, who had been a dad, had put his daughter to bed at a reasonable hour.

Clomping up the steps of the staff quarters, Clay walked quietly down the hall to his room. He showered quickly, hot water, then cold, and put himself to bed, lying on top of the bottom sheet, with the top sheet folded away so he could feel the cool breeze across his skin.

His hair was still wet, and would get pushed into stiff positions that come morning, he'd have to comb out with water. Or maybe he'd leave them to use as an icebreaker with Austin, as in, *Hey, have you seen my hair? Wild, no?* And then Clay would laugh and Austin would laugh, and it'd be okay between them once more.

Deep in his heart, he knew it would take more than a simple joke between friends to fix everything.

When morning came, he used a washcloth to scrub the sleep out of his eyes, then shaved, and looked at himself in the mirror. He was still the same Clay, with his hair sticking up in the back, but now his eyes looked dim.

Happiness was only a truth telling away, and if Austin said no to giving Clay, and perhaps the ranch, a second try? Then Clay would just have to move on, though he didn't imagine he'd go back to the bars. The thought of it, him taking his pants down for a stranger who wasn't Austin, had a hollow ring to it now.

Dressed and ready to go, Clay pulled on his cowboy boots and marched down the stairs, walking along the path to the main lodge for breakfast. The whole way he looked left and right. and though he'd not a single idea what he was going to say, he was going to find Austin and at least try to start things on the road to something better.

It was much to his surprise when he turned the corner around the main lodge and saw Austin coming toward him at a fast clip. Bea wasn't with him, and maybe she was already inside and Austin was on his way back to his cabin to grab something for her they'd forgotten.

But no. Austin saw him and picked up his pace, and met Clay at the edge of the glade, his hand reaching out, though he didn't touch Clay, as he might have done in the past.

"Hey," said Austin. "I'm glad I found you. I wanted to talk to you."

Half of Clay remembered the last time Austin had wanted to talk to him about his intention to go back to the city, to leave the ranch, to leave Clay and what they'd shared far behind him. But Leland had urged him to give this a chance, to throw away his own pride, even if just for a minute, so that's what he was going to do.

Besides, Austin was obviously fresh out of the shower, freshly shaved, bright as a new penny, his eyes that rich dark green Clay was coming to love so much. With that shy smile thrown in, Austin was hard to resist, so Clay stopped fully and vowed to put his whole heart in the ring.

"Hey," said Clay. "How're you doing? What do you want to talk to me about?"

Austin stopped, his body drawing up, his expression a little shocked.

"I wasn't sure you'd be willing to listen, after I was such a jerk about everything."

"You weren't a jerk," said Clay, shaking his head. "You were just thinking of Bea, about her future. And that's a good thing. I just didn't want you leaving and forgetting about me." He wobbled that last word and, realizing this, his face got hot and he was sure, quite sure, he was currently the saddest, most pathetic schlub on the planet.

"I'm not leaving," said Austin, and this time he reached out to take Clay's hand in his. "I rethought everything. I was thinking small. I was limiting Bea's future by wanting what I already knew, rather than being brave and trying something different. Bea's happy here. I'm happy here, with *you*."

"You are?"

"Yes, I am. And I just want to be with you, come what may. Leland said—"

Clay laughed, then shook his head at Austin's questioning gaze. "Leland gives a lot of advice, and usually it's pretty good."

"It is." Austin smiled and then moved close, as though the words he was about to speak were meant only for Clay. "He told me to just tell the truth, and that was after he gave me a powerful description of Bea with the wind in her hair, a confident and strong young woman. And all because of growing up on the ranch. *This* ranch."

"He told me," said Clay, swallowing over the thickness in his throat. "That you were under a lot of pressure, and that I needed to go easy on you. To understand what it's like to suddenly be the sole provider for a nine-year-old girl."

"You're good with kids," said Austin. "I've seen you. And you're good with her."

"She's a sweet kid," said Clay. "Takes after her dad, I'd say."

"Does that mean you'll give me another chance?"

Austin looked hopeful as he asked this, his eyes wide, his whole body still, as though prepared to turn and run at the first rejection.

"Of course," said Clay, moving close enough that the toes of their boots touched and he could lean forward and kiss Austin very gently on the mouth. "Of course *yes*."

Austin sighed and kissed Clay right back, and the sigh moved through Clay and then back again, until its sweetness ribboned around them both.

"I want to go on another date," said Austin, drawing back a little bit. "So I can tell you everything. So we can start again."

"Sure," said Clay. He nodded and moved even closer.

"But I don't know who'll watch Bea, this time," said Austin. "I can't keep asking Jasper and Ellis."

"They love having her, you know," said Clay in response to this. "But heck, let's take her with us. We don't need anything so formal as getting a sitter, it'll just be the three of us. We can take Ladybelle out and find another good painting spot and then get kraut burgers after."

"You make everything so easy."

"I'd like to make you easy," said Clay, laughing. "See what I said there? *Easy?* As in—"

"Yes, yes, I know, I do. And I thank you for being patient with me."

"As long as you need, sweet man," said Clay, his hands moving to Austin's hips. "As long as you need." Then he looked down at Austin's hands and smiled, took those hands to his mouth and kissed them. "I love the new pink look you got going on."

"That's Bea's nail polish," said Austin, blushing. "I figure to be a good dad, I needed to join in things she'd like to do. So I did. Feel like most of a fool, but I did it."

"If it makes you feel any better, she can paint my nails any time, though I prefer something a little brighter. More red."

Austin moved into Clay's arms and hugged him tight, and they stood that way for a good five minutes, with Clay hugging Austin right back.

29

CLAY

*M*onday mornings were especially busy on the ranch, with guests still settling in. Stella did her best to problem-solve lodging issues, calling on Clay every other minute, it seemed, to haul extra towels, pillows, and trash cans.

It wasn't really the work Clay liked to do, as he preferred to be in the barn helping Brody with the guests as they met their horses for the week. But after breakfast Leland had asked Clay to help Stella in particular, in addition to her regular staff, and all of this took Clay further from the barn and the office, where Austin was likely to be.

As for Bea, he spotted her in the arena, trying to help Brody like she worked there, and at one point, as he passed with armfuls of towels, he saw Leland going over to her. Next thing he knew, Bea was on a horse, her little straw cowboy hat perched on the back of her head, taking lessons and enjoying herself like everybody else.

"We'll find her interesting work to do," Leland had said in confidence to Clay earlier. "Willing to help with that? We'll all help of course, but I figured you'd be most interested."

"Yes," said Clay. "I am."

"We'll have a meeting about it later," said Leland, and then he tipped his hat at Clay, finger to the brim, and walked off, his long legs making big strides as he headed to the barn.

It was like Leland to make it seem as if absorbing a young child into the life of the ranch was as easy as breathing. Normally, they had a twelve-year-old limit put on young guests, and Bea was only nine. A courageous and energetic nine, but still.

The cell phone in his back pocket rang just before lunchtime, as Clay was about to head to the barn, completely done with domestic chores and ready to shovel horse shit and groom horses and all the grubby work. He wanted to throw himself into that and get all sweaty, and then he wanted to find Austin and plant a manly kiss right on him. Except the ring tone was Maddy's, so he stopped in the shade of the roofline of Cottage #1 and answered it.

"Hey there," said Maddy, in a rush, like she usually was on Mondays. "Got a FedEx envelope here addressed to Austin. I figure he's going to want this sooner than later, and I can't get him on his phone. Can you—"

"Sure, I'll get it and deliver it." Clay nodded like she could see him, excitement building. Only one person needed to send something overnight to Austin, so the envelope had come from Mona and contained the custody papers. Signing them and returning them would take a load off Austin's mind, and that was worth Clay delaying his return to his regular ranch hand duties. "I'll be right there."

Tucking the phone in his back pocket, he trotted up the road from the cabins to the main road, and then to the office. He clomped up the wooden steps into the shade of the porch of Maddy's office and went inside. Maddy was already standing up, holding out the mostly white envelope, a smile on her face.

"Looks like we're not going to lose him," she said. "Leland told me a little bit."

"Thanks, Maddy," he said. "I'll find him."

As fast as he could, he headed to the barn, where Austin was likely to be, passing beneath blissful shade before stepping out into full sunshine again. Only once he'd passed the main lodge, he saw Austin and Bea headed to their cabin, with Austin walking close to Bea, his arm around her shoulders.

"Hey!" Clay hurried to catch up with them. Once in the glade on the dirt path leading to the cabins, he saw Bea's face was red, and that she'd been crying. "What's up? What's wrong?"

"She just overdid it this morning," said Austin. "Trying to keep up with Brody and getting in the way. Luckily Leland was there, and luckily the horse whose legs she was going between wasn't bothered. We figure it'll be a good idea to have her go to Sue Mitchell's day camp most days, most mornings, at least. And then we'll figure out the rest of it. Right, honeybee?"

Bea nodded and sniffed, wiping her nose on her sleeve.

"Can I help?" asked Clay as he held out the envelope. "Look what I brought you."

"You just did." Austin smiled. "Looks like I need to wire that money to Mona."

Austin took the envelope as Bea held up her hand for Clay to take, and together they walked to the cabin. Once inside, Austin rinsed a washcloth with cold water and carefully wiped Bea's face with it. Clay raced to get her a glass of cold water, which seemed to help her hitching breaths almost right away.

"Listen, Bea," said Clay as Austin sat down to tear open the envelope and sign the custody paperwork as fast as he could. "Why don't you and me and your dad go out together tonight? We'll find a view and your dad can paint and after that we can get kraut burgers."

"Dad never lets me use his paints. And Mom doesn't like me painting because it's messy," said Bea as she scrubbed her eyes. Then, as if distracted by a new idea, she asked, "What's a kraut burger?"

"Well," said Clay. He propped himself on the arm of the easy chair, close to Bea's chair at the kitchen table without overwhelming her. "I think your dad would be okay with it and, if you like it, we'll get you your own paints."

On the heels of that, he thought of adding, *and your mom's not here*, but that would pile too many new ideas onto Bea. She might not need reminding, just then, that she wasn't going to live with her mom anymore. Anyway, she didn't need to worry about what Mona thought. Just like he was going to make sure Austin knew he didn't need to worry about what Mona thought.

"Shall we sit here and braid your hair for a minute?" asked Austin. "Then we can go to lunch. And Clay, if you could get Maddy to FedEx this for me, overnight, and put the receipt on my desk. The ranch doesn't need to pay for my personal business."

"Sure," said Clay. He picked up the form with Austin's tidy signature on several pages of a stack of documents. "But will you wait lunch for me?"

"Yes," said Bea. She stood up and leaned against Clay, turning her face into his shirt, and he was almost undone by this trusting gesture.

"She's a little worked up, still," said Austin. "Maybe we should skip lunch, or bring it back here."

"No, I don't think so." Clay touched the top of Bea's head, so small beneath the cradle of his palm. "Don't hide her away just because she's had a bad morning. Right? Don't hide her away. Don't hide yourself away either."

"Okay." Austin stood up and kissed Clay over Bea's head, not hiding it, but it was so quickly done, Clay responded in kind, smiling when Austin smiled at him. "We'll wait on the steps for you, after I braid Bea's hair."

"Sounds good."

Not waiting, Clay hustled down to Maddy's office, and breathless, handed over the forms to her and passed along Austin's message about the receipt. Then, almost running, he made it to the main lodge to find Austin and Bea sitting in the shade of the top step.

Bea's hair was done in a thick braid down her back, and she was saying something to Austin, laughing. When she saw Clay, she ran up to him and grabbed his hand.

"Dad said that you're kissing friends now," she said, tugging on his hand to get him up the steps as fast as possible. "I saw you kissing each other before. It was gross."

"It can be gross, sometimes," said Clay, wrinkling his nose as though overcome at the grossness of it all. "But I like kissing your dad, in spite of that."

He smiled at Austin to get him to join in the fun of it, the easy way Bea seemed to have accepted that he and her dad were now dating. Austin seemed as relaxed as Clay had ever seen him, those shoulders finally coming down to a more normal position, and the smile Austin gave him in return was warm and slow and not the least bit hesitant.

"Let's go to lunch," said Austin, and together they all mounted the steps and went inside.

Sitting between the two of them, Bea chattered away to anyone who would listen the whole time they were eating, and after they bussed their trays, Clay had to dash up to the barn, there to clean out box stalls and haul horse shit, and to find Leland to ask him for the evening off.

"Do you mind, boss?" asked Clay, peeling the hay from his shirt front.

"No, I don't mind," said Leland. "Always say you should take time off when you need it. Where you headed?"

"We're going to find a view so Austin can paint." Clay ducked his head, searching for more hay stuck to his person. "I was figuring to drive us out to the ridge. Then after, the three of us are getting kraut burgers in Chugwater."

"Taking Bea?" asked Leland. He reached up to the hooks where he kept the keys. "Might be too much for Ladybelle. Take the F150, as it's a little rugged up there and you wouldn't want to get stuck with her in your keeping."

"Thanks, Dad," said Clay, joking.

"Welcome, son," said Leland, joining in.

The rest of Clay's afternoon lagged despite him being right where he wanted to be, in the barn, working with horses, helping Brody get a group of guests ready for a little trail ride before the rains came, led by the ever-stoic Quint. But finally, finally, he could set his tools and responsibilities aside to go to his room for a quick shower, a fresh t-shirt, tight but not too tight, and to run a cloth over his boots. He dabbed on some cologne, a dragged a comb through his hair, and he was almost dizzy as he walked down the stairs, feeling that this was going to be a very special night.

While it wasn't their first date, not really, it was the first one where Austin had full custody of Bea, the first one where Clay knew his own heart had been handed over, the first one with the three of them. He might not be ready to be a single dad, but he sure was ready to be there when Austin needed him.

The two of them were waiting for him on the path beneath the trees, hand in hand, expectant, smiling when they saw him. Austin had a sage green t-shirt on that Clay had never seen him wear before. It set his eyes to a deeper green, his hair to burnished copper. Over his shoulder was looped a black canvas bag that no doubt held his paint things.

As for Bea, from somewhere she'd gotten a tie-dyed t-shirt and her hair was in two braids over her shoulders. Both of them wore their straw hats, and Clay's heart leaped, seeing them like this, and he closed his eyes for a minute, so he could remember them this way forever.

"You okay?" asked Austin.

"Just taking pictures with my head," said Clay just before kissing Austin right in front of Bea.

"Gross!" Bea hopped up and down, tugging on Austin's arm. "We're supposed to be painting, not kissing. Kissing's for later. Let's paint!"

"Okay, okay," said Clay. He drew Leland's truck keys out of his pocket and swirled them around and around. "Let's ride!"

Together they went up the service road to where the truck was parked, and as soon as Clay had opened the driver's side door, Bea leaped in and sat on the small divider between the seats.

"That's not a seat for little girls, honeybee," said Austin. "There's no seat belt."

"But I want to ride in the front like I did in the yellow truck." Bea crossed her arms over her chest, looking like she was trying to imagine she weighed a zillion pounds so they couldn't move her.

"It should be okay," said Clay. "We're just going up to the ridge and maybe down into the valley a little way. Later on the road, sure, she'll sit in back."

"You're spoiling her," said Austin.

Clay just smiled and got into the driver's seat, and Austin, shaking his head, got in as well.

"My job is to spoil her, I do believe," said Clay. Then he added, "On the main roads you get in back with a seatbelt on, okay, Bea?"

"Okay," said Bea, seeming well satisfied she'd gotten her way.

Driving as carefully as he had ever done, Clay guided the truck up the road to the pasture, stopping to let Austin undo the gate. Then, after they'd driven through, he paused to let Austin close the gate before getting in the truck again.

After that, it was a slow, slightly bumpy ride to the ridge, from which could be seen the unbroken line of foothills and behind that the range of mountains, starting with Iron Mountain and all the way up till they disappeared on the horizon. To the right was the flatness of green, grassy fields sloping up and sloping down, but always remaining low beneath the blue, cloudless sky.

A bit of a breeze accompanied them halfway down the ridge to a spot that Clay knew, a flat bit where they could park the truck and get out and Austin could paint. There wasn't anywhere for him to go to give Austin his privacy, but this time, somehow, that didn't seem to matter.

Austin simply gathered the black canvas bag from the back seat and took out his paint things. Then, to Clay's surprise, Austin handed to him and to Bea each a pad of watercolor paper, a small tray with little squares of watercolors, a paintbrush, and put in each paint tray's well, a bit of water.

"Now," said Austin. "You paint and I'll paint—"

"And then we'll have a contest!" shouted Bea, splashing her water all over her shirt.

"No, no," said Austin as he patiently filled her little well with more water. "We're not going to judge the paintings. We're just going to enjoy doing them and seeing what everybody came up with."

"I like it," said Clay.

While he could paint the broad side of a barn with ease, he was not an artist and this wasn't a task he was good at. Still, it was fun to find a place to sit near the edge of the small dirt parking lot to where the land sloped down and down, and then to swirl the paintbrush in water. To smear the brush in the dry blocks of paint, and then to whoosh the brush across the paper.

He did his best to mimic the enormous amount of sky compared to the green high prairie, and was well pleased when Bea came to sit beside him, echoing what he was doing. She had a bright blue smear of paint already across her cheek, and her paper contained large blocks of shapeless color.

Her smile was bright and when she bumped her head against his arm, his heart swelled, for that was the gesture she did with her dad when she was happy or too full of emotion to express herself with words.

A bit of wind tugged Bea's paint tray out of her hands. When Clay leaped for it before it went over the edge of the ridge, his own paint tray flopped upside down, the water drying into the earth inside of a heartbeat.

"There's dirt on it now," wailed Bea, holding up his tray.

"Doesn't matter," said Clay as he sat down next to her once more.

He showed her his painting, broad stripes of blue for the sky covering most of the paper, with a thin line of green at the bottom. Grey and purple to the left for the mountains. It was a dumb painting, really, for there was no light source, no indication that the sun was shining, but Bea took it from him and held it up to the sky.

"You made it look exactly like what it is," she said. She wrinkled her nose as she handed him her painting. "Mine is just blobs."

"True," said Clay, taking the painting to admire it, holding it to one side so the colored water wouldn't drip on his jeans. "But they're colorful blobs."

Off by himself, Austin was silently painting, and Clay wondered if he was painting the landscape alone, or if he was adding them into it, two shapes on the edge of the ridge, suggestions in paint, a ghostly cowboy and a ghostly daughter.

And indeed, when Austin was done, that's exactly what he showed to them both. Only instead of being colorful blobs or a painting that was a wash of color only, Austin's painting had a form to it.

He'd painted the far horizon, but used all the colors he could see, evoking the energy in the view, the vibrant light and, looking at the painting, Clay could imagine he'd caught the cool breeze in the colors, as well. And then, yes, he'd included two small shapes in the lower right side of the painting, under which he'd signed his name.

"Thank you for suggesting this," said Austin. He handed the painting to Bea, then took their paintings from them to look at. "There's a lot of love in these," he said, nodding slowly like Clay imagined an expert in New York might do. "They're wonderful. Now, who's hungry?"

Austin packed his paints carefully away while Clay, even more carefully, helped Bea into the back seat of the F150 and made sure her seat belt was buckled and that her hands were in her lap before he shut the door.

It was then that he and Austin could share a moment, just a moment, to stand close and kiss. Their lips met, and Clay gently pulled Austin to him, grabbing onto Austin's belt with a tug until their hips met as well.

"Is that a paintbrush or are you just glad to see me?" asked Clay, teasing and soft as he felt Austin's erection against his, layers of cloth between them.

Austin looked at him, his eyes wide, reflecting all the green of the valley below.

"I don't know," said Austin, almost whispering. "I was just so relaxed, so damn happy to be here with the two of you—It's been happening in the mornings, now, too. Do you think it will stick around? Will it go away and come back?"

"I don't know," said Clay with a shrug, not letting go of Austin. "If it does, it does. It'll come back. We've got time."

Just then, Bea knocked on the window, and mouthed the words, *Ug, kissing,* at them, but she was smiling too, showing that she was teasing.

Clay kissed Austin, then, more urgently than before, cupping the back of Austin's head in his palm, sighing into the kiss as he listened to his body's response. Strange how good it could feel to be aroused by love in addition to passion. Strange to be standing in the sunlight, loving on this good man, though he had to laugh at Bea's expression that they were *still* kissing.

"C'mon," he said, pulling back, licking the taste of Austin's mouth from his lower lip. "Let's go eat before we all starve to death."

They all got into the truck and Clay drove slowly down the ridge, let Austin open and close the gate, then drove even more slowly down the main road of the ranch.

Along the roadside, guests were headed to story hour around the fire pit, and though Clay had the urge to stop and help them set up, as he'd done many times before, he kept his foot on the gas and kept on going. There would be many more story hours around the fire pit, all summer long, but this was their night together.

Clouds had formed over the mountains, and when the sun dipped behind them as it slowly went down, the sky became streaked with soft-edged shards of blue-pink and purple-blue and swirled with echoes of circles of clouds drifting on the high breeze.

"Think you can paint that?" asked Clay, pointing through the windshield.

"I'd like to try," said Austin.

He rolled down his window, and Clay rolled his down and turned off the air conditioner so they could drive with the breeze coming through the window. Bea unbuckled herself to come forward in the cab. She was leaning over until her hands were on the edge of the open window, so Austin took her in his lap as they went slowly along the backroad to Chugwater, which was, as everyone in the truck knew, completely against the rules.

"Just till the main road," said Austin.

"Just till the main road," agreed Clay, slowing down to drive even more carefully than ever. But it was worth it to see Bea's face as she looked at the waving grass and the blue skies, and the lone grouping of cattle beneath the slowly shining and slender iron windmill above a metal tank of water that flashed a reflection of the sky as they drove past.

Finally, at the point where the dirt road turned into pavement, Bea obediently clambered into the back and buckled herself in, which was when Clay could speed up and deliver them to Chugwater, where he pulled up in front of the Chugwater Soda Fountain.

"They have shakes too," he said as they all got out.

He looked down the road to where the Stampede Saloon was, where cars were gathering beneath the lights in the front parking lot. And where someone, perhaps, was in the back parking lot between the saloon and the railroad tracks waiting for dark and looking for a good time.

He'd have to tell Austin more about all those other men and how Clay had imagined he'd meet someone nice that way. But maybe not today. Today was for painting and kraut burgers and introducing Bea to Wendell, the very much loved and very much stuffed elk on the wall of the soda fountain.

"Let's eat," he said, opening the door to the soda fountain, and bowing to Bea as though she was a little princess, which she was, at least in his eyes.

30

AUSTIN

*T*he first thing to happen to Austin after he'd had breakfast with Bea and packed up her little backpack with overnight stuff and waved her off as Sue Mitchell's dun-colored and well maintained Travelall pulled out of the parking lot was that his phone went off, signaling he had a text.

Pulling out his phone, he tapped the text messenger icon and read the message.

Leland says Bea at sleepover?

The reason Leland had known was that he'd gotten a call from Sue about the sleepover and had passed the news to Austin at breakfast. With Bea sitting right there, there was no way he could have said no. And no way he would have wanted to.

Clay's text was a question, though he ought to have known that any news coming from Leland was one hundred percent accurate. Beneath the simple question was another, more complex one, as Clay was following up on his suggestion earlier that week that they should fool around some more.

If Bea was out of the cabin for the entire night, the time was probably right for them to get together, though he went a little cold at the thought of it.

Bea always came home from being with the Frontier Girls all bright and cheery and somehow more steady within herself. Same with the day camp that Sue ran, which Bea had attended on Tuesday and Wednesday that week.

Now it was Thursday. Bea would be gone all day and all night. Clay knew that, and now Austin needed to take the next step. He'd already said yes with his heart, but his body wasn't so sure.

Yes, he was ready at the same time he knew he was very much not ready. Still, Clay deserved an answer. Maybe this was the same cross-roads moment he'd experienced when he'd discovered Mona was cheating on him. The same decision he'd had to make when he'd been offered the accounting job at Farthingdale Ranch. Yes or no. Left or right.

Though, come to think of it, with each step away from Mona, he was cutting himself off from her pull on him. He could do anything he liked, really, as long as Bea knew she was loved. He could take her with him wherever he went, except there was nowhere he'd rather be than right where he was, standing in the parking lot in front of Maddy's office with his cell phone in his shaking hand.

Clay would be good to him, kind to him. Being a man, being who he was, Clay wouldn't think, at least probably wouldn't think, that anything about Austin was icky or needed fixing.

Austin hadn't been naked in front of another man since he took gym in his college days. But showering with a bunch of other guys as they laughed over the score of a basketball game was different from sliding between the sheets with one man. One very handsome man with a charming smile and easy-going manner, not to mention those sweet dimples.

On the other hand, if this was to be his first time, he would rather it was with Clay than anyone else, anywhere, ever. So, though his hand was still shaking, he pulled the phone close to his stomach, as though someone might try to peek over his shoulder, and typed a response with his thumbs.

Yes, he texted. *You, me, and an empty cabin.*

He pressed send, then typed, *Sry, that didn't come out as suave as I meant it.*

Then he waited, jiggling the phone in his hand, laughing to himself about the fact that if they were both standing around with their phones, surely they could just call each other. But this was more fun, and yes, that was the point, wasn't it?

That was the way it was when he was with Clay. Fun, easy, a genuine pleasure. Surely being in bed with this man would be, really, more of the same? And who didn't want that? Not him, that's who.

His phone beeped, and he opened the text messenger and read *Snds like a porno if you ask me.*

Shuddering, knowing that was the last kind of message he wanted to send, Austin gave in and dialed Clay's number. Clay picked up right away.

"Hello, there," Clay said, and it was easy to hear the smile in his voice. "I'm here with a pile of horse shit if you want to meet me now. Or, you can wait till after dinner, when I've had a chance to take a shower and spruce myself up."

"I'll take you any way I can get you," said Austin before he could think it through. "Oh man, that came out wrong, too."

"It came out fine," said Clay. "You're going to be fine. How about this? I'll shower when I'm done for the day, and I'll meet you at the main lodge for an early dinner, and we can go from there. Hold hands and stuff. Maybe make out, like we did before, only this time on your couch. It doesn't have to be more than that, right?"

"Right," said Austin, though he kind of felt it had to be more than that. Why was he making this good man wait? "That sounds good to me."

"All right then," said Clay. "Just be prepared. I have the nicest ass in the tri-state area."

Then with a laugh, Clay hung up, leaving Austin staring at the phone, a goofy smile on his face and a pleasant anticipation of how it would go. Them making eyes at each other, flirting at dinner. Making out in the light of the ruby-colored table lamps. And then to the couch, when they'd get each other all hot and bothered. What could be more natural than that? Nothing.

Sticking his phone in his back pocket, Austin glanced up at the bluest sky, then slipped into the shade of the porch with a sigh before going back into the office. There, he made himself work hard, not letting himself be distracted.

Yes, Clay texted him every hour on the hour with funny emojis and misspelled commentary about how much horse shit there was and how Brody seemed to prefer a horse's company to Clay's. Dutifully laughing under his breath, Austin replied to each and every text.

By the time Maddy wanted to shut the office for the evening, Austin was more than ready to bid her goodnight before walking back to the cabin, where he took a shower, shaved, applied too much cologne, then hopped in the shower again. Luckily there was plenty of hot water and towels, and soon he dressed in his newest blue jeans, his cowboy boots polished, his nicest snap-button shirt tucked in beneath his belt, and off he went to dinner, whistling.

As he mounted the wooden steps to the main lodge, he looked up and there was Clay, dressed for a night on the town, wearing his newest blue jeans, and a snap-button shirt of the palest gray that brought out the blue in his eyes. The overhead light shone on his blond hair, and he was as bright as a new nickel.

"Man, I love you in that shirt," said Clay as they got in line. "Gah. How am I supposed to wait till we start making out?"

"We could skip dinner," said Austin, squawking a bit at the last word when he realized what he'd just said.

"No," said Clay, tugging on Austin's belt as they moved forward. "You need at least some toast in your belly, or you'll be all in knots and that's no fun."

"I don't know what I'm doing," said Austin. He shook his head, and scuffed his cowboy boots along the wooden floor as he wished he had more guts and that he'd quit acting like a twelve-year-old boy about all of this. "I'm normally not this timid."

"You're a—" Clay leaned close, his mouth brushing against Austin's ear. "You're a virgin in these woods, and I mean to treat you like bone china."

"You said bone," said Austin in his best Beevus and Butt-head voice, sniggering, in spite of the cape of nerves that seemed to rise and fall all around him.

Clay laughed hard at this, tears squirting from his eyes, and it seemed all he could do to muffle himself with his hand over his mouth, out of courtesy for all the guests in line for dinner.

"You're the best, bruh," said Clay, still laughing. "Just the best."

They were still jocular as they reached the buffet, and though Austin knew he needed to eat, he couldn't focus on anything in any of the warming trays. In the end, he got what Clay got, which was lasagna dripping with cheese and sauce, and a little bit of salad, to keep things healthy.

As they sat at their favorite spot, a table just for two, it felt so normal, so much a part of his everyday life, that Austin felt he could take a breath. Could eat his dinner, and look at Clay and smile and not feel like he was marching to his own doom. Because he wasn't. This was Clay, sweet, adorable, good-looking Clay who always looked at Austin like he was everything Clay ever wanted.

The cape of anxiety lifted from him, finally, as they bussed their trays and headed out of the dining hall and down the wooden steps. They weren't walking hand in hand, as it seemed important to be more discreet than that, but they both paused at the same time to look up at the coming sunset, dusk dropping down in shades of violet, a faraway cloud on the horizon, dark and dangerous, flickering silent lightning amidst the virga.

"Man," said Clay. "I bet you could paint the hell out of that." He bumped his shoulder against Austin's.

"I can try," said Austin, leaning into the bump. "I'm going to stay and try."

Gently, Clay took Austin's hand and led him along the path and through the glade of trees, a soft sigh of a breeze pattering across the leaves of the cottonwoods as they shook themselves into the cool of the evening.

At the steps of the third manager's cabin, Clay paused, looking up at Austin, waiting, it seemed. Then Austin figured it out.

It was his cabin, so he should lead them inside. From there, maybe Clay would be kind enough to take over, but right now he was waiting, wordlessly asking permission to enter. It was to be, in the end, Austin's decision.

He took a breath and shrugged his shoulders, like a fighter prepping to go in the ring. Then he laughed at himself as he gestured to the door.

"Hey," he said as casually as he could. "Nobody's home tonight, so why don't you come in and we can hang out." He dropped his head. "I should have practiced that more. I sound like a twelve-year-old kid."

"To me," said Clay as he raised Austin's chin with his fingers. "To me, you are perfect. And yes, I'd love to come in and hang out."

Together they climbed the wooden steps, and Clay waited while Austin unlocked the door. The cabin was a bit stuffy, so he opened the windows, but kept the shades halfway. He turned on two of the ruby-glass lamps and shut Bea's door. All the while, Clay watched him from the door until Austin bent to tug off his cowboy boots, at which point Clay moved forward to help him.

"You need a boot jack, looks like," said Clay, kneeling down to manfully pull the boots off.

"And a Carhartt jacket, as I recall," said Austin. He held onto Clay's shoulder with one hand and propped himself against the wall with his other hand to balance himself.

And became unbalanced when Clay stood up, his body close, so close that Austin would have fallen back had Clay not reached out to curve his arm around Austin's waist.

"Aren't you going to take your boots off?" asked Austin, the squawking sound returning.

"Cowboys do it with their boots on," said Clay in his most exaggerated drawl. Then he laughed, kissing Austin. "Right?"

"Right."

Not knowing what he was agreeing to, it still felt very agreeable to be led to the couch by Clay, who plopped himself down and then patted the empty seat beside him. He toed off his cowboy boots and sighed when Austin slid into place, and pulled Austin to him, half on top of him, chin tilted up as though waiting for a kiss.

All at once, having gotten over some invisible hurdle, it felt good and natural to bend close and kiss Clay, his heart rising as Clay kissed him back with warmth and energy, joy and acceptance. And when he collapsed against Clay's body and Clay's arms went around his waist, he filled with delight at Clay's sigh, which seemed to come from his soul, and the expression on Clay's face, blue eyes half-lidded, a flush to his cheeks.

"You're very tall for a monk," said Clay, playing the game between them. "And I bet you are pale beneath those robes."

"I have freckles, and—" Austin paused. "And Mona says—"

Clay stopped him with a finger to Austin's mouth.

"Listen to me," he said, fierce. "I do not care what Mona says or thinks or does. I. Do. Not. Care. All I care about is you, and now, hearing about those freckles and whatever else you got going on underneath those clothes, I want to lick and kiss you all night. All freaking *night*."

With a twitch of his shoulders, Clay flipped them both over so Austin was beneath Clay. The weight of another man's body on top of him, solid with muscle, dense thighs pressing on his own was new but welcome.

That Clay's erection was brushing his hip settled him, and he tipped his head back and sighed, as though he'd come a long way and climbed a tall, very rugged mountain. The peak wasn't yet reached, but with Clay pressing him into the couch and kissing his throat, there was nothing standing in his way.

Clay's body surged against his, and Clay was making a small sound, like a growl or a hum, intent on the kisses along Austin's neck, thumbs digging into Austin's ribs. The whole of him, all that energy, moved into Austin like Clay was intent on charging him right up to the point where he'd explode.

This was not a teenage make-out session. It was a prelude to sex between two men, and his body, in response to this realization, rather than shying away, seemed to pulse from within, desire pushing everywhere in him, everywhere.

"I felt that," said Clay, almost mumbling as he kissed lower down Austin's neck. His fingers fumbled at Austin's snap buttons, which came easily undone, each button making a clack-slap sound.

"I felt it—" Austin reached for Clay's shirt, echoing what Clay was doing, letting Clay lead the way, but following so close behind that if he went any faster, he might be leading the way. "—too."

He was hard. His erection was pressing against the buttons of his blue jeans, so hard, like it meant to force his way out if Austin didn't take care of it, and fast.

He was hard, just like Clay was.

Grunting under his breath, he pushed Clay back and unsnapped the remainder of Clay's pearl-snap buttons, then went for his belt buckle, huffing out a breath when he couldn't get it undone quickly enough.

Part of him was charged with anxiety that he'd be moving too fast, be too rough for Clay, like Mona always complained about—but no. He wasn't with Mona. He was with Clay, and when he got Clay's belt undone, Clay's mouth fell open and his eyes were glazed.

"Shit," said Clay, seeming not to realize he was speaking. "The monk ravages the Viking. An' I'm the Viking, right?"

"You can be anything you want," said Austin low as he rose up between Clay's thighs, spreading them apart with his knee.

It felt natural to dip down to undo the button and zipper on Clay's jeans, to spread Clay's shirt to display his chest, powerful and wide from real work, a sprinkle of blond hair along his breastbone. But when his hands touched the elastic of Clay's boxers, he paused.

"Don't stop," said Clay, lifting his head up. "What're you stopping for?"

"This is the hard part for me," said Austin, his voice perfectly clear without a single tremble. Yet he was trembling inside, shaking all over like he couldn't stop.

"Okay." Clay held himself very still, then said, "I could go down on you first, right? Take you all the way. Swallow everything. Show you how it's done?"

"I've had it done. I know how it's done." Austin sank back on his heels, his heart pounding, his head whirling. He was trying to clear his thoughts but surely this wasn't the time for that? Surely he'd dallied enough, and had already said yes. So why was he stopping?

"Maybe—" Clay took one of Austin's hands and kissed his finger-tips. "Maybe close your eyes and just feel your way through. I have a very pretty penis, by the way, but I don't want it to overwhelm you."

"Pretty?" asked Austin, distracted by the idea of what made a pretty penis.

"It's the most beautiful penis you will ever lay eyes on." Clay nodded as though satisfied he'd made his point.

As usual, as always with Clay, laughter bubbled inside of Austin, taking down walls of anxiety, waves of self-doubt, all in one fell swoop.

"You're the most—" said Austin, bending close to kiss Clay's slightly round belly. "The best. You're the *best*."

"Does that mean you're going to close your eyes and try to suck my dick?" asked Clay, eyebrows going up as he pretended to be quite serious.

"Yes." Austin nodded, making it a promise. "Yes."

He closed his eyes and let his fingers pull at the elastic of Clay's boxers, tugging them down, not opening his eyes as he felt Clay shimmy beneath him. He felt Clay tugging his briefs and blue jeans down to his thighs.

Austin inhaled the scent of another man, naked before him, warm and up close. He leaned in, fingers trembling a little, and took Clay's erection in his hand.

Warm, that's what Clay was, warm and solid beneath a layer of tender, silken skin. Which was what his own cock felt like, back in the day, back when he used to get erections like every other man. What was different here was the fact that Clay was waiting, staying still as Austin stroked him, petted him a little bit.

"Your mouth is quite close, you know," said Clay, his voice very quiet. "Just another half inch and you'll be there."

That particular half-inch was his own hurdle to master, and Clay shouldn't be made to wait any longer than he already had waited.

Taking a breath, Austin leaned even closer, propping himself up on one hand as he tugged on Clay's cock and opened his mouth. Pushed out his tongue to encounter warm skin, tasting the bit of salt, the linger of soap, the scent of Clay, what he smelled like between his legs, the most intimate part of him.

Gathering all of his courage, Austin took another breath and opened his mouth to take Clay's cock close, his tongue padding the bottom, his lips suctioning tight. Clay tasted good, felt good, and the idea of it, what he was doing, what he'd been brave enough to do, rushed through him like a blessing, like a cool breeze on a hot day. Like everything it should feel like. Good and sweet and full of a growing passion.

"Oh, man," said Clay, his groan making the words furry-edged and soft. "Oh, man, oh, man, oh, man."

This praise soaked into Austin like welcome rain on dry land, urging Austin to do what he wanted, what felt right. To give Clay all the pleasure he deserved, without Austin's own inhibitions in the way.

He sucked harder with his mouth, using his hand to grip and release the base of Clay's cock, which might be pretty standard stuff in the big scheme, but to him it was wild. His belly quivered, and his thighs trembled as they held him up, but he sucked and twirled his tongue around the head of Clay's cock and vowed that he'd soon be brave enough to open his eyes and see just how pretty a penis it was.

But for now, he concentrated on Clay's responses, the wordless sighs, the high-pitched sounds, the way Clay's body surged beneath him, the tremble in Clay's thighs, the quiver in his belly. When he felt Clay's cock tighten, he tightened his grip around the base, then went loose. Tight and then loose, all the while sucking softly, almost teasing.

And felt, just before it happened, all of Clay's body tighten, his cock stiffening before releasing a warmth into Austin's mouth.

Surprised at the taste of it, Austin pulled back, his eyes wide open, the back of his hand against his mouth so as not to spill any of it. And then swallowed as Clay watched.

"Oh, holy shit," said Clay, breathing hard as sweat dappled his chest, and his pretty penis lay lax and curled on his belly in a nest of dark gold hair. "Holy *wow.*"

"Well," said Austin, shrugging as he looked down at Clay's nakedness, awe rippling through him at what he'd just done. "You do have the prettiest penis I've ever seen."

"I've also got a very nice ass," said Clay, sitting up on his elbows. "Would you like to see *that?*"

"Yes," said Austin, putting force into the word like he'd been trying to convince Clay of this fact for hours.

Clay shimmied fully out of his clothes to kneel naked and vulnerable on the couch with Austin. Then he tugged Austin's shirt off him, humming contentedly beneath his breath, and undid the shiny buttons on Austin's jeans. And from there, tugged on the elastic of Austin's boxer-briefs.

"Ready for the next bit?" asked Clay in a completely conversational tone. When Austin nodded, shaking, Clay quite slowly, but steadily, pulled Austin's jeans and boxer-briefs down to his thighs, and very matter-of-factly, helped Austin stand to take them off and guided him to kneel on the couch again.

"Are these the freckles you spoke of?" asked Clay as he ran his hands over Austin's bare shoulders. "And is this your penis?" he asked, making a little joke of the question.

Austin nodded, holding his breath, and then, all at once the joke went out of Clay's voice.

"All this time," he said, sighing as he cupped Austin's ribs, then curled both of his hands beneath Austin's balls as reverently as though holding jewels. "You've been hiding this beautiful, beautiful body from me."

The words, like some kind of spell as they accompanied the gentle stroking of Clay's fingers, pushed Austin's cock to more hardness, and then more. And more until his cock was standing against his belly, familiar and strange all at once.

"I don't suppose," said Clay in a conversational tone as he bent to kiss the head of Austin's cock, inhaling Austin's scent before straightening up. "Don't suppose you'd like to fuck me with this one day."

To emphasize what, exactly, Austin might want to fuck, Clay let go of Austin and turned, brushing his white, dimpled ass against Austin's thigh. Which was when Austin's body, having perhaps decided that enough buildup was enough, tightened up, his belly dipping as his balls tightened, and he came in short, white streams over Clay's hip.

"Shit." Austin did his best to clench the base of his cock, but it was too late, he'd wasted his first time with Clay.

But Clay, being Clay, laughed low and pulled his shirt up to wipe his hip, then he pulled Austin on top of him. Their limbs tangled together as Austin's body thrummed slower and slower as he breathed to calmness in Clay's arms.

"My ass was just so beautiful you couldn't help yourself, right?" asked Clay, kissing Austin's ear.

"That's for certain," said Austin, the words jerky and hard to say.

"Well, that has to be about the best compliment I've ever gotten." Clay swept the hair back from Austin's damp forehead. "What do you say we wait a little bit an' then have another go."

"It might be more than a bit for me." Austin took a breath. "But if you're willing to wait—"

"I am willing to wait forever," said Clay, stoutly. "You've got a great mouth, I tell you what. And you smell good. All over. *And*, I'll have you know."

Austin looked up as Clay paused.

"You, my friend, my dear Austin," said Clay, his eyes steady as he looked down at Austin. "You have the prettiest penis I've ever seen. Next to mine, of course." Clay nodded, as though pronouncing a well-known truth.

"Really?"

"An' I bet you taste good, too." Clay kissed the top of Austin's head. "Can't wait, nope, cannot wait."

Settling into each other's arms on the couch, a slight skim of sweat drying on their skins, Austin could relax now that the hard part was over. And it hadn't even been that difficult, not with Clay gently guiding him through it, being there, being Clay, every step of the way.

Then, in a short while, they fooled around a little more, kissing and groping each other like teenagers, then hot and sweaty, moved to the shower. There, Clay, in the stream of water, went on his knees and sucked Austin's cock until he came in hard pulses that felt like they were pulling his spine hard all the way to the front of him.

Watching Clay, still on his knees, blink against the water as he licked his lower lip was enough to make Austin's knees buckle and to wish somehow that they could do this always.

"Can I spend the night?" asked Clay as he stood up and turned off the shower.

"Sure," said Austin. He reached for a towel and satisfied himself with buffing Clay all over with it before he dried himself off, blushing as Clay watched. "But you'll have to leave early before Bea comes home."

"Can do," said Clay, strutting out of the bathroom naked as the day he was born, his feet making squeaking noises on the wooden floor as he went, his bottom bright and shiny with dampness. "C'mon," he called. "Time for bed. Time for more fooling around."

The breeze coming in the open window stirred the curtains, bright against the deepening night outside. Clay clambered into bed as Austin flicked off the light. Clay patted the spot beside him, which Austin went to as fast as he could, eager, now, to hold Clay in his arms and to be soothed by Clay's presence in the dark.

When they were settled together, each holding the other, Austin opened his mouth to say something, only he yawned. And then Clay yawned. After which a gentle silence fell, shifted only by the sound of leaves moving against leaves, of the wind on the hillside grasses.

When the sun hit Austin's eyes the next morning, he heard the front door slam and pulled the bedsheet over them both, reflexively, for the bedroom door was wide open. Bea's footsteps could be heard, the clunk of her backpack as she dropped it on the floor. A pause. A shuffle as Bea took off her cowboy boots while she, no doubt, took in the litter of jeans and shirts and underwear and cowboy boots all around the living room.

"Good morning, I'm home," called Bea. "Did you guys have a sleep-over, too, Dad?"

"Yes," said Austin, weakly. He cleared his throat and tried again. "Yes, Clay and I had a sleepover, but he needs to go to work now so could you go to your room while we get dressed?"

"Fine." Bea's stomping footsteps could be heard, followed by a door closing.

Knowing that the coast was clear, though for how long was unknown, Austin shooed Clay out of his bed. Together the two of them hustled into their clothes, and were only without their socks and boots by the time Bea determined she'd had enough of being in her bedroom when more exciting things were happening elsewhere.

"Can we go to breakfast now?" she asked, her hands on her hips as she looked at them. "And could somebody help me braid my hair? Mrs. Mitchell had so many little girls over, I didn't want to ask her."

"I'd be happy to do it," said Clay, completely nonchalant, it seemed, despite the presence of a nine-year-old in their midst. "Got a comb? Here's a chair. I'll do your braid while your dad puts on his boots and thinks about what he's going to get done today."

Gratefully, Austin sat in one of the wooden chairs at the small dining table. Bea sat in the other while Clay combed out her long, strawberry blonde hair, as gently as he might do with a skittish mare. But Bea was the furthest thing from skittish and she seemed to be half falling asleep as Clay separated her hair into strands and began to braid it.

"Maybe I'll get a horse lesson today," she said to nobody in particular.

"Maybe you will," said Clay. He looped the elastic band around the end of her braid, then flipped it over her shoulder. "You're ready. Let's go to breakfast. Austin, get your boots on."

Clay shoved his feet into his boots, as though to show Austin how it was done. Then he opened the door and took Bea's hand in one of his, and Austin's hand in the other.

"All right, let's go," he told them, tugging them to the outside. "I don't know about you, but I'm starving."

Then, hand in hand, they walked along the dirt path through the shady green glade of trees. Together like a little family, and Austin's heart filled at the thought of it. How they might always be this way, sharing the simple moments.

EPILOGUE

$\mathcal{N}$ear the end of the season, on a Saturday night in September, when the length of arid days was offset by the cool nights, the scent of autumn teasing the air, Clay took a shower. But it wasn't just *any* shower, it was his first shower in manager cabin #3 with Bea on a sleepover. Thus, he took a great deal of care hanging up the towel he'd used, and the washcloth, so mold wouldn't grow. So Austin would never regret inviting Clay to stay.

For Austin, just last week, had invited Clay to move into a cabin with him and Bea, and Clay had accepted on the spot. It had taken him only a day to shift his stuff from his little room on the third floor of the staff quarters to the little cabin beneath the trees, and the whole while he'd been just about coming out of his skin with excitement.

He and Austin had gone on a string of dates over the summer, each more satisfying than the one before it. Each date had been filled with long drives to vista views, and quick drives to the Diary Queen in Chugwater, along with quiet walks along the river at sunset, and evenings filled with loud laughter in the dining hall on puzzle night.

Sometimes they brought Bea with them on those dates, and sometimes Bea wanted to go to the forge so she could be babysat by Jasper and Ellis. There, she insisted on doing her share of whatever work they offered her, as though unaware she was a small nine-year-old girl who didn't have to keep up with them when they trimmed the river or hauled bags of coal in Jasper's truck.

For some reason that neither Austin nor Clay could understand, the forge fascinated her, as did the horses in the barn. And once she'd discovered the tack room, it was all they could do to keep her out of there, or convince her that saddles laid on two by fours for storage weren't actually meant to be sat on.

Other times Bea had day-long outings with the Frontier Girls, of which she was now a proud member. Almost every day since she joined them, she'd been bugging Austin for someone to make her a frilly flower-sprigged dress with a bonnet to match so she could be like the rest of the little girls. Though Clay had only moved in a week ago, she'd already figured out that if Austin said no to the dress and bonnet, she could try asking Clay to say yes.

He had no willpower with her, no willpower at *all*, which meant that Austin had to get on the phone with Maddy to track down someone who could help. Maddy, in turn, had pointed them in the direction of Ginny, Leland's mom, who was currently sifting through her old patterns to find something suitable.

Tonight, Bea was having a special sleepover with two specific girls from the Frontier Girls group, Lisa and Ruth Anne. The three little girls would be at Ruth Anne's house, though from what Clay had gleaned, Ruth Anne lived with her doting grandparents, as her parents had sadly passed away. Not to mention, Austin had it on good authority that Bea would not be returning till late on Sunday.

He and Austin had time. They had tons of time, and now it was time for Clay to gird his loins and speak up about what he wanted.

He missed getting fucked up the ass like crazy, and now that the two of them, him and Austin had dated for a few months, and now that he'd moved in, and now that they'd spent the last week getting used to sleeping in the same bed every night—it was time.

Austin was very easy to live with, and between the two of them they'd smoothed out the rough spots brought on by compromising where the kitchen scissors should be kept in the kitchenette—which really had been the biggest point of contention thus far—Clay knew he didn't want to put it off.

Especially not since Austin, strong and tall, took every private opportunity to corner Clay. He'd press him to the wall, his long arms blocking Clay's escape, and kiss him till Clay's legs threatened to go out from under him. Other times, after Bea had taken her shower, and after she'd begged Clay to braid her hair in a fishtail braid so she could dream of being a horse (a request Clay was always powerless to resist), they would tuck her in, turn on her nightlight, and have the evening to themselves. Usually they made out like teenagers, and sometimes it turned into something more.

The couch in the cabin wasn't the biggest couch in the universe, but when Austin sat at one end, and patted the space beside him, it was more than Clay could resist. He'd run and leap and plonk himself down with half of him in Austin's lap. Sprawled across Austin's broad chest, he'd lay his head in the curve of Austin's shoulder. Austin's whole body would welcome Clay, curving in echo so all of Clay fit against Austin's body as though Austin had been carved to accept him.

Frankly, Clay wondered why he'd ever thought stand-up sex in an alley behind a second rate bar had been the way to spend his energy. As near as he could figure, though, he must have gotten his ideas about how to find love from those porno films he used to watch. Totally unrealistic, those films made like an easy lay was the first step on the path to following in love. But oh, how wrong he'd been.

It was better this way. Better with the three of them in the cabin together, in the mornings in the kitchenette, where Bea had determined they might have a little mini breakfast together of cinnamon raisin bread and Irish Breakfast tea, an odd combination she declared Jasper and Ellis had shown her.

There was a four burner stove, and a fridge and all, but with the dining hall so handy, Austin confessed to Clay that he'd not really thought about making meals at home. Clay was all for it, so mid-week of their first week, they'd purchased a small selection of groceries.

"Let's make our own pancakes," Clay told Bea on Friday morning. "And put as many chocolate chips in them as we want."

Which probably hadn't been the best idea, as a nine-year-old's idea, let alone a young ranch hand's idea, of a good chocolate chip to pancake batter ratio probably wasn't quite balanced. The first batch they made had turned into chocolate goo. Austin had just laughed and they made another batch, which they all enjoyed very much.

During that first week, they'd mostly eaten dinner in the dining hall, though on Friday evening, magically, Austin had raced to to bring back a large artisanal-type pizza pie from the Rail Car. This turned out to be too spicy for Bea, but plenty fine for Clay and Austin, and after they made her a peanut butter and jelly sandwich, they all sat on the front porch and ate dinner together as the cool of the evening came down.

If Bea had Clay wrapped around her little finger, Austin had Clay wrapped around his heart. The joy of waking up each morning in Austin's arms after making out—and having sex—beneath the sheets the night before, went beyond whatever he could have imagined, had he dared to imagine something so peaceful and domestic and sweet.

The only thing Austin seemed to want from Clay, beyond a whole lot of dick sucking, which Clay was *always* happy to oblige, was for Clay to take better care of himself. That included putting towels on the rack when he was done, and teeth brushing and flossing every day, along with vegetables at most meals, and less fountain sodas and Bugles on road trips and more iced tea and grapes.

All of this was a bit more mothering than Clay was used to, but was accompanied by sweet kisses on his nose, and gentle fingers carding his hair back from his eyes.

Best of all was in the evening when Austin's gaze would grow quiet and careful. He'd look at Clay like Clay was the most adorable, the most handsome, the most desirable man to *ever* walk the Earth. All of this stroked Clay's ego good and fine. And when Austin's arms came around him, he felt wrapped up in warmth and light and love and knew he could do anything, *be* anything, he wanted to be. All he wanted to do was to be near Austin, always.

Which made the conversation Clay wanted to have with Austin fill him with trepidation. Would Austin, who'd never been with a man other than Clay, and who had horror stories about Mona and their sex life that he finally shared with Clay, be willing to give Clay what he needed?

But then, did Clay really need to be fucked up the ass or was it merely something he wanted?

And how was he going to broach the subject with a man who had moments of blushing timidity about sex woven in among his growing boldness, his desire for Clay expressed in kisses and looks and long, lingering touches right before Austin tackled Clay to the bed?

Maybe he should do what Leland always advised, which was to just come out with it and tell the truth.

He gave his still-damp hair a quick pat as he heard the front door to the tiny cabin open, and Austin called out, "Honey I'm home!" like he was the lead role in an old black and white sitcom about small town living. Clay smiled at himself then raced through the small living room to help Austin with the two grocery bags he was carrying.

"Did you get the right kind?" asked Clay. "It's important because Cap'n Crunch is the best. Cap'n Crunch with Crunchberries is a sad, disgusting nightmare, especially for a small kid who is still growing."

"Yeah," said Austin, laughing as he followed Clay into the kitchenette. "She's going to flip *out* when she learns that Sunday night dinner is going to be sugary cereal and ice cream."

"And why are we doing this again?" asked Clay, as they put everything away. "Seriously, even I know that much sugar isn't good for her."

"Because," said Austin, after he kissed Clay on the nose. "She's a good kid, and she deserves to totally have her way sometimes, and sit in her Lilo and Stitch pajamas, and stuff as much sugar into her mouth as she wants while watching *Moana* over and over till she passes out."

"So—" started Clay, thinking that this might be a good way to begin a conversation about what he wanted. "So, you think people should go all out sometimes? With having what they want, I mean?"

It might have been the phrasing of the question or it might have been the tone in Clay's voice, but Austin shut the fridge, his hands going still as he looked at Clay with those beautiful green eyes of his.

"Are we talking in general terms here?" asked Austin, all of his attention focused on Clay. "Or is it something more specific than that?"

As always, Austin liked for things to be laid out, either in numbers or lists. Which might have made him sound really anal retentive at one point, but now Clay knew him better. He felt he knew Austin so well, in fact, that when he told Austin which one it was, he knew Austin would shift his attention to better get to the heart of the matter, to better give Clay what he needed.

"More specific," said Clay. His hands went in his pockets, and though he was barefooted, he scuffed his toe along the wooden floor and shrugged. "Specific about me, I mean."

"Oh?" asked Austin, his voice growing soft. "Is there something I've done wrong?"

Mona's mark had left very deep scars inside of Austin to the point where, when Clay wanted something, Austin immediately jumped to the conclusion that he was in error for not figuring out by osmosis what Clay needed.

Clay knew he needed to disabuse Austin of that notion, and to do that, he was going to have to lay himself bare. He was going to have to peel a little skin back and make himself vulnerable. In short, he was going to have to tell Austin the truth.

"No," he said. "It's not something you've done or not done. It's something I need. Okay?" Clay took both of Austin's hands in his, then placed them on his chest. "I need it and it's hard for me to tell you, being that you're a new gay an' all."

"I'm not *that* new," said Austin, scoffing.

"Well, you're new to this," said Clay. "Or am I mistaken that you told me Mona never liked butt stuff, so you never did it."

"Butt stuff." Austin side-eyed Clay as he leaned back against the fridge, pulling Clay with him till they were hip to hip. "Go on."

"To begin with," said Clay, forcing a bit of a laugh. "My anus is not bleached, so let's be clear about that."

"Okay," said Austin. "Why does that matter?"

"So here's the thing—" Clay nodded, doing his best to look Austin straight in the eyes as he told his truth. "Before you, I liked to have these one-off flings with strangers. Behind the Rusty Nail and the Stampede Saloon. Remember? I told you that, right?"

"You mentioned it, yes," said Austin. "You were doing that when you were the randy ranch hand before you became the almost-not-tall-enough Viking."

"I thought I could find love that way," said Clay, the words coming out in a rush. "And of course I was wrong, but I miss it—"

"What do you miss?" asked Austin. He pulled Clay even closer and kept him there, his arms around Clay's waist. Their hips pressed together, their hearts beat together, and in that moment it seemed as though Austin had already said yes to whatever it was Clay wanted, without Clay having to say a word.

He was going to say the words anyway. Biting his lower lip, he tensed all of his muscles like he was going to have to walk through fire.

"I miss getting fucked up the ass," he said, almost pulling out of Austin's arms as though in preparation for Austin shoving him away. "I miss standing with my hands pressed against the dirty bricks, getting pounded—I miss it, I miss it, I miss it, an' I know it's a lot to ask, but was wondering if we could try—"

He was almost squinting as he looked at Austin, preparing for the worst, preparing for the big fat no that Austin might give him. But, in the midst of this, he realized Austin was looking at him with some tenderness, his eyes soft, his hands still firm around Clay's waist.

"I'll probably be terrible at it," said Austin, looking away, and then back at Clay. "But I can try. Do we need—do you have—? And how do I—?"

"It's like regular fucking, but it's like—" Clay paused to kiss Austin and then to kiss him again. "I'll just be blunt," he said. "You have to open my ass up, on account of you have a rather big dick an'—"

"It's not *that* big," said Austin, blinking his surprise.

"It is a bit," said Clay. "It's big and it's gorgeous, so prep is important. I've got plenty of lube, and all you have to do is, well, you push your lubed fingers into me and ease the way for that big dick of yours. Then you can pound me into the mattress. Sound good?"

"Sounds rather clinical when you put it that way," said Austin.

"It isn't," said Clay, hoping he'd not made a mistake in asking or in how he explained it. "I'll love it no matter how you do it, if you don't mind trying."

"I don't mind." Austin ducked his chin to kiss Clay on the mouth, and then again, more softly. His eyes were the deepest green, his face flushed, perhaps by anticipation, perhaps with pleasure.

"Do you want to close your eyes again, like we did before, and do it by feel?" asked Clay, kissing Austin right back.

"No." Austin shook his head, his eyes half lidded as he cupped Clay's face in his hands. "I want to see you. I want to see everything."

This was so brave, Clay wanted to just stop and hug Austin till the end of time. But the process was already begun because now he was worked up, and wanted to be out of his clothes and face-down on the mattress as soon as was humanly possible. And he wanted Austin fucking him even sooner than that.

With a gentle hand, Clay led Austin into the bedroom, leaving the ruby glass-topped lamps lit while turning off the overhead lamp so the bedroom was in semi-darkness but there'd be enough light to see. Clay opened the little drawer on the nightstand to reveal three condoms in gold foil packets that glittered in the slanted light, along with a small bottle of lube, which they'd used before when messing around.

Nothing in the drawer was a surprise, but Austin's indrawn breath was a little loud, so Clay turned to tug on Austin's hand and kissed him on the neck, right below his ear, and whispered, "You've got this."

"I've got *you*," said Austin, drawing his body to its fullest height, the line of his jaw firm. He pulled on Clay's shirt. "Now, let's get you out of those clothes so I can ravish you."

Austin undressed himself and Clay at the same time, layer by layer, his expression serious as he bent to his task. When they were down to their skins, Clay could have stood forever admiring Austin's long muscles covered by pale skin, the line of his hip leading to his groin. The tender curve of his inner thigh, dusted with dark hair. All of him was lovely, just as he ought to be, and Clay knew he was the luckiest man alive.

Clay found himself smiling goofily as Austin drew him to the bed and positioned Clay exactly where he wanted him, which was face down.

When Clay felt Austin kneel on the bed, and felt the warmth of Austin's hand on the curve of his ass, he knew that he was experiencing the best love, the purest love. That Austin had come through so much, through such a nasty time with Mona, that he'd be willing to be gentle, to take the lead, take control, just to give Clay what he wanted was the most amazing miracle.

"How much do I use?" asked Austin, opening the small bottle of lube with a snicking sound.

"As much or as little," said Clay, his words muffled by the pillow, his heart thumping into the mattress. He wanted to give Austin words of confidence because every time Austin touched him, it was always just right, done with patience, and care, and most of all, love. "Whatever feels right. No condoms, if that's okay."

Austin's weight shifted, and Clay felt a kiss in the small of his back. Every square inch of skin felt like it was standing up and screaming for joy, and the anticipation, while killing him, was another layer of pleasure beneath that.

The coolness of Austin's fingers along the back of his thigh almost made him jump. When Austin knelt between both of Clay's thighs, pushing his knees apart, he almost came there and then, but stiffened his belly and held his breath because he wanted it to take a good long while. Wanted to experience all of this with edgy intensity all the way through him—this, Austin's first time fucking him.

"Tuck your knee up," said Austin in that serious, slightly bossy way he had that always made Clay's limbs weak, started his blood to simmering. Then his whole body snapped to attention when Austin patted the inside of his thigh, right above his bent knee, then circled his fingers around Clay's balls, just like he knew what he was doing. "A little more, please."

It was like Austin to say please, and later he might say thank you, but right now, he was in charge or at least it felt that way. Clay almost jumped when he felt the cold lube along his crack, quickly warming to skin temperature, but not quite enough fast enough to let him forget it was there.

"I'm just going to get to it," said Austin, pausing, stroking his fingers along Clay's skin. "My heart is beating so fast, I'm not sure how long I'll last."

"Could come from just this," said Clay, the words coming out a little muffled by the pillow. "Just do it. Whatever. Just do it."

Austin's fingers, tucked between Clay's butt cheeks, circled his anus, then circled again. And again. He raised his hips to give Austin more access, shifted his hips, squirmed against the sheets. Austin's other hand came to press in the small of his back, bossy and sure, and Clay's cock pulsed and pulsed again before he could stop it, sending shivers through him, his hips curling forward.

The warmth of Austin's body pressed close along his back.

"Oh, my," said Austin, kissing the back of Clay's neck.

"Ah, fuck it, I couldn't hold it," said Clay, half growling, half laughing. "Just fuck it. Just fuck me. Hard. An' is it okay if we pretend we're in an alley—or maybe I shouldn't—"

"Does that make me the one night stand in this scenario?"

Clay opened his eyes to see Austin's face close to his, Austin who had bent down to make sure of Clay.

"No." Clay shook his head. "Never mind that. I didn't mean to make a game of this. I just wanted—wanted what I wanted."

"Well, then," said Austin, straightening up. "Let me go ahead and give it to you."

As Clay knew from watching Austin working, when Austin got to business, he meant it. Which meant that when Clay felt Austin's lubed fingers, Austin didn't wait, but circled around Clay's anus exactly twice, and then those long fingers, first one, then two, were inside him, pushing, pushing, pulling, then pushing again.

More lube came out of the small container with another solid snicking sound of the lid when it opened and closed. Austin's weight shifted down as Austin's scent, sweet and salty, known and loved, swirled around Clay. He closed his eyes all the way and sank into the sensation of Austin's cock, a dense, silky weight, lowering then pushing in, just a bit, just the tip, Austin's fingers slipping out to make room.

All those mechanics, the physical details slipped away as Austin pushed inside of him, the thickness of his cock, the slick head, the lube, the patience—all of it rolled into the trust between them. The sweetness of such closeness. The patient, steady thrust and pull of Austin's body, the response of Clay's own, willing, opening up. The meeting of their two hearts in this physical way. The love, pure and strong and good—wove between and around them both, binding them together, making Clay's heart pound, joy filling him.

The best part, truly, the best, was listening to the soft sounds Austin made as he fucked Clay good and hard. Like music, a small, sweet melody of effort and joy, and when Austin's fingers clutched at Clay's hip, clutched with enough strength to perhaps leave marks for the morning, Clay wanted to roll to his back and grab Austin and lift him high and shout to the heavens.

For when was the last time Austin had made love to anyone like this? When was the last time Austin had shoved his rock hard, beautiful and huge penis into anyone? Ages and ages. *Ages.* And now Clay was the lucky, lucky recipient, his body open and ready for those final hard short thrusts. Ready for the warmth to trickle down the inside of his thighs. Ready for Austin to pull out and land hard, collapsing on Clay's back, his hands stroking Clay's thighs as he sighed.

"Jesus wow," whispered Austin. "You're so tight. And hot. No, I mean, literally, hot. The inside of an ass is *hot.*"

"Mine is the only ass you will ever know," said Clay, whispering, as though saying his vows. "The only ass you will ever need."

"And the prettiest ass, as well," said Austin. By now he'd adjusted himself, resting on the back of Clay's thighs, his balls warm on Clay's skin, the light touch of his penis leaving a trace of dampness. "What say you we take a shower and then try this again. And this time I'm going to go even slower."

Clay's cock gave a jump to alert him that it was willing if he was.

"You got it," said Clay. He smiled as he raised himself up on his elbows, turning to look up at Austin, who was looking flushed and a little smug, well pleased with himself, as he should be. "This can also be done standing up in a shower, I'll have you know, though it does get a little slippery."

"Any way you want it," said Austin. Leaning down, he peppered Clay's back with kisses, his palms cupping Clay's ass. "Any way at all."

The purest form of love, it seemed, was not in the taking, but in the giving. And this time, upon impulse, Clay did roll to his back, clutching Austin's thighs to make sure Austin knew that he was not to roll off, but to stay in place. Then he looked up at Austin, at that handsome, serious face, those gorgeous freckles along his shoulders, the red-gold hair that dusted his chest. All of Austin was all around him now, like a cape of muscle and strength.

"I love you," Clay said. "You give me everything I never knew I needed. I love you."

Austin's eyes shone brightly as he bent down to kiss Clay on the chin, on his mouth, on his nose.

"You are my love, my heart." Austin's mouth moved softly across Clay's lips as he said this. "My always."

For a moment, Clay lay perfectly still, absorbing the moment into his soul. Then he shifted, his skin laced with sweat, semen drying between his legs.

"Is it shower time?" asked Austin.

"Yes, it is," said Clay. "Let's shower. And while we shower, I'm probably going to bend over and pick up the soap."

"Oh, I wish you would," said Austin, his lovely mouth curving into a smile. "I wish you would."

"I will, my love," said Clay. "I most certainly will."

The End

Thank you for reading!

If you enjoyed this book, please consider leaving a rating (without a review) or leaving a rating and a review!

Want to read more about romance at Farthingdale Ranch? Check out The Wrangler and the Orphan, Book #4 in the Farthingdale Ranch series.

JACKIE'S NEWSLETTER

Would you like to sign up for my newsletter?

Subscribers are alway the first to hear about my new books. You'll get behind the scenes information, sales and cover reveal updates, and giveaways.

As my gift for signing up, you will receive two short stories, one sweet, and one steamy!

It's completely free to sign up and you will never be spammed by me; you can opt out easily at any time.

To sign up, visit the following URL:

https://www.subscribepage.com/JackieNorthNewsletter

facebook.com/jackienorthMM
twitter.com/JackieNorthMM
pinterest.com/jackienorthauthor
bookbub.com/profile/jackie-north
amazon.com/author/jackienorth
goodreads.com/Jackie_North
instagram.com/jackienorth_author

AUTHOR'S NOTES ABOUT THE STORY

I've not done a lot of what I'd call "chatting up the story" while writing The Ranch Hand and the Single Dad, because writing it was a lot more challenging than I had thought and I needed to hunker down and get 'er done.

When I talked about the story to Wendy (who is always a wonderful sounding board), it was fun to imagine a single dad on a ranch, a nerdy red-headed accountant, and the randy ranch hand he falls in love with. Which is what the story turned out to be, only not the way I'd pictured it!

For starters, I got caught up in the logistics of what an accountant would need to do to organize the accounts and help bring the ranch back from the brink and to straighten out their troubled accounting practices. (Bill Wainwright does not like writing things down or getting receipts, which surprises no one.)

And then, Austin (the nerdy red-headed accountant who is straight and newly divorced) needed extra handling, as it's been a while since I wrote an "out for you" romance.

As I worked, the story got longer and longer and longer - and sweeter, as though while I spun it out, it turned into cotton candy. So this one is low steam and sweet as honey. There's a lot of hand holding and kissing and the joy of a friendship turning into love, and I think you'll enjoy it very much.

A LETTER FROM JACKIE

Hello, Reader!

Thank you for reading *The Ranch Hand and the Single Dad,* the third book in my Farthingdale Ranch series.

If you enjoyed the book, I would love it if you would let your friends know so they can experience the romance between Austin and Clay.

If you leave a review, I'd love to read it! You can send the URL to: Jackienorthauthor@gmail.com

Jackie

facebook.com/jackienorthMM
twitter.com/JackieNorthMM
instagram.com/jackienorth_author
pinterest.com/jackienorthauthor
bookbub.com/profile/jackie-north
amazon.com/author/jackienorth
goodreads.com/Jackie_North

ABOUT THE AUTHOR

Jackie North has written since grade school and spent years absorbing mainstream romances. Her dream was to write full time and put her English degree to good use.

As fate would have it, she discovered m/m romance and decided that men falling in love with other men was exactly what she wanted to write about.

Her characters are a bit flawed and broken. Some find themselves on the edge of society, and others are lost. All of them deserve a happily ever after, and she makes sure they get it!

She likes long walks on the beach, the smell of lavender and rainstorms, and enjoys sleeping in on snowy mornings.

In her heart, there is peace to be found everywhere, but since in the real world this isn't always true, Jackie writes for love.

Connect with Jackie:

https://www.jackienorth.com/
jackie@jackienorth.com

facebook.com/jackienorthMM
twitter.com/JackieNorthMM
pinterest.com/jackienorthauthor
bookbub.com/profile/jackie-north
amazon.com/author/jackienorth
goodreads.com/Jackie_North
instagram.com/jackienorth_author

Made in the USA
Coppell, TX
10 December 2024

41972752R00193